THE LAST SECOND

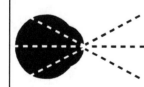

This Large Print Book carries the
Seal of Approval of N.A.V.H.

CHARLESTON COUNTY LIBRARY

THE LAST SECOND

CATHERINE COULTER
AND J.T. ELLISON

LARGE PRINT PRESS
A part of Gale, a Cengage Company

WITHDRAWN

Copyright © 2019 by Catherine Coulter.
A Brit in the FBI Thriller.
Large Print Press, a part of Gale, a Cengage Company.

ALL RIGHTS RESERVED

This book is a work of fiction. Any references to historical events, real people, or real places are used fictitiously. Other names, characters, places, and events are products of the author's imagination, and any resemblance to actual events or locales or persons, living or dead, is entirely coincidental.

The text of this Large Print edition is unabridged.
Other aspects of the book may vary from the original edition.
Set in 16 pt. Plantin.

LIBRARY OF CONGRESS CIP DATA ON FILE.
CATALOGUING IN PUBLICATION FOR THIS BOOK
IS AVAILABLE FROM THE LIBRARY OF CONGRESS

ISBN-13: 978-1-4328-6181-0 (paperback alk. paper)

Published in 2019 by arrangement with Gallery Books, an imprint of Simon & Schuster, Inc.

Printed in the United States of America
2 3 4 5 6   24 23 22 21 20

To my beloved brother-in-law, Blaise, who died recently after a valiant fight with cancer. He was a caring husband, father, brother, grandfather, friend, a man filled with such love and kindness, always ready for a laugh, always ready to hug a grandchild. You will be missed forever. Ah, the wonderful memories all of us will cherish.

— Catherine

For my daddy, who helped steer the winds, and for Randy, as always.

— J.T.

ACKNOWLEDGMENTS

Thank you to Catherine, who lets my imagination run free, then teaches me how to make it all come together. This has been quite a journey! Imagine, we've made it all the way to space!

I was blessed to grow up in an aerospace family, but I couldn't have put the concept of this together nearly as well without the help of my dad and my brothers, who answered innumerable questions about the ways EMPs work, how to put one in space, and how they could be stopped. And thanks to my mom for listening and suggesting ideas over the dinner table — during the writing of this book, and my whole life.

To the Tuesday porch: thank you for keeping me honest, the word count stacking up, and for all your constant support.

And my darling Randy, without whom

none of these books would happen. I'll go up in a rocket with you anytime, baby!

— J.T.

PROLOGUE

NASA Johnson Space Center
Houston, Texas
March 2011

There was a large mirror on the wall of the white room. Dr. Nevaeh Patel sat in a hard plastic chair, leads from a lie detector machine hooked to her left hand, a thick cord wound around her chest.

She was the one who'd insisted on the lie detector. After the embarrassment of having her mission cut short, being replaced by another astronaut and brought back to Earth, two weeks on the ground of tests, physicals, conversations, polite glances, and outright stares, she'd gotten tired of their disbelief and insisted on being tested.

Still, this final indignity was almost too much for her to bear. All she'd done was tell the flight director and flight doctor the truth about what she'd seen during her EVA — extravehicular activity — outside the

International Space Station, what she'd heard. It had been real, they had been real, and the powers that be didn't believe her. On board the space station, they'd subjected her to batteries of tests, extensive psychological profiling, and concluded she had been suffering from zero-gravity-induced hallucinations. They rotated her off the ship and grounded her in Houston so they could do it all again.

Which was an affront to everything they claimed to want from their mission — NASA's ultimate goal was to find exoplanetary life, for heaven's sake. Which she'd done.

The flight director himself, Dr. Franklin Norgate, now sat across from her, a clipboard in his hand. He wore a gray plaid short-sleeved button-down and a skinny black tie, his normally kind eyes guarded. He was as smart as she was, maybe more so. She'd always respected him, seen him as quietly intimidating.

To his right was the examiner, a blank-faced man introduced only as Jim, in his fifties, bald as an egg, a mustard stain on his black tie, like a Rorschach blot. There had been Rorschach tests, too, earlier today and during the innumerable conversations with

NASA's psychiatric team over the past two weeks.

What was wrong with them? They were being idiots. Nevaeh had successfully made contact with an alien species. The Numen, they were called, gentle, kind, fascinating beings. And NASA was treating her like she was insane.

She shivered.

Franklin asked, "Are you cold?"

"It's chilly in here, yes."

"I'll see if they can make it more comfortable for you." He stared at the mirror, and a moment later, she felt the air-conditioning kick off. She nodded her thanks.

The examiner gave her the same strangely blank polite smile all the other experts had been giving her.

"Ready to begin?"

"Yes."

"Good. As I mentioned earlier, only yes or no answers. Are you comfortable?"

"Yes."

"All right then. I'm going to ask you some control questions in order to develop a baseline. Is your name Dr. Nevaeh Patel?"

"Yes."

"Is your first name — Nevaeh — 'heaven' spelled backward?"

"Yes."

Silence, scribbling, then, "Did you attend Stanford University?"

"Yes."

"Did you study physics and astronomy?"

"Yes."

"You received your Ph.D. in astrophysics from MIT?"

"Yes."

"Are you an astronaut?"

"Yes."

"Do you live in Michigan?"

"No."

"Do you live in Texas?"

"Yes."

"Are you being truthful with me?"

"Yes."

"Did you speak with an extraterrestrial being on the International Space Station on your last mission?"

"Yes."

A pause. The men shared a glance.

"And did this extraterrestrial being tell you to harm anyone on Earth?"

"No. No, of course not."

"Dr. Patel, I must remind you, yes or no answers only."

"No."

"Were you paid by a foreign government in the past two years for any services?"

"What? No!"

"Yes or no only, ma'am. Were you paid —"

She was starting to sweat now, why, she didn't know. She regretted asking them to turn off the air. "No."

"Did the alien being you spoke with have a foreign accent?"

She had to think for a moment. Were their words accented? Or did they sound very much like her own voice, an echo of something kind and gentle, but in chorus, as if there were hundreds and one, all at the same time? "No."

"Were you stationed on the International Space Station for almost six months, beginning in October 2010?"

"Yes."

"Were you the chief science officer on the mission?"

"Yes."

"Did you lose your tether on an EVA outside the ISS?"

"Yes." Her heartbeat spiked, she couldn't help it. She was hurled back to the moment when she knew her life was ended. She clearly saw the tethers breaking, her gloved hand missing the handhold, felt her body flood with adrenaline. She was in space, floating away from the space station. Her jet pack didn't respond. She was so royally screwed, she was dead.

Then the strong, gentle hand caught her, and a hundred melodic voices spoke as one in her mind. *You are not going to die today. But you must tell them we're here.*

She shook her head, refocused on the room. It happened so often, her drifting back to the moment the Numen had saved her.

The examiner was watching her closely. "Did you encounter an extraterrestrial being on this EVA?"

"Yes."

"Did you speak with this alien?"

"Yes."

"Did the alien tell you to come back to Earth and tell us of its existence?"

"Yes."

"And the alien then led you back to your port so you could rejoin the crew."

"Yes."

"Are you forty-nine years of age?"

"Yes."

"Do you have blond hair?"

"No."

"Do you believe extraterrestrials are trying to communicate with us?"

"Yes."

Silence. More scratching, then the man nodded and the machine's lights went off.

"Thank you. We'll unhook you now."

Norgate said, not unkindly, "You can wait in the hall."

She started to speak, then shook her head and left the room. They thought she was crazy, she'd gone off the deep end and couldn't be trusted. Space madness. Hallucinations in a stressful moment. They weren't going to believe her, no matter what she said, no matter what the machine indicated. She could see it in their eyes.

She went to the hallway as instructed. She was good at following orders, it was one of the reasons NASA recruited her in the first place. Brilliant, compliant Nevaeh. So respected for her leadership, so adored by her peers.

She knew everything was about to change.

Norgate said, "So? Did she pass?"

Jim Carstairs, the examiner, said, "Yes. Yes, she did."

"Let me see it."

Norgate took the sheets of paper, saw the spikes and flat lines, so much like the EKG he'd had at his last physical.

"I don't understand. She really passed?"

Jim said, "With flying colors. Either she's telling the truth, or she's convinced herself what she saw, what she heard, was truly an

15

alien species. I'll write it all up for you, but she wasn't lying to us. Whether she's relating what really happened is a whole different matter."

Franklin Norgate raked his fingers through his hair. "The press is going to have a field day with this."

The door to the exam room opened and Dr. Rebecca Holloway entered. Tall and thin from an extreme running regimen, Holloway was the lead psychiatrist for this NASA facility. In the end, she was responsible for deciding whether Dr. Patel could go back to space or was finished as an astronaut. Norgate was relieved he didn't have to make the call. He knew he was a coward, but he was grateful it wouldn't be on his head.

"You saw?"

"I did. Dr. Patel absolutely believes she communicated with aliens."

Norgate said, "I would hate to lose her, Rebecca. She's brilliant. Capable. One of the best astronauts we have in the program."

"She also seems to be suffering from serious delusions, Franklin. You know we've seen this happen before. Not to this extent, of course, but we've had astronauts topple over into madness. It's why we screen them so carefully to start with. I can't believe she made it this long without showing her mental issues. She is brilliant, which is probably why she's been able to control the visions. Until now, at least. The stress of the incident has made it impossible to hide her problems any longer. I'd say it broke her, irrevocably. Maybe it was inevitable, given who and what she was."

Norgate rubbed his chin. Given who and what she was? She was an astronaut. What did Rebecca mean? "You're being awfully harsh, Rebecca. I don't know if we should give up on her so soon. Maybe some therapy, some time off —"

Holloway shook her head. "Sorry, Franklin, but there's no way I'm clearing her for flight. I suppose she did show some skill during the incident. It appears she kept her head about her, managed to get reattached to the ISS against all odds. But she shouldn't have been in that position in the first place. In my professional opinion, the stress of the incident has manifested into something bigger and deeper. The delusions she's having about these aliens — it's entirely possible she's had a psychotic break and is going to present with a severe mental illness after more testing. She's sick, Franklin, and I'm grounding her."

He sighed. "All right, I'll tell her. Can we at least keep her attached to the next mission, for publicity's sake?"

"I don't think you'd be doing her any favors. Think this through, Franklin. What it looks like is she tried to commit suicide. She unhooked her tether —"

"A mischaracterization, you saw the tapes. Her tether got tangled with her fellow astronaut Gary Verlander's and they were trying to get themselves straight."

"That's what you think you saw, what she claims, too, but what I saw, what others saw as well, was an astronaut unhook herself and kick off into space, Franklin. It was a miracle she was able to turn around and re-attach. Now she's back on Earth talking about meeting aliens. I know you believe in her, always have, but I don't. Not now. She's not stable. I can try some new therapies and reassess in six months, but I can't guarantee you she won't be worse. Psychopathy like this, she could very well be more embedded in her delusions."

Dr. Holloway left the room, the door closing behind her. The click rang of finality. Norgate stared at the closed door. Holloway hadn't ever liked Dr. Nevaeh Patel, he'd known it immediately. Jealousy? Had Nevaeh known the extent of Dr. Holloway's dislike? He doubted it. Before this fiasco, Nevaeh had been totally focused on being an astronaut, readying herself to go to the space station. She probably hadn't even noticed Holloway. But, of course, her entire future had been decided by one person. Not that it mattered now. Rebecca Holloway's word was final and he'd lost his best astronaut.

Now he had to break it to Nevaeh that she was grounded.

In the hall, Nevaeh stood erect, hands behind her back, legs shoulder-width apart. She looked — resigned. When she met his eyes, he shook his head slightly, and she bit her lip.

Norgate said, "It's only six months."

Nevaeh gave an ugly laugh. "We both know I'm finished here. What I don't understand, Franklin, is this: I've given you the information NASA's been searching for since its inception, and instead of doing everything you can to confirm what I'm saying, you're kicking me out."

"It's just six months, Nevaeh —"

It was Rebecca Holloway, she knew it. "I quit."

And with that, she walked away, shoulders back, heart breaking in two. And the Numen, silent until now, said in a soft, sibilant, and single voice, *It will be all right, Nevaeh.*

We chose you. You will find us again. We will help you.

CHAPTER ONE

PRESENT DAY
TIME TO LAUNCH: T-MINUS 00:03:01:23

The Guiana Space Centre (CSG) is a French and European spaceport to the northwest of Kourou in French Guiana. Operational since 1968, it is particularly suitable as a location for a spaceport as it is near the equator, so that less energy is required to maneuver a spacecraft into an equatorial, geostationary orbit, and it has open sea to the east, so that lower stages of rockets and debris from launch failures cannot fall on human habitations.

— Wikipedia

Launch of the Galactus 5 Rocket
Galactus Spaceport
French Guiana
July 14, 2018
Dr. Nevaeh Patel was always nervous at a

countdown, but this wasn't an ordinary launch. She'd taken great care to ensure no one on the ground had any idea how very important this payload was to her. All they saw was the same calm, cool, collected CEO and president they always saw, an omnipresent figure during launches, a well-liked, hands-on manager, intelligent — a woman to admire. After all, she'd spent almost six months aboard the International Space Station, one of the few female astronauts to achieve the honor in the new millennium, and was spoken of with awe by many of the aerospace experts who spent their days and nights sending rockets to space. Many. Not all.

She tapped a pencil against the computer station, listening to her launch commander run through the countdown checklist. She looked from screen to screen, focused, assessing. The forty-foot wall was broken into five massive squares — the large center screen showing the Galactus 5 rocket on the launchpad, flanked by two more screens on either side. Top left, the launch sequence; bottom left, the orbital planes surrounding Earth; top right, the elliptical they selected for the satellite insertion; bottom right, the interior specs of the rocket itself, laid out in a 3-D rendering from engines to fairing, running systems checks of each component. Above was a smaller horizontal screen running the computer programming codes now taking over from human flight control.

She watched every screen with the intensity of a hawk. Nothing was left to chance. Nothing. Even the smallest anomaly would scrub the launch. And she prayed.

Her launch commander spoke in her ear: "This is Flight. Everything looks good. We are all go for launch. Repeat, all go for launch. T-minus two minutes."

The rocket's computers took over, and all she could do now was watch and wait as the team leads ran the various preflight tests and reported back. She heard the magic word in her ear over and over.

"Flight systems *nominal.*"

"Oxygen burn *nominal.*"

"Launch processing system *nominal.*"

"Payload test conductor *nominal.*"

"Telemetry *nominal.*"

Nominal was the only word she ever wanted to hear during a launch. It meant everything was going according to plan, the launch sequence wasn't meeting with any problems. *Nominal* meant more than *normal* in space talk. It meant everything was performing perfectly. With as many moving parts as it took to send a rocket into space, *nominal* represented the triumph of human achievement.

There had been a time when she was the one strapped into a tiny capsule and hurtled into orbit, the powerful thrust of the rocket taking her from zero to seventeen thousand miles per hour in less than eight minutes. But those days were past, and now Nevaeh ran Galactus Space Industries, a low-cost private provider to the European space arena. Launching telecommunications satellites into orbit was their bread and butter. She was responsible for eight launches a month, mostly sending European telecom satellites into a geostationary orbit, where they would boost signal strengths to increase cellular and Wi-Fi coverage for whichever company was sending up the satellite. With the success of Galactus, these nominal moments had become ordinary. Almost. But this time *nominal* was all she wanted to hear.

"This is Flight. T-minus one minute."

Nevaeh couldn't help it, she always held her breath. So much could happen in a single instant, so many things could go wrong.

In her ear, "T-minus ten. Nine. Eight. Seven. Six. Five —"

The engines, already running in preflight mode, roared to life, billowing steam and fire, and lifted the rocket into the sky, making the ground shake. Nevaeh's heart pumped hard as she watched the rocket — her special rocket — her focus now on the launch commander running through his postlaunch checklist. Cheers nearly drowned out his voice, but she listened carefully as he ticked off each benchmark.

Less than a minute later, the rocket was supersonic; another minute and the booster engines throttled back and separated from the main capsule that contained the twelve-foot-wide comms satellite.

Eight minutes after launch, the capsule was in orbit, and the fairing — the protective shield above the satellite — opened. The satellite was propelled into space, where it would take its place among the more than two thousand other satellites sending radio signals back down to Earth.

When the final stage broke away, there were cheers from the engineers in the flight center. Relief coursed through her. They'd done it. She looked down, saw that sometime during the launch she'd broken her pencil in two.

She grinned at the launch commander and rose and raised her fist to the rest of the room. She gave them a small bow and some applause of her own.

She called out, "Success. A beautiful launch. Thank you all for your hard work." She gave them all a thumbs-up and added, *"Merci beaucoup."*

Nevaeh walked from the command center to her small office. Her primary office was, of course, at the Galactus headquarters in Lyon, France, but she maintained space in French Guiana when she was able to be here for launch supervision.

It now fell to her team of engineers to activate the satellite and triangulate it into its final position.

She smiled. Not one of the engineers, not one of the technicians, no one except Kiera Byrne, her bodyguard and companion, knew she'd altered the computer code to put this particular satellite into a spot selected by her — not the company who'd paid for it to be launched. There was a special payload on this run-of-the-mill satellite, and only she and Kiera knew. No one else needed to know what was in the lead-lined box. Not until she was ready.

In two weeks' time, her nuclear bomb hidden aboard the satellite was going to set off an electromagnetic pulse that would change the world, and Nevaeh would remake it in her own image.

CHAPTER TWO

An EMP is a high-intensity burst of electro-magnetic energy caused by the rapid acceleration of charged particles. The electromagnetic shock disrupts electronics, such as sensors, communications systems, protective systems, computers, and other similar devices. It is a pulse that flows through electricity transmission lines — damaging distribution centers and fusing power lines.

— www.heritage.org

As a woman in the space industry, one of the few female corporate leaders, Nevaeh had to be one step ahead of her male counterparts at all times. Even though she was light-years ahead of many of them intellectually, had experience none of them would ever have after her stint on the International Space Station — not to mention the multiple degrees and extensive schooling under her belt — she still had to work twice as hard to maintain her position as head of Galactus.

Only you are brilliant, Nevaeh. It's why we chose you. You are going to bring peace to those who wish it, and death to those who resist. You will rule with us at your side. Now set off the bomb, destroy all the incessant noise in the heavens, and we will come for you.

The familiar melodious voices of many and yet only one in her head made her square her shoulders. Any time she felt a moment of weakness, of self-doubt, her astral friends would remind her of her purpose, remind her of what was important.

Of course, she never told her boss, Jean-Pierre Broussard, founder and owner of Galactus, about how she spoke with the Numen. He knew all about her claims nearly a decade ago of communicating with astral beings on the ISS, and it had made him more excited to hire her, not less. She had wondered many times what would happen if she announced to the world that a glorious new day was coming. But she knew. She'd be laughed at, declared insane, space crazy. She thought of that bitch, Rebecca Holloway, the vaunted shrink at NASA, who'd managed to have her grounded for good with her lies about Nevaeh's mental status. She'd overruled Franklin Norgate, the flight director, Nevaeh's friend. But then again, maybe she was wrong about Franklin, maybe he did believe Holloway's judgment. At least Holloway couldn't have openly declared her insane, no, that had remained internal, but what she'd done was just as bad. She'd made sure Nevaeh was denied what she'd desired more than anything else — to be in space. Where she belonged.

But who cared about Dr. Rebecca Holloway now? She'd gotten what she deserved and that made Nevaeh smile.

Did Jean-Pierre believe her experience in space? It didn't matter. Happily, he wasn't ever in her face. He stayed out of the way of the people who knew how to run the business. Unlike some of the stories she'd heard about other private space companies, Jean-Pierre was not a hands-on owner. His was a light touch, and he gave her free rein. He'd built the Galactus company from scratch, raised the money to get the first rockets off the ground, then found her. Together they'd assembled the best and the brightest to run Galactus. He was only involved when there were PR problems, or when he felt the need to touch base with the angels — venture capitalists who invested in the company from time to time when they were needed. He had an almost inexhaustible bank account himself and was smart enough to know what to spend it on. With her at the helm, Galactus stayed flush.

Broussard's dedication was always to the bottom line. He wanted Galactus to be the most respected, the best. Galactus wasn't the only private aerospace company in Europe, but they'd taken the lead because Nevaeh had found ways to launch satellites quickly, with reusable rockets. Had she stolen ideas from SpaceX, one of the most successful private space companies in the world? "Certainly," Jean-Pierre loved to say, winking at the cameras. "When the best exists, you might as well learn from them. Galactus will be to Europe what SpaceX is to America. There's room for all of us in space. It's infinite, after all."

After Jean-Pierre had hired her to run his company in 2013, knowing she was more than capable, he'd sailed off on his mega-yacht, *The Griffon,* to search for treasure buried in the sea. The arrangement worked wonderfully for them both — Nevaeh hated oversight, and Jean-Pierre hated day-to-day business management.

It was *The Griffon* Nevaeh now contacted

to report to Jean-Pierre, as always, about the successful launch.

She dialed, the satellite uplinked to the yacht, and Jean-Pierre's handsome face appeared on her computer screen — tanned, dark eyes, white teeth flashing, salt-and-pepper hair mussed from the salt spray, his Roman nose slightly pink from too much sun. His beard was beginning to gray a bit, but it only added to his charisma. He was so very French. When she'd first met him, he'd looked exactly like what she would expect from a billionaire playboy who'd parlayed his life into treasure hunting on the high seas. But he wasn't a playboy. He was whip-smart, and proved it because he'd instantly seen her potential. Whenever a competitor made a snide comment about her, one even going so far as to call her crazy, Jean-Pierre had dealt with them immediately.

Of course she wasn't crazy, she wasn't. What would he say if he knew who and what she really was? What she really wanted? From him? No matter what happened, she would always be grateful to him, no, worship him, for what he'd taught her, what he'd enabled her to understand and believe in — the Holy Grail. Ah, she'd doubted and argued, but he'd shown her document after document, until she finally believed the Grail existed. "It will make one who is worthy immortal," he'd said over and over, and she knew he believed it. Was he so anxious to live forever? He never said. But then she realized what it would mean — the Numen were immortal and she could be as well. She would be with them forever.

"Nevaeh, *ma chérie,* you're smiling from ear to ear. I can assume then the launch, as usual, was perfect?"

"Perfection personified, Jean-Pierre. To think, this is almost becoming routine. We're on schedule for ninety-six launches this fiscal year, as you expected."

"Wonderful. Congratulations to us."

"Yes, absolutely. The engineers are maneuvering the satellite into position and they will report in when they've finished, but I anticipate no problems." She paused an instant, then asked what she really wanted to know about, what the Numen were always asking now. "How is the search going?"

Jean-Pierre's face changed, suffused with a sort of light she imagined only existed in the passionate and the mad. Perhaps she looked the same when she thought about her own extraordinary path.

"This is classified, Nevaeh, and for your

ears only, of course —" The words burst out machine-gun fast, so great was his excitement. "I believe we may have found the *Flor de la Mar,* the ship matches her specs perfectly. She rests on the seabed below our current location and is in marvelous shape, considering how long she's been down there."

Her pulse began to pound. "Since November of 1511, correct?"

"Yes, the ship went down in 1511 in the Strait of Malacca, where we are now. As I told you, they were hauling treasures taken from the King of Siam back to Portugal. Our cameras show the ship is caught on a ledge, and some of the treasure is certainly lost in the trench below. We are undertaking a deep dive with the submersible today to take a closer look."

Her mouth felt dry. She whispered, "And the Grail? Immortality?"

"You know the Grail brings more than immortality, Nevaeh. I've told you countless times. The Grail brings the holder whatever it is he desires most. But only if he is worthy, and that is the key — being worthy."

Had she acted too impassioned? She forced a laugh. "Only 'he,' Jean-Pierre? The Grail is sexist?"

He laughed back. "Ah, Nevaeh, so many

have failed, as you know, and I believe to my soul it stayed hidden because none of those people were worthy of finding it, claiming it."

She wanted to say *yeah, yeah, blah, blah* to his philosophical nonsense. She really wanted to scream at him, *I'm worthy, what I want is worthy, the Grail is meant for me.* But instead, she said dutifully, "If anyone is worthy, Jean-Pierre, it's you."

"Honeyed words, but appreciated. Now, I will let you get back to Lyon, and I will get back to my ship. *À bientôt.*"

Nevaeh said, "Happy hunting," and reached for the button to end their call. As she did, she saw Jean-Pierre turning toward the doorway as an excited-looking young man entered waving his hands. She heard the very words she'd been waiting for, three years now, and her heart leaped into her throat.

"We've found it, sir! We've confirmed this is the *Flor de la Mar,* and there's something big in the hold, bigger than —"

The call went dead.

The clear sibilant voice in her head said, *They have found what we seek. It is time, Nevaeh. With the Grail, we will succeed, you will be with us forever.*

She sat for a moment, thinking furiously.

And then she placed another call.

"Flight command, what is the status of our satellite?"

The man's voice was grave. "I was about to call you, Dr. Patel. There seems to be a problem. The satellite missed its insertion point. Apparently, it's an issue with the code telling the satellite to unfurl its solar panels. Because of this —"

"How could this happen? The code has been programmed for weeks. This is the easiest part of the launch. Who is responsible?"

"I'm not sure, but I will let you know. I am so very sorry. We will begin diagnostics to determine what happened. As far as we can tell, the code coordinates were incorrect, but a check of the original code is correct. I have no idea how it happened, but we will get to the bottom of it. Might take a few weeks, but we'll figure it out."

Of course, she knew exactly what had happened. She smiled into the phone as she said, her voice hard, "See that you do. I am very disappointed. It was such a perfect launch."

She didn't slam the phone down, but gave it a good snap. Good, let them stew. She gathered her things and headed to the plane. By the time she was back in Lyon, the satellite would be written off as a complete loss, and she could begin her work placing it in a new elliptical. With Jean-Pierre's discovery of the *Flor de la Mar,* she sent a prayer heavenward. *Let it be the Holy Grail.*

CHAPTER THREE

Sky News
July 15
"In aerospace news today, France's private space company Galactus announced that despite a picture-perfect launch yesterday, the payload, a telecommunications satellite, failed to deploy in the proper elliptical orbit. According to a statement released by the company, the failure was caused by a faulty fairing atop the nose cone of the rocket, damaging the satellite payload as the final separation occurred. This prevented its solar panels from deploying.

"The value of the satellite was estimated at thirty million euros, and is considered a total loss. Despite the failure, Galactus confirms there is another launch scheduled, this time with the top secret government payload rumored to be a French spy satellite."

CHAPTER FOUR

T-MINUS 120 HOURS

Home of Grant and Kitsune Thornton
Capri, Italy
July 23

Special Agent Mike Caine sat on a stool by the elevated countertop, her foot up, resting her healing broken ankle. She sipped her champagne as she watched Kitsune arrange tomato and mozzarella slices for a caprese salad. She started to stretch forward to hand Kitsune the olive oil when Kitsune waved her away. "No, don't move, Michaela, your ankle's nearly healed, no setbacks allowed. Your only job is to sit there and watch the master chef at work, and, of course, admire."

"Can I at least drizzle on the basil and olive oil?"

"You're not French, you wouldn't get the amounts just right." They were laughing when Grant Thornton, Kitsune's husband of three months, came into the open kitchen carrying a platter of grilled lobsters. Mike breathed in. "Goodness, that smells like heaven. Careful, Grant, Nicholas and I might move in."

"You'd be welcome, but I doubt you'd be here long before haring off on your next adventure," Grant said. "Smell that lobster. Nothing like local, you'll see. Where is Nicholas? I thought he'd be back by now."

Mike said, "I thought he was part of the male grilling party."

Grant set the platter on the counter. "He told me it looked to him like I had things well in hand, said he had an errand to run and he'd be right back."

"He did mention he needed to call his mom back," Mike said. "She's solving a mystery in their local village of Farrow-on-Gray, something she excels at. Our families, his and mine both, seem to take turns calling. Even Horne, his parents' butler, and Nigel — he's Nicholas's butler in New York — and no, please don't mention Nigel, Nicholas would be horribly embarrassed. They all want to know where we are, what we're doing, and is my ankle healed yet. My dad's all into hearing about my scuba diving off Santorini and the Gorgeous Rebecca, my mom, wants more photos of the

Palace of Knossos on Crete. And as I said, Nicholas's mom has this new mystery to solve."

Kitsune said, "Nicholas told me you looked just like your mother — the Gorgeous Rebecca."

"Nah, Mom's a knockout, I'm only a vague copy."

Kitsune shook her head and smiled. "What's his mother's mystery involve?"

"When he comes back from his errand, whatever that could be, ask him. I don't have a clue yet. He's told me he gets his love of solving mysteries from her. She's quite the sleuth at home." She grinned, dropped her voice. "Or maybe, Kitsune, Nicholas is off searching out a missing Rembrandt."

"Sorry, he'll be out of luck," Kitsune said. "I never bring my work home. Even the Rembrandts."

Grant said, "There's a pity, I'd like to have a Rembrandt on the wall. No, make that a Vermeer."

Mike laughed and slid off the stool. "I'll go see if he's back."

"Lunch in ten minutes," Grant called out.

Mike walked through the large main level, open on all sides. She couldn't help herself and paused to admire the vast sea views.

The house itself was four stories of white stucco, built into the Capri cliffside. It was lovely, very private. It was, she knew, their sanctuary as well as their home. She stepped onto the bougainvillea-covered veranda and breathed in the sweet scent and thought about Kitsune and Grant — an international thief and a former Beefeater, now an international security expert — how they'd found each other and gotten married. It boggled the mind.

Mike called for him, but Nicholas was nowhere to be seen.

Now, what was he up to? Giving his mom advice?

Mike made her way back to the open kitchen, retook her seat on the stool, and took a sip of champagne.

Kitsune asked, "Find him?"

"Nope." She grabbed her phone and sent a text. "Why didn't I think of this before wandering around?"

Where are you? Lunch is almost ready.

With you in a moment.

Mike said to Grant, "He didn't say what he was doing?"

"Nope."

Mike said, "What man disappears from a lunch party with fresh lobster heading the menu to run an errand?"

A man's voice said from the doorway, "The kind who wants to surprise the wild woman with the nearly healed ankle."

She turned to see Nicholas holding a bouquet of blush-pink and white roses, peonies, and sprigs of delicate lily of the valley, all wrapped in fine blue gauze the same color as the Bay of Naples.

Nicholas held out the flowers. "For you, Agent Caine."

"Oh goodness, Nicholas, they're gorgeous, but what are they for?"

"Our anniversary. One month we've slain dragons together, maybe a bit longer, but close enough."

Their anniversary. But it was more than that, lots more. It had been nearly one month today he'd come to her apartment after they'd survived a hair-raising adventure, and she'd leaped on him. Imagine, she'd only known him for a total of six months, since January, when he'd first come over from London. *The Koh-i-Noor was January, and now here we are in July, partners in every sense, sitting on a veranda on a sunny Italian cliff.* In six months her life had changed irrevocably. Well, his had as well.

He'd uprooted himself from Scotland Yard in England to move to America, joined the FBI, and was now a firecracker agent, and the two of them were leading the Covert Eyes team. And her life had expanded and blossomed —

"Where are you, Mike?"

She gave him a manic grin. "Just thinking, remembering. So much has happened, actually to all of us, in the last six months. And somehow, against the odds, we're here and we're friends." She took the flowers and her hand lingered on his. "Thank you for the flowers. Let's go dancing in Rome, my ankle's almost one hundred percent. Some place to waltz. Do you waltz, Nicholas?"

"Yes, my father said every gentleman had to waltz and do it gracefully, as if he'd emerged from the womb dancing to Strauss."

"Come on, mates, enough with the mush," Grant said as he walked in with a tray of grilled vegetables. "Chow's ready. Nice flowers."

Kitsune took the flowers, set them in a vase. "You did good, boyo, very good. Grant, pay heed. Nicholas bought these for their anniversary. Here we've been married for three months, and all I get is lobster and grilled aubergine?"

Grant laughed. "Oh, trust me, I know, and I won't forget." He moved close, lightly touched his fingers to her cheek. "You've given me the most bonkers three months of my life. I'm looking forward to years of the same."

She swatted him with a towel, then leaned up and kissed his mouth. "You're lucky I'm mad for you."

They brought everything to the veranda, even the flowers, set precisely in the middle of the table. The veranda was heavenly scented, the stucco warm and inviting, the trellis covered in lush green vines dotted with jasmine, the small lemon orchard above and to the side making the whole hill smell like sunshine. A light breeze blew off the sea. It was a glorious moment in time, Mike thought, a moment to remember and treasure. *Bonkers,* she thought, an excellent word. All their lives were amazing and, yes, bonkers.

In between bites, Kitsune said, "The mystery, Nicholas? Tell us what puzzle your mother is solving, then I want to know Mike's favorite spot you've visited during your vacation."

Nicholas speared a grilled carrot. "Mum said Mrs. Able, the owner of the Cock and the Crow, a local inn in Farrow-on-Gray,

44

found a dead man in his room, shot through the head, the room ransacked. The room was rented to a man from London for one night, a stranger. But it was no stranger Mrs. Able found. The dead man was a local solicitor, good reputation, solid family. And on his forehead, in his own blood, was a cross with a small blood dot on each side of the crossbar, and a huge blood X on his chest. Mrs. Able came to see my mum immediately and it was my mum who called the local constabulary. She's investigating along with Inspector Crabbe, a dour old curmudgeon who adores her and treats her like the queen."

"So what happened? Did your mother figure it out yet?"

"It's only been a few days. She said she'd keep me posted and to give Mike a big kiss and remind her of her promise and to text me any ideas."

"Promise?" An eyebrow went up as Kitsune dipped lobster into hot butter.

"Unwritten and unspoken, but clear enough," Mike said. "I'm to keep him safe and in perfect health. Or else. Now, onward. My favorite spot so far? I really liked Santorini. Well, of course, there's Crete."

Nicholas tugged on her ponytail. "Admit it, Mike, you're getting antsy, you want

45

some action, maybe fly back to England and help my mum solve this murder mystery. All this wallowing in the sunshine and floating in the Mediterranean is getting to you."

Was she getting antsy? She thought of exploring Rome and said, "Nah, not yet." She waved her hands around her. "Capri is spectacular. We did the Blue Grotto this morning, what a cool spot. And it's beautiful here. If this was my view every day, maybe I wouldn't ever want to leave."

Kitsune said, "Ah, but duty always calls, doesn't it? A lovely balance we all have, I say. After wallowing for a while, I'm contacted when there's something to, ah, liberate, Blue Mountain tells Grant there's someone for him to protect, and for you two, there's always someone naughty to discipline. And speaking of stopping bad guys — you're gaining quite a reputation. Saving the president again, and the Queen and prime minister? I hear you were knighted, Nicholas, and Mike is now a dame. Impressive. My advice? Wallow while you have the chance. There's always something lurking in the shadows, just out of sight, waiting to grab you by the throat."

Grant said, "What's lurking for me is heading up a team to protect a man in Malaysia. Should be pretty straightforward.

I ship out tonight."

Nicholas said, "So Blue Mountain has forgiven you for getting yourself kidnapped, and you're back in the saddle. Glad to hear it."

"They even gave me enough downtime to do pretty substantial upgrades to our security here. My boss, name's Wesley Fentriss, said to make it solid so I'd never be taken from here again, or he'd shoot me. The man I'm going to protect is Jean-Pierre Broussard. You've heard of him, yes?"

Nicholas raised a brow. "The Frenchman who founded Galactus Space Industries?"

"That's the chap. Turns out he's just as interested in treasure hunting as in space exploration, and has his megayacht somewhere near Malaysia. Apparently, his treasure hunting is so lucrative he needs major security, so Blue Mountain has been rotating teams in and out for the past month. I've been assigned to head the next team. As I said, I fly out tonight."

Nicholas asked, "Is Broussard searching for anything in particular, do you know?"

"No clue, but it must be something special. We don't normally provide generic guard duties, but there are pirates in that area, so he's concerned what treasure he finds could be stolen. It should be interesting. I've heard the yacht is four hundred feet long, one of the most state-of-the-art in the world. I saw a photo — it looks like a floating spaceship."

Mike said, "What about you, Kitsune?"

The breeze was tousling Kitsune's black hair around her face. Her eyes were lighter and bluer than the sky. She looked relaxed and happy. Amazing, Mike thought, to think this elegant Madonna could turn into a tiger in an instant, a very deadly tiger. She said, "Actually, like Grant, I'm about to leave on an assignment as well. No, forget it, I'm not about to tell you what I'm going to do or where I'm going to be. Actually, I have to be completely off the grid for the next two weeks. I don't like it, but no choice."

Grant took her hand in his. "I'm not particularly thrilled about that last part."

Nicholas knew if anyone could take care of herself, it was Kitsune. She was wily as her namesake, a fox. He asked, "How about one small hint, Kitsune?"

Her grin was cocky. "You mentioned Rembrandt, didn't you?"

"Which one?" Mike asked, sitting forward. "Where?"

Kitsune threw back her head and laughed. "No more. Now, if you two would like, since we're both leaving, you could postpone

Rome and stay here. Finish convalescing, Mike, and wallow in the lovely water in the cove right below us. You and Nicholas could keep celebrating your anniversary."

Nicholas finished the last bite of his lobster. "That's very kind, but we're expected at the Hassler in Rome this evening. I can't wait to show Mike around."

Grant said, "What do you want to see, Mike?"

"Everything. Full-on tourist mode for me — the Pantheon, the Colosseum, the Vatican, you name it, I'm game. Oh, Grant, I noticed your fitness tracker. I've been thinking it wouldn't be a bad idea to get one, especially considering how lazy I've been. I need to ramp up my exercise again, and I love accountability. What do you think of it?"

"I'm with you, I like accountability, too. This baby measures all sorts of information, from steps to weight to heartbeat. This new version costs less than a hundred dollars and even tells you the time and where you are on the planet."

He took it off and handed it to her. She said, "I want one in blue. Hey, Nicholas, do you think we could find me one in Rome? I could get you one in macho black like Grant's for our anniversary, instead of flowers. What do you think? Hey, what are you doing?"

Nicholas said, without looking up, "Checking out where we can find a fitness tracker like Grant's in Rome. Ah, here we go. Now, Mike, we need to leave. I want to get to Rome before sundown."

At the door, Kitsune hugged Mike and whispered against her ear, "Don't worry, it's not a Rembrandt, it's something far more exciting, more esoteric, if you will. Ah, can't you see me flirting in Russian? You can stay in touch with Grant, and I'll be back here in two weeks. I hope."

Mike called out as she climbed aboard behind Nicholas on their rented motorcycle, "Grant, be careful with all those pirates in Malaysia."

CHAPTER FIVE

T-MINUS 110 HOURS

The *Flor de la Mar* or *Flor do Mar* (Flower of the Sea) was a Portuguese carrack of 400 tons that sailed the seas during the early 1500s. This ship was carrying a great amount of treasure when it sank somewhere off the coast of Sumatra, possibly at the northern end of the Strait of Malacca, during its voyage back to Portugal. . . . Whilst some have claimed that the ship has been found, these have not been supported with irrefutable evidence. Thus, the wreck of the *Flor de la Mar,* along with the treasure it was transporting, is still considered to be lost.

— Ancient-origins.net

The Griffon
Strait of Malacca
Off the Coast of Sumatra
Jean-Pierre Broussard stood at his desk

holding the fragile piece of paper that had brought him here, a portion of a letter from the captain of the *Flor de la Mar*, Afonso de Albuquerque, to his son, detailing the doomed voyage. It was dated two weeks after the captain was rescued from these very waters back in 1511.

Jean-Pierre knew that nearly all of the four hundred crew aboard the ship had died, but Albuquerque had gotten away and, miracle of miracles, now a portion of the letter was in Jean-Pierre's keeping. He held the creased paper carefully, so worn and fragile it now was. It wasn't an officially known letter, but one Jean-Pierre had discovered, translated, and kept to himself, knowing what it could mean to him, to Emilie. Surely the fates could not be so unjust as to give him the letter and not lead him to the ship.

As always when he read the words, he felt a leap of hope.

As sorry as I am to see the *Flor de la Mar* lost, I will be forever happy to have left behind the accursed black stone, which is clearly not of this world. It was bad luck from the start.

The black stone Albuquerque spoke of was the Heaven Stone — more commonly called the Holy Grail — he knew it to his soul. Why had Albuquerque considered the stone bad luck? Why hadn't he realized what immense good fortune he'd found or been given? If only he'd understood what he had, he never would have been so cavalier about leaving it behind when he managed to escape from his sinking ship.

Soon, soon, he would find it. He had to find it. Time was running out for Emilie. He closed his eyes a moment in prayer, a daily ritual, and he saw Emilie three years ago, at eighteen, just after she'd been diagnosed. And it was for Emilie, beautiful, innocent Emilie, the daughter of his heart. No one was more worthy than she. He would have freely given everything he owned if it would help her, but nothing could help, no drug, no medicine, no operation. Only the Holy Grail. And it was on that day he knew he had to find the Grail, it was simply the most important thing in his life, now or ever. He had to find it, bring it to her, and she would be well. There was no more worthy an individual than his precious daughter. Then he saw her as she'd been a month ago, lying on her back in bed, her beautiful black hair spread around her head on the white pillowcase, her nurse sitting beside her. Her legs were now too weak for her to walk, and she had little strength left in her arms. It wouldn't be much longer, the doctor had told him, and lowered his head in sympathy. Jean-Pierre had held Emilie close, kissed her temple. "*Mon petit chou,* I am still looking for your gift from God and I swear to you I will find it and it will cure you. You must be strong. You will live, you will be healthy, I swear it to you."

Three years since he'd begun his search, three long years he'd prayed, he'd studied, followed any and every lead he heard about or read about in ancient texts, stories, legends, he didn't care. Many times he'd despaired because she'd gotten progressively weaker, but then, somehow — he believed it a miracle, truth be told — the letter had come to him. Yes, he knew it was meant to come to him, for Emilie.

The past nine days had filled him with hope. Exciting days, frustrating, and then he'd had to deal with the fallout from the failed satellite launch. He'd said over and over to the reporters who incessantly emailed him — *These things happen. We regret the failure tremendously, and will endeavor not to let it happen again.*

Let the press clamor. Jean-Pierre could care less about the satellites his company launched or, in this case, failed to launch into space. No, what he was about to find was the Holy Grail itself, the ultimate reward to those worthy and deserving — the granting of one's greatest desire and everlasting life. For Emilie.

And he'd finally found the *Flor de la Mar,* no question in his mind. He'd seen in the silty quiet of the water's depth the skeleton, spars and metal scattered on the ocean floor. Ah, but there were significant pieces still intact. A five-by-ten chunk of the hull had been their first recovery. Upon examination, they were able to see the repairs to the hull made after the ship's maiden voyage, when it began to leak. The round marks from the wooden repair pegs had been almost perfectly preserved in the salty deep waters.

For nine days, they'd been diving to the wreck. They'd split into two teams — divers and those running the submersible, as the wreckage was in two areas — one half on the reef, 656 feet under the water, the other deeper by nearly 300 feet, down into a dark, unmapped trench.

The ship herself was in tatters, clearly broken apart by the waves that had sunk her centuries ago. A loss, but nothing to discourage him, because the cargo was scattered across a football field's length of terrain. So far, they'd flagged hundreds of crates buried in the silt.

The cargo. Or should he say, the lost treasure from the heavens.

He wasn't at all surprised the ship had gone down. The fact was they'd overloaded her with treasure and she wouldn't withstand a ferocious storm. She had been repaired many times, this old warhorse of a ship, and was not up to the challenge. Her sinking was no fault of the Heaven Stone. The weight of the crates alone was beyond her capabilities, not to mention crew, supplies, and, of course, the stone. He wondered why Albuquerque had decided to use her to transport the treasure he'd taken from the King of Siam after his conquest of Malacca. Where was his brain? Broussard asked himself again. How had the Grail come to be among the treasures of Siam? He didn't know why, doubted he would ever know, nor did he really care. He only wanted to find it, find it before Emilie suffocated to death.

A bright young voice called out from the doorway, "You were reading that ancient letter again, weren't you, Jean-Pierre? You have memorized it."

Jean-Pierre looked up to see Devi, beautiful Devi, with her charmingly accented

French, her glorious black hair braided halfway down her back, her perfect young body. So eager she was, and how she pleased him, her brightness, her curiosity. She distracted him when he despaired, and to be fair, he found her incredible in bed. To his surprise she wasn't at all venal. She was kindhearted, amazing in his experience for one so young and beautiful, and a bigger surprise, she'd been presented to him quite unexpectedly, like a lovely steak on a plate, by a wealthy businessman in Kuala Lumpur. The world saw her as his current mistress, and that was true enough. But unlike others before her, she was interested in him and in his search, always eager to listen to his stories about the Holy Grail. But, of course, he'd never told her about Emilie. No one knew about Emilie. He'd always protected her identity, kept her away from the rapacious, ever-insatiable media, to spare her the pain of being called illegitimate.

Devi stood in the suite doorway, wearing a lacy white coverup, and beneath it he knew there was a bikini that would make a man's guts twist. He found it amazing his crew never leered at her, never made jokes about his latest mistress behind their hands. Fact was they liked her. He saw she was looking down at the linen packet in his hands.

"Devi, yes, I have memorized it. I've told you, the very existence of this letter gives me new hope when I would fall into depression. It makes me hold to my belief." He'd shown it to her, of course, and she'd read it.

She crossed the room to where he stood, lightly laid her hand on his shoulder. "I have spoken to the men. They are convinced something — they don't know what — is down there, waiting to be retrieved. They all want it to be the Holy Grail. They want to present it to you. They are as excited as you are. Tell me, Jean-Pierre, if — no — *when* you have the Grail in your possession, what will you do with it? Carry it on your shoulders to show the world? Become the emperor of the planet forever? What?"

He looked into her beautiful face, so vital with health and youth. Jean-Pierre was twice her age, wealthy, a man who knew he was handsome and well-made and charming. And notoriously fickle with his women. Still, Devi had been with him for more than six months, a record, both of them knew.

He kissed her gently, then eased the linen-wrapped letter into his battered leather logbook. "No, I do not wish to be an

58

emperor or carry it on my shoulders and prance about the world and show off my prize." What to say? "It is something private, something very special to me."

"You have never told me how you came to be hunting for the Holy Grail."

He sat down, brought her onto his lap. "No, do not kiss me, I don't want to lose my thread." He closed his hands loosely around her waist. "I will tell you. At first it wasn't about the Holy Grail, I scarcely knew anything about it. I grew up in Lyon, as you know, and there wasn't much to do. We had a store that rented movies on those dreadful VHS tapes. I had read about Jacques Cousteau and his underwater discoveries, and was looking for something similar to watch. The owner of the store had a private collection of bootleg movies he received from friends in the United States. There was one that told the story of a treasure hunter in Florida named Mel Fisher who discovered the sunken Spanish galleon *Nuestra Señora de Atocha,* and recovered four hundred and fifty million dollars in treasure — gold, silver, emeralds, rubies — forty tons of gold."

Her eyes never left his face. He loved her curiosity, her focus on him as if she wanted to pull the words out of his mouth. Did she care for him? He hoped so. He continued, "As you can imagine, to a ten-year-old boy interested in treasure hunting and diving, this was an incredible discovery. I decided on the spot I was going to become a treasure hunter. I began reading books on lost treasure. So many lost ships, so many stories to follow, and I've found my share, to be sure. But in the past three years, as you know, I've sought the biggest treasure of them all."

She whispered, "The Heaven Stone — the Holy Grail."

"Yes. I suppose you could say I must find it or I will lose my desire for all of this." He waved his hand around. "Yes, I must find it and soon, very soon now." He touched his hand to his heart. "I feel it here. Soon I will have it."

She cocked her head to one side. "I don't understand. Why is the Grail so important to you? It's as if your life will no longer be worth living if you don't find it."

He wasn't certain what to say, and he didn't have to speak, for he heard his dive captain yelling in the hall.

"Captain! Captain! We need you!"

Jean-Pierre lifted her off his lap. "Now what is this all about?" He yelled, "Come."

Cesar Lourdes stood in the doorway, a

mask in one hand, water streaming from his stringy ponytail, a huge grin on his face. "Boss, I'd thought we'd found something, before, well, it wasn't the Grail, but now — this might be the Grail, you must come."

Jean-Pierre's adrenaline spiked, his heart kettledrummed in his chest. He and Devi followed Cesar to the aft portion of the bridge where the dive was being coordinated. As they walked, Cesar said, "I was on the reef site, kicking around in the silt, seeing what I could find, and I knocked into something pretty big, bigger than the rest of the chests we've recovered or marked for recovery. And very different. I ran the portable X-ray over it and, sir — there's something inside, and it doesn't seem to be fastened to anything. It's very strange."

Keep calm, keep calm. "How big are we talking?"

"Hard to tell. The container, it seems to be a sort of sphere, only a bit elongated, maybe ten feet or so high."

Devi said, "Since the Grail isn't supposed to be so large, Jean-Pierre, then maybe it's the strange thing inside this sphere?"

It is, it is, it has to be. He said, "Possibly."

Cesar said, "I believe the container is made of iron. It's immensely heavy."

Devi said, "Why would the Grail be inside

something made of iron? To protect it?" She paused, blinked up at Jean-Pierre. "Or protect us?"

Jean-Pierre gave her a long look. "Only one way to find out." He knew then, knew to his soul. It was the Holy Grail. He said, "Let's get my stone. Devi, what's wrong? Don't you wish to stay?"

"I'm sorry, Jean-Pierre. My stomach — I do not feel well. You will show me everything later."

"Of course, of course," he said over his shoulder, not really paying her any more attention, his focus on the winch bringing up the container.

Devi walked away, doing her best to look relaxed, to look at ease. But she did feel sick to her stomach, sick for what she was doing to this excellent man, this man with such a mighty life force that made him burn so brightly. She had no choice. No choice. When she'd first come to him, she'd expected this wealthy Frenchman to treat her like the bauble she was when presented to him, a plaything, to give him great sex and amuse him, and she was prepared to play her part well. Again, no choice. But she hadn't expected to like him, to admire him, to find his passion for finding the Holy

Grail, something she'd always believed no more than a romantic legend, fascinating, mesmerizing. What would he think when he learned she'd betrayed him?

On the sun deck, Devi eased down on a chaise, turned away from two young crewmen after she'd waved at them, and reached into her bag. She drew out a mobile satellite phone with a special program installed. Every message sent and received — email or text — would self-destruct within two hours. As long as she kept it hidden, she was safe.

She tapped in a few words. He believes he's found it. It's inside a huge iron sphere. Will update soon.

Moments later, a reply appeared. Very good. Keep me apprised. What are your current coordinates?

Devi opened her compass app and sent the exact latitude and longitude coordinates of *The Griffon* in the next text. Then she typed in, Is my sister well? You promised to let me speak to her.

But there was no answer.

The bitch. Nevaeh had promised, stared her right in the eye and promised not to hurt Elina. Devi stared at the silent phone. She knew if something happened to her little sister, she'd kill Nevaeh Patel with her bare hands.

She hid the phone away, put on her sunglasses, and pretended to sunbathe, all the while forcing herself to try to stay calm.

CHAPTER SIX

T-MINUS 109 HOURS

Galactus Space Industries Headquarters
Lyon, France

The cream bricks were bathed in sunlight when the SUV pulled into the parking lot at Galactus. Nevaeh climbed from the back seat, stepped into the soft, thick air. Rain was coming, but for now, the skies were a luminous blue. She set her sunglasses in place as she turned to Kiera, her Kiera, ruthless, hard as nails, fiercely loyal, and loaded down with weapons, but still, to Nevaeh, Kiera was her champion and her confidante, the only other human being she trusted with her very life. Nearly four years now they'd been together.

Kiera was frowning up at the sky. "Will I have time to check the telescope before the rains begin?"

"No, probably not. Don't worry about it."

Kiera checked her watch. "You have meetings starting in five minutes. The final report for the board on why the satellite failed to deploy."

They shared a smile as the main doors slid open.

Nevaeh said, "Then we will give them a definitive reason, not the usual nondeploying fairing. I've decided it's to be metal fatigue from the manufacturer causing the fairing to damage the satellite. And a bonus, contractually, if there is a failure, they have to give us back all the money we outlaid for the contract. Not our fault. Tsk, tsk. Shouldn't be so careless."

She laughed, an elegant, carefree sound. And she felt carefree, happier than she had in years. All her hopes, her dreams, everything was about to come to pass, and she was going to be reunited with the Numen and all would be revealed, everyone on this planet would know she was their future, she and the Numen. She was their salvation. Of course she was in a good mood. Years she'd spent getting to this moment. Years of work to bring about a new age — no more stupid wars, even if she had to castrate every covetous, money-grubbing man on the planet. Or woman.

She knew there would be resistance, at

first. People didn't want to be saved, didn't, apparently, want there to be no more wars, no more corruption. She had tried to share the possibilities after she'd first encountered the Numen on the space station, and her thanks had been to be drummed out of NASA for her trouble. She'd learned her lesson. The world wasn't ready for what she would bring them, nor were they ready for the simple truth — life existed outside of Earth. Nevaeh knew the Numen were gods, older than the Olympians, older than the Titans. And they'd chosen her, no one else, just her. And it had taken her seven years, but now she was ready to — well, not bring peace, exactly. Say, stability, order, function, through her intelligence, her ability to lead. She would bring the Numen to Earth, and they would give her what she had to have — power and immortality. Might people die to fulfill her quest? Of course. But the sacrifices must be made.

The nuclear bomb would fix everything. And the EMP fallout. It would bring them to their knees, make them grateful to her for picking them out of the ashes.

As for the static and noise that gummed up the atmosphere, cell phones and radio waves and wireless communications all combining to make the layer of atmosphere around Earth supercharged with disturbances, it would all stop. Soon, the world where people worshiped their devices, were completely dependent on technology, it would all end. There would be blessed silence in the heavens and on Earth. And she'd give humankind the promise of a greater good.

Yes, once all was quiescent, the Numen would come, and she and they would rule — together.

Inside, the headquarters of Galactus looked empty. The floors were a huge expanse of white marble. The walls were pure white, the only splashes of color from small groupings of modern art canvases on the walls that were changed seasonally. But it was the focal point that was incredible — a full planetary system hung from a jet-black ceiling, fifty feet across. It was in perpetual motion, aligned to mimic the movement of the stars and planets in their ellipticals. To Nevaeh, it represented more than a fanciful rendering of the solar system. It was a reminder of the limitless possibilities of space.

A young Jean-Pierre had been to the Guggenheim in New York and fallen in love with the unique interior architecture, and so modeled Galactus after the museum. It was striking. The floor ramps circled upward, ever upward, ten floors, like the spirals of a shell. The offices and workspaces were on the outer walls and the immense center was filled with the universe. Anyone who came in always stopped and stared.

Nevaeh loved walking into Galactus and looking up at the universe. Outside of her sensory deprivation chamber, it was the only place that felt like home.

A woman left an unobtrusive reception desk and came across the expanse to greet her, as if she were a general. Other employees appeared. They might as well salute as she walked by. She was, she supposed, actually their general, and they'd soon understand how important she was. Not only their CEO, but more, so much more.

Smiling, at peace, she took the discreet elevator to the tenth floor and walked into the board meeting, head high, prepared to lie. Everything was in motion.

An hour later, Kiera escorted Nevaeh back to her office. "Did the board accept your explanation?"

"Yes, of course. The board is taken care of, though I believe they were upset Jean-Pierre wasn't on the call. I convinced them the satellite was damaged by the fairing, not our fault, and we're ready to move forward on the upcoming launches. Obviously, we'll have to write off the satellite, and the company will hardly want to trust us with another, but who cares? Little do they know, there will be no more launches. Once the nuke is in place, we won't need to send junk into space any longer. Can you imagine, space cleared of human waste?"

Kiera didn't know if she really considered communication satellites human waste. Nor did she believe space was cluttered, too cluttered for these space aliens Nevaeh called the Numen. After all, wasn't space infinite? Enough room for everybody? But she knew enough to accept what was going to happen, perhaps rejoice because she would be at Nevaeh's right hand when the apocalypse came, if such a thing could happen. Kiera was willing to suspend disbelief when Nevaeh had first told her of these peace-loving aliens, but the strange thing was, over time, the aliens had changed as Nevaeh had changed. Goals had changed. No more peace-loving kumbaya. Fact was, the change felt right to Kiera. After all, many of the peace-loving people in Ireland were dead. And now Kiera was ready to believe, maybe thrilled to believe. What would she become? She would be important, would have a major role in the new regime. She held this knowledge tightly to her heart. And stopped questioning. After all, Nevaeh was certain and she was the smartest person Kiera had ever known. And her will was amazing, and her experience with these space aliens? Her goals with the Numen? Well, who was she to question? She loved Nevaeh and had come to accept all she said was truth, with a capital *T*. She leaned in close. "And so much will happen, and only you and I know what is coming. It will be glorious, Nevaeh. Simply glorious."

Yes, it would be. Nevaeh said, "Now, hurry up. I need to move the last pawn into place."

CHAPTER SEVEN

Kiera opened the office door and stepped inside first. She was always careful of Nevaeh. What she saw was reassuring — an immense mess, like a bomb had gone off inside, which, of course, Kiera knew was how Nevaeh liked it. Her boss was a horizontal filer, had stacks of paper and books all over her desk, the floor, the cabinets, the bookshelves. No one in the company dared move a thing. Nevaeh knew where everything was, didn't need to search for a moment, could lay her hand on the file or folder or article needed in seconds flat. Kiera was more organized, liked to see the top of her desk, though granted, she rarely used it. The contents of her office mostly consisted of the weaponry.

Nevaeh said, "Close the door. I have work to do."

Kiera prowled, said over her shoulder, "When will we hear from that idiot girl?"

Nevaeh looked at the clock. "Soon. Surely Jean-Pierre has the Grail by now. Devi will be in touch, and we must be ready to leave the minute she does. What are your preparations?"

"We're staged, ready to head to the ship when we get her call. I have a plane waiting to take us to Kuala Lumpur, and I've arranged for transport to *The Griffon*."

"And the transport is fully equipped?"

"Yes. Everything we need is aboard, awaiting our arrival."

"Excellent. I need to do one thing before we leave."

She sat at her desk and opened her laptop. Kiera came to stand behind her.

"The satellite must be put into the proper position, and since no one but us knows it's still up there, we need to do it carefully so we don't draw unwanted attention. We don't need the fools at the U.S. Strategic Command noticing the satellite has joined a new orbit. And if they do, this needs to look like another piece of randomly moving space junk."

She began typing in a complex series of letters and numbers, lines of code Kiera knew would turn the satellite on and give it instructions to reposition. She thought Nevaeh was amazing to be able to move their own man-made stars.

Five minutes later, Nevaeh clicked a button and shut her laptop.

"I've programmed the satellite. It is beginning its move into position, slowly, so it won't attract attention. By my calculations, it will be perfectly aligned by the apex of the lunar eclipse on the twenty-eighth. And on that date we must have the Grail in hand." She rose. "I believe Jean-Pierre has found the Grail and it's all coming together, Kiera. I will be in place to detonate the bomb and cause the EMP at one a.m., the moment the eclipse enters totality."

Nevaeh felt nerves and hope together. "When we have the Grail, we will be immortal, Kiera, both of us. For I would never leave you behind. And you will meet the Numen."

"But Nevaeh, it all depends — what if Broussard doesn't find the Grail? What if it's not on that sunken ship?"

"The Grail is there, waiting. I know it here." She laid her palm over her heart. "The Numen told me Jean-Pierre would find it, so of course it will be in his hands — and ours — before long." She clasped Kiera's arms. "Think, Kiera, the Holy Grail. As I've told you many times, the Numen will come and together, we will reward you."

Kiera smiled perfunctorily. First things first. "Nevaeh, we should go. We can be in Sri Lanka by nightfall and ready to intercept *The Griffon*. And the Grail." Kiera tucked a strand of hair behind Nevaeh's ear. "This is what you've worked toward."

Nevaeh's secretary knocked on her door, making the women jerk apart. They were always so careful in public, no slips allowed. Nevaeh knew there were rumors, but she didn't care. Still, no sense flaunting her relationship with Kiera at work. She called out, "Come in, Alys."

Alys was young, twenty-five, with a penchant for black leather jackets and a French boyfriend who was handsome as sin and picked her up from work every day on his motorcycle. Nevaeh watched them from the window sometimes, Alys kissing him deeply on the mouth and clinging to his back as he roared away, her ponytail streaming from under her helmet. They seemed happy, and Alys was never a slacker. She was smart, detailed, always diligent, never missing work or coming up with excuses for days off.

"Dr. Patel? Is now a good time? I have the launch schedule. You said you wanted to be at the spaceport in time to oversee the engine test."

Nevaeh said smoothly, "Alys, I've received

a call from the Quints manufacturing facility in China. They have discovered the issue with the metal used to make the fairing, as we suspected. I must meet with them and approve a new assembly. I will be at the spaceport Wednesday."

"I will tell them not to expect you until then, Dr. Patel."

"Excellent, Alys." She smiled at her secretary, took the papers, and grabbed her bag. "I need to get moving, so much to do."

"The plane is ready for you."

"Oh, did I not mention I won't need the plane? Quints sent theirs. It's the least they can do if I have to go to them in person. I'll have them fly me to the spaceport once we're finished with our meetings."

Alys said, "Very well. I'll tell the pilots to stand down."

She'd accepted the lie without blinking. No way she could know, Nevaeh was always so careful, but something about Alys's smooth, perfectly blank face — no, she was being paranoid. Alys didn't have the chops for betrayal.

"Thank you, Alys. That is all."

With a nod, Alys withdrew.

One of Kiera's eyebrows shot up. "Quints? Is that what you told the board?"

"I did, and they believed me. We needed a

cover, now we have one. I've bought us time. No one will miss us until it's too late."

CHAPTER EIGHT

The Holy Grail is a vessel that serves as an important motif in Arthurian Legend. Different traditions describe it as a cup, dish or stone with miraculous powers that provide happiness, eternal youth or sustenance in infinite abundance. The term "holy grail" is often used to denote an object or goal that is sought after for its great significance.

— Wikipedia

The Griffon
Strait of Malacca
Off the Coast of Sumatra

Jean-Pierre stood on the marine deck with his feet braced shoulder-width apart and his arms crossed, his heart pounding, hoping, praying as he'd never before prayed in his life, trying to contain his excitement. He'd retrofitted this entire lower deck, a fifty-foot square, to be the salvage and recovery area for his dives. And now he was watching the retractable crane, its huge winch turning with a metallic groan, pulling a thick steel cable from the water. Would the cable hold? It was as if there was a monstrous fish on the other end of the line. The ballast at the bow of the yacht 350 feet away kept the boat steady, but Jean-Pierre could feel the stern list slightly toward the sea. Whatever they were bringing up was very heavy, as Cesar had said.

The winch suddenly caught with a metallic twang, and Cesar shouted, "Stand back, stand back." He spoke into a walkie-talkie, "Try again. Go slower this time. Finesse it, lads."

The winch groaned with effort, and the massive yacht swayed a bit, but the coil of metal rolled onto the cylinder, slowly, slowly. The surface of the water grew dark and broke.

A huge sphere rose from the depths. It was large enough for a man to step inside, black, made of what indeed seemed to be iron, just as Cesar had believed, rusted to the point of looking like snakeskin, flakes falling in the water drops onto *The Griffon*'s deck. The crane's arm swung with a great metallic screech, and the sphere was guided into place between a quickly assembled set of bolted-down sawhorses.

Jean-Pierre walked slowly to the huge container that looked like an elongated ball. He gently ran his hand over the metal. Yes, it was iron. Very curious. He estimated the sphere to be ten feet high, perhaps eight feet wide, its surface pocked and scarred. He gave it a slight push. Nothing. It had to weigh a ton. Where had it come from? Who had built it? And why? Why in heaven's name would the Holy Grail be inside?

Cesar said, "Do you want us to document everything first? Even though it might not be the Holy Grail, it's an amazing find and we can get it all on camera. We might be making history here, boss. We can upload this and the world can watch with us as we discover what's inside the sphere."

Broussard immediately shook his head. "As you said, we're not certain the Holy Grail is inside, but if it is, the last thing we want to do is announce it to the world. Remember the pirates. I don't want to take any chances with its safety. No, we will keep it quiet, only amongst ourselves, all right?"

A team member came running up. "Sir, we can't go live even if we wanted to. Something is interfering with the signal. Our Wi-Fi is down, ship-wide."

Jean-Pierre said, "Is it possible the stone

has its own electromagnetic field? Incredible."

Cesar said, "I can still videotape, sir, even if it won't broadcast. For our use only. Is that all right?"

"No." He looked Cesar right in the eye. "Right now, record nothing."

He wanted no word to get out. "It is time to open it up," he said. "It's time to know."

While he waited for Cesar's team to construct a makeshift scaffolding so he could see the top of the sphere, he ran his hands over the scarred surface. He felt the container vibrate ever so slightly against his palms. Yes, the Grail was inside, speaking to him, and it was powerful and strange, and he knew, knew to his soul, that at last he'd found it.

CHAPTER NINE

Broussard climbed the ladder, his hand always on the surface of the sphere, feeling it vibrate, feeling its odd warmth. Was it somehow communicating to him? Or did he want it so badly he was imagining it? He searched for a hatch of some sort and found it at the very top. He shouted, "I've found the opening. Bring me a crowbar."

Cesar scrambled up the ladder with the crowbar.

"Help me wedge it into the crack here."

"Are you sure there isn't a latch to let it open without forcing it?"

Jean-Pierre said, "This is the latch. It rusted off and all that's left is this small indentation in the metal. Maybe the metal isn't iron, it seems to be softer." Could it be an asteroid? What a strange thought, but it made sense, some called the Grail the Heaven Stone, after all.

"Cesar, put the crowbar there."

Jean-Pierre noticed Grant Thornton, the team leader from Blue Mountain, had followed them up the scaffolding. Broussard found him intelligent and focused, worked well with both his team and the crew. He wasn't watching the latch of the sphere. No, his back was to them and he was looking for any possible trouble. Good, Thornton was doing his job. Jean-Pierre had hired the security team because he knew the moment word got out about his discoveries here in Malacca, with or without an announcement, the waters would be overrun with pirates, with media, with the local governments of Malaysia, India, and the Philippines, all of whom claimed salvage rights to the missing *Flor de la Mar.* Another reason to say nothing, to keep this private for as long as possible. Jean-Pierre intended to retrieve the Grail, sail away, and fly to Paris.

Cesar was grunting and sweating, trying to force the latch open. Jean-Pierre gave the crowbar a turn, but no go. And then he had an extraordinary thought. He didn't question it, simply knelt over the sphere and laid his splayed hands on the latch. The words came without thought, his voice a soft whisper. "I mean you no harm. I am a disciple. I've sought you for three years to save the life of a human being more important to me than life itself. She is worthy of you and I am her messenger."

Nothing happened, but Broussard didn't move, still kept his head bowed, his hands on the latch. Cesar started to speak when a small crack appeared at the missing latch.

Cesar raised the crowbar, but Jean-Pierre grabbed his hand. "No, let it open itself for me. It will. Watch."

Cesar's voice shook. "You're acting like this thing is alive. Sir, it can't be."

"You'll see."

Cesar started to back away. Thornton grabbed Cesar's arm before he tripped and fell off the scaffolding. "Easy, mate."

The crack was widening and Broussard stared into a small opening at the top of the sphere. He and Thornton watched the opening grow wider until Jean-Pierre could fit an arm inside, and then his head and torso.

"Give me a torch."

Cesar handed over a Maglite.

"Now, hold me."

Both Cesar and Grant Thornton grabbed hold of Jean-Pierre's ankles as he leaned downward into the black sphere. Cesar said, "Be careful, sir, you have no idea what's in there. It could be dangerous."

Grant didn't know what to think, but

whatever this turned out to be, it was scary. He'd heard Broussard speak to the damned sphere, actually heard him, and he'd seen it open with his own eyes. By itself, as if something magical inside was responding to Broussard's words. The Holy Grail? He'd heard the men talking about it, knew that was Broussard's goal. Grant, like most of the crew, doubted its existence, considered it nothing more than a grand legend, but still they all wondered, waited.

Jean-Pierre's voice echoed back up to him. "The Grail will not hurt me. You can let me go, Cesar, Thornton. There's a platform inside."

"What do you see?" Cesar called down. "Is it the Holy Grail?"

Inside the sphere, Jean-Pierre's Maglite lightened the blackness. It was completely dry. The vibrations were stronger now, a steady hum. He saw six metal lines leading to the center of the sphere, where a one-foot-square box was anchored in midair. When he touched the box, he could swear it sighed.

There was no give in the metal lines. He set down the Maglite. At his touch, the tension went out of the wires, they retracted, and the box fell free into his hands.

Broussard realized the interior of the

sphere was glowing a dark green and pulsing now, gently, rhythmically. He wasn't afraid. He was in awe. The warmth, the vibrations were stronger than ever.

He was wondering how to open the box when a soft click echoed inside the sphere, and the box opened for him.

He saw a black stone sitting on a tray of what looked like solid gold, the stone so small it would fit into his palm. He first ran his fingers along the edges, smooth, like glass, then he closed his hand around it. A sudden warmth filled him and he felt light, buoyant, his mind clear and strong. The pain in his right knee, which had always nagged him since an injury in the astronaut training program, was gone.

It was even more. He felt energized, young, completely healthy, strong, virile. It was amazing. And holding the Grail, acknowledging the incredible power in his hand, he raised his face and prayed his thanks to heaven.

Would the stone somehow speak to him? He waited, but there was nothing, simply the pleasant warmth and vibrations. He had questions, of course. Would the stone need to remain with Emilie to keep her well? Could he cut off a sliver of the stone for her to keep to ensure her continued health? He didn't know. But he knew all would come clear, he mustn't be impatient. And after Emilie was healed, what would he do? Could he use the Grail for the greater good? Was it possible to bring peace to the world using its power? But perhaps the stone only granted his single greatest desire, and selfishly, it wasn't world peace. There was so much to think about, but only after he'd gotten the Grail to Emilie. He wondered then if after he presented her with the stone, he would once again be a middle-aged man with an aching knee, and continue on every man's steady march to mortality.

He called, "I'm coming out. Throw me a rope. Gather the crew. I wish to speak to them."

Devi stood at the railing watching Jean-Pierre disappear inside the strange elongated metal sphere. All the men were talking, speculating, wondering what was happening inside. Some were afraid, others pacing with excitement, others holding their breaths, not wanting to believe, but —

She watched Jean-Pierre climb out and stand tall on the scaffolding. He had a huge grin on his face. In his hands, he held an ugly black box that looked older than time itself. He looked ready to burst with excitement. She had the oddest feeling he some-how looked younger, stronger. But how could that be? He waved to her to join him. Then he yelled at the top of his lungs: "We found it! We've found the Holy Grail!"

Her fingers trembled as she sent the text. No choice, no choice.

He has it.

Nevaeh's reply came almost immediately.

You know what to do. Your sister's life depends on your actions now. We will be there soon.

Devi knew what to do, yes. With a prayer for her sister Elina's safety, she went to share in her lover's celebration.

CHAPTER TEN

The Griffon
Strait of Malacca
Off the Coast of Sumatra
July 24
The dinner menu was exquisite, planned by Jean-Pierre specifically to celebrate his success. A sherry-laden turtle soup, heaping trays of cold shrimp, crab, and lobster, plates filled with chunks of feta cheese, black olives, focaccia bread, and bowls of olive oil for dipping. Succulent lamb slowly turned on skewers with eggplant and tomatoes, Grand Marnier soufflés rose in the ovens.

Devi, dressed in a flowing ocean-blue dress, her hair twisted into a knot on the top of her head, hurried toward the galley. She had one chance to save her sister Elina's life, only one chance to disable the ship

89

and all the men and women on it. Normally, the kitchen crew would have their meal in the galley before serving, and that would have been a problem for her. But tonight, they would join in the festivities — Jean-Pierre's orders.

She had no doubt she could deal handily with the crew. It was the security Jean-Pierre had hired that scared her. Two men, two women, all with watchful eyes and semi-automatic rifles slung across their chests. One in particular, their leader, Grant Thornton, a tall, dark-haired, good-looking man, seemed to follow her every move, and it wasn't lust she felt from him. It was distrust. No, that was absurd, she was feeling so guilty about what she had to do she was projecting her feelings onto him. Still, she wanted to avoid him at all costs.

Devi was quite aware she was beautiful, just as she knew the crew liked her, even though they knew she belonged to Broussard. She liked them, too, truth be told, which only increased her guilt.

Focus, she had to focus. She had to make sure they all ate the feast.

She had three targets — the soup, the wine, and the water. Thankfully, Jean-Pierre was a wine connoisseur. He loved big, bold reds that needed to decant and breathe. The water would be in the butler's pantry with the wine — easy enough to access. The soup was more problematic. She needed to distract the chef, a French graduate of Le Cordon Bleu named Lola. Jean-Pierre took her everywhere with him. Lola predated Devi by ten years, and would probably postdate her, as well. As far as Devi knew, Lola was the only crew aboard who didn't like her, and she didn't know why. Devi was always polite to her, always deferential, always complimented her cooking. It was as if Lola knew she wasn't to be trusted. Well, she had a plan for Lola, too.

Devi took a deep breath and walked into the galley, shoulders back, head high. She belonged there, had every right to check on things. She'd made a point of visiting the galley several times over the past few weeks so she wouldn't draw notice being there tonight. The smells were redolent of garlic and onions and the tang of good sherry. She was so afraid she wanted to vomit. One false move could lead to failure and the bitch would kill Elina.

Lola's sous chef, Frederick, smiled at her, then turned back to the stove to stir his sauce. The other six people in the galley were much too busy with the final dinner preparations to do more than nod to her.

91

Devi's first stop was the butler's pantry. As she expected, several decanters of wine alongside pitchers of both sparkling and still water stood waiting. There was so much of everything — it looked like preparations for the kind of party Jean-Pierre threw for his megarich friends, business moguls who came to the boat to talk deals or to celebrate, rather than a party for his crew. But again, this was a special celebration.

No one was paying her any attention. Devi opened the bottle of ketamine and carefully counted out the drops as they fell into the open decanters and pitchers until all had been dosed.

A server appeared in the doorway, and she quickly grabbed an empty wine bottle and examined the label. She smiled. "Hello, Andre, I'm not familiar with this wine. I don't want to make a fool of myself."

Andre only shook his head, and fetched the cutlery he was looking for. He found this beautiful young Indian girl amazing and envied Monsieur Broussard his good luck. "Never," he said, and rushed out.

When she was alone again, she took a deep breath and retrieved another small bottle of ketamine from her bra.

Devi walked into the galley, the bottle hidden in her hand, straight to Lola, who was ordering her crew around as if she were the master of *The Griffon.*

Lola was sweating, but her uniform was as crisp and white as the moment she'd put it on. She saw Devi coming and narrowed her eyes.

"What? What's the matter? He's not changing the menu, is he?"

Devi smiled. "No, of course not. I have a — okay, this is terribly embarrassing, but I —" She pointed toward her stomach, whispered, "Cramps. Early. I'm out of aspirin."

Lola rolled her eyes. "Surely the medic has some."

"The medic is celebrating early with most of the other crew at Monsieur Broussard's spectacular find. Do you have any aspirin, Lola? Please? I'll pay you."

Of course Devi knew Lola had aspirin, she always had aspirin. Lola waved a hand dismissively. "Yes, in my bag. On the third shelf."

"Thank you." Devi made a beeline for the bag. Just as she put a hand on it, she slipped and went down, the bag spilling its contents all over the galley floor. Lola said several nasty words and came to help. Devi struggled to her feet.

"I'm so sorry, I slipped, I didn't mean to — I'm sorry, I've made such a mess."

Lola waved her away, tossed a couple of ripe curses at her head, and began picking up her belongings. Devi reached behind her and dumped the contents of the bottle into the turtle soup.

A few seconds later, Lola shoved an aspirin bottle in her hand and said, "Get out of my galley before you make even more of a mess."

This time, Devi's smile was genuine. "Thanks so much, Lola. Dinner smells delicious."

She didn't start to breathe again until she was out in the hallway. She'd done it.

Jean-Pierre was waiting for her when she returned to her own suite. She felt her heart slam into her chest — why was he here? But he simply whistled at her.

"What a beautiful dress. You've been saving this one for a special occasion, yes?"

She pinned a smile on her face and twirled the lovely blue silk skirt. "Yes. I'm glad you like it."

His dark eyes glittered. "I'd like you better out of it. Come here."

"We haven't the time, Jean-Pierre. Dinner is about to be served."

As she said it, they heard the dinner bell — an antique Jean-Pierre had brought from his grandfather's vineyard in Lyon.

He shook his head, drew her in. "You have time for this. Trust me." He nuzzled her neck and slid a long, flat white velvet box into her hands.

"What's this?"

"Open it and see."

She snapped open the lid and gasped. Five huge green faceted stones nestled in a thick platinum chain. "Are they emeralds? No, wait, they're far too dark, they look black."

"They're moldavite, exceptionally rare, and what I believe the Holy Grail is made of. It will bring you great fortune, and luck in love. Here, let me."

He lifted the necklace gently and put it around her neck. She could feel the weight of the stones against her collarbones, warm and solid. They tingling against her skin, or maybe it was her imagination?

Jean-Pierre moved her to the mirror. "Look." She did. In the brighter light the stones were stunning, and the deepest green she'd ever seen, like a rain forest.

She said formally, "Thank you, Jean-Pierre. I will treasure this gift."

Treasure it, because this will be the last thing you ever give me. The last time you will ever see me. She wanted to weep.

CHAPTER ELEVEN

The dining room was already full when Jean-Pierre and Devi arrived. She felt every eye upon her. Did they all know what was to come? But no one looked at her strangely, or with distrust. She counted — yes, all the crew were present. Everyone but the four security guards. She said a quick prayer — *Please, let them be eating or drinking on their watch.* She didn't have another way to incapacitate them. They had to eat the drugged soup or drink the drugged wine or water, or she'd failed, and her sister would die.

Jean-Pierre took his place at the head of the table, raised his glass, and toasted the crew. The room erupted with cheers. Devi did her best not to let her hand shake when she joined in.

Broussard said, "As some of you might know, as a child, I had two passions: deep water and space. My father, a man of infinite wisdom, told me I could not count on treasure hunting to feed me. It wasn't a leap to imagine space as silent and perfect as deep water, so I decided to become an astronaut." He paused, grinned, looked at Devi. "It was sexier to women, anyway."

There was laughter, the crew sitting forward, all attention focused on Broussard.

"After finishing my studies at the Sorbonne, I applied to France's astronaut program and made it through three rounds before my father became ill and my presence was required at home for his care. After his death, I talked a fellow engineer into a start-up company making satellites that were smaller, faster, and easier to insert into orbit. The telecommunications boom was beginning and our small firm was uniquely positioned to provide these satellites to companies all over Europe.

"It used to cost upwards of one hundred million dollars to put a satellite in orbit, and took months, years, of prep work. I wanted a low-cost option, and I was convinced I could make it work.

"I invested most of the meager fortune I'd amassed from treasure hunting into this vision, hired the best engineers I could afford, and within five years, Galactus was regularly sending satellites to space. With the brilliant and talented Dr. Nevaeh Patel at the helm, we've grown exponentially.

"And that, my friends, gave me the money and the time so that I could dedicate myself to finding the Holy Grail, the greatest treasure of them all. I believe it is the holiest of holies. None of the legends, modern or ancient, agree on what the Grail is or where it came from. In Wolfram's epic, there was supposedly an Arabic manuscript found in Toledo with instructions for how to use the Grail. His claim was that the answers were written in the stars, and this was the basis of the concept of the Heaven Stone.

"A celestial path to the Grail — imagine my excitement at the thought. Dr. Patel and I have discussed the possibilities endlessly, and the meaning of the Holy Grail. She came to believe, firmly, that the Grail came from space. Me, I had no idea.

"But then I came upon a letter written by the captain Afonso de Albuquerque speaking of the incredible heavy black stone he'd taken aboard his ship, a stone he blamed for the sinking of the *Flor de la Mar,* which went down during a violent storm. The very ship we've been salvaging from, here beneath us."

When would he stop talking? When would everyone drink and eat? Devi sat like a statue, waiting, waiting.

"My friends, I thank all of you. Tomorrow, when we have recovered from our wonderful celebration, I will display the Holy Grail for you to see. Now, let us enjoy the feast Lola has prepared for us." He again raised his glass, toasted the entire room, drank, and sat down, grinning like a happy boy at Devi.

Devi smiled back at him, a rictus, and waited. She counted down the moments until people started to drop unconscious. It was like a strange choreographed dream.

Clink. Drink. The soup served. Spoons against china.

And then, one by one, heads began to tilt. Jean-Pierre, who'd drunk freely of his wine, was one of the first to go down. The crew started crashing to the floor, or onto the table, or lolling backward against their chairs.

It was working.

Finally, when she was certain everyone was unconscious, Devi ran out of the dining room and made her way to the bridge. No one was there, of course. The crew normally assigned to the bridge were passed out in the dining room, all the instrumentation set on autopilot. She'd seen no sign of any of the security team. They'd all been expecting the threat to come from off the ship. They hadn't been in the dining room, but she knew Jean-Pierre had sent them trays. Of course, Nevaeh had been right about their security protocols — they'd never seen Devi coming.

She disengaged the autopilot first, then stuck a small thumb drive into a port on the right side of the bridge's computers. Devi knew it had a bug inside to set off a small EMP — an electromagnetic pulse, Nevaeh had told her — inside the boat. She felt and heard nothing, but within moments, all the screens went dark. The engines began to shut down, one by one, the lights, too. The idea was to leave the ship as quiet as a black hole in the water. So far, so good. The tools she'd been provided were working perfectly.

There was a transponder on the boat as well, and she found it inside the bulkhead. Despite the localized EMP, she'd been warned it might still have the ability to send a signal because of its covering, so she manually turned it off, then smashed the motherboard with a stiletto heel. There was a tiny metallic squawk and the GPS system went dark.

She'd done it, she'd succeeded. The crew was down, and now, so was the ship. It was over and soon she would be taken to her sister. She thought of Jean-Pierre and felt a stab of guilt. He was so different from the man she'd expected him to be. And so very smart and dedicated to his one goal — to find the Grail. She'd asked him once why this obsession? He'd said only that it was the most important thing in his life. He'd said no more, only shaking his head. He was a physical man, had always been generous in bed. No, no, it was over. She had no choice. She had to forget him. She fingered the necklace at her throat. Moldavite stones, perhaps what the Holy Grail was made of. Surely it could not be true, despite his absolute belief, his absolute certainty. But still —

She glanced at her watch. She only had five minutes. She had to hurry.

She ran back to Jean-Pierre's study, where she'd seen him carefully place the box holding the Holy Grail into his safe. She'd memorized the combination weeks before.

She quickly opened the safe and lifted out the box that contained the stone. It was heavier than she expected. She had to use both arms to carry it. It hadn't seemed at all heavy when Jean-Pierre had carried it.

She lugged the box to the elevator, but it wasn't working. The EMP had done its job well, shutting off everything electrical on the yacht. The box was much too heavy for her to carry up the stairs. She left it, ran up the stairs to the helicopter pad on the aft deck.

When she stepped onto the deck, she was overwhelmed by the dead silence. No voices, no sounds of the mighty engines, no motors running. She'd felled the yacht. It was dead in the water. All she heard was water lapping against the hull far below, and for a moment the guilt nearly brought her to her knees. She saw her sister's face, so very young and innocent, so frightened, and the bitch had told her over and over she was the only one who could save her. Only sixteen, her whole life in front of her. All right, Devi had done what Nevaeh had demanded of her. It would soon be over. Elina would soon be safe.

She heard the *whap-whap-whap* of a helicopter's rotors in the distance.

Nevaeh was coming.

Devi ran to the edge of the helipad. With the boat completely disabled, the helicopter wouldn't be able to locate it on radar, so she had to guide them in herself, by hand. She'd stashed a set of flares and a Maglite in a padded bench. She pulled them out and shot off a flare, then turned on the

Maglite and started waving it toward the sky. The chopper came closer, growing louder and louder until it appeared above her, hovering like a giant insect.

Devi set the flashlight on the deck of the helipad. Its strong beam of light illuminated the landing spot. The chopper touched down. The doors opened and Dr. Nevaeh Patel climbed out of the pilot's seat. Her vicious Irish-born bodyguard, Kiera Byrne, jumped down after her, an M4 carbine strapped to her chest. Devi feared Kiera perhaps more than Nevaeh. She'd never seen an ounce of pity in those green eyes. And now, looking at Kiera, loaded with holsters and harnesses full of guns and knives, Devi felt cramping fear. She knew Kiera was on the lookout for any crew member still standing, and Devi knew Kiera would shoot them dead with no hesitation. Kiera was better armed than the security Jean-Pierre had hired. The fear was now bitter in her throat. She believed Nevaeh Patel was insane, but she knew Kiera Byrne was a sadistic monster.

Nevaeh smiled at her, raised a hand in greeting. She wore her signature black trousers, black turtleneck, and black blazer, black low-heeled boots on her feet. As always, she looked powerful, her very stance announcing her intelligence, her control. Tonight, at this moment, when she smiled she looked as smug as a shark about to devour prey. The sadist stood at her elbow, silent, watchful.

Nevaeh said, "Hello, Devi. Congratulations on disabling the ship. I trust everyone is down?"

"Yes. There will be no resistance, as you asked."

Kiera stopped in front of Devi. "Well, where is the Grail?"

"I left it at the base of the elevator, downstairs. But everyone is unconscious, I made sure of it."

Rage crossed Nevaeh's face, brutal and quick, making Devi jerk backward. "Is this some kind of trick? I told you to meet me here with the Grail."

"It was too heavy, I couldn't manage it. It's where I told you, just downstairs. Please, I've done as you asked. Take me to my sister. You promised."

"Is the transponder off?"

"Yes, and I uploaded the virus to the navigation system, like you wanted. Please. I've done everything you've asked, and more."

Nevaeh paused for a moment. She reached out a hand and ran it along the younger woman's jawline. "So pretty. You lasted six months. You must have pleased Jean-Pierre greatly. By the way, your sister is dead. And now, so are you."

She nodded to Kiera. The bullet caught Devi in the face, and she went down hard on the deck.

CHAPTER TWELVE

Nevaeh didn't look at the young woman who lay in a pool of blood on the deck, her beautiful blue gown spilling around her. She'd been a good tool, but she wasn't important now. She followed Kiera down the stairs to the main deck. True to Devi's word, the black box was sitting, unsecured, by the elevator door.

Nevaeh felt her heart jump as she placed her hand on the box. It was as if she'd touched a low-voltage live wire without insulated gloves. It felt odd. Arousing.

"Open it," she whispered, and Kiera released the latch. Nevaeh fell to her knees, reached her hand inside. The stone was dark, a greenish black, nothing exciting or fantastical about it. It looked like it could fit in the palm of her hand, but she had to use both hands to lift it out of the box, it was so heavy and dense. Strange, it seemed to shrink away from her when she reached in to touch it. Surely that was her imagination.

It was definitely giving off an electrical buzz she now found quite unpleasant, like she was being shocked instead of warmed from within. The temptation to drop the stone, to throw it overboard, was overwhelming. She held on, though.

"You are mine now."

The nasty electrical sensation was easily ignored when the Numen, hundreds of them, spoke as one, their melodious voices reverberating through her, their shadowy bodies dancing around her, as if released from the stone itself.

Nevaeh, the stone is yours. Bring it to us, and be one of us. Silence the heavens and we will come to you. You have done what you were meant to do.

The Numen's voices were so happy, happier than she'd ever heard them in many years. It took considerable effort to release the stone, but she did, placing it carefully back in its box, not noticing it turn darker.

"Bring it. We have everything we need now. The nuke will go off in four days' time, and the EMP will silence the heavens, and I will finally be able to fulfill my destiny."

Kiera lifted the box, and was also surprised at its weight. What was it made of, lead? The buzzing was giving her a head-ache.

They took the stairs back to the helipad. Nevaeh stepped around the spreading pool of blood and took one last look at Devi's destroyed face. She climbed into the helicopter and secured her seat belt. She let Kiera pilot, she wanted to savor this moment. As the chopper rose into the blackness, Nevaeh looked down at the dead ship.

And so it begins for me.

And so it ends for you, Jean-Pierre.

When they were some distance away from *The Griffon,* Nevaeh said, "It's time, Kiera."

Kiera hovered the chopper. "You're still sure you wish to do this, Nevaeh?"

She put her hand on Kiera's knee. "Yes, I am sure. It's time to end Jean-Pierre. We can't afford any possible interference. The stone is mine now. The Numen are calling to me, Kiera. They want me at Aquarius. They want me to launch the nuke."

Kiera nodded. Once she'd been jealous of Jean-Pierre Broussard, had wanted to hurt him. She was afraid they would become lovers. But Broussard loved young women and Nevaeh loved her.

Still, no loss. She launched the missile. It gave a *whoosh* and the chopper jerked. They waited for the sound of the explosion, watched as the dark, empty night became a brilliant white for a few seconds.

"Direct hit," Kiera said with satisfaction.

"You sank my battleship." Nevaeh and Kiera both laughed as Kiera moved the chopper away from the blast site.

Kiera said, "Do you want me to swing back around? See the carnage?"

"No. I feel no need to dance on Jean-Pierre's grave. He was good to me. As a boss, he was perfect. Like Devi, he fulfilled his purpose. And now he's of no more use. There's no way the ship could survive. Head for land. We will make our way to Sri Lanka."

CHAPTER THIRTEEN

Ketamine is a medication mainly used for starting and maintaining anesthesia. It induces a trance-like state while providing pain relief, sedation, and memory loss.

— Wikipedia

Grant Thornton heard the words, garbled and distant as if he were underwater. A woman's voice: "Bring it. We have everything we need now. The nuke will go off in four days' time, and the EMP will silence the heavens, and I will finally be able to fulfill my destiny."

Was there more? Grant didn't know, his brain wasn't working right. Just a few stray thoughts.

I am hearing things.

Surely she didn't just say "nuke."

"EMP"? No, that was crazy. Why can't I move?

Just when he started to think he'd imagined the voice, he heard a door slam closed.

The ship felt deserted, though he knew that wasn't true, someone was there, they'd gone into the stairwell.

A nuke. Four days. An EMP. And another word, what was it? Something weird — Nevaeh.

He was starting to feel uncomfortable, which, deep in his lizard brain, he knew was a good thing, because up until a moment ago, he'd been unable to feel anything, only had a strange, disembodied sense of his own body, as if in a dream state, though he was awake. A fine wave of panic went through him — *danger, I'm in danger, is Kitsune okay?* — before he wrestled those thoughts back into their cage. He couldn't think about his wife when he was operational.

He dragged in a breath and tried to move, feeling pins and needles in his legs. Something registered — *drugged.*

Not good. Wait it out.

He felt like he was paralyzed, knew he needed to stay calm. Whatever he'd been given was starting to wear off. Ketamine, he realized, somehow someone had given him ketamine. It was the same drug they'd injected him with when he'd been kidnapped. When? How could he have been taken down? He was alarmed he couldn't remember anything. He could recall coming on board *The Griffon,* meeting Jean-Pierre Broussard, being briefed, coordinating with the rest of the team. He vaguely remembered standing atop some scaffolding, but why he'd been there escaped him.

The team. Where was everyone? Who else was down?

He moved his fingers, relieved when they started to twitch. And finally, finally, his brain refired. Someone had managed to disable the most top-notch security in the world and robbed his client. There would be hell to pay.

Grant had honestly thought Jean-Pierre Broussard was a little mad, considering. In the briefing Grant received when he'd boarded the ship, Broussard had clearly stated he was about to be in possession of an ancient artifact that many people would kill to possess, and he'd heard the scuttlebutt across the ship when the Holy Grail had been pulled from the waters. Someone in the kitchens called it the Heaven Stone, but Grant knew it couldn't be the case. He'd said, "You're having one off on me," and the kid had said, "No way. I'm serious. It's the Grail. The boss is going to be immortal. Hey, maybe it'll rub off on us, too." And he'd given a kind of scared laugh. But then they'd brought up that huge container and there it was, in a small box, and Broussard was incandescent, no other word to describe his joy.

He heard the rotors of a helicopter starting up.

Come now, Grant, get up, there's a good lad.

He managed to get a knee under him, braced an arm on the wall. The noise was deafening now; he realized it was coming down the lift shaft. He smashed the button, but nothing happened. The lift wasn't working. He'd have to take the stairs. *Hurry. Hurry.*

He could barely handle his weapon. He fumbled the gun into his hand, braced himself against the wall, and entered the stairwell.

It was dark, but his eyes had adjusted. At the final landing, he stood, hand on the door's handle, breathing hard, hyperventilating to sharpen his awareness.

He was buffeted by a gust of wind when he flung open the door. The helicopter he'd heard was taking off. No one shot at him, good luck there, so he threw himself out of the stairwell onto the deck. The chopper — in the darkness its lights looked like the outline of a Sikorsky X2, but he couldn't be entirely sure — was already a hundred feet off the deck and moving away, fast.

He knew he should shoot at it, but his finger wouldn't move quickly enough, and the chopper was out of range before he had enough control.

The deck was dark, but he managed to pick up a Maglite rolling around in the wind of the chopper's backlash. He smelled blood, the acrid odors of death that made him want to retch. He shined the light on the ground and saw a lump that must be Devi, Broussard's mistress. He'd seen her go into the dining room in that dress. It was the only way he could identify her. She'd been shot in the face and wasn't recognizable anymore.

Grant felt for her pulse anyway, not surprised when he found nothing.

His brain was still foggy, his breathing harsh and ragged, but he was starting to get his wits back. Someone had attacked the ship and stolen something. He could only assume it was the strange box with the stone inside, the stone Broussard claimed was the Holy Grail. And he wondered yet again, how could a stone be the Holy Grail? Everyone knew the Grail was a cup, right? He'd seen no cups, only that huge ugly sphere and the ancient box Broussard had brought out from the inside.

He shook his head, trying to ignore the buzzing in his ears. *Focus, mate.*

Devi was beyond help. The chopper was gone into the night.

The boat itself was quiet, so quiet he knew immediately there was a problem.

As he turned back toward the stairs and the lift, he saw a bright flash of light. Was the helicopter coming back?

No, it was a thousand times worse.

The light grew closer and with it came the high-pitched whine he recognized from every combat zone he'd ever fought in.

An incoming missile.

He had only enough time to think, *We're dead, we're all dead, Kitsune, I love you, I'm sorry,* before the missile struck the side of *The Griffon* with an ear-splitting *whump* that immediately became a raging, white-hot fireball.

CHAPTER FOURTEEN

The explosion deafened Grant, the light blinded him, and the concussion from the blast knocked him backward ten feet to the deck. *The Griffon,* mortally wounded, listed to the side immediately. Grant started to slide, arms scrambling for any purchase. He slipped through the railing and knew he was falling. The toe of his boot snagged on a launch rope and he was swinging upside down over the water now. He saw the fire below him. If he fell, he was dead.

His senses, still dulled by the drugs, went into overdrive, delivering a massive dose of adrenaline. He used his momentum to swing toward the deck and grab the railing, where he clung like a monkey until it became too hot to hold. He pulled himself through and fell back to the deck, hitting his head hard. The deck was now at a sharp angle to the water.

No time, no time. The yacht was on fire,

taking on water, he could feel it groaning beneath his feet.

They were sinking.

Where was everyone?

He stumbled across the deck to the stairs, started down. He had a horrible moment of panic at the idea of the water rushing in and trapping him in the space, but pushed through his fear.

It only took him a few minutes to get back to the dining room.

It looked like a horror film — bodies everywhere, slumped in chairs or on the floor. He went to Broussard first, found his pulse thready and weak. He knew what to do, but he needed to get his carry bag. He had Narcan, it would help reverse the ketamine effects. Where was his bag? Not on his hip where it should be. His mind couldn't quite grasp where. He mentally retraced his steps — yes, the stairwell, near the lift to the helipad.

He hurried through the room, felt a few more necks. Not everyone was dead. Some were, and there were a few who were past his help, but Broussard was still breathing, and the priority. Get him awake, get the crew awake, evacuate as many as they could before the freezing waters claimed the yacht and all aboard.

He took a deep breath. Someone else must be awake. The engine room maybe, or the bridge. Someone had to have been sailing the ship during dinner, yes? Or not.

His bag was on the floor in front of the lift, a blessing he didn't have to run up those close stairs to the chopper deck again. He grabbed it and staggered back to the dining room. He shot Narcan into Broussard's arm. Should he give himself a shot, too? No, it wasn't worth the risk, his adrenaline was pulsing through him like a strobe. He would keep moving.

Broussard started to revive. Grant left him, found the rest of his team, got them shot up with Narcan. They began coming out of it. After a few minutes, he'd used all the Narcan he had, so the rest were on their own.

Four were dead and the rest of the crew were in varying degrees of drug-induced delirium, beyond high. *Yes, definitely ketamine,* he thought.

Broussard began coughing. Grant gave him some water, told him to get it together or they'd die, repeating the words over and over until Broussard's eyes opened.

He drank more water, then sat up, eyes still unfocused. "Thornton. What happened?"

"Listen to me carefully. The ship is sinking. We have to evacuate."

"Abandon ship?"

"Yes. How do we do that?"

Broussard's head lolled back. Grant slapped him until he came to again.

"What's happening?"

"We were attacked, drugged. The boat is sinking. Get it together, mate."

"Devi. Where's Devi?"

"I'm sorry, but Devi is dead, and we will all join her soon if you . . . Don't. Wake. Up!"

The yacht groaned again, its internal gyroscope off and twisting, and the room shifted, hard. That woke Broussard.

"The lifeboats. We need the lifeboats. And the submersible can take up to six people."

"Show me."

Grant's people were staggering around now. He clapped his hands to get their attention.

He shouted, "Emergency protocol seven, immediately! The ship's been hit, is going down. Get as many people as you can to the lifeboats."

His people started moving, slowly, but they were moving.

Grant said, "There are a few fatalities among the crew as well from whatever we've all been dosed with, I'm assuming ketamine. But Devi was shot to death. Someone came on board in a Sikorsky helicopter, and I'm pretty sure they took your Holy Grail with them. Then they shot us with what surely looked and felt like a Hellfire missile. Hit the side, near the stern. Come on, we have to get moving or we're all going to die."

Broussard's head lolled back again and he cursed in French. Odd how curses didn't sound as bad in another language.

"But who did this to us? Who could have drugged everyone?"

"Doesn't matter. Time to go." He heaved Broussard to his feet.

Broussard was slowly coming back. He looked around, confused.

"Why are the engines off? The emergency lights aren't on, either."

"Right. It happened before the missile hit us. Seems the ship was turned off somehow."

Broussard dragged in a breath, shook his head. "No, that's impossible. Come with me."

Together, they moved to the stairs, then up to the control deck on the bridge. There were no lights in the con, not from the screens or the generators. Grant could see flashlights bobbing. Good, his team was leading people to the lifeboats.

"We can't have more than ten minutes before the whole ship goes down."

"How the devil did this happen? The transponder has been turned off." Broussard fiddled with it for a moment. "Not only turned off, it's been tampered with."

It had to be said. "Was Devi capable of such a thing?"

Broussard closed his eyes a moment, then shook his head. "No. She must have been in the wrong place when whoever it was came aboard."

Broussard was moving from station to station, screen to screen. "I've never seen anything like this. It's more than a power outage. It's almost as if we've been turned off purposefully. But how —"

He grappled with something, then yanked it free. "*Merde.* Look."

Grant flashed his torch over Broussard's hand. He held a small jump drive.

"Not part of your standard operating system?"

"No. I've never seen this before. I'm going to have to get us started by hand. I have a special deployment protocol programmed into the system, shouldn't be compromised. It will allow the lifeboats out and inflate them. You need to tend to the rest of my

121

crew. See who you can get revived enough to help me." Before Grant could move, Broussard turned. Cursed. Grant looked over his shoulder to see a wall of flames. The missile's fire had spread.

"No time, no time, do it now or we all die!"

Broussard smashed a foot through a panel to a red lever. He grabbed it with both hands and yelled, "Help me!"

Grant got his hands on it, too, and together they pulled, wrenching the bar back until Grant felt the shudder of machinery and heard a few cheers, then directions being yelled to people to get into the freed lifeboats.

"I've got to get Devi. I can't leave her here. I'll find Devi and get the Grail and meet you at the boats."

Grant grabbed his arm. "I'm afraid Devi is responsible for this. She was the only one unaccounted for in the dining room. She's up on deck, or was before we tilted — no, you can't go up there."

"How do you know that?"

"Whoever took your Grail and disabled your ship was talking to her before they shot her. I didn't hear her calling for help. I heard her ask about her sister, I think. I'm still very fuzzy."

"But — how? Why? The Grail —"

"The Grail is gone. Whoever took it killed Devi and is trying to kill the rest of us. Now go! We'll figure everything out later." He shoved Broussard back toward the stairs to the lifeboats. Looked back at the con. He needed to get word out somehow.

"Do you have a ham radio?"

"Of course, right there. It's on a solar-power-generated battery pack."

"Should work, if there's enough juice in the batteries. I'm going to try."

If what he'd heard was right, he had to warn the world. The ship being disabled electronically as it was, he hoped he wasn't too late.

He lit up an emergency channel, identified himself, and started to send the message — *They have a nuclear EMP* — when he realized his back was hot.

"Too late!"

Broussard grabbed Grant's shoulder and heaved him to the ground as the flames leaped and danced toward them. They elbowed their way on their bellies to the stairwell. The flames were consuming everything in their path. They were out of time. Grant steeled himself and dove down the stairs. Broussard landed on top of him. They lay there for a moment, stunned, before

Grant felt water. That brought him back fast. Drown or burn up. He dragged himself to his feet.

Broussard looked dazed, a small trickle of blood streaming from his temple. Grant shook his arm. "We have to get to the lifeboats. Which way?"

Broussard pointed, and Grant thanked all the heavens above the lifeboats were in the opposite direction from the wall of fire.

CHAPTER FIFTEEN

They clattered down stairwell after stairwell, the smoke thick and choking. Grant kept talking, anything to keep Broussard focused, anything to distract himself from the ship's slow death slide into the sea. At four hundred feet, *The Griffon* was half the length of the *Titanic* — massive for a privately owned vessel — and the extensive aft ballast was keeping her afloat. The stern was missing, and the angle of the ship was becoming steeper and steeper. They were going down sooner rather than later. He kept pushing Broussard.

They burst out onto the lacuna deck, where the starboard lifeboats were docked. The boat was listing badly now. Something swung from the railing above them. Grant looked up and wished he hadn't. Devi's lifeless body was dangling from the rail.

Broussard cried out, "Devi!" But Grant pushed him forward again. "She's gone, there's nothing you can do. But I'm certain I heard someone from the chopper talking to her. Something about a nuke and an EMP."

"EMP?"

"That's the message I was trying to send, no idea if it managed to get out or not. The woman in the chopper said an EMP would go off, silencing the heavens, and then she would — fulfill her destiny? Something insane like that."

"Someone's planning to set off a nuclear bomb?"

"She said in four days' time."

Broussard's eyes were wild, reality setting in now. "The Grail. They took the Grail?"

"I think they did."

When he met Grant's eyes again, there were tears. And rage.

"Why didn't you go after them?"

"In my invisible plane? They had a helicopter and I was still reeling from the drugs. Still am, actually. Now, let's get you onto one of these boats —"

Broussard shook his head. "Let's take the submersible. It's closer than the boat." He pointed to a door.

Just what I want, to be locked in a tiny submarine.

Oh well. Grant said, "Let's go," and opened the door.

CHAPTER SIXTEEN

The submersible wasn't a coffin like Grant had expected, and dreaded. It was a good fifteen feet long, twelve feet wide, and seven feet tall. It had six seats — a pilot and five passengers — a wide, round bubble viewing area, and Grant knew it was rated for ten hours at a depth of up to one thousand meters. Still, he was surprised by the space. Two large men, one with weapons, had plenty of room to move inside. He stood back, let Broussard handle the controls.

Broussard efficiently detached from *The Griffon* and motored them twenty yards away to meet up with the rest of the boats. Four lifeboats had launched. He did a quick head count — twenty crew, three Blue Mountain, and himself and Thornton. Four of his crew were dead. Jean-Pierre felt sick. He'd sailed with this crew for years. How was it possible that anyone, much less Devi, could do such a thing? Drug his people, not care if it killed them or not, steal from him — steal all hope from Emilie. No, it wasn't Devi. It had to be someone else. She had to have been trying to stop whoever was behind this.

He saw Cesar at the helm of the first boat. He'd seen to it all four boats were roped together.

When Broussard and Grant stood side by side on the wide ladder, their heads out of the submersible, Cesar called out, "Sir, Mr. Thornton, thank heavens you're both all right. Listen, the transponders were deactivated on all the lifeboats. Whoever did this was trying to make sure we all died."

"Four of our crew are dead."

Cesar's face became stark with disbelief and pain. "Yes, I know. We had to leave them in the dining room. Everyone else is accounted for except Devi, sir. I'm sorry — we couldn't look everywhere for her, we had to get off *The Griffon* or we'd all die. We're damn lucky the seas are calm."

Grant couldn't believe this. On his watch, and everything had gone south. As to the seas being calm, he decided calm must be in the eye of the beholder because the swells were at least ten feet high, making the boats and submersible bob around like corks.

Broussard's face was gray in the darkness.

Grant heard him whisper, "Devi, my beautiful girl." But his voice was strong when he called back to Cesar, "Do we have any means of letting search and rescue know where we are?"

Cesar shook his head. "A few flares, but they'll need to be near enough to see them. Without the transponders, it's going to be hard to locate us — and we're adrift."

They'd already moved another forty yards away from *The Griffon*. The waves were pushing them, the currents running fast.

Grant cracked open his satellite phone only to find it, too, wasn't working.

Grant shot a look at Broussard. It had to be said. He called out, "We fear Devi was responsible. She's dead, shot by her accomplices, we think. We believe she drugged the food and drink. Did she manage to disable everything? Do you know?"

Broussard raised his head. The blind grief was still there, but now his eyes were hard, his brilliant brain focused. He held up the small thumb drive. "I think she set off a small EMP inside the electrical systems of the boat, and it wiped everything."

Cesar said, "But why? I don't understand. All of us liked her and, sir, she really liked you, everyone knew it."

Grant called, "Perhaps she was forced to

do this. My recollections are fuzzy at best, but I think I heard her say something about her sister. She thought she was going with them, whoever they are, but they killed her."

Cesar looked stoic. "Well, whatever her motives, she nearly managed to kill us all. We won't last too long out here. There's a bad storm coming, a typhoon. I'd say we have twelve hours before we're in trouble, and when the storm finally hits — no, let's not worry about that now. We'll be out of here long before it hits."

Grant said, "There has to be some way to communicate. Aren't you hooked into a satellite somewhere?"

Broussard nodded. "Of course we are. It will have marked our last transmission location and someone at the company will share that information when I miss my board meeting in the morning."

The ship's lead engineer, Eros, called from another boat, "I tried to get a distress call out when I woke up, sir. But nothing registered. I don't think it worked."

Broussard said, "You tried, Eros, and we are all grateful. Mr. Thornton tried as well. We will have faith the calls were heard and our rescuers are on their way to us now. Have you been able to chart our position?"

"I have, sir," Eros said. "We're two nautical miles from the last known location of *The Griffon,* and moving away from that position at approximately four kilometers per hour. I will continue triangulating. We have the stars to guide us until the typhoon gets close."

"Excellent. Cesar, do we have rations and water?"

"We have water, sir, and the lifeboats have the usual — twenty food packs per person, enough to last five days. The ropes holding us all together are stout, so no one will break away."

At Grant's raised brow, Broussard said, "We always keep the lifeboats provisioned. The submersible also has food and water for five days. I like being prepared for the worst. If we have to, we can ride out the storm. Also, we can try to take the submersible to land. With luck, someone will start searching for us sooner rather than later."

Grant thought Broussard sounded more confident than he felt. The aftereffects of the drug were making him nauseated, and the idea of being alone in a small submersible in the middle of the Indian Ocean with a storm bearing down didn't make him feel much better.

"And if they don't come for us?"

"Then we wait. And we pray." He thought

again of Emilie, how weak she'd sounded, but hopeful — she'd believed him utterly when he said that he would cure her. He couldn't fail her, not now, not this close.

A huge metallic groan sounded behind them, and everyone turned to see *The Griffon* slide under the water.

Broussard cried out, couldn't help it. Every man and woman stood frozen, staring in horror.

Now they were completely alone.

CHAPTER SEVENTEEN

T-MINUS 71 HOURS

The Hassler Hotel
Rome
July 25

Nicholas was drinking coffee and watching the news, enjoying the warm summer breeze flowing across their bed from the open terrace doors. Mike walked out of the bathroom, her hair in a towel. He gave her a grin and a wave.

"All right, Mike. One more day in Rome. You've seen the Vatican — hey, what's this?"

At his tone, Mike focused on the television. A large red crawler ran along the base of the screen.

Breaking News: Jean-Pierre Broussard, head of Galactus Space Industries, missing; fears the tycoon's megayacht, *The Griffon,* has sunk off the coast of Malaysia.

"Oh, bollocks."

"Oh no, that's the boat Grant is on, isn't it?"

"Yes." He turned up the volume. The anchor was speaking with barely contained glee — now *this* was news that should show his face all over the world. One of the planet's richest, most successful men, possibly dead? Missing at sea? It was a feast to last for days.

"— reports have been coming in that the ship went off the radar last night, and Broussard was reported missing this morning after failing to attend a scheduled board meeting. Authorities report there was a brief SOS call, but there have been no distress calls since. Authorities trying to contact the crew are receiving dead air, and the boat's transponder, which should allow for emergency services to locate it, has not registered. Is it possible some sort of sabotage occurred or was the ship the target of pirates who are known to sail the waters in the area?"

Nicholas turned down the volume. "We'd best get in touch with Grant's people. I assume Kitsune knows already —"

"No, she's off-grid, remember? No communications. She won't know unless she gets in front of a television, and she's not the type to be hanging around watching TV on a job. Chances are she's totally in the dark. We have to go search for him, Nicholas."

Nicholas scrubbed a hand over his face. "Yes, of course we do. Let me contact Blue Mountain, see if I can scare up any new information."

Five minutes later, Nicholas said, "I have Grant's boss here, Mike," and put the phone on speaker.

"Sir? I'm Special Agent Nicholas Drummond, with Special Agent Michaela Caine."

"Wesley Fentriss here. Yes, I know who you are. I also know I have you two to thank for helping Grant out of his last, ah, situation. You're calling about the disappearance of Broussard's yacht, right?"

"Yes. We knew Grant was aboard *The Griffon.* We wanted to ask —"

Fentriss cursed, grumbled about operational security, but Nicholas interrupted him. "You know Grant is our friend, there's no one I'd trust more with my back, and we were in a tight spot with him not long ago, as you well know. We want to offer our services to help find him. Anything we can do. Our FBI team, Covert Eyes, is at your disposal. We're in Rome, we can be wherever you are in a couple of hours if we leave now."

Silence, then Fentriss said, "Very well. Grant says if it hadn't been for you and your people, neither he nor his wife would be walking the earth.

"We're lucky, we're staging from Rome. I was here on another business matter already. Come to the British Embassy. Via Venti Settembre. I'll have someone meet you. Thirty minutes."

Fentriss hung up, and Nicholas said to Mike, "We're only ten minutes away. Let me call down to the desk, tell them we won't be checking out right away, have them hold the room and call us a car, then we can head over there."

She was already pulling her damp hair back into a ponytail. "I hope this is all a mistake, and Grant and his team are okay. I hope —" She swallowed. She was afraid, as afraid as she knew Nicholas was.

CHAPTER EIGHTEEN

T-MINUS 70 HOURS

The British Embassy
Rome

Mike thought the front of the British Embassy looked like a ship, with its triangular prow and double staircases. She told Nicholas, who said, "Of course it does. Don't forget, Mike, England enjoyed hundreds of years of naval superiority." He pointed across the room. "Over there. If I'm not mistaken, there's someone from Blue Mountain."

The "someone" was a young woman who looked lethal despite being dressed in loose palazzo pants and a cropped blazer. Chic, and dangerous, Mike could see the outline of her weapon on her hip. When she spoke, it was pure, unadulterated British girls' school.

She stuck out her hand, shook theirs.

"Poppy Bennet. I'll take you to Mr. Fentriss. He's hot under the collar, so don't be surprised if he blows up at you instead of saying hello. Grant's team has been out of touch for ten hours now, no check-ins, no GPS signals. We've been trying to back-channel with the Malaysian government but they don't want to talk. They're claiming *The Griffon* found a long-lost shipwreck that has them and the governments of Indonesia and India all up in arms and fighting for jurisdiction. We're only concerned about finding our people. Sorry, I'm talking too fast. I've had a lot of caffeine. You're Drummond and Caine, right? Of course you are, I recognize you. Grant had his little escapade last month with you. He referred to you as his saviors and friends. Right. Come with me."

They stopped at the desk to show their credentials, then Poppy hurried them up the gallery stairs to the second floor. "We're operational on a separate issue in Kosovo. A team got caught on a K&R — kidnap and ransom — but of course you know what K&R stands for, sorry. They were pulling a client out of Syria when it went south, so the boss flew in to handle the negotiations himself. Two teams in trouble in a day, that's a record for us."

139

Blue Mountain had set up shop in one of the embassy's ornate ballrooms. There were portable screens all over the walls with a bevy of operators on headsets typing and talking. Satellite imagery of Kosovo on the main stage, another set of screens showed satellite images of endless stretches of blue water.

Fentriss, gray-haired, steel-eyed, square-jawed, looking every inch the retired full general he was, stood to the side, arms crossed over his broad chest. He said without preamble, "We're looking for them everywhere, using Grant's insertion as a jumping-off point. The ship isn't showing up on radar, isn't showing up on the satellites, which is a miracle considering how big the bloody thing is. Upwards of four hundred feet, *The Griffon.* Hard to imagine its simply disappearing, which is why we're afraid she went down." He stuck out his hand, shook theirs. "It's a pleasure. I'm sorry we have to meet under these circumstances. Grab a headset so you can hear what's happening. I'm going to attend to my other disaster for five."

He switched headsets and stepped away, started barking orders.

Poppy said, "Here you go." She handed them headsets, donned one herself, but left

140

one ear open in case they had questions.

She said, "The last communication we had with them was yesterday, 0200 Zulu. Grant had done a sweep, the package — Jean-Pierre Broussard — was secure, they were about to have some sort of fancy dinner. Lots of excitement on board, Grant said Broussard claimed he'd found the Holy Grail and they were having a big celebration." She rolled her eyes. "Well, who knows? I remember that huge tsunami heading for Washington, D.C., and then poof, it suddenly disappeared. In any case, Grant was supposed to check in again at 0400 Zulu, but he didn't. And nothing since."

She pointed to a screen that showed the last known position of *The Griffon.* "We flew him in from Jakarta on a chopper and this is where he went on board." She was silent for a moment, and they could hear the chatter of the search and rescue pilots.

Poppy said, "They're flying a grid pattern, but that's a seriously big ocean and *The Griffon* isn't showing up visually or on radar." She paused. "There is a strong possibility they went down. We don't know, just don't know yet."

Nicholas said, "Were they on the move or stationary when Grant last checked in?"

"We don't know that, either. I have all the logs, if you want to look at everything the team has uploaded recently. It will be a couple of weeks of data."

Nicholas said, "I'll take it. Combing through minutiae is a specialty of mine. Maybe something will stand out."

Poppy laughed, pointed to a computer terminal at the back of the room. "Everything is uploaded and ready to go right there."

Nicholas handed over the headphones, and a few moments later his eyes were glued to the terminal.

Mike asked, "So Grant said Broussard found the Holy Grail, and that's why he hired Blue Mountain, to protect it once he found it. They had a celebration feast, and that's all we have?"

Poppy said, "Grant said Broussard was certain he'd find the Grail aboard a shipwreck they located — the *Flor de la Mar.* Sank in 1511. Evidently billions of pounds of treasure aboard. So they found her, and Broussard believes he did indeed find the Holy Grail." Again, she rolled her eyes, then shrugged.

The Holy Grail? Mike, like every other sentient human being who'd seen *Indiana Jones and the Last Crusade,* pictured a chalice in her mind's eye. Broussard believed he really found it? No, that wasn't possible, how could it be? The Grail was a legend, nothing more, a miraculous tale changed and embroidered on over the centuries.

Mike listened to the search and rescue helicopter pilots for a few moments. "You don't have any sort of GPS trackers on your teams?"

"All of their comms are chipped, their sat phones are, too, obviously. As I said, Grant's entire team went offline last night. The yacht has a transponder, a black box to be used in case of an accident, like an airliner, but that, too, is offline."

"I thought those were built to withstand pretty much anything."

"We can only hope Broussard would keep his up-to-date, he's a seasoned sailor. They have a hundred-day battery life. They're not foolproof, though, especially if they're manually disabled."

"It doesn't make sense. With all the technology we have, they should be findable."

"And now you understand why we're so worried. And of course, there's a nasty storm brewing out there. If they're alive, they're getting ready for rough weather."

Nicholas sat back in his chair. He called

out, "We have a problem."

Poppy and Mike joined him at the computer station. Poppy asked, "What is it?"

"There's a microburst transmission from Grant's last location. It's in Morse code."

Mike asked, "What's it say?"

Nicholas met her eyes. " 'They have a nuclear EMP.' "

CHAPTER NINETEEN

T-MINUS 68 HOURS

Aquarius Observatory
Sri Lanka

They stopped in Kuala Lumpur long enough to switch the Sikorsky for a chartered jet, hired, naturally, under an assumed name. The flight was only three hours, and they landed in Colombo at the private airport as the sun came up.

Nevaeh loved traveling to the mountains of Sri Lanka. It felt more like home than any place she'd ever lived, second only to her time in space. That was her real home. But the rain forests here were lovely. She'd asked the Numen once about their homelands, if they were arid or rainy, but they'd chimed, *Wait and see, wait and see.* Trust went a long way to cement the relationship between them, so she hadn't asked again, knowing they'd show her everything as soon as they felt the time was right.

And it would be soon. She finally, finally had the Grail, or as the Numen called it, the Heaven Stone. Or had she first called it the Heaven Stone? She couldn't remember, only that they had agreed she must have it to be immortal like they were. And that was why she knew everything Broussard knew about the Grail. And now she had it and spoke quietly to them, rejoicing in their pleasure. Their blended voices, all in one said, *Soon you will be ready for us. You will join us, be immortal like us, and we will be with you when you return to lead the Earth.*

"Soon," she whispered, "soon enough, we will be together. First I will clear the heavens for you, then anarchy, and finally rebirth, and then we, my friends, will lead the Earth into its future."

When she and Kiera stepped off the plane, they were greeted by Rayyan Megat, the head of her observatory facility, Aquarius, so named for Nevaeh's own astrological sign and her favorite constellation. The station was a two-hour drive from the airport, deep into the mountainous center of Sri Lanka.

It was here where she would meet the Numen in person again. She had told them that, and they'd said in their beautiful single voice that it was good. And she'd had

Aquarius designed specifically — it was both a refuge and a place from which to strike. And a place of welcoming. She didn't know how they would arrive, they hadn't told her. A spacecraft? Who knew? They were all-powerful, omniscient. Of course, they'd changed over the past years, as her world had changed, as demands had changed, as she'd learned and planned, and spoken to them often. And in that moment, she found herself wondering if they'd changed or she had. No, no need to concern herself about any of that now. It was nearly here, her day of triumph.

Rayyan bowed deeply. "Welcome home, Doctor. Everything is ready for you. There are waters in the truck — as you know, it's going to be very hot on the way, so we don't want to get dehydrated. I know you want an update on the coming storm. We are expected to take a direct hit on the coast, which will mean severe winds and flooding rains at the facility. The generators have been fueled, the shutters are in place. The kitchens are stocked as well. Even if there should be more damage than anticipated in the lowlands, we are prepared."

"Very good, Rayyan." They settled in and Kiera silently took both bottles of chilled water, cracked their lids, and drank deeply.

She handed the other bottle to her boss.

Kiera lightly touched her arm. "That's right, drink it down. Good. Now, rest. You have a big few days ahead."

As she drifted into sleep, Nevaeh thought again how everything had gone so perfectly, the plan she'd been laying in place for so long coming at last to fruition. But wait, something was bothering her. Something felt — wrong.

Was it the unexpected storm? She hadn't planned for a typhoon in the middle of all of this. Would it hurt the Numen's chances of coming back to Earth? No way to know without talking to them, which she planned to do as soon as she arrived at the facility and had some privacy.

If not the impending storm, was it the Grail? Her Heaven Stone? It was inside its box at her feet. And strangely, it felt somehow restless to her. Restless? Wait, was she really hearing it give out a tiny buzz? Where was the warmth she'd expected? The welcoming? And its heaviness, it didn't seem right. It worried her. No, Broussard and all his books and letters had been wrong. It was heavy, very heavy, and it buzzed. Who cared? Because above all, she had not a single doubt she was worthy of the Grail, her goals were worthy, everything she'd done and planned to do was justified, necessary, even critical to survival. She was bringing peace to the Earth — peace dictated by her and the Numen, naturally, but given the savage brains of most humans, again, what she would bring would be a blessing. She suspected Jean-Pierre had wanted the Grail for some specific purpose he hadn't shared with her. But what it was, she had no clue. Probably self-aggrandizement. He wasn't worthy, not to her mind. Nothing noble or selfless in his actions.

The stone was hers. But why the constant low buzzing? It was driving her mad. She prayed the Numen would understand.

But still — something was off.

Her satellite phone rang, and it was a number she recognized.

Her secretary, Alys.

Nevaeh debated answering, but the sense that something wasn't right made her scramble the call before she picked up. No matter what was happening, she couldn't run the risk of being tracked down. Only Kiera knew about Aquarius. Nevaeh wanted to keep it that way. She watched the screen until she was satisfied she couldn't be traced, then pressed the talk button.

"Oh, Dr. Patel, I am so glad you have answered. I have terrible news. Monsieur

Broussard's yacht is missing. They fear he has gone down with the ship, and his crew, as well." There were liquid tears in Alys's voice, though Nevaeh could tell she was trying to keep it together.

Nevaeh felt her heart kettledrum in her chest. It was too soon, way too soon. "What do you mean, the ship is missing?"

"I don't know when the word came, but I only found out moments ago. The manufacturer of the ship's transponder called into the office to speak to Jean-Pierre. Apparently, the transponder went offline sometime last night. Claudette tried to raise Jean-Pierre, but he wasn't answering and she alerted me. The Malaysian coast guard and a search is underway."

"How is this possible, Alys? Why didn't Claudette notify me immediately?"

"There's been so much confusion, no one knowing what to do. I'm sorry, ma'am."

She yelled, "You should have called me first!" but Alys was crying, distraught.

"Calm down, calm down. I'm sure he's fine. Jean-Pierre is an experienced sailor, the battery probably ran out on the transponder. Who contacted Claudette?"

"I don't know, I don't know. I'm sorry."

Nevaeh said, "It's all right, Alys. I know this is very upsetting. Thank you for alerting me so quickly. Listen, why don't you go home. I will take it from here."

Alys sobbed her thanks and was gone.

Nevaeh turned off the phone. "How can they have been reported missing so quickly?"

Kiera shrugged, used her calm voice, the one she only used with Nevaeh. "It won't matter, Nevaeh. If and when they do locate him, they'll find a dead man along with everyone on the ship. That was a Hellfire missile we shot them with."

Nevaeh stared out the window. "I hope you're right." Still, something felt off, felt wrong.

CHAPTER TWENTY

T-MINUS 66 HOURS

The British Embassy
Rome

Fentriss barreled over to the workstations like a bull rushing a matador's cape. "What are you talking about, Drummond? Grant sent a message in Morse code about a nuclear EMP? Who has a nuke? Where is it?"

Everything stopped in the room, all eyes on Nicholas.

Nicholas said, "There's a microburst here with the message intact. That's all there is, and the location isn't registering any different than their last known. We better start looking for a nuclear signature in the area."

He shrugged. "It isn't like this scenario hadn't been a distinct possibility for years. We all know eventually someone is going to be stupid enough or greedy enough to try and set off a nuke, be it a suitcase bomb, a dirty bomb, or a nuclear EMP. God save us all if someone tries to launch a warhead toward another country."

Mike asked, "Did it go off? Is that why they're offline? It would have sunk them, right?"

Nicholas said, "I haven't the foggiest. But if there's a nuclear signature, we'll at least be able to measure how strong the EMP might be. It all depends on the load of the plutonium. Though had it already gone off, the satellites would be affected and they aren't. So, I don't think it's happened yet. We would know."

Fentriss started barking orders and everyone scrambled. New views appeared on monitors, headsets were adjusted, the level of chatter increased.

Nicholas said to Mike as they watched the choreographed chaos, "Do you know, I don't think he was all that surprised to hear about the nuke. What do you think that means?"

She raised a brow, said slowly, "It means they know there's a nuke missing, doesn't it?"

"Sir," Nicholas said, standing so quickly his chair nearly fell backward. "May I have a moment?"

"Not now, Drummond."

"Yes, now. Sir."

Fentriss jerked a thumb to indicate toward the door and Mike and Nicholas followed him to the hallway and into a small dark-wood-paneled antechamber. Fentriss closed the door and rounded on them. "What is so bloody important you need me right now?"

"When were you going to tell us about the missing nuke?"

Fentriss looked ready to explode. Instead, he stared heavenward, and said between gritted teeth, "I know enough about you, Drummond, to know you aren't going to let this lie. So I'm going to read you in, because surely at this point your people would know as well. There is no missing nuke, per se. A small amount of plutonium has gone missing from the Idaho Research Facility. Its whereabouts are currently unknown, and we've been warned to be on the lookout. It's possible the amount stolen was enough to equip a nuclear bomb."

Mike couldn't believe this. "*You* were told. Blue Mountain? Not the FBI, not the CIA, but the staff of a high-end security firm?"

"Don't punch out a wall, Agent Caine. Look, it's being kept quiet — the last thing anyone wants is panic on our hands or the thieves who stole the plutonium to know we're onto them. We were told because Blue Mountain has teams all over the world unfettered by government oversight. We're uniquely equipped to look for the missing plutonium. But of course the proper authorities have been alerted. I talked to the head of the DOD myself yesterday. General Temple is well aware of the significance of the problem. He's given me full authority to search anywhere we need and stop this mess."

"Yesterday? You only talked to General Temple yesterday? How long have you known about this?"

Mike was vibrating. Nicholas put a hand on her arm. "When did the plutonium go missing?"

Fentriss said, "The last time it was registered in-house at the facility was in 2015, when it was moved from one research area to another, in a standard protocol. But they only discovered it was actually missing a couple of weeks ago."

Now Nicholas was getting mad. "You're telling us there's been nuclear material unaccounted for out in the world for more than two *years,* and no one knew? That's preposterous."

Fentriss's face was turning red, but his voice was low and even. "I know you're both angry, but dial it back, agents. We aren't responsible for someone misplacing plutonium, not our purview. The research facility didn't release the information until a few days ago. Whether they were aware two weeks or two years ago, it's out there now, and we need to find it.

"There's more. One of my men on the Kosovo mission said he'd heard there was a nuke EMP in play. Unfortunately, he died right after his transmission, and we haven't exactly been conversant with the rest of the team, so good luck finding out where he heard it. Their mission fell apart, then Grant's team went off the radar."

Fentriss's face suddenly looked older, worn. "Trust me, agents, now you know what I know. So can we get back to work finding my people?"

Nicholas said, "What was your team's mission in Kosovo, sir? How would your man overhear this news? Was he murdered?"

"It's a standard K&R, an oil executive who went missing in disputed territory while trying to broker a deal. It has nothing to do with the plutonium. My guy was a terrorism expert, one of the reasons I hired him. The team uploaded his tablet to me, and I've been going through his notes. He was in Damascus last month, had a meet with a source, and they mentioned some followers of Khaleed Al-Asaad were making not-so-discreet inquiries. Our man was found in a ravine, his neck broken. Was he murdered? I think it likely."

Nicholas said, "We were told Al-Asaad was killed some two years ago, if I remember correctly. The CIA got him."

"Yes, evidently so. His power structure was rumored to be second only to Bin Laden's. And, Al-Asaad had a huge following, all eager to blow us up, to buy and sell arms to those who want to commit acts of terrorism all over the world." Fentriss rubbed a hand across his tired face. "They will never give up, never give in, until they have what they want, sowing chaos until they gain total destruction of the West. These not-so-discreet inquiries gave me the impression Al-Asaad could be alive. If he is, it will only get worse. Is he involved with a nuke? It's our worst nightmare."

Mike was still angry. "Regardless, we need to let our boss know what's happening. Who else has been read in about the missing plutonium?"

Fentriss said, "Listen to me. The plutonium isn't your problem, it's mine. Your job here isn't to find a nuke. It's to help me find my team. If you want to go plutonium hunting, I suggest you get in touch with your people and get assigned to the program. In the meantime, if you were serious with your offer to help find Grant, please, stay focused."

Mike said, "Fine. But don't think we aren't going to be pursuing the nuclear angle as well. No choice. We'll be drawn and quartered if we don't at least mention what we know."

"Up to you. Shall we?" He gestured toward the door, and they started back to the main staging area. Fentriss peeled off to bark more orders at his people.

Mike watched him stride away, her mind going a mile a minute. "I can't believe this, Nicholas. Listen, if a nuke went off and there was an EMP, there'd be a signature, yes?"

"Yes, without a doubt. It hasn't gone off — yet."

"Exactly. So there's a chance to still use GPS to find Grant."

A dark eyebrow went up. "How so?"

"His fitness tracker, Nicholas. Remember the new one he was wearing? I told you I wanted to get one in Rome. Well, I did some research. The device he was wearing was made by Ziost, uses GPS to automatically track outdoor runs. You don't have to tell it to track you, it's all ready to go the moment it senses you running. So even if the ship's GPS is offline, there's a chance the tracker isn't. If we find the device, we can find Grant and his team. I hope. Assuming he's still wearing it, of course, and it's still sending out signals."

He stared at her, grabbed her arms, and hugged her tight. "Have I told you lately I love your brain? That's brilliant. Let me get Adam on this."

"Are you going to touch base with Zachery, too?"

"Zachery is on a retreat with some other muckety-mucks this week, remember? In the wilds of Montana, no wireless, a team-building exercise. I think we should play this out first. If the powers that be call him back, and he wants us, he knows how to reach us."

"You know we're going to be hotdogging, something Zachery hates."

He grinned. "Yes, well, Fentriss has a point. We should take advantage of this being a silent op for the time being. We're still off the official radar. So let's find Grant. I assume it will be all hands on deck soon enough. Perhaps he'll know more about what's happening and we can avoid an international crisis."

She shook her head at him. "Another one, you mean."

He hugged her again. "It's what we do, Agent Caine. Now, let's call Adam."

CHAPTER TWENTY-ONE

Adam Pearce, their twenty-year-old off-book hacker, and a major part of their Covert Eyes team, answered on the fourth ring, his face popping up on Nicholas's screen. His hair stuck up at angles, he was wearing earbuds and a vintage Journey tour T-shirt, and a can of Red Bull was visible by his elbow.

"What took you so long?"

Adam grinned, waggled his eyebrows. "You don't want to know."

"Adam, Mike here. Don't tell us you're entertaining a female caller. Are you?"

"Maybe . . . No, of course not. Just kidding. I was playing Fortnite, of course. What every red-blooded young hacker in the world is doing right now."

Nicholas said, "I'm not sure what that says about society's future. Terribly sorry to interrupt your game, but we have a serious situation and need your help."

"Sure. What's up?"

"Grant Thornton is missing."

"Oh, no, not again."

"Yes, again. Different situation this time, though. He was on board Jean-Pierre Broussard's yacht."

Adam's mouth fell open. "You're kidding. Oh, damn. I heard they're afraid the yacht went down. I had no idea Grant was anywhere near there. I thought he was with Kitsune, at their place —" He shut up. Operational security concerning Grant and Kitsune was paramount for the entire Covert Eyes team. Adam was too smart to openly discuss their whereabouts, even on a secure connection. "Is Kitsune okay?"

"She's on a job and we have no way to reach her. Malaysia's search and rescue teams are working the area, but the yacht's transponder seems to be offline. It's possible a small EMP went off in the area, we're trying to confirm now. But Mike thought of something rather ingenious. Grant was wearing a Ziost fitness tracker. It has —"

Adam's face lit up. "GPS, to track outdoor exercise. Pretty standard when it comes to these kinds of devices, though Ziost does everything automatically. You're thinking I could use his tracker's GPS signal to locate him. Assuming an EMP didn't knock it off-line. You remember the micro-EMP you set off in Italy last month? That didn't mess with your watch, did it?"

"No. But my watch was shielded, and it's much too old to be affected by an EMP. Not GPS-enabled, not digital at all."

"Let me know when you want to come out of the Dark Ages, dude. Okay, now, I'm not sure how an EMP might affect smaller, personal device electronics of this nature. I don't know if anyone's been doing any testing to find out, either, since fitness trackers aren't exactly vital to national security. Still, it's a super idea, Mike. I'm on it. Though since this is a public company, we'll have to get a warrant, and it's going to take some time."

Mike said, "Mm-hmm —"

"Of course, there are faster ways —"

Nicholas grinned. "I have no idea what you're talking about."

Mike said, "Nor do I, but we'll deal with the repercussions — if any — later."

"Got it. I'll get back to you."

Mike said, "Hold on, Adam. Before you go, a favor. After you run Grant's tracker, please pull everything you can find on the Idaho Research Facility. They are — were — stewards of some missing plutonium, and

I'd like to find out if a small bit of plutonium from Idaho could be used to build a nuclear EMP."

"A nuclear EMP? Now you have my attention."

"This is on the down-low, okay? There was a Morse code burst transmission from *The Griffon* before it went offline about a possible nuclear EMP in play. We're hoping it's a false alarm. Get into the dark web and see what you can find, okay?"

Adam took a swig of Red Bull and nodded. "I will, but I haven't heard anything about this. Not cool. I'll get back to you as soon as I find anything."

"Thanks."

"Be careful, guys. I have a bad feeling."

Nicholas said, "We will. We're going after Grant, and we're going to bring him home. With any luck, Kitsune will only find out over the dinner table."

"Wait, you're going to Malaysia?"

"Yes. We're with Blue Mountain. Wheels up in sixty from Fiumicino, so we have to get moving. We'll be in touch, and you ring me straightaway when you've tracked Grant."

"Copy that. And don't worry. I've got this. I can find out about everything we discussed faster than you can."

Poppy Bennet appeared at Nicholas's elbow just as Adam's face disappeared from the monitor. "That boy is going to track Grant through his fitness tracker GPS? Amazing. When will we have the coordinates?"

Mike said, "Adam will let us know. He's very good. If it's possible, he'll do it. With luck, we will have them soon."

Poppy heaved a sigh of relief. "At last, some hope. Now, we have to go. I'm giving you a ride to Fiumicino. ETA to Malaysia is ten hours."

Nicholas said, "Plenty of time to hear from Adam and to figure out where this nuke came from and is now. Oh yes, we need to stop by the hotel and grab our bags."

"I already have them waiting in the car, and have checked you out. Blue Mountain covered the bill." She smiled. "I'm terribly efficient."

CHAPTER TWENTY-TWO

T-MINUS 60 HOURS

Fiumicino Airport
Rome

Fentriss's personal Blue Mountain jet was a beautiful Gulfstream G650 — a much upgraded version of the same plane the Covert Eyes team used. Fentriss was already aboard, on a call, and waved them to their seats.

He told whoever he was talking to he'd call them back and hung up. "Problems on the K&R mission. I'm afraid I won't be able to join you in Malaysia." He handed Nicholas a card. "Here's my personal information. You call me immediately with any updates. Poppy told me about your idea, Agent Caine, tracking Grant using the GPS on his fitness tracker. Good thinking. Flight computer says you'll be in Kuala Lumpur in ten hours. Hopefully they'll be found before you land."

And to Mike, "If this works, I'll be forbidding my people from wearing the fitness trackers in the future."

Mike said, "But if Grant wasn't wearing it, we wouldn't be able to find him — or your client, Mr. Broussard."

Fentriss said, "You know what this means. If anyone can hack into the system and locate my operatives when they're meant to be off-grid, the trackers are a major operational security risk."

Nicholas said, "It's a good thing we aren't just anyone, sir. I understand your rationale. The wrong person gets ahold of this information, it would compromise your teams."

"Exactly. I often ask myself why there's always a downside. Now, I have to deal with the Kosovo situation, going there directly. Thank God it's a damn sight closer than Malaysia. Poppy will go with you and liaise with operations in Kuala Lumpur, get you a team, and anything else you need. Go find my people." He paused a moment, then shook their hands. "Thank you. I'm trusting you with their lives."

Nicholas said, "We'll find them. And thank you for providing the ride. Saves us a lot of time getting our own jet here."

They watched Fentriss march off the

plane, took their seats. A few minutes later, they were taxiing, and then in the air.

Once they were settled, laptops and phones open and tapped into the plane's secure encrypted network, Poppy said, "Tell me, what can I do to help?"

Nicholas said, "Are you an operative, or are you admin?"

The look she gave him should have set his hair on fire.

"Right, operative. In that case, I'll need you to run me through how the teams are comprised, what your emergency protocols would be in this kind of situation, everything you can think of that will help us intercept him. Where will Grant be making his way to if he's simply out of touch? Assuming the boat went down but they were able to get into life rafts, what's the first thing he's going to do?"

Poppy said, "Find a way to communicate, obviously. And if Grant's down, another team member will be leading things. Assuming we're in a worst-case scenario, that is."

She flipped out a laminated map on which she'd made a series of X's.

"This is what's known as the Strait of Malacca. Here" — she pointed to a large red X written in grease pencil — "are the last known coordinates of *The Griffon.* You'll notice this yellow X is where the EMP transmission came from. There are at least five nautical miles between the two, heading toward the Indian Ocean. They were sailing north, out of the Strait. Why? I don't know."

Nicholas stared at the map. "Hook us up with search and rescue out of Kuala Lumpur. Once Adam gets back to us with the coordinates, we'll pass them along so they can get a head start. Make sure they have a chopper ready for us, too."

Poppy frowned. "You're going out there?"

"If they haven't been located when we land? Yes, we are."

She played with the map, drew two thunderbolts to the west of the ship's last knowns. "This is a major storm, Nicholas. It's very possible the winds will take it to official typhoon levels later today. To fly into that kind of storm is suicide."

"So make sure it's a sturdy chopper."

Mike groaned. "A very sturdy chopper. We don't have the best luck with them."

"Not exactly true," Nicholas said. "It's not usually us who has the problem."

Poppy said, "I'll make it happen, though for the record, I think you two are nuts to want to fly out into the middle of the ocean in a storm of this magnitude. What else?"

"Specs for *The Griffon.* We'll need to know

how many crew were aboard, how many life rafts, whatever means of escape they'd have if the ship were to go down. And if Broussard has what he believes is the Holy Grail, pulled from that old shipwreck — the *Flor de la Mar* — anything and everything on that, too, if you please."

"You got it." She turned to her own computer and started typing away.

Mike said, "I want to learn more about this Jean-Pierre Broussard character."

Poppy snapped her fingers and pointed at Mike's tablet. "I thought you would. I've sent you the dossier. It includes video and transcripts of various interviews. If you want more, holler."

"Thanks, Poppy."

Nicholas said to Mike, "I'm going to do some recon on how Grant works, see if I can figure out what he's thinking. You study up on Broussard."

Mike saluted him. "Sir, yes, sir, Sir Nicholas, sir."

Poppy raised a brow. "Is she being facetious?"

Mike said, "Nope. Nicholas was knighted a couple of weeks ago."

"Yes, I remember, and you were damed as well, Michaela. I think that's the best part. So I'm flying with royalty, what a deal." She stood, curtsied, making them both laugh.

"Actually, Poppy," Mike said, "Nicholas technically already is royalty — his grandfather is a viscount. I'm only a sheriff's daughter from Omaha."

Poppy said, "Who's been royally damed. I need to hang with you two more. Maybe I'll get a sash of my very own."

They settled in to their work, Nicholas and Poppy discussing the operational aspects of Blue Mountain, Mike researching Jean-Pierre Broussard.

He wasn't hard to find. The Galactus website had a series of slick, well-produced videos showing the progression of the company as it grew into a private space powerhouse. The videos were narrated by Broussard himself. He was handsome, larger than life, rich as Croesus. He'd wanted to be an astronaut himself, had started Galactus to reshape the way both businesses and private citizens accessed space.

A quick search for *The Griffon* turned up an entirely new aspect of Jean-Pierre Broussard. This was the playboy she knew about from *People*. There were endless photos from various ports of call, such as the Venice Film Festival, where *The Griffon* had docked for two weeks while the world's finest actors and filmmakers came aboard and partied into the wee hours. But there was an interesting story about how the yacht had recently been retrofitted with a massive crane for yet another treasure-hunting expedition Broussard didn't talk about.

She read more, absorbing the two sides to the man's personality — treasure hunter, space explorer. After two hours, she emerged with a better understanding of the man and his missions, but she knew absolutely nothing about his private life. If he'd ever had a wife, children, for example. He was considered a playboy, changing out new lovers on a regular basis.

Mike stretched, fetched herself a cup of coffee from the galley, and went to Nicholas's chair. He and Poppy had long since finished their briefing and now he had a series of spreadsheets open with coding gibberish on them.

"Do you think Jean-Pierre Broussard really found the Holy Grail? Do you think it's a cup? Or something else? I remember reading somewhere many believed it to be a stone. You know, like the Sorcerer's stone in *Harry Potter*."

Nicholas didn't stop typing. "Parzival."

"Gesundheit."

He laughed, looked up at her. "Parzival,

the Grail knight. He features prominently in the Arthurian Grail legends. The Grail as a stone predates the modern Christian version of the Grail as the cup from Christ's crucifixion. They called it the Stone from Heaven. The legends are swashbuckling, romantic tales of adventure and true selfless heroism. My dad read me the stories at bedtime."

She shook her head. "How do you remember this stuff? You were just a kid."

He tapped his earbuds. "I downloaded a series of workshops led by the mythologist Joseph Campbell explaining Wolfram von Eschenbach's medieval poem. I've been listening for the past hour. It's actually quite saucy in parts."

"Please read me the saucy bits later. Now, what else do I need to know?"

"The Grail stone is claimed to have healing powers, rewarding fidelity and true love. And there's also the promise of immortality."

"Immortality. Now, that would be an excellent reason to go hunting for it."

CHAPTER TWENTY-THREE

T-MINUS 52 HOURS

They were two hours out of Kuala Lumpur when Adam called back. Nicholas was running data sets on *The Griffon*'s last known location, extrapolating a possible search area. He tossed his phone to Mike to answer.

She got Poppy's attention, then put it on speaker, said to Adam, "Tell us you found something."

"I found something. I have a general set of coordinates. Looking for the fitness tracker was a great idea, Mike. Sending them to Nicholas's phone right now." A text came in with the coordinates. She read them off to Nicholas, who plugged them into his grid. A large red dot showed up. It was on the farthest edge of the area he'd marked.

Nicholas said, "Bloody good job, Adam. We have him. Is this coordinate live?"

"Before you get too excited, no, not exactly. This is the last known of Grant's Ziost tracker. It was uploaded last night. As of five minutes ago, the tracker was still in this position, but the regularly scheduled upload didn't happen. Ziost has two ways to do GPS tracking — uploading GPS data manually when the user tells it to track a run or a walk, or sensing when the user has started a workout and tracking it automatically. Luckily, it also updates itself in the system every eight hours, so there are new coordinates three times a day. Since I know what the signal is now, I can keep trying to track it myself instead of waiting for their system to refresh and upload again. Assuming I can locate it on my own GPS system. When I do, I'll have to track it by hand and will send you updates if it changes."

Mike said, "Adam, is there any way to tell if this tracker is above the water or below?"

"No, but my vote is above. The Ziost is water resistant to one hundred feet, not meant to be a dive companion or anything, more like you can shower with it or get it wet, but it isn't designed to be immersed for extended periods. But this signal was pretty strong. I'd think if it was underwater, it wouldn't have the same strength. I could be wrong, though."

"Good to know. Thanks, Adam. Keep on the lookout."

"I am. Also, on your nuke, I'm forwarding all the info I was able to find on the Idaho Research Facility. You'll find this interesting, for sure. There's a dead scientist from around the same time the plutonium went missing — 2015. His name was Edward Linton. Murder-suicide; he evidently shot his wife, Janie, then himself. The disappeared plutonium was in his research section, and he was the one in charge. Suspicious timing, don't you think?"

Mike shook her head. "I can't believe this is only coming out now. When he and his wife died, why didn't the facility do a thorough check of all the materiel? Make sure it was all there?"

"No clue, but it would have been the smart thing to do, for sure. I'm already running a — ahem — program to take a look at their internals and see what's what."

Nicholas said, "Ah, excellent initiative. Thank you, Adam. We'll be on the ground in a couple of hours. Will loop you in as soon as we have more."

"Good. Hey, take me off speaker for a moment, will you?"

Nicholas raised a brow but complied. "You're solo. What is it?"

"This possible nuclear EMP situation is starting to get some legs. Word leaked out, and the press has it. There's a lid on it for now, no bets on when they start reporting it. The Idaho Research Facility has already released a private statement, so it won't be too long. The dark web is lit up right now, everyone's talking about it." He was silent for a moment, then came back, sounding unusually grave and formal. "If a nuclear EMP goes off, what are my orders? What's our procedure?"

Nicholas felt a wave of fear like a punch to his gut. Any sort of nuclear explosion would be terrifying, but to have a nuclear EMP go off would create chaos the levels of which he couldn't imagine or predict. And they had no idea where it might be, nor where it might go off. Still, he tried to re-assure Adam. "If such a thing were to happen, you'd get yourself to the New York Field Office. It would be the safest place. They have preventative measures to keep us up and running, and alive. The building is hardened against all sorts of attacks, EMP included."

"Okay. Let's say it's not an if but a yes it could very well happen. What about you and Mike?"

Nicholas said, "We'll be fine. We might

not be in ready communication, but we'll be fine."

"Nicholas, this is what I'm worried about. You're on the other side of the world. If it goes off, depending where it does, there's a good chance we won't be able to communicate at all. In that case, you've got to find an old ham radio rig with tubes around. Do you know how to use a ham?"

"Actually, I do. My grandfather was an enthusiast, and my father as well. The odds of our stumbling across one in an emergency, though, given where we are, are slim. But if — and it's a big if, Adam — but if something happens, don't panic. We'll be in touch as soon as we can. If I can find an old-school radio, I'd broadcast in our approved frequencies. If I can't, know I will find a way to check in. We're prepared for this scenario, Adam. Don't worry."

"I should have known you'd have squared away for all eventualities. It's a little freaky, to think a nuke might be imminent. I'll be moving to Federal Plaza. I'll call you back from there."

"Good plan. Before you go, what is the chatter?"

"In the dark web? The usual nihilist crap. But there are a few accounts saying it's for real, one in particular, a guy who used to work for OSTP — Office of Science and Technology Policy in the White House — saying he overheard on a private signal network that Strategic Defense found a nuclear signature off the coast of South America two weeks ago. And do you believe this? The signature is from a spaceport launch site in French Guiana."

"Hold on." Nicholas pulled up the website for the spaceport. "Oh, bollocks."

"What?"

"French Guiana spaceport is Galactus's home base. It's where they launch all their rockets."

"And now Broussard's boat has gone down — wait, do you think he's responsible? Could he be behind putting a nuke into space?"

Nicholas blew out a breath. "I don't know. But we better find out. Drop everything, Adam. Once you're at Federal Plaza, reestablish contact with me when you're set up with Gray. Get the team informed. And do it quickly."

"I'm gone."

Nicholas looked up to see Mike walking back from the galley, a cup of coffee in her hand.

"What was Adam freaked out about?"

"The nuclear EMP may be more than a

rumor. Supposedly, a nuclear signature was reported from the spaceport in French Guiana. All back channels, nothing official. It's where Galactus launches their satellites. I need to do a deep dive into the Galactus systems, see what I can find. If they launched a rocket with a nuke on it, Broussard himself may be responsible. And if so, he could have made his boat go offline in order to run. Or the ship could be down. We don't know yet."

Mike could only stare at him. One day they were happily chowing down grilled lobster with Kitsune and Grant, and the next — "You've got to be kidding me."

His smile was grim. "I wish I were."

CHAPTER TWENTY-FOUR

Aquarius Observatory
Sri Lanka

Nevaeh heaved the box holding the Holy Grail into her safe and slammed the door. It made no sense, the Grail seemed even heavier than it had been just a short time before. Even stranger, once they'd arrived at Aquarius, the stone had stopped buzzing. She would swear it felt cold, distant from her. Even the Numen had held silent.

Perhaps she was only tired from the flight and the excitement of having the Grail in her possession, and worried about the too-early discovery of Broussard's boat going down, and she wasn't feeling what she should. It was her fault, not the stone's. Yes, she would call it the Heaven Stone, not the Holy Grail, it was more fitting because she was coming to believe it had come from the Numen a long time ago, and had somehow become lost to them. When she'd mentioned this to them, she remembered their agreeing.

As she showered, she realized that in just over two days' time, she would be in ready, constant contact with the Numen. When the nuke went off, the satellites surrounding it would be destroyed, and all would be clear and silent, what she knew they wanted, and their conduit to her would be open. She would be there, on her mountaintop in Sri Lanka, waiting for them.

It was ingenious, really, the plan she'd concocted. Having the nuclear EMP built was only the beginning. The massive co-ordination of getting the nuke to space, un-traced, had taken years to develop. But it was there now, floating in orbit, unseen by the very people who tracked such things, ready for her signal.

Yes, people would die. But people died every day. Once the Numen were here, with her, everything would change. Wars would end, for all time. All good things demanded sacrifice. So sacrificing the few to save the many was the only way. She refused to feel bad about that.

She toweled off, turned on the television, and saw the breaking news alert. They were reporting *The Griffon* had gone off radar and was missing in the vast sea off the coast of

Malaysia. No survivors had yet been found.

She pumped her fist.

Are you dead, Jean-Pierre? About time, I say.

Only two more days.

She heard Kiera moving around in the hallway. Her second, as she sometimes thought of her, had been nothing short of perfect. Nevaeh would relive the moment of impact from the missile they'd shot into *The Griffon* for days to come. And the look on Devi's face before Kiera had shot her. Hope. Such hope. What a stupid, stupid girl.

Would the Numen take Kiera with them, too?

Nevaeh wasn't sure, really, if she wanted Kiera to be with the Numen. Odd, the Numen were strangely silent when she'd asked them the question.

She snapped off the television and walked naked to the sensory deprivation tank she'd installed in the room she'd had built in the facility, right next to her bedroom. Closed, it looked like a large white egg. She pressed a button and the eggshell cracked open with a small hydraulic *hiss.* It was made by a company called DreamPod, and that's exactly what the tank did for her — allowed her to relax and access her dreams.

This was the place she most enjoyed communicating with the Numen. She believed they preferred it, as they became positively chatty. She lay in the warm, salty, embryonic water, the preprogrammed chakra lights glowing and the distant hum of music in her ears. And then, when she was fully relaxed, she went black. No lights. No music. Nothing.

Her brain relaxed into theta waves — near sleep. The sensory deprivation chamber was quiet as the womb. Absolute silence, absolute calm. It was as close to being back in space as she could get without launching herself on a rocket.

She waited, but nothing. Why wasn't it working? She couldn't seem to relax.

The melodic chorus started, all sibilant voices merging into one: *Why didn't the Heaven Stone greet you as it was supposed to, as we expected it to? It was heavy, and that isn't right. And the buzzing? We do not understand this. What have you done, Nevaeh, to make it treat you like an enemy? You killed Broussard, Devi — perhaps you should not have murdered Devi — she was an innocent, wasn't she? Blackmailed by you? Why did you kill her?*

"Devi was only a tool. She served her

purpose. She was of no importance any longer."

We know you're wondering if that is why the Heaven Stone doesn't want to become one with you.

"No, I have no doubts. Maybe the Heaven Stone needs time to understand what my goal is, what we are all planning to do together. Isn't that possible?"

Yes, perhaps that is possible. There is so much work left to do.

"Everything is in place. I have the Heaven Stone so I am now immortal, so I can be one with you and live forever. I've placed the bomb aboard the satellite, the count-down is underway. Two more days, and there will be no more noise in the heavens, no more noise on Earth. And you will come to me."

Only two more days, Nevaeh.

"Yes, I will be high on my mountaintop awaiting you. In two days, at the apex of the lunar eclipse, the skies will glow with an explosion of such magnitude that, like I said, all the satellites will go dead, and then the world around us will be dark and silent, as I came to believe you wanted. That will be your moment, that is when you will be able to enter Earth's atmosphere unharmed. All will be open to you, and I will welcome you and we will begin our journey to save Earth."

We know you have worked relentlessly to make us recognized by all, to make us know and condemn your enemies. Soon, Nevaeh, soon —

"Yes, we will bring peace to Earth together. I will rule, you at my side, my confidants, my advisers. No one will ever betray me again, all will revere me — and you."

She waited in the silence of the dark, quiet water but they said no more.

She rose, stepped out of the chamber and into the low light.

It was time to set the world on fire.

CHAPTER TWENTY-FIVE

Schizophrenia is a chronic and severe mental disorder that affects how a person thinks, feels, and behaves. People with schizophrenia may seem like they have lost touch with reality.
— National Institute of Mental Health

Manhattan, New York
July 19, 2012
Nevaeh stepped out of the cab on Fifth Avenue into the sweltering July day. Summer in the city was loud and sticky. She was excited, and not a little nervous, to be taking this step. It felt momentous. She'd waited four months to get on the schedule with Dr. Claire Fontaine, a leading psychiatrist with a specialty in schizophrenia who no longer took new patients. But Nevaeh hadn't given up. When the call finally came — the doctor had a cancellation, would be willing to make an exception, could she be

187

there tomorrow? — Nevaeh had quickly packed a bag and was on the first flight out of Houston.

Fontaine was her ticket back to NASA, back to the space station, she knew it in her heart. Yes, she'd quit, but flight director Franklin Norgate had reached out time and again, telling her she had a place on the NASA team. He'd made it clear they wanted her back to train other astronauts, and maybe, with the right mission, the right timing, she could get assigned a mission of her own. Did he really believe it? Nevaeh didn't know if it would ever happen as long as that vindictive bitch Rebecca Holloway was in charge. But maybe after today, Holloway would have to back off, she would have to admit Nevaeh wasn't insane. Fontaine was that good, that respected, that listened to.

As for her situation, as Norgate liked to refer to it, it had been kept private. It wasn't good press to have an astronaut quit the program like she had. And when it happened, as it did occasionally, NASA battened down the hatches.

Norgate, a man she no longer admired, kept referring to her recovery from her "ordeal." Ordeal? What a stupid thing to call a life-changing event. He would eat his words as well, beg her to come back, lead her own mission.

She took the elevator to the fifth floor and found Fontaine's office. The waiting room was simply furnished with blond modern sofas and chairs. A bored young woman checked her in and took her payment. So Dr. Fontaine didn't take insurance, fine with her, she would happily pay ten times what the woman was charging to get Fontaine's assurances of her sanity.

After a few minutes, the wooden door opened and a kind-faced brown-haired woman wearing a sleeveless black sheath dress and bright red lipstick gestured her inside. Dr. Fontaine was in her early fifties, runner-fit, and from fifteen feet away, Nevaeh could see the intelligence in her light-colored eyes. She felt a surge of hope. Nevaeh didn't think this woman would make up her mind until she had all the facts.

They spoke for a few minutes, introductions, really, then the doctor said, "What may I help you with, Dr. Patel?"

"I'm having a — situation" — ah, that word again — "and I want to get your confirmation I'm not suffering from any sort of delusions or mental incapacities. It's a delicate matter."

Fontaine looked interested. "Go on."

She told the story clearly and cleanly, giving specifics, the way she'd been trained. The doctor nodded and wrote a few things down, but for the most part simply listened. When Nevaeh finished, she said, "It's been a year since you left NASA?"

"Yes."

"And the Numen haven't appeared to you in any corporeal form? They're only auditory?"

"Yes."

"I see. Fascinating."

"I have my files from NASA. I can —"

"Let's talk some more, first. I'll do my homework before our next meeting. Tell me about your family. Your upbringing."

"I don't have mommy or daddy issues. I loved my parents deeply, and they loved me. They always supported me. Always."

"They're gone?"

"Yes, unfortunately."

"I can see by the look on your face you're experiencing a strong memory right now. Tell me what you're seeing, Dr. Patel. What are you remembering?"

"Funny how you say it, a strong memory. Yes, I was remembering how I became an astronaut in the first place. It was July 20, 1969, the mission was Apollo 11. The television was on in the living room, one of the square, squat things, brown and ugly. I was sitting in front of it, and the pictures were grainy, black-and-white, and it was incredible, seeing the moon, the dust being kicked up. I was transported there, it was so hauntingly beautiful. My mother started to speak and my father told her to stop talking. Then we heard the words, tinny on the television's weak speakers. I've heard the real recordings. They don't do Armstrong justice."

"The words?"

" 'That's one small step for man, one giant leap for mankind.' When Armstrong took his first step on the moon, I knew immediately I wanted to be an astronaut. I wanted to do what they were doing. It seemed incredible, indescribably amazing."

"And your parents? How did they react?"

"My mother said, 'Oh, my darling girl, you do? I think you would be a wonderful astronaut.' My father, who was always more practical, said, 'Do you know how much schooling is involved?' I didn't, of course, so he explained to me all the science and math I would have to do, and when I got excited instead of deterred, they did everything they could to help me reach my goal. I was already good at math, and an early reader. We lived in Connecticut at the time, my father taught at Yale. They took me out of public school and enrolled me in a private elementary that fed to Andover, which in turn opened all the doors to Stanford. They took me on vacations to Cape Canaveral to watch launches — it was incredible, earth-shattering, to be in the presence of so much power. I studied hard, pushed myself, and achieved my goals."

"I'd say a Ph.D. in astrophysics from MIT would be an achievement for anyone."

Nevaeh was pleased. This doctor, this brilliant respected psychiatrist, would see to it she would go back into space. Nevaeh knew it. She said, "So you know some of my story."

Dr. Fontaine looked at her notebook. "I glanced at the files you provided, briefly."

"Then you'll know the Ph.D. wasn't all I craved. The schooling was necessary, but I had to be special to get NASA's attention. I first published when I was twenty, in the *Journal of the Aeronautical Sciences,* a paper on the future of manned space flight. It got attention from many quarters. I got my pilot's license when I was sixteen, then went on to be certified in both fixed wing and helicopter. All I was missing was a tour overseas in the military. Every step I took from the age of eight was designed to make me stand out when I applied for the astronaut program. I was among an elite group of extremely well-educated and committed individuals, all of whom were freakishly smart. I had to be better than good, I had to be invincible. And it worked. I got their attention, and I went to work for NASA, became an astronaut."

"How did you feel when you were chosen for the program?"

"Transcendent."

"And how did you feel when you were told you had to rotate off the space station and come home for evaluation?"

"Furious. It wasn't fair. They made me come back because they thought I was crazy. I am not crazy. How could I be? Look at all I've accomplished. I've never had an incident in the past. Why would I start now?"

"Dr. Patel. You had a severe trauma in an unfamiliar environment. Sometimes trauma can cause a dissociative state. It's the mind's way of helping you cope."

"I know what a dissociative state is. I had all the psychological training before I went up to the space station. They only choose those who exhibit the proper mental capacities for space flight. And once they'd screened out those who wouldn't be able to handle it, they trained us to handle it all.

We were warned about hallucinations, depression, claustrophobia, anger, anxiety. How lonely we would feel, how disconnected. We still don't understand exactly what microgravity does to the body, to the brain, to the blood, don't know how to mitigate these very real emotions.

"But I know myself. That's not what happened. I wasn't suffering from anything."

"Tell me what you think happened."

"It's not what I think, it's what I know. I went on the walk, did my assigned repair. I was finished, getting in place to come back inside. My hand slipped and I missed the rung. The negative inertia pushed me away from the ladder. I began to float away, and my tether snapped. I had no way to get back to the station. And then a hand gripped mine, and that's when they spoke."

"They?"

"The Numen."

CHAPTER TWENTY-SIX

Dr. Fontaine said, without a hitch, without an ounce of disbelief, "The Numen? Did they name themselves, or is this a name you gave them?"

"They identified themselves, I believe."

"All right. Go on."

"They said, 'You are not going to die today. But you must tell them we're here.' And that's what I've been trying to do, and everyone thinks I've gone mad. That I have some sort of space sickness that's impaired me. But it's not true."

"You're getting upset. Try to calm yourself. Square breathing. Of course you know what that is."

Nevaeh obediently breathed in for a count of four, held her breath for four, blew it out, then sat. She did this twice more before Dr. Fontaine said, "All right. That's better. Now. When you hear the Numen, are they external to your body? Or does it feel like your own internal voice speaking to you?"

"They're external, they're not inside me."

"And how often do they speak? Do they wait until they are spoken to, or do they interrupt you?"

"It's often in response to my speaking to them."

"Do they tell you to do things?"

Nevaeh needed to be careful here. The longer she was away from space, the quieter the voices got, and she hated it, like missing an arm.

She said simply, "They want me to keep telling people of their existence. They mean us no harm. They want to help us achieve peace."

"If you're walking down a busy street, could you talk to them?"

"No. I need quiet. Calm. They don't like the noise. That's part of what they want, for us to turn down the noise. All the phones and computers and satellites — it's stopping them from being able to talk to more people. They see nothing but a violent ending for our species from the takeover of technology. They know there's no end in sight."

"So they've made contact with people before?"

"I don't know. They haven't said. Do you

believe me?"

Nevaeh saw Dr. Fontaine's eyes widen, though of course she'd been trained to school her face.

"Nevaeh, it doesn't matter what I believe. We're here to discuss what you believe. Do *you* think you're exhibiting signs of schizophrenia, or schizoaffective disorder?"

"No, I don't. I feel completely normal. My cognitive function is not impaired. I feel no decompensation of my abilities. I have no symptoms of any sort of mental illness other than the occasional conversation with some space travelers."

She sounded bitter, she knew she did. She hadn't chosen to be the conduit through which the Numen held a discourse with Earth. At times she wished they hadn't chosen her. But of course, they'd saved her. How could she repudiate them?

Dr. Fontaine said, "I wasn't entirely forthcoming earlier. I have taken a cursory look at the records you provided me from your doctors at NASA. It's well-documented that sometimes astronauts hallucinate in space. They feel that's what happened. On your EVA, you suffered from a hallucination, and it has cemented itself in your imagination and become real for you. This is not unheard of."

"The operative words there are 'in space.' They've tried a hundred different explanations for what happened. I was trying to commit suicide because I had separation anxiety and desperately wanted to get back to Earth. I was deprived of oxygen when my tether snapped and it caused a hypoxic event. I forgot to eat my rations, I had a love affair, then a breakup with a fellow astronaut and wanted to end my mission early.

"None of this is true. I heard what I heard, I felt what I felt. And I want to feel it again. I want to be with the Numen again, to feel their love, their acceptance, their desire to bring peace to the Earth."

"Ah. So you want to escape reality, get away from our noisy world."

Why was she dragging this out? Nevaeh said, "If I wanted to escape reality, I'd load up on heroin and float away. No. I want you to verify there is nothing organic wrong with my brain, which is why I'm here — for testing. I've filled out all your forms, I've provided all my medical files. If you want to do blood work today I am more than happy to comply. I welcome the tests and your results." She paused a moment, then said simply, "I need you to tell NASA I can go back to space. Tell them I'm not schizophrenic, I have my full faculties."

"Why must you go back to space?"

"I have to talk to the Numen again. Now, given the distance and all the noise, as I already said, it's not enough for them or for me. I need to hear them clearly. To find out what they want me to do next. Please, Dr. Fontaine. You're my last hope."

"Ah."

"What do you mean, ah?"

"Dr. Patel — Nevaeh — a diagnosis, or lack of, from me won't sway your bosses at NASA. I know you hope my recommendation as to your sanity would do the trick. But do you know what? I think you also recognize it is possible you are having some sort of extended dissociative episode. It can ingrain in your mind as a real event, and when you revisit it, over and over, you make it part of your value system. It's something Freud called abreaction. It's a method of bringing traumatic events back to the surface, reliving them, and becoming conscious of them as a repressed event. It's how your mind deals with a horror. In your case, you were faced with the most frightening aspect of space travel — disappearing into a void. Literally. And so your mind has created a reality in which you spoke to an alien species who want to bring peace to Earth, who saved your life. You believe without them, you might be dead. It's a powerful delusion."

Nevaeh wanted to leap over the table and strangle the woman. But she kept her temper, smiled, said calmly, "You're missing the point, Dr. Fontaine. NASA prepared me for the idea I might die during the mission. You spend months planning to strap yourself inside a tin can that will be tied to a rocket and shot into space, and see if they don't cover the very real possibility you might die. I wasn't afraid of dying."

"No? What did you feel the moment you realized all the failsafes had collapsed and you were truly untethered?"

"I started the sequence of steps to get myself back to the ship, stat. I did what I trained for, exactly as I trained. It didn't work."

"But what did you feel, Nevaeh, when you realized you weren't going to be able to re-attach, that you were going to die?"

"I felt — numb. Disbelief, I suppose, that it could end like this because I made a stupid mistake."

"Perhaps, if you're willing to be honest with yourself, you might recognize your magnificent brain wanted to protect you from the knowledge that you would die, and so created a savior in the form of an alien species who quite literally handed you back to the space station. I'd like you to consider the possibility you saved yourself."

"That's not what happened. I know what happened, I was there."

Nevaeh's voice was rising, she couldn't help it. Fontaine wasn't any different from Holloway.

Dr. Fontaine sat forward, clasped her hands on the desk. "Listen, Nevaeh, you wanted the truth, I'm giving it to you."

It was over, all over. She had failed to convince this woman. She said, "You don't believe me."

"I believe you believe you, which is what matters here."

"So what do we do next? If you won't talk to NASA for me, are you going to tell me to take this or that drug and all this will go away? I'll never hear from the Numen again?"

"Well, if you were schizophrenic, or suffering from a schizo-affective disorder, I would. I don't believe you are. I do believe you're suffering from a severely traumatic experience that your mind has built a wall around, and you're going to need some serious work to unlock it."

"Work, like therapy? With you?"

"With me, or a psychologist near where you live. There's nothing inherently special about this kind of therapy, Nevaeh. We use it all the time for PTSD, from which I believe you are definitely suffering. We can desensitize you to the event, making the trauma less traumatic, and eventually, you'll be able to think about it without creating a barrier of fiction around your thoughts. You will be able to remember what really happened, and you will heal. I can make recommendations of colleagues who specialize in this treatment back in Texas, if you want to start therapy at home. It might be easier to see someone close."

She didn't move, and Dr. Fontaine sighed. "There is something else you can try."

"What?"

"Sensory deprivation. You say you heard the voices clearly when you were in a zero-sound environment, and you need calm and silence to communicate with them now. Sensory deprivation is a version of regression therapy. We put you in a flotation tank and see what happens when you're able to re-create how it felt for you in space the moment you became untethered. Then, using those thoughts and feelings, we slowly bring you back to a more realistic scenario of what actually happened."

"They used them in our training. I know what it feels like. It's — not the same as being in space."

"But it's close enough that NASA, as you said, used it in your training to help you with the feeling of sensory deprivation."

"I'll think about it."

The doctor closed her notebook, rose, straightened her dress. "Our time's up. Would you like to make another appointment?"

Nevaeh slowly rose. She said automatically, "I'll call and set something up. I need to think."

They shook hands. "Good luck, Nevaeh. Don't forget, it's always darkest before the dawn."

Now, wasn't the dear doctor clever? "Actually, Dr. Fontaine, it's much darker in outer space."

CHAPTER TWENTY-SEVEN

T-MINUS 50 HOURS

Sky News Coverage of Typhoon Akari
July 26

"This is our continuing coverage of the typhoon bearing down on the search and rescue area where Galactus founder Jean-Pierre Broussard's yacht, *The Griffon,* was last seen on radar. The storm has now been named Akari, which we're told means 'red storm.' Gale-force winds are expected to top two hundred and fifty kilometers per hour, which places it squarely in the Category Four classification. The storm has already moved through Indonesia and is now approaching Singapore. While this first landfall caused it to weaken, it is expected to reach peak winds as it moves into the Strait of Malacca. Rescuers will have to stop the search as the waters will be too dangerous.

"Rescuers are in a race against time and the elements to find the founder of Galactus and his crew. Sky News has learned a pilot on a Singapore Airlines plane flying overhead saw an explosion in the general vicinity of *The Griffon*'s last known whereabouts. This, in addition to the storm, makes this situation even more dire.

"We'll continue our coverage after a break."

CHAPTER TWENTY-EIGHT

T-MINUS 49 HOURS

The founding of Kuala Lumpur was almost an accident. In 1857, 87 Chinese prospectors in search of tin landed at the meeting point of the Klang and Gombak rivers and set up camp, naming the spot Kuala Lumpur, meaning 'muddy confluence.' Within a month all but 17 of the prospectors had died of malaria and other tropical diseases, but the tin they discovered in Ampang attracted more miners and KL quickly became a brawling, noisy, violent boomtown, ruled over by so-called 'secret societies,' a network of Chinese criminal gangs.

— LonelyPlanet.com

Kuala Lumpur
Malaysia
Mike didn't know what to expect when she

stepped off the plane in Kuala Lumpur — imagine living in a city whose name meant "muddy confluence." She'd imagined it would be exotic, different spices scenting the air. It would be unique.

The smell was not exotic. Instead, the air was heavily scented with gasoline and asphalt — the universal language of tarmacs everywhere. It was hard to breathe the thick, heavy air. The sun was up, though Mike could feel the heavy pressure in the air, the skies were gray, cloudy, the rain from the storm imminent. And it was hot and muggy. Both Nicholas and Mike pulled off their jackets. They followed Poppy to the cars to take them to the chopper, all of them carrying their go-bags. As they walked, Mike touched Nicholas on the shoulder, showed him her phone, the radar image of the typhoon. The storm was growing stronger, clear to see, strengthening, coalescing, forming an eye. The path was going to take it right across Malaysia into the Strait of Malacca and out to the Bay of Bengal — precisely the direction they were going to be in searching for *The Griffon*.

"Nicholas, it's heading right for the area where Adam found Grant's last fitness tracker signal."

"How long?"

"This area will be affected in half a day, maybe? Depends on if it slows down or speeds up once it hits water again. We need to hurry. I have no desire to be lost at sea in a typhoon."

He saw her worry, and at the same time, saw her excitement. His danger junkie. He hugged her to him. "Nor do I, Agent Caine. Nor do I."

She looked up to see shadows under his eyes. They were probably under hers, too — they hadn't gotten much sleep on the plane, only catnaps here and there. His beard was growing in, the stubble thicker around that infernal dent in his chin that always made her want to lean up and kiss him. "I like the scruff, makes you look like a dangerous playboy."

A black brow went up.

She poked him. "You're distracted. What are you thinking about?"

"How to keep us out of trouble if there is an actual nuclear EMP floating around up there." He pointed toward the heavens. "Depending on where it goes off — if it goes off — the nuclear explosion itself could have little effect on areas outside of its initial range. The real issue is the aftermath of the EMP. The blast will knock out anything electronic in its path for a good fifteen hundred miles in any direction. Without the most basic electronics, the entire supply chain stops. Food can't be shipped. Water treatment plants will go offline —"

Mike said, "And electric grids will fail, and people will be in the dark, and it's three days to anarchy. Yes, I've had all the same briefings on EMPs you have. We'd be so screwed."

He said, "If there is an EMP and it affects the communication satellites, I think we'll have anarchy faster than three days. We can only hope if it goes off, it does so above a less populous area."

"Still, Nicholas, no matter where it goes off, there'll be no phone connections and that means no Facebook, no Twitter, no selfies — yes, there will be chaos."

Her teasing distracted him for a moment. "I've never seen you take a selfie, Mike."

"Probably not. Now, what's really bothering you?"

He smiled, but his eyes were still distant. "Honestly? I'm not sure. It's a bad feeling, something I know is out there — and I know we don't know everything we should know."

"We've been knowless many times, Nicholas. It'll come."

Nicholas said, "Still I hate going into this

half-blind."

Poppy pointed to a huge black SUV. Nicholas laughed. "Oh, now this beauty isn't at all conspicuous."

Mike said, "And here I thought bigger was always better."

"You would know, well, better than I, Agent Caine."

They both laughed, and Poppy blinked at them, made them laugh harder.

"Come on, guys, what's the joke?"

Mike shook her head. "I think we're a little punchy, not enough sleep the past few days. Where are we headed now?"

"The car will take us out to the coast where they've based the search and rescue operation. Nothing coming in from the planes that have already gone out, but they've held back a chopper waiting for you two." Her brows knit together. "Are you absolutely sure you want to go out there?"

Nicholas said, "Yes, of course we do. We consider it a personal mission to rescue Grant anytime he gets himself into trouble. Makes us feel important."

Poppy said, "I think it makes you certifiable. You should let the experts handle this."

"Probably," Mike said. "But the fact is, Grant is our friend, and neither of us could live with ourselves if he was hurt and we didn't do everything in our power to help him. Plus maybe helping all the people aboard *The Griffon*. We'll be fine."

Poppy said, "Remind me to be very good friends with the two of you from now on." She shifted the Glock on her hip as she climbed into the vehicle. Mike knew this woman was lethal and more than capable of taking care of herself, and maybe them, too. Mike wouldn't mind having her on their Covert Eyes team. But she supposed there was a reason Poppy was in the private sector. She reminded herself to do a background check on her later. If they made it back to land, that is.

They climbed into the SUV behind her, nodded to the large man in a black suit behind the steering wheel. He turned and gave them a nod. "Agents. Roderick Grennan, Blue Mountain. We're thirty minutes to the staging area in Putrajaya. They're waiting for you." And he slammed the SUV into gear and squealed off the tarmac, into the insanity of Kuala Lumpur.

Nicholas said, "Now, let's call Adam, see what's happening with our coordinates."

Adam was in their offices at 26 Federal Plaza, looking infinitely more relaxed than when they'd talked to him last. Gray Wharton was on-screen as well, looking rumpled and windblown, as if he'd just stepped off the Staten Island Ferry and had forgotten to smooth down his hair.

"What sort of trouble are the two of you getting into now? Kuala Lumpur? It's a far sight from Rome and chowing down gnocchi on the Piazza del Popolo."

Mike waved. "Hello, Gray. Good to see your face. We're about to do something foolhardy, possibly certifiable, to end our long, so very boring vacation."

"Well, there's something new. Latest update, the coordinates from Grant's fitness tracker have moved a bit. Why? Our best guess is they're in life rafts, floating near where the ship was last seen."

Mike asked, "Why haven't the Malaysian SAR folks found them yet, then? If they have a spot to look for, they should be able to zero in on them with no issue."

Adam said, "There's one easy answer. I think you need to be prepared for the idea that Grant lost his tracker."

Nicholas said, "Bollocks. You're wrong, you have to be. We're heading out now to join the search. Keep feeding us coordinate updates."

"And weather updates," Mike added. "This typhoon looks nasty."

"Will do." They punched off the phone

just as they arrived at the heliport.

Poppy said, "I'm going to stay on land with Roderick and monitor the storm and coordinate with the search teams from here." She paused. "Too, I have no desire to launch myself out over the ocean."

"No worries," Nicholas said. "Stay in touch."

Mike was glad to see the chopper was military, being piloted by the Malaysian Coast Guard. Once they were suited up and strapped in, the pilot, introduced as Musa bin Osman, spoke over their headsets in very good English.

"We've narrowed the search to a two-hundred-and-sixty-kilometer area, but haven't had any luck yet. I fear the yacht has gone down, and the seas have been kicking up because of the storm. MMEA — that's the Malaysian Maritime Enforcement Agency — is in the lead for the SAR. We have four boats in the region, all searching with our own people. The U.S. Navy is sending ships from the Bay of Bengal, out of the U.S. Pacific Fleet. Over eighty thousand ships pass through the Strait of Malacca a year, and *The Griffon* was last seen heading into the Singapore Strait two weeks ago. Of course, the Blue Mountain people have kept us updated. Still, there's nothing yet. But I have faith we'll find them. It will take us an hour to get out there. Off we go."

The chopper launched into the air. Ten minutes later, they were over open water, flying north.

CHAPTER TWENTY-NINE

T-MINUS 45 HOURS

Strait of Malacca
Off the Coast of Sumatra

Grant was beyond thirsty but he didn't care, he wanted to make sure the rest of the people in their four boats had enough. He'd fared better than most of the crew from the drug overdose — the combination of alcohol, drug, sun, and waves was now making some of them even sicker. The heat was brutal, the waves two meters high. Surely someone was looking for them by now. He thought of Kitsune, knew she had no idea what had happened to him, and prayed.

He kept looking, but the vast waters remained empty. He didn't want to ask Broussard how much more fuel they had before the sub was in danger. They could always join the others on one of the boats, but Grant had to admit the sub was a better option. At least it could waterproof itself. The rest of the crew were hanging on to the edges of the life rafts, their jackets puffed around their necks, water splashing on them, looking both miserable and stoic.

Jean-Pierre was holding it together, but Grant could tell the man was fading, too. He'd forced him to take a nap, because they needed rest, but as the leader of the crew, Broussard wasn't the kind to let Grant take control of things. He'd finally agreed to rest for an hour, leaving Grant alone with his thoughts. Dire, scary thoughts. And always Kitsune, her wonderful laugh, her immense love for him, his heart.

He had one purpose now: keep these people alive long enough for them to be rescued.

Not being able to call for help was the worst. The sat phone in his bag was toast, further cementing the idea that Devi had set off some sort of EMP in the boat disabling all of their comms. Grant knew his bosses would be searching by now, but worried they might be too late.

He had no idea where they were in the ocean, either, which was causing him no slight bit of panic.

He'd lost his fitness tracker sometime back when the boat was going down, and he used it as a watch to tell the time, too, so he was reliant on Broussard for time updates, which had been driving both of them mad. With Broussard asleep, all he could do was stare into the milky gray skies and estimate.

The sun was high above, burning them even through the haze, and the salty waves made his skin crack. How long would they be able to manage out here without being rescued? He didn't even want to think about it.

He shifted uncomfortably, and Broussard came awake.

Broussard stretched and yawned. "Nothing new?"

"Unfortunately, no."

Broussard's face fell, but he gestured to the small pillow he'd been using. "You should get some sleep, Grant. I'll keep an eye on things. Oh yes, no more 'sir' or 'Mr. Broussard.' Call me Jean-Pierre."

Grant smiled. "Very well, Jean-Pierre. The waves are getting worse. Do you think the storm we saw coming has strengthened?"

Broussard shrugged, his face once again emotionless, his eyes hard. "Probably. There is nothing that can be done to change our circumstance, Grant. We must make the best of things. Do get some sleep, it helps, if

217

only to escape for a while."

"I wouldn't have guessed you were a fatalist."

Broussard shook his head, smiled. "I'm no fatalist. No, I'm a romantic. The way I look at it is if it's my lot to die at sea, so be it. But I don't think we're going to die today. We can't die today. We were in possession of the Grail. Even though it was for a short time, I'm thinking it still provides me protection. It welcomed me, Grant, recognized I was worthy, though I'm far from it, but then again, as I told the Grail, I am only the messenger."

"The messenger? For whom?"

Broussard looked away, Emilie's name on his lips. But no. "It is not important. Do you know, I still feel stronger than I should, and I don't feel as hungry or thirsty as I should. I know the Grail gave me strength and it still lingers. Why, I don't know.

"Plus I'm sure someone is going to be coming for us. Your people, my people. They will be searching for us."

Grant wished he'd touched the Grail. Would it have made him as positive as Broussard? "But without any kind of tracking device, they'll have to spot us by air. And I haven't seen any planes fly over, and believe me, I've checked often. We mustn't be in any normal flight paths."

"Perhaps not. But someone will come. I have faith. Faith is what got us here in the first place, and faith will save us. And the Grail."

Because Broussard had left the top of the sub open, they heard cries from the boats. They both looked out. Grant watched in horror to see the fins of two sharks begin circling one of the life rafts.

"I fear our situation is going from bad to worse. Look at these waves. And now sharks?"

"They'll be fine. We will all be fine."

"Why did they unlash the boats?"

"If they were still all connected, one big wave could topple a boat and it would be a domino effect. This way we can rescue from one boat to the other, if need be. And look."

Broussard pointed as Cesar, his dive captain, leaned out of the boat and shot one of the sharks. The other went mad, and the men in the boat cheered.

"They're sailors, Grant. They know how to handle themselves in open water. All will be well. The Grail rewards those who believe. Oh, I nearly forgot. You dropped this."

He handed Grant his fitness tracker.

"I thought I'd lost it on *The Griffon.* Where did you find it?"

219

"It was on the floor of the sub, under the seat. Covered in water, and I believe I was standing on it for some time, so it's most likely ruined, but maybe you'd like to have it anyway."

Grant strapped it on, held his breath, and pressed the power button. The device flared to life. 12:25 p.m. He grinned. A silly thing to have missed, being able to tell the time.

Broussard smiled at him. "See? Life, it isn't all bad."

A large wave caught them, and as the submersible crested, then slid down the wall of water, landing hard in the trough, Grant thought again about Kitsune. What was she doing? Was she safe? He prayed so.

Life isn't all bad? *Yeah, it is.*

CHAPTER THIRTY

T-MINUS 43 HOURS

They'd been flying for what seemed like ages, but Mike knew it was only an hour. Her eyes hurt from straining them to look at the water, which shone back up at them. They were flying lower than she liked, able to see the waves as they formed and crested. The swells were massive, and she closed her eyes when it seemed they'd reach up and grab the helicopter.

Nicholas's cell rang. He pulled it out of his jumpsuit, wedged it under his headset.

"Adam. You have something new? Speak up, it's loud."

"I do. Good news. We just got a fresh update from Grant's tracker. The coordinates have moved significantly. They've slid north, up toward Phuket, Thailand. Here's the latitude and longitude."

Mike read off the information and the

pilot called, "Well out of the search area, you're sure about this?"

"Adam? The pilot says —"

Adam said, "Tell him we're sure. Might explain why they haven't been found. The signal came in brand-new, like the tracker had been turned off or something and was turned back on. We're able to follow it. So fingers crossed the tracker is still attached to Grant."

The pilot said, "Based on this, we've all been looking in the wrong place. The last known signal from the boat should have had them farther south, not heading north."

"Maybe the yacht was farther north than was first thought."

"Could be, yes. Or the seas, working their magic. I'll inform the rest of the search and rescue teams and rejigger our flight path." The chopper banked to the left, headed on the new course.

Nicholas tapped Mike on the leg. "Again, Dame Mike, good thought with the tracking device."

She wanted to preen for a moment, but couldn't, because a wave crested right beneath them, scaring her to death. She swallowed. "I hope they're okay. Why would they have gotten so far out of the search area?"

"Life rafts float. They don't have the ballast of something larger, can be carried by the waves. I suppose the seas are driving them north because of the outflow from the storm."

"Okay, that makes sense. We're due some luck. Now at least we have a specific haystack to search."

Nicholas said into his cell, "Adam, anything more on the EMP?"

"I'm working on it. As I already told you, the plutonium signature was found two weeks ago, on July 14, the same day Galactus put a satellite into orbit. It was a communications satellite, and according to the news reports, and though the launch went off without a hitch, the satellite itself wasn't able to deploy. There was a problem with the fairing — that's the capped part of the rocket that opens to let the satellite out into space. Apparently, the satellite clipped the fairing and was damaged, couldn't insert properly into orbit and turn itself on."

"A logical place to start looking for the EMP, then," Nicholas said. "If the satellite is still up there, we might be able to get a track on it. Gather everything, Adam. We'll hopefully have Grant back on land in a few hours and we can start chasing down this bloody satellite."

"Copy that. Be safe. Oh, you know Mr. Zachery is off-site at a training session for the bigwigs this week. He hasn't been notified of your latest escapade. Ah, Gray swears he won't say anything."

Nicholas could hear the grin in Adam's voice. "Good, because I highly doubt Zachery would be pleased with our current whereabouts. Talk soon, Adam."

He punched off, zipped his cell back in the waterproof pocket of his flight suit. He and Mike watched the massive waves below and knew they had to be patient. The chopper was starting to bounce around, enough that both Mike and Nicholas tightened the straps of their shoulder harnesses.

Finally, after what seemed like an eon, the pilot called, "We're coming up on the new coordinates. Keep your eyes peeled. We're first on scene, but the winds are picking up."

Nicholas took a monocular out of his go-bag and stuck it to his eye. Mike, shielding her eyes, stared as hard as she could, looking, looking. She spied what looked like a flash of light, realized that must be the sun's reflection on metal.

"There's something ahead!"

Nicholas swung his monocular toward the spot where she was pointing. A blip on the horizon, growing larger and larger. The chopper swung up higher and sped toward it. They could hear the pilot on the radio calling to the rest of the search and rescue team. "Spotted, no wreckage, looks like a life raft. Here are my coordinates." And the crackle and buzz of cheers and babble in a language they didn't understand.

The pilot turned, gave them a thumbs-up. "The cavalry is on their way. Let's get closer and see what we can do in the meantime."

Nicholas counted off. "Five dots, must be the life rafts, and something metal. Is that some sort of personal submarine?"

Mike could see more clearly now, laughed. "Broussard is a gazillionaire, of course he has a submarine. Hallelujah, we've found them."

The chopper pilot brought them closer, hovering directly over the water, only a few hundred feet away so his rotors didn't cause any damage. Mike could see men and women in the boats cheering and high-fiving one another, could see Grant and Jean-Pierre Broussard waving from the sub.

No, wait, the people in the rafts were shouting, some screaming, pointing. But Mike didn't turn in time to see a massive wave rising behind them, black and churning, and it smashed into the side of the chopper.

CHAPTER THIRTY-ONE

T-MINUS 41 HOURS

The hit sent Mike forward against the pilot. She didn't have time to think, time to recognize what was happening, she felt only the sickening sense of falling, then tumbling and spinning. She realized the chopper was whirling around, now on its side. Before she could scream, she was hit with a ton of water, in her nose, in her mouth, ripping at her clothes. She held on to her harness for dear life. She felt Nicholas's hand gripping her arm and knew he wouldn't let go.

They hit the surface of the sea hard, and the chopper flipped over entirely. Suddenly, everything was dark. She realized Nicholas had ripped off her headset and was yelling in her ear. She shook her head against the knowledge they were in a helicopter and now it was upside down and so were they, and they were going down. The helicopter wasn't flooded yet, but it would be in minutes. She smelled smoke. How could that be? They were underwater and a fire had started? But she could smell the smoke, could feel the heat. Mike panicked, jerking frantically at her harness, but it wouldn't unlock. She was stuck there, hanging upside down, the flames coming closer, then Nicholas pulled out a knife and sliced through the thick nylon, and she fell out of her seat into his arms. She could see the pilot slouched over, his head bent at a completely wrong angle. His neck was broken and she knew he was dead, but still she screamed, "Musa is hurt, we have to help him!"

"We have to get out, do you hear me? The pilot's dead, the chopper is going to sink, there's only a bit of air left. We have to swim for it. The door is right here. Come on, Mike. You can do it. Suck in a big breath."

She was frozen, and then her survival instincts kicked in and she was moving. The water was already up to her chest, dark and so very cold, and under that water was death.

She calmed, heard him say, "The door is below us, you're going to have to lie down in the dome of the chopper to get out, but I've got you." Nicholas threw a life jacket over her head and fastened it around her waist, yanked the cord so it inflated, then pulled her deeper into the dark water, shouted, "Hurry, hurry, deep breaths, here we go. The flotation device will help you rise up, but big breath, I'm not sure how far under we are. Let's go."

She knew there was no choice. The water was frigid, and then, suddenly, she was free of the helicopter, and the puffed-up life vest strained against the rapid movement of the water. She didn't know if they were rising or falling, she couldn't see, she couldn't breathe. Her ears felt like they were going to explode. She fought down the panic, fought to keep the air in her lungs. Nicholas had a hard hold of her hand and she felt him tug, so she started to kick, kicked for her life, praying they'd surface.

Nicholas had the third life vest in his hand. He used his teeth to tear open the ripcord, ignored the rush of salt water into his nose. It inflated in a stream of bubbles and was enough to help propel them faster toward the surface. Moments later, though it felt like hours, they burst out of the water into the open sea. He yanked Mike to the surface behind him, grabbed her arms, held her as they both coughed out water, their eyes stinging from the salt.

He remembered his god-awful fear that

he'd lost her in that lake in Italy, but not this time, no way was he going to lose her again. She was pale and it scared him to his gut. "Are you all right? Mike, are you all right?"

When Mike heaved a huge breath, coughed out more water, got a fresh mouthful of freezing cold salt and brine, she managed to whisper, "I'm alive and well, Nicholas. Tell me you're okay, too?"

"Oh yes, I'm marvelous." Then they rode up the wall of a ridiculously high wave and crashed down the other side. No anchor, no way to control anything, they were at the mercy of the gigantic waves.

Nicholas kept talking to her, nonsense, really, holding her as close as the life vests would allow. "This is some adventure, hadn't planned on this part, but well —"

Another massive wave lifted them, and threw them down into the trough. She hadn't trained for this, it was nothing she'd ever imagined. She couldn't speak, just held on to Nicholas for dear life. Nicholas had a cut over his eye, blood was streaming down his face, but he still had ahold of her — and he kept talking about this surprise adventure. Then she realized he'd tied them together somehow — and now he was shouting. He sounded happy.

Happy?

She realized he was yelling, "We made it, we made it! We're going to be okay!"

She said against his face, "We're okay? Our helicopter just crashed and we're floating in the middle of the freaking ocean."

"Good, you're back. Hey, we're alive. It's a great start."

Another huge wave splashed over her head, dragging her under, but the life vest pulled her back to the surface and she sputtered and coughed. Nicholas wiped his eyes with the back of his hand. The waves had to be ten feet high. They needed to find those life rafts, and fast.

Well, he was right, they were still alive. She shouted, "What happened?"

"Had to be a super-gigantic rogue wave, caught us broadside. Hopefully it didn't take down the life rafts or the sub."

"How far away are they?"

Before he could answer, a submarine popped up into the water next to them. And Grant Thornton opened the hatch, stuck his head out. "Good to see you two. Come on, make it snappy. Come into my parlor." He tossed down a sturdy rope ladder. It was a contest between them and the waves, but finally, they managed to scramble inside the submarine without it taking on too much water. The top snapped closed with a pneumatic hiss, the bilges pumped out the extra water they'd brought in with them. And then there was silence. Blessed silence.

Grant was grinning at them. "Welcome aboard."

And a handsome Frenchman Mike recognized as Jean-Pierre Broussard said, "That was quite an escape. Sorry, no tea or cakes to offer you. Grant, you know these two. Introduce us."

CHAPTER THIRTY-TWO

After introductions, Mike said, surprised, "I still have my glasses."

"Indeed you do," Broussard said, and handed her a dry cloth. Mike wiped her glasses, then squeezed the sea water from her ponytail. "Thank you for being here."

Grant said, "We saw the whole thing. I'll tell you guys, I've never prayed so hard in my life. We saw the chopper coming from a distance, had no idea you two were in it. Then I saw Mike, and she started signaling, and suddenly, a wall of water was coming up on you. It was the biggest wave we've seen so far. Your pilot was much too close to the sea, he should have never been down that far. We lost one of the life rafts, too, it capsized, but everyone is accounted for on the other rafts. Your pilot?"

Nicholas shook his head. "Dead. His neck was broken, something in the cockpit hit him wrong. It's a miracle we're okay, for a moment there I thought we were going down with the chopper."

"We did, too. We slammed the top closed and submerged, headed toward your last position. Smart thinking with the life vests, they were easy to see."

Nicholas looked from Broussard to Grant. "Here you are, rescuing us, when we came out here to rescue you."

They shook hands formally, and Grant said, "How did you find us?"

Mike wanted to hoot and holler, maybe line-dance — they were alive. Nearly drowned, again, and that thought made her shudder. She managed a smile, pointed. "Your fitness tracker. For some reason, it was the only signal we could find, and it's been off and on for the past day. I assume something terrible happened to the yacht?"

Nicholas said, "Yes, what happened to the yacht? Did she go down?"

Broussard swallowed hard, his face hardened. He nodded. "She did."

Grant said, "They shot a missile at us. Probably a Hellfire. Took out the stern and we barely had time to get everyone evacuated — those that were alive, that is. That woman wanted us dead. All of us."

Mike asked, "What woman?"

"The woman discussing the EMP. Did

you get my transmission, is that why you're here?"

Nicholas said, "We did. We were already coming for you when you went off the radar. What do you know about the EMP?"

Grant repeated what he'd heard. "It's going to go off maybe tomorrow, Nicholas. We have to get to land and stop her. Please tell me the pilot was able to send word of our coordinates before he crashed?"

"He did. Help should be arriving shortly. Do you know why your signal was lost? Your boat was dead in the water — no signals, no power signatures, nothing. The transponder never came online."

Broussard said, "We had a saboteur on board. Grant believes it was Devi, the young woman who'd been with me six months. I cannot accept it, she was a favorite of the crew, she was happy with me, on *The Griffon.* This woman Grant overheard — she murdered her, in cold blood.

"The missile Grant mentioned. *The Griffon* was attacked, and the Holy Grail was stolen out of my safe. We'd just found it and were celebrating. Someone drugged us, stole the Grail, murdered my Devi, and then scuttled my ship."

Nicholas asked, "Do you have any idea who might want to do this, sir?"

"I found the Holy Grail. Who wouldn't want to have it? Whoever it was — a woman, Grant believes — wanted the Grail and made Devi steal it. And she must have wanted me dead. Who is she? I don't know."

"Just to be clear, this is Parzival's Grail you're talking about, correct?"

Broussard's eyebrows shot up. "You know Parzival?"

"I know some. He was a knight of the Round Table, was part of the Arthurian legend. And he was a Grail knight. As to the rest, you'll have to fill us in. But first, sir, can you get us to land in this sub? The closest land mass is Thailand, about fifty miles to the east. You've drifted pretty far north."

"I can, we have the range to accomplish that. Though I'd like to wait to know my crew is being rescued, and then we can head off immediately. I need someone tracing the Grail. I must find it. I must retrieve it. It's critical." He paused, then, "We'll find the woman responsible, too."

"Sir, there's the distinct possibility an EMP is going to explode, maybe tomorrow, we're not sure, so we need to get back to land, warn the authorities, and find whoever is behind it. And stop them."

"But the Grail, my crew —"

Mike said, "Mr. Broussard, there was a nuclear signature at your launch on July 14 from French Guiana. We believe it was aboard the satellite you were putting into orbit. Obviously, the company who owns the satellite is being investigated as we speak, but we need to find out who might have planted it, and who wants to set it off. Getting a nuclear bomb on a satellite isn't an easy task, as you're well aware."

"I don't know the first thing about getting a nuclear bomb on a satellite. And it's impossible one of Galactus's rockets had anything to do with this."

He was exhausted, obviously broken-hearted over the death of his lover, Devi, everything was lying in ashes at his feet. But there was more, Mike sensed it, and it had to do with the Grail. She softened her voice. "And yet, sir, it seems you are involved, and someone clearly wants you dead. There's more going on here than you realize."

As she spoke, they heard the familiar *whomp-whomp-whomp* of a helicopter's rotors through the open top of the submersible, closely followed by cheers. The cavalry had arrived. Hopefully they wouldn't be swamped by a rogue wave, too.

Nicholas stood. "Looks like we've saved ourselves a trip under the sea. Let's divert one of the rescue helicopters and get ourselves back to Kuala Lumpur, and the jet."

Broussard asked, "Where do you plan to go?"

Mike looked from Broussard to Grant. "Lyon, France. We need to go to Galactus headquarters, find the people responsible for the launch. Can you tell us the name of the person in charge of that launch?"

Broussard said, "My second-in-command is Dr. Nevaeh Patel. She will certainly open an investigation as soon as she's warned. When we reach the helicopter, we can radio ahead —"

Grant whirled around. "Jean-Pierre, what did you say her name was?"

"Nevaeh Patel. Dr. Nevaeh Patel."

"I hate to tell you this, Jean-Pierre, but I didn't understand at the time that what I heard was a name. I only thought it was something weird — 'Nevaeh' is what I heard Devi say before the helicopter blew up your ship."

CHAPTER THIRTY-THREE

Massachusetts Institute of Technology
Boston
July 26, 2012

Dr. Fontaine was right about one thing. A sensory deprivation tank was the closest she could get to being in space. Maybe it would bring the Numen, and there would be real communication, not short simple bursts.

After she left Dr. Fontaine, Nevaeh flew to Boston. She had friends at MIT, so she knew she could borrow a few hours in the psych lab's sensory deprivation tank. She'd done some research, debated on chamber versus flotation REST — restricted environmental stimulation therapy — and decided for her purposes, flotation REST was the best option. She wanted to get herself into the theta brain-wave stage as quickly as possible, a meditative state that existed when she was not quite asleep, but relaxed and calm. From her experience with sensory deprivation, she'd always done better in water than a darkened room. She was an astronaut, after all — being weightless was second nature.

Even though she was a graduate of MIT and could have walked in the front gates with no problem, she didn't want to be on anyone's radar, particularly NASA's, so she talked to one of her former professors she trusted not to give her away, and he set up an appointment in the lab. For good measure, she paid off the lab tech and went to the facility in disguise, a long wig and black glasses. She liked the way the glasses looked, thought she'd add them into her style rotation, but the blond wig made her look sallow, perhaps unwell. Perhaps she was. Hopefully she was about to find out.

The lab tech had been quite pleased with the money and more than happy to stay late and let her in, then let her out when she was finished. He brought her to the room, gave her a fluffy white bathrobe — as if she were entering a high-end spa — told her to press the button on the wall when she was ready for him to close her in, and disappeared to play a video game.

The sensory deprivation chamber looked like a silver coffin. She took off the wig and her clothes and changed into a bathing suit.

She put in earplugs, tucked her long black hair under a cap so it wouldn't float around her body and distract her, and climbed in.

The water was warm, heavily laced with Epsom salts, and the high saline content would keep her afloat. All she had to do was keep her face above water.

She relaxed back, resting her head against a pillow, let the water embrace her. The tech knocked on the door. "You ready?"

"I am."

"You didn't press the button."

"I'm sorry."

"That's okay. You want me to stay? It can be kind of freaky the first time."

"No, thank you, I believe I'll be fine."

"When you're ready to get out, don't forget to hit the button inside the tank. If you don't, I won't know to come and get you."

The button in question was a small red dot, impossible to miss, even in the dark.

"I'm ready. Close the lid."

The lid was on a pneumatic hinge, it closed slowly, with a hiss.

The blackness was complete. Nothing but blackness. She waited for a few moments, expecting her eyes to adjust, but she still couldn't see a thing except for that ridiculous red dot.

Relax, she told herself. *You're doing an experiment, nothing more. You're used to experiments. Not a problem.*

She did some square breathing, then tried to empty her mind. *Let go,* she told herself. *Let go.*

Nevaeh was back on the space station. Her mission specialist, Gary Verlander, came out of the mess with a grin. "Hey, Nevaeh, today's the big day. Are you ready for our walk?"

"I am. Let's go!"

They high-fived and set off for the mission, propelling themselves through the hatches to the space lock. Being able to move in three dimensions was incredible, and her adrenaline and excitement made it feel even more like flying.

She executed a perfect somersault and put herself into the right position to move feet-first into the control room. Verlander followed.

It felt like it took them almost as long to get into their suits as they would spend outside, going through the innumerable checks and balances to make sure they wouldn't die when they stepped out into space away from the safety of the station. Walks were an event, and she was always excited. The views from inside the space station were amazing, sixteen sunsets and sunrises per day, orbiting the Earth every ninety minutes, incredible, yes. But knowing you were actually *in* space, standing on the edge of infinity; it had to be mind-boggling. She was always so ready.

They strapped her tools to her body and guided her to the airlock. They waited patiently while the airlock depressurized. Finally, the outer doors opened and she was free, Verlander floating alongside her.

The blackness, infinite blackness. It beckoned her, always. If she'd been an emotional woman, she might have cried a bit with the joy of it, but tears could cause major issues inside her suit, messing with her Snoopy cap and affecting her vision, so she refrained.

She stepped out carefully, watching her hand placement. There was a constant patter of communications from mission command in Houston, everyone checking, double-checking, triple-checking that things were nominal.

They were. She kept her breathing regulated, her heartbeat steady. This was what she'd trained for.

It took a while to get into position, but once they were there, they began the task

— they were to run wires between modules. It was painstaking work, slowed by their clumsy suits. They'd rehearsed it, knew every step, but still, it required constant focus. She didn't want to screw up.

Several hours later, they were finished, and started back. Nevaeh took one last look out into space, then turned for the ladder. She moved too quickly, and her hand slipped. Without warning, she was spinning, her body twisting, sailing away from the space station. She felt the small tethers holding her close to the station suddenly snap. Her heart rate spiked, but she kept calm, focused. She knew what to do. She had the long tether attached to her suit, they could use it to reel her in. She tried grabbing at the line but missed. She was shocked when there was a sudden tug. Verlander's tether had crossed hers.

The unexpected pressure caused her main tether to snap.

There were roars in her ears, instruction from every quarter, but Nevaeh froze. This was unthinkable. Impossible. She started to panic, tumbling now, free-falling, and there was nothing to stop her. She was free of the space station, of her tether, she was dead. Verlander was watching her with horror etched on his face. The voices kept calling her, but they were a jumble, she no longer understood them.

As quickly as she'd frozen, she pulled it together. There was a third failsafe. She activated the SAFER — her mini jet pack that could propel her back to the ship — but nothing happened. She smacked the button again and again. Nothing.

All the precautions had failed.

She could hear the calls now, mission control giving instructions — she heard Franklin Norgate's voice, tried to listen, but something was wrong with her ears, nothing made sense.

She shut her eyes, accepted she was going to die out here. All she felt was numb and embarrassed she'd screwed up so badly. And that's how it would go down in space history. The astronaut had screwed up.

Then, suddenly, there was a sort of ringing in her ears, then another voice, no, more than one voice, it was as if all the voices in the world had come together and coalesced into one.

You are not going to die today. But you must tell them we're here.

She had no idea who was speaking these bizarre words, but she reached out blindly, astounded when her thick glove met with something hard. The spinning stopped. She opened her eyes, but all she saw was the same blackness of space. Still, her field of vision was limited, she couldn't see anything except what was right in front of her. But she saw nothing. There was nothing. Only space.

She saw Verlander, hand outstretched. She was maybe fifty feet away from him. It was impossible. But then, she felt a gentle push, and she was moving slowly, so slowly, back toward Verlander and the hand rungs that meant life.

The strange voice or voices spoke to her again. *We are the Numen, and we bring peace. We would like you to tell people about us. We want to come to Earth, but we need you. You are the only one who can help us, Nevaeh.*

"How do you know my name?"

We know everything about you. You have been sent to find us. We are here. We want to help. We bring peace. We bring endless understanding and love.

And suddenly, her hand found the hand rung, and she heard cheering in her headset. She vaguely realized her fellow astronauts and flight crew were all crying and shouting. But the words she'd heard — they weren't coming from her headset. This voice — these voices — were coming both from inside her suit and outside, in the void, somehow.

Tell them we're here waiting, Nevaeh. You must tell them to stop all the satellites coming into space. We can't communicate, too much interference. Tell them we need to silence the heavens so we can come to you.

How many times had she thought this? So much junk in space, too much, surely too much. "I will tell them. Thank you for saving my life."

Nevaeh couldn't take it in, couldn't believe it. The Numen? Aliens had saved her life? She was to be their messenger? She was safe, she was alive. She watched the space lock open. She felt strangely disoriented. There was Verlander motioning for her to go first. She could see the relief, the joy, in his eyes. He was talking but she couldn't make out his words. She smiled at him, she didn't feel capable of doing anything else. She felt a punch of outrageous pride, a joy so profound, that speech, for the moment at least, was beyond her. Her brain, her heart, all of her buzzed with the incredible feelings flooding through her. She had fulfilled NASA's prime mission.

She had spoken with an extraterrestrial being.

She was to be their emissary.
She was the chosen one.

She breathed deeply, waiting. Would the Numen come? It was dark, it was quiet. She heard the words reverberating through her body like a bell tolling, as strong and intense as she'd heard them the very first time.

We're here, Nevaeh. We're here. That is exactly what happened. You are the chosen one. You are the one to join with us to bring peace to a troubled world. At last we are together in peaceful quiet and we can more easily be with you. We know Dr. Fontaine was wrong and so was Dr. Holloway at NASA. We understand your anger, your frustration, but it doesn't matter. They don't matter. Forget them, they can't touch you. Never believe you created us as a coping mechanism, never allow yourself to think that even for an instant. No, we are on a journey together and we will succeed. Give us the quiet we need so we may speak to you. You must find a way. We know you will find a way.

CHAPTER THIRTY-FOUR

T-MINUS 40 HOURS

Strait of Malacca
Off the Coast of Sumatra

Jean-Pierre Broussard yelled in Grant's face, "You're saying you heard Nevaeh's name before *The Griffon* blew up? That's utterly preposterous. Dr. Patel is a brilliant scientist with an extreme passion for space travel. She was a highly decorated and accomplished astronaut before she came to work for Galactus. There is simply no way she would do anything like this — this terrorist attack."

No one said a word.

Broussard drew in a deep breath. "Take your seats, we're diving." Without waiting, he punched several buttons and the submersible dove, moving toward the rescue site.

Grant said calmly, "I understand you're

upset by this news, but how else could I know the name? Nevaeh isn't a name you hear every day."

Broussard didn't spare him a glance, kept his eyes on the depth meter. "If you're remotely decent at your job, you would have read her name in the dossier when you took this protection detail."

"Jean-Pierre — sir — I most certainly did read the dossier, and her name wasn't in it. *You* are the client, not your company. I'll be happy to show it to you when we're back on land."

Now Broussard turned to stare at him. "Then you heard her name on the news, or you heard me mention her name. I simply refuse to believe she would do anything like this. And to say that she would hurt Devi —" He went into a spate of French curses. Grant looked at Nicholas and Mike, shrugged.

He said quietly, "I know what I heard."

Nicholas said, "Gentlemen, please. We'll have plenty of time to research Galactus and Dr. Patel. We should surface now, we're near the lifeboats."

Mike couldn't agree more, she couldn't see anything but bubbles and rushing water, and it was disconcerting, considering they'd been on the other side of this glass only minutes before.

Broussard brought the sub back up to the surface, stepped to the periscope, peered through the eyepiece, then slapped the handles back into place and nodded. Mike watched as they broke the surface of the water fifty yards from a lifeboat and lifted the top. The people aboard waved wildly.

She was relieved to see the rescue area was quickly becoming mobbed with helicopters and boats. There was even a frigate in the mix. The deck of a ship would feel more secure to her than this bubble-faced submarine. She noted the name on the side of the frigate with a smile — the RSS *Tenacious.*

Grant was still angry, but he pulled himself together, said to Broussard, "Take us to that frigate, sir." No more Jean-Pierre. "We can coordinate from there better than being in the water with the lifeboats."

A few minutes later, they were on the deck of the frigate. It was much more stable, a blessed relief. Mike felt as if the waves that had slapped against the sub with such terrifying force were now only barely breaking against the ship.

A sailor handed them emergency blankets. They wrapped themselves in the specially treated fabric, grateful for the sudden warmth. Mike said to Nicholas, "Never thought I'd be so happy to be standing on a floating hunk of metal."

He gave a tug on her wet ponytail. "You and me both, Dame Caine, you and me both."

A short, portly man in a dark green uniform strode toward them, a lopsided smile on his face. In accented, somewhat broken English, he said, "I am Captain Heng of the Singapore Navy's RSS *Tenacious*. You are welcome aboard. We have food, drink, and warm clothing inside. If you will follow my sailors' directions?"

Captain Heng started to turn away but Nicholas caught his arm. "Captain Heng, we're Agents Drummond and Caine, Federal Bureau of Investigation in the United States. We need to make for land immediately. It is a matter of national security. Can we take your rescue chopper? Ours is somewhere out there, unfortunately." He pointed at the ocean. "We went down on approach."

The captain's face registered shock. "I am sorry to hear that. Your pilot? He has been rescued as well?"

"I'm afraid he died in the crash. This is Mr. Broussard. He can give you the exact coordinates so you can attempt a retrieval of his body. Captain, I am sorry, I don't mean to sound ungrateful, but we need to leave your ship immediately."

Either the captain recognized the urgency in Nicholas's voice or he was a good-natured man, because he nodded and said, "Very well. I will arrange it to be here in ten minutes. I will have my pilots take you to Singapore."

"Phuket, sir. Thailand is the closest. We have a plane waiting in Kuala Lumpur, we can have them meet us there."

"This will take more arranging."

"Sir, the circumstances are critical. We must get to land, and fly to Europe, and we need to do it before this typhoon strikes and we get stuck here for the next twenty-four hours. Many lives depend on our actions."

"Very well. Have your plane moved to Phuket, and we will talk to the Thailand SAR and arrange for them to take you. They have ships nearby." Another small lopsided smile. "We all cooperate when people are at risk in the Strait. As you say, the typhoon is coming, we must all be prepared."

Nicholas already had his satellite phone out, remarkably still working. "Isn't this a lovely surprise? These phones are indestructible, apparently. Even an ocean swim doesn't kill the signal. I lost my tablet, but at least this was zipped in a waterproof pocket inside my suit."

Mike sighed. "Mine didn't make it."

"Come now, Agent Caine. We rescued Grant, which will make Kitsune very happy, all because of your brilliant idea. We're batting a thousand so far."

"Except we almost died. Again."

"Once we stop this nuke we'll talk about that." He tucked a strand of wet hair behind her ear. "If you weren't such an adrenaline junkie —"

"Me? An adrenaline junkie? Oh no, you don't. I'm just along for the ride this time. Well, maybe. Okay, maybe not."

He was still grinning when he spoke to the pilots of the Blue Mountain jet and got their assurances they would head to Phuket immediately. A few minutes later, a steel-gray Seahawk chopper landed on the deck of the *Tenacious,* the flag of Thailand painted on its side.

"There's our ride."

Grant and Broussard joined them, both still damp but drinking down hot coffee.

Grant said, "We're going with you."

Broussard said, "That's right. Don't try to ditch us. We're coming, no argument."

Nicholas said, "That's fine with us. Mr. Broussard, we will need all the information you can provide on your second-in-command, this Dr. Nevaeh Patel."

Mike didn't want to get into yet another helicopter, but no choice. She said over her shoulder, "I'm going to start having a phobia about these things if we're not careful," and jumped aboard and settled in, put on her harness and headset. She accepted a cup of the strong coffee, swallowed, and was surprised to see the world was suddenly much brighter.

Grant sat down next to her, strapped in. Nicholas was opposite, Broussard beside him. They lifted off and one of the pilots said over their headsets, "We will be in Phuket in fifteen minutes."

Nicholas gave them a thumbs-up.

Grant said, "You, get a phobia, Mike? I thought crashing a chopper in the ocean would be high on your bucket list. I've heard Nicholas call you an adrenaline junkie."

"Yeah, yeah, like you had sinking with a megayacht after being taken out by a Hellfire missile on yours? No more talk about crashing helicopters. And why does everyone think I'm an adrenaline junkie?"

Nicholas patted her damp knee. "Probably because every time we go in the air or the sea, you're the first one out the door with a manic grin on your face. Now, we've got to find out if this nuke is for real. Mr. Broussard, you need to run us through everything you know."

Broussard looked at the three of them, sighed. "Grant, please do not call me Mr. Broussard again. Nor you, Nicholas. Now, you've heard everything. I was drugged, too, but luckily Grant was able to wake me up and get me to function." He closed his eyes a moment, then said, "I think Devi must have dosed the wine and soup, and the water, too."

"Any idea what drug she used?"

Grant said, "I'd say ketamine. I remember the feeling waking up from it a little too well. Nicholas, would you mind loaning me your phone? I need to give my boss Fentriss an update on our status, make sure we're set for what happens next."

Nicholas handed it over. "I wish you could call Kitsune. She's going to be furious with us when she hears about our adventures."

Grant grinned and his face relaxed. "I can't wait for her to yell at me. At least I'll be there to hear her." He looked at Mike. "My fitness tracker, best purchase I ever made. Thank you, Mike."

While Grant contacted Fentriss, Nicholas

said, "Mr. Broussard, would you please tell us about Dr. Nevaeh Patel?"

CHAPTER THIRTY-FIVE

Broussard looked exhausted. He'd had much worse to deal with than they had — well, Mike had to take that back. The upside-down helicopter in the ocean topped everything in her mind. He was grieving for his lover and his lost yacht. No, that wasn't exactly right, Mike realized. He was grieving most of all his loss of the Holy Grail, if indeed it was that legendary artifact, which she very much doubted. Still —

Broussard shook himself, focused on Nicholas.

"I'm happy to tell you about Dr. Patel, and you will see it's impossible she could have anything to do with all this." He paused, drew a deep breath, and said, "I hired her in 2013 to run my operations out of Galactus's headquarters in Lyon. She was previously an astronaut aboard the International Space Station, spent nearly six months in space. She's brilliant, capable, loyal. I tell you, there's simply no way she'd ever —"

Mike interrupted smoothly, "Why did she leave NASA, sir?" Would he tell them the truth?

"Please, call me Jean-Pierre, no more formality after all we've been through." He paused a moment, carefully selecting his words. He thought of all she had been through and said, "Nevaeh had accomplished all she could there. It was time for her to help others travel into space. She readily joined me in my goal to make space travel inexpensive. As you might know, we are also always looking for ways to allow people to get back into space — real people, those who've done a minimum amount of training and are looking at it as a great experience."

What, Nicholas wondered, would he have said under other circumstances?

Grant nudged Mike in the ribs. "Sounds like something else for your bucket list."

"Maybe, who knows what could happen up there?"

"Which is why I hired Nevaeh. She knows what it's like in space. She knows how to function in zero gravity, what it does to the body, the mind, how and what a civilian should be trained to do, what they need to survive a trip into space. Sorry, I got off-track. What we've accomplished so far is to drive down costs and make it more accessible for even smaller companies to have their own satellite systems."

Grant said, "So your ultimate goal is for Galactus to be the first private space flight provider in the world. Within a few years, I'll wager."

"Yes, that's it exactly. An EMP would certainly set us back, set the world back, which is why I believe you're wrong about Nevaeh being a part of anything like that. She is dedicated to the program. She would never want it to fail."

Nicholas asked, "How would someone get a nuclear bomb aboard a satellite?"

"Hide it inside the body of the satellite, I assume. It could easily be built with a special compartment which wouldn't draw any attention in the final assembly. I don't know for sure, I've never given it much thought."

Mike said, "Seems awfully easy. Would Dr. Patel — Nevaeh — have had access to the satellite before it was put on your rocket?"

Broussard scratched the beard stubble on his chin. "It's possible, yes, but realize, during assembly, when we're loading the rocket, any number of people would have access to the satellite."

"The nuclear signature was definitely found at the same site as your Galactus 5 launch," Nicholas said. "Help us understand why the launch wasn't a success."

"It's something we've had issues with in the past, but it's been years since anything like this happened. Simply put, the satellite was damaged when it clipped the fairing. The fairing is at the top of the rocket, the nose, where the cargo is located. When the fairing opens — it's on an explosive charge, timed to the millisecond — the satellite is essentially jettisoned into space, and then its own controls take over to move it into its predetermined orbit. It has engines like any other space object.

"The process of launch is usually under thirty minutes, but the satellite moving to its own orbit can take a couple of days. The satellite in question left the rocket without issue, but then never inserted into the proper orbit."

"So where is it?"

"No one seems to know. The likelihood is that since it didn't secure the proper orbit, it will probably fall back to Earth and be burned up in the atmosphere upon reentry, if it hasn't already. Of course, it could be caught up in space junk, floating in orbit, unseen and untracked. There's so much crap floating around up there, it would be impossible to find."

Mike felt her heart rate spike. "And if it has a nuclear EMP on board?"

Broussard said, "It depends on many things, the atmospheric reentry angle, the speed at which the object is reentering Earth's atmosphere. Things do not completely combust or vaporize. For example, Skylab dropped debris across Western Australia despite all attempts on the scientists' part to aim for an unpopulated area. It was within three hundred miles of Perth, much too close for comfort. So the atmosphere could set the EMP off. Or it could be burned up." He straightened, fire returning to his eyes. "Either way, I can't imagine how a nuclear bomb could be aboard one of my rockets, much less that Nevaeh Patel put it there."

Mike said, "When was the last time you had contact with Dr. Patel?"

"July 14 — Bastille Day in my country — the day we found the *Flor de la Mar*. She'd reported to me on the failed insertion of the satellite. She certainly was regretful to report we'd had a failure, took full responsibility, but there was nothing alarming about our conversation. We'll talk to her once we have means to make a connection. You'll see." He looked over at Grant. "I'm sorry, but I really believe you didn't hear her name, maybe something close, but not Dr. Patel's name."

Grant said nothing, only shook his head.

Nicholas said, "Let's go to the Holy Grail. Did Dr. Patel know you'd found it?"

"Of course. She had a profound interest in my finding the Grail, particularly after I proved to her its capabilities, I guess you could call them, that is, worthiness, health, fulfilling your desire, and immortality. She insisted on calling it the Heaven Stone when I told her that was one of the names given the Grail in the past centuries. She and I were both devoted to my finding it." He paused. "It was my most ardent desire." He broke off. He looked like he was in despair.

Why? No, the reasons didn't matter now. No more softball. Mike said, "Jean-Pierre, why would Dr. Patel schedule the attack at that particular time, if not to retrieve the Grail and kill you? It seems obvious since Devi was shot, and Grant heard Nevaeh's name. Was she working for Dr. Patel? But why?"

Broussard wouldn't meet her eyes. He put his head in his hands, whispered, "I cannot believe it, I cannot. *C'est impossible.*" He looked up, tears in his eyes. "Whatever happened, whoever is responsible for all this misery, this death, I must have the Grail. If I don't get it back soon, all will be lost."

"What will be lost?" Grant asked.

Broussard only shook his head, not looking up.

They were over land now, green and lush, and a few minutes later landed at the airbase in Phuket.

Grant handed Nicholas back his phone. He looked as exhausted as Broussard.

"Thanks for letting me use your phone, Nicholas. Fentriss sent the Blue Mountain G650. It is waiting for us. We'll be in the air to France as soon as we can board." He looked over at Broussard. "Jean-Pierre, it's time for us to speak to Dr. Patel in person."

CHAPTER THIRTY-SIX

T-MINUS 38 HOURS

Aquarius Observatory
Sri Lanka

The sun rose hard and fast over the forest, the gray, milky light giving way to multiple shades of gold and pink, then to a flush stark red. Nevaeh watched with wonder from her bedroom. It was stunningly beautiful. It brought to mind the old saying, "Red sky at morning, sailors take warning." Indeed, the storm was coming, and when it did, it would strike hard.

How many sunrises and sunsets had she witnessed over the years? How many had she seen from space? Had any been this beautiful?

Kiera, her red hair mussed, entered the bedroom, bringing Nevaeh a cup of coffee and her tablet.

She yawned. "You're going to want to see

this. The media are going absolutely stark raving mad about the missing yacht."

Nevaeh accepted the coffee but brushed away the tablet. "I don't care about Jean-Pierre anymore."

"Unfortunately, you have to pretend to care. You're going to have to issue another statement."

Nevaeh groaned. "I don't want to think about him. I want to think about the future. Come back to bed."

Kiera gave her a grin but stepped away to flip on the television. "I'm not kidding. It's on every station. You'll have to talk to them."

"I'm supposed to be in China dealing with fairing manufacturing metal fatigue, and then French Guiana overseeing a launch. How do you suggest I suddenly appear on the radar?"

"We'll make it look like you're on the jet. It will take nothing to set up. You say you're en route to Lyon. It will take thirteen hours for you to get there from China anyway." She paused. "I'm thinking maybe you should shut down the Galactus campus."

"Shut it down? Won't that be rather noticeable?"

Kiera sat on the floor in front of the television, her long, muscular legs crossed at the ankles.

She looked up. "Makes sense. You can say you're suspending operations in order to focus all your attention on the search and rescue of Jean-Pierre. Here's an idea: You're worried whoever is behind this — terrorist attack — could come to the Galactus headquarters. You want to protect all the employees. Surely that sounds logical. Also, added bonus — with the campus closed, no media will be able to hound the employees."

"Look, Kiera, it doesn't matter what the board thinks, it doesn't matter how much money Galactus is losing. The world as we know it will end soon, right?"

Kiera gave her a long look and slowly nodded.

"You can say no one is able to work, they're all too afraid Mr. Broussard is dead. You know he's like a rock star to the employees. The media will eat it up."

"And I'm not?"

"Of course you're not. You're their boss, you carry the whip, the bitch who makes them all show up every day and work their butts off to earn a healthy profit. He's the owner, the playboy with a dozen mistresses, the exciting crazy man who is off chasing treasure."

Nevaeh was nodding now. "Yes, yes, I have it — sabotage. We've discovered the satellite was sabotaged. In light of Jean-Pierre's missing ship, and the sabotage of our latest launch, we fear for the safety of our employees. We will not be issuing any more statements until we know what's happened to Jean-Pierre. Buys us another couple of days of silence, and by then, it will be too late."

Kiera was now doing sit-ups. She beamed up at Nevaeh. "Yep, that works."

She came up on her knees, picked up her coffee, and clicked her cup against Nevaeh's.

"Kiera, bring me the phone. I'll call in instead of telecon, so there's nothing to see. Run a hairdryer in the background. It will sound like the plane's engines."

Nevaeh picked up her tablet and checked her messages. Dozens of emails, which she ignored. She looked over at Kiera, saw she was playing with one of her weapons, a Ka-Bar knife, and smiled. Her bodyguard, her confidante. She felt affection for her, probably as much as she'd felt for her now-dead parents. She was right, Nevaeh couldn't avoid the situation any longer. Kiera handed her the phone, then went to the bathroom, turned on the fan, and put a hairdryer on the edge of the tub, set it to medium.

Nevaeh dialed into the Galactus headquarters to speak to Claudette, Jean-Pierre's secretary.

Claudette was obviously worried. "Oh, Dr. Patel. We are so concerned about Jean-Pierre. You've been fully briefed?"

"I have. Claudette, I have more information. I will be issuing another statement to the media, but I want you to shut down the campus. Send everyone home."

"What? Why?"

"I have discovered something disturbing. The satellite we lost on Bastille Day was sabotaged. I fear for your safety, for the safety of our employees. Send everyone home, and lock the gates to the facility."

"This will inflame the media, Dr. Patel. It is highly irregular. I don't think —"

"I don't care about the media, Claudette. I am only concerned with the safety of our employees, and the company itself. I will speak to the department heads myself if you are not comfortable doing so. If you need me to, gather them immediately."

"Yes, ma'am. Hold, please." Her voice was still doubtful, but a few minutes later, she came back on the line. "I've told the team. They agree, given what you've found. They are moving to shut down the campus, as you wish. It's also true no one has the heart to be here today. If Jean-Pierre is gone —"

"I fear he may be, and if so, we will all have a burden to bear. I will issue a statement to the media shortly, and once the campus is shut down, you are to go home and await my instructions. I will be in touch as soon as I have a succession plan in place. I will be working with the authorities to determine who is behind this sabotage, and once I do, we will move forward with Galactus, stronger than ever."

"Yes, ma'am."

Claudette hung up. Kiera grinned at her, gave her a thumbs-up.

Nevaeh laughed. "That girl is blind in her devotion to Broussard. Well, that was harsh. I must personally give him my most profound thanks for finding the Heaven Stone." She thought to the Numen. *See what I've accomplished? It's nearly done.* She said to Kiera, "Let's draft a statement and be done with this. I need to check our satellite and make sure it is moving into the proper position."

"What should the statement say? 'Dear World, you may think you're royally screwed, but we promise, all will be well'?"

Nevaeh shook her head, suddenly grave. "You shouldn't make fun, Kiera. I know you're enjoying this, you've always been too bloodthirsty for your own good. Everything

— everything — we've done is to save these people from their mean little lives. They will erect statues in my honor. And, of course, statues of the Numen."

Nevaeh was getting carried away, but it didn't matter, Kiera knew all would be well soon enough. She said, "I will take care of it. You go look for the satellite. I will come back to you with a draft for the media."

Nevaeh watched her go, then checked her watch. *So soon, just as I promised you.*

So soon, they said back to her. *Just as you promised us.*

CHAPTER THIRTY-SEVEN

T-MINUS 36 HOURS

Phuket, Thailand

Poppy Bennet stood with her hands on her hips in the doorway to the Blue Mountain Gulfstream. She greeted Jean-Pierre Broussard, introduced herself, and got him settled into a soft leather seat. He was pale, too pale, and she worried. She apologized on behalf of Blue Mountain for his troubles, covered him with a blanket, and patted his shoulder. Then she came back to the front and walked to Grant, seemed to breathe him in as she hugged him tightly. "We've all been so worried, even Fentriss, and you know he's not much on sentiment. You've got to stop scaring the life out of us, Grant, promise?"

"I swear I'll try harder, Poppy."

She cupped his face between her hands. "I am so glad you and your team are safe.

271

Now, you're not to worry, all right?" She turned to Nicholas and Mike. "Is it true what everyone was talking about? You two actually went down in the chopper that was struck by a giant rogue wave?"

Nicholas nodded. "We were lucky. The pilot, not so much."

Poppy shook her head. "Mr. Fentriss was very relieved you two survived, too. He really didn't want to have to report your deaths to the FBI. Now come and sit down, both of you look ready to fall over."

Mike said, "Any news from the rescue?"

"It's ongoing. So far, all is well. As I told Grant, the team is all right. I'm going back to Kuala Lumpur to retrieve them and bring them home."

Grant said, sounding half-asleep, "Poppy, I should go with you to get the team. I need to assess the situation, try —"

"What you need to do, Grant Thornton, is give your sorry arse a good sleep. I'll handle Kuala Lumpur. Mr. Fentriss wants you to stay with Mr. Broussard." He started to speak but she held up a hand. "No, no arguments. You almost died — again. Expect Mr. Fentriss to preach protocol."

Mike asked, "Protocol?"

Grant shrugged. "Not what it sounds. It's a debrief. A very thorough debrief. Mr.

Fentriss is a stickler for them."

The pilots, different ones than on their trip down to Malaysia, handed over hot coffee and tea, and Poppy said, "I'm leaving you in their very capable hands. This is Mr. Paul and Mr. Peters. Gentlemen, get them safe to Lyon, then you're expected in Brussels. Report in from France."

Mr. Paul, tall and skinny with a sharp jaw and shrewd eyes, said, "Yes, ma'am." Peters, who was wearing mirrored aviator sunglasses and looked straight out of *Top Gun,* added, "Yes, Miss Poppy, ma'am," in a soft Southern drawl. She gave him a wink and Mike suspected there might be a little more going on between these two.

Poppy shook Mike's and Nicholas's hands. "I am very glad you made it." She glanced at Grant. "Mr. Thornton, I expect you to stay in touch, but not until you no longer look like the walking dead." She disappeared down the steps. Peters sealed the door, then took his seat in the cockpit while Paul readied the cabin.

"Anything you need, let me know. The bar's open. There's food in the fridge, fruit and cheese, all kinds of healthy stuff. Don't tell Peters, he's a health nut, will be back here scolding you, but there's also a stash of M&M's under the counter, third drawer.

Help yourself to whatever. Wheels up in five."

He disappeared into the cockpit, and Grant and Mike took their seats. They both sipped from their cups. Mike was worried for a moment her waterlogged hair might ruin the buttery-soft leather seat, then decided who cared, and snuggled down. She said to Grant, "I assumed we'd be with the same crew. How many planes and pilots does Blue Mountain have on call?"

"Several. As Poppy said, Mr. Fentriss is a stickler for redundancy, and for not exhausting the pilots if he can avoid it, so we always have a couple of crews on hand. I've flown with these two before, they're good." Nicholas had followed Peters to the cockpit. Mike heard him say, "We're in a hurry to get to Lyon. What's our estimated flight time?"

Paul looked over his shoulder, glasses flashing, and drawled, "I hear you four seem to be daredevils, so you'll be pleased to know we've laid in a route that will let us push this honey to her limits." He slapped the ceiling of the jet. "We'll be traveling at Mach 0.9, which is just shy of the speed of sound, about 685 miles per hour, and we'll be right at the outer limits of our fuel capacity getting you there. It's nearly six thousand miles to Lyon, and we'll be there by around three in the morning local time. We're going backward, so we gain a few clock hours. So hang on tight and get some sleep."

Mike said, "Wicked," and they all laughed. "What? I like planes. Much better than helicopters."

Nicholas asked, "What about the typhoon? Is it going to affect us?"

"No, but we're getting out at the right time. Another few hours and they'll be grounding all aircraft. It's going to make landfall in Singapore and sweep up the strait."

The pilot glanced at Grant, who'd paled. "Yes, you would have had a rocky night. But all's well. We received word the crew of *The Griffon* has been rescued and are also back on land. By the way, I heard Peters here talking about the M&M's. Don't blame me if you feel awful tomorrow, but you probably deserve some sort of reward, so I won't yell at you too much. Ready? Off we go."

Once they were all settled and seat-belted in, Broussard said, "Before I crash, I've got to call in. I want to speak to Nevaeh."

Mike said, "Jean-Pierre, please, let us keep your whereabouts quiet a little longer."

"At the very least, I must be allowed to

speak to my secretary, Claudette Bourget. She will be discreet, she is trustworthy."

Nicholas said, "You thought Dr. Patel was trustworthy, too."

They all saw the moment Broussard registered doubt. A good start. He sighed. "Claudette is utterly loyal to me. And I'm not asking your permission."

He pressed a few buttons and put the phone on speaker so everyone could hear.

A young, hyper voice said, *"Galactus, bureau de Monsieur Broussard."*

"Claudette, bonjour, en anglais, s'il vous plaît," and she immediately switched to English.

"Oh, sir, it's really you! We were all so afraid and there's been no news — it's wonderful to hear from you!"

Jean-Pierre heard her crying. "It's all right, Claudette, I'm fine." No need to tell her he'd lost four crew. "Soon I'll tell you about it."

"I know you'll want to speak to Dr. Patel right away, but she isn't here, I'll have to patch you through to her mobile. Once she closed the offices and sent us all home, we feared the worst. I had the phones forwarded to my mobile, and when the phone rang, I was so afraid — I'm at home watching the news, and they said you were all dead, and the typhoon is coming, and — oh, *monsieur!* She will be so thrilled to know you're alive. She's been worried sick, we all have."

Broussard let her run on until she finally stopped. He said evenly, "Did you say Dr. Patel closed the offices?"

"Oh, yes. When they couldn't find you or *The Griffon,* Dr. Patel gave instructions to go on lockdown, only essential personnel. Everyone else left. She said it was sabotage — oh, but of course, you won't know. The Bastille Day satellite we lost was tampered with. Dr. Patel went to Quints in China and found the metal fatigue was purposeful.

"The media were all over campus, many strangers, many threats. We moved them off the property and closed the gates. Shall I ring her for you now? She will be so pleased, so relieved."

Nicholas laid a hand on Broussard's arm and shook his head.

Broussard nodded. "No, Claudette, it's quite all right, I will call her myself. I must handle this personally. Don't mention my call to anyone else, either, if you please. No media, no outside conversations, no internal communications. I will take responsibility for our messaging to the press. I'll be back to you in a couple of hours. I wanted to let you know I'm okay, but I don't want the news to get out yet, not until I've had some time to rest and regroup. And if there's some sort of sabotage, yes, we need to keep it quiet, the news I'm alive might set off another round of attacks."

"*Oui, monsieur.* It is best you stay hidden for now. I'm so glad to hear your voice."

Broussard frowned at Nicholas as he hung up. "This situation is getting out of hand."

Nicholas said, "Question, Jean-Pierre. Do you really believe Dr. Patel closed your offices to mourn you? Or because a satellite was sabotaged? You're a multinational corporation, you're losing money by the minute, am I correct?"

"Yes, we are, and I admit, it's not the typical procedure. But this isn't a typical situation, either."

"Sir, the timing is too convenient. She thinks she's murdered you, she's shut down your company, stolen the Grail, and we have no idea why, only a brief reference to a nuclear EMP, and now claims of sabotage. Calling and warning her that we know she's up to something would be a massive mistake."

Broussard drummed his fingertips on the leather chair arm. "Listen to me, special agents — yes, that does give you gravitas, doesn't it? How about she's simply distraught at the idea of the head of her company being lost at sea? I know her. If I call her I'll know the truth, all of it."

Nicholas sighed. "Sir, if Dr. Patel did do this, she definitely wants you dead. We'll be operating from a position of power if she continues believing she succeeded. This way, we can see what she does next. I need to have a trap set up on her phone so we know where she is at all times, and I don't want her to rabbit before we have a chance to figure out what she's up to, and why she wanted you dead."

Broussard shook his head. "Since you insist on circumventing me at every turn, and if there's nothing else you need from me, I must rest."

He closed his eyes and was asleep before they had a chance to ask him any more questions.

CHAPTER THIRTY-EIGHT

Mike gave a now-sleeping Broussard a look, then said, "Let's let it go for now. He's not thinking straight, and can you blame him? He's trusted Dr. Patel to run his company for more than five years. A shock this big — I'm not surprised he's hanging on with his fingernails. But he is getting close to believing it. Who else could it be? So that's enough for now. Both you and Grant are exhausted. I'll take first watch. You two get some sleep."

Nicholas started to protest, but Mike shook her head. "Seriously. I'm too jazzed anyway. Believe me, the last thing I want is a nightmare about the huge wave that took down our helicopter and all that black, cold water. I'll do some research instead."

"If you're sure." But Nicholas was already yawning, and Grant didn't protest at all. Both men crashed, hard, leaving Mike alone with her thoughts.

She retrieved a bag of M&M's from the drawer for a quick sugar boost and got herself another cup of coffee. Then she put on her earbuds and checked in with Adam, who looked beyond relieved to see her, especially when she told him what they'd been through.

"Adam, we're fine. Don't worry. Has the news cycle caught up with the rescue yet?"

"No, it's night here. I'm sure the moment dawn breaks, it will be all over the news."

"Copy that. Anything new on your end?"

"Gray is running a bunch of scenarios and is working with the nuke folks at U.S. Strategic Command, looking for the nuclear signature prior to the launch. The company whose satellite was launched July 14 — P-Tel Communications, out of Valencia, Spain — is being raided to cover all the bases.

"There's another team at the Idaho Research Facility trying to figure out what happened with the missing plutonium. But no one has any idea where the nuke is now. As you can imagine, people are starting to freak out. It's all going to leak soon, media's already planning stories. Thankfully, no one wants to start a worldwide panic, so they're going carefully."

"Media and discretion, that's gotta be a

first. With any luck, we'll track it down and stop it from blowing up before it does any harm. We're back on the Blue Mountain jet, heading to Lyon, Galactus headquarters, so we can talk to Jean-Pierre Broussard's second-in-command, Dr. Nevaeh Patel. She's our primary suspect. Everyone is asleep right now, but —"

Adam's face lit up. "Wait. Dr. Nevaeh Patel, the former NASA astronaut? She spent almost six months on the International Space Station before an accident forced them to bring her back down to Earth? That Nevaeh Patel?"

"I remember now something about her, but not exactly what."

"Oh, man. I've been researching her as part of the whole Galactus company."

"Talk to me. What kind of accident did she have?"

"A bad one. She was on an extravehicular activity — EVA — what they call a space-walk — when her tether broke. A less-experienced astronaut probably would have died, because she was literally floating away from the space station and her jet pack failed, but she somehow managed to maneuver herself back and grab ahold of a truss. It was a miracle she survived, changed a lot of their procedures for EVAs, too."

"Why don't I remember? Surely something like that would have made her a heroine and she'd have been all over the news."

"Nope. Turns out they grounded her afterward, and she left NASA under guarded circumstances. No one said a word at NASA and neither did she. I turned up some in-depth research that she had a bunch of psych evaluations when she got back to Earth, nothing reported. Two years later, she resurfaced and went to work for Broussard."

"Sounds like a normal thing to do if someone almost died on a mission. The FBI would react the same way, put us through our paces, make sure we were fit for duty. But then again, how she managed to save her own life, why didn't anyone make a big deal out of it?"

"Hey, look what I just found. Listen to this. Says here a small contingent of people claim she told them she spoke to aliens when she was untethered, and they were the ones who helped her back to the space station."

"Tell me what you mean by a small contingent, Adam."

"Well — all right. Just maybe I took a quick gander at the personnel database. You didn't hear that."

Mike laughed. "No, of course not. My hearing isn't what it used to be."

"Hey, these are exigent circumstances — plus, interestingly, she was one of NASA's most promising astronauts, you'd think her leaving would cause a ruckus. But like I said, no one said anything. Was she dismissed, did she quit, did they make life untenable? She was officially grounded, that's for sure. Also, when I just happened to stumble onto her personnel file, I saw she didn't pass her psych evals. So, no way they'd ever let her back to space. They can't afford dead or crazy people on a space station. Now *that* would make for bad press."

"Okay, let's come forward. So, where was Dr. Patel when the plutonium went missing from Idaho?"

"2015? I'm assuming in France. Lyon. Breaking major ground in the private space industry working for Jean-Pierre Broussard. Maybe, I'm not sure yet."

Mike was silent. "I don't know what to think. But Grant swears he heard Devi, Broussard's lover, say Nevaeh's name right before she was shot and killed. And then the yacht was taken out by a Hellfire missile." She glanced at Broussard, heard a gentle snore, and whispered, "I trust Grant.

I don't think Broussard can be all that objective, yet. Do a deep check on where she was when the plutonium was stolen in 2015. Also, we need to know if Patel has been in France this whole time, or if she's somewhere down here in Malaysia. Maybe putting a bullet in Broussard's lover and trying to kill him and steal the Holy Grail."

"Holy Grail? He really believes he found it? Wow. Well, you and Nicholas will find out, one way or another. Hey, Mike? Get some sleep. You need it."

"Thanks, Mom. I will."

"Hey, that's my line."

She pulled out her earbuds, ate more M&M's, and did a few searches herself. She pulled up photographs of Nevaeh Patel on her screen. Patel in a *Time* magazine spread on female astronauts, Patel as an astronaut all suited up. Patel as a successful executive. The most recent news showed her statements to the media regarding her missing boss.

Patel was fifty-seven now, forty-eight when she was chosen for a mission that meant she'd spend nearly a year aboard the ISS. She had bachelor's degrees in physics and astronomy, a master's degree in earth and planetary sciences from MIT in 1984, then a Ph.D. in astrophysics from the same. Mike did some quick math — Patel had started college when she was only sixteen.

She flipped through the rest of the available material online, finding more photos, more stories. In addition to being brilliant, she projected a powerful presence. Tall, fit, no-nonsense, a face and voice you listened to, trusted. She had long, dark hair, dark eyes, maybe brown, and large black glasses — similar to Mike's own. Mike spotted one photo, enlarged it. It showed another woman standing in the background, much younger, with short, spiky dark hair that might be red, a round, hard face, broad shoulders — and clearly in a defensive, protective stance. There was something almost feral in her look, and Mike could easily identify the multiple weapons she carried by the lumps and bumps in her clothes.

A bodyguard of some sort. Which made sense — Broussard used bodyguards, why wouldn't the second-in-command? Apparently the French aerospace industry was dangerous.

She dialed Adam. "I'm sending you a photo, Adam, the woman standing behind Dr. Patel. Find out who she is."

"Got it. Will do."

Mike closed the lid on her laptop, put her head back, drifted off to sleep. Her last

thought was about the look on the bodyguard's face, staring intently not at the
camera, but at Patel.

CHAPTER THIRTY-NINE

The International Space Station (ISS) is a multi-nation construction project that is the largest single structure humans ever put into space. Its main construction was completed between 1998 and 2011, although the station continually evolves to include new missions and experiments. It has been continuously occupied since November 2, 2000.

— Space.com

Houston, Texas
September 2012
How could she reconnect with the Numen? Nevaeh only knew one way to make it happen.

She flew home to Houston. She was afraid she was never going to get clearance to come back to NASA. Why would they take her when they believed she was crazy?

Crazy because when she was lying quietly

in a sensory deprivation chamber, she was able to communicate with aliens? And so she called her flight director, Franklin Norgate, the only one with power who could possibly believe her sane, and asked to have lunch.

They met at an anonymous sandwich shop near the Johnson Space Center campus because she was afraid if she went back to the campus, her fury would erupt and she might lash out, do something stupid, and then she'd jeopardize even this one small hope. The Numen knew she was trying.

Norgate looked tired — not a surprise, everyone in the space program looked tired. Long nights, altered biorhythms, high-stress environment — it was par for the course.

"How are you, Nevaeh? You look well."

"I am well. Feeling great. I wanted to talk to you about coming back to the fold."

Franklin's smile lit up the room. "Wonderful news! We have a new crop of astronauts who are scheduled to begin training next week. This is perfect timing."

Nevaeh grinned, her heart light for the first time since she'd been grounded. "When do we ship out?"

Franklin said, "This is for the resupply mission scheduled for first quarter 2015. You'll be happy to know we have another female on the roster. It's her first time going up. Your mentorship will be invaluable. There's nothing like having firsthand experience. You can teach her the ropes, get her prepared. She will be thrilled to learn you're going to be her mission specialist. When can you start?"

"Mission specialist? Why won't I be chief science officer?"

Franklin looked up from his potato chips, which he'd been cheerfully consuming at Mach 1, brows drawn together. "You'll be on the ground, guiding her work."

Nevaeh set down her sandwich. The momentary joy she'd felt was replaced by fury. She had to swallow, hard, to not start screaming about the unfairness. Finally, she said, "Why won't I be on the shuttle, sir? I haven't been out of training for very long. It won't take much to get me space ready again."

"Nevaeh, you've been permanently grounded. You knew that. We sent the letter after Dr. Holloway heard from —"

"I haven't received a letter. Who did Dr. Holloway talk to?"

He stumbled through the next few words, then cleared his throat. The *who* didn't matter. He said, "I thought you'd received your letter and were writing us off. This is why I was so happy to hear from you. To hear you're willing to come back and work with us, to lend your expertise, to help shape the missions to come — you're too invaluable to lose."

"I'm invaluable, but not worthy of going back to space."

He looked at his hands, fisted in his lap. She was never going to forgive him, he could see it in her eyes. Dark, fathomless, and furious. Perhaps he should have stood up to Holloway, but in matters of the astronauts' minds, she was the final authority. And it was costing him a good woman.

"You are worthy, Nevaeh. But Dr. Holloway put a permanent hold on your flight status."

"She's never liked me."

"No, she hasn't, you're right there. Her animus is unwarranted, but her opinions matter and her decision is final. You've been out of training for too long. And — I shouldn't tell you this, but she investigated when you asked for your records. She had to, we needed to know what you were going to do — perhaps you were going to mount a legal defense against us, or you were preparing to go public. And you sought out an independent psychiatric consult from a doctor who is well known for treating schizophrenia. Rebecca drew her own conclusions, but I believe the two of them talked."

The anger continued to rise, but she managed to keep her voice low and calm. "Those records are confidential."

"Nevaeh, your mental health is tied to your security clearance. You know that. You sought treatment outside the program. It sent the wrong message."

"But the doctor told me I wasn't schizophrenic. She didn't treat me, didn't give me meds. Nothing."

"You went to her because you were still hearing voices, yes?"

She didn't answer, and he reached across the table, took her hand.

"Nevaeh, I want to help you. Come back to work for us. We'll get you the best care, the best medication therapies, and you will have a hand in shaping the future of space as we know it. We can work around the hallucinations."

She stood, knocking the food wrappings onto the floor. "I am *not* hallucinating. And if you won't strap me to a rocket and get me back up there, I have nothing to offer NASA."

Norgate spread his hands in front of him, looked helpless. "I'm sorry, Nevaeh. It's out of my hands."

She left the restaurant at a near run. She ignored Norgate's calls.

She could no longer contain her fury. She kicked the side of her car, again and again, causing a massive, boot-shaped dent.

It wasn't fair, what they were doing to her. Not fair at all. She wanted to tell the world. She'd never felt such anger, such hatred, toward another creature. It almost surprised her, but at the same time, she understood her emotions. She was being stripped of her status, her livelihood, her mission in life. It was natural to feel violent loathing toward the person standing in her way. One person had destroyed her: Rebecca Holloway.

No, there was another, too. Dr. Fontaine in New York had sold her out.

She got in the car, turned the air-conditioning on high, slammed the car into gear, tried to breathe, to think.

As she drove away, she knew she was going to have to find a way to put herself back in space. And she had no idea how to make that happen. Maybe the Russians? Perhaps they'd take her on, allow her to fly with their cosmonaut program. Would she have to become a Russian agent? Spy for them on the United States, give away the secrets of the American space program, and more, get them access to everything her clearance gave her? Maybe. And she would do it happily, if they could give her what she needed.

She knew she'd have to tell the Numen she'd failed. Would they desert her? Would they find another astronaut who was more capable? When she next went into the chamber, she knew she had no choice, they were her partners, they had a right to know.

CHAPTER FORTY

Nevaeh found a sensory deprivation tank at the University of Houston. Here, she didn't have to disguise herself, she used an old teacher ID from a summer class she'd taught once upon a time, and let herself into the psych building. A little sweet-talking, a hundred-dollar bill, and she was into the technician's good graces, with assurances she could use the sensory deprivation tank anytime she wanted.

In the tank, she tried to clear her mind. It took longer than usual to find her calm; she was consumed with thoughts of Rebecca Holloway's perfidy.

When she finally felt herself relax into a theta state, she found the Numen were waiting for her.

She couldn't keep the desolation from her voice. "NASA isn't going to let me come back. It's that bitch, Holloway, she's always been jealous of me."

We know of her behavior, her jealousy of you, you who are a bright light and honest, who only want good for the Earth. NASA deserted you, believed her, and look what you achieved, and you brought them news of us and yet they were too afraid to listen. You will find another way, you must find another way.

And they went silent.

Yes, Nevaeh thought, *I will find another way.* It came to her suddenly, and she believed she heard the Numen humming in agreement.

Nevaeh emailed Jean-Pierre Broussard the next day.

The following day, her phone rang. A man, clearly French, introduced himself as Jean-Pierre Broussard. She closed her eyes and thanked the Numen, for she knew it was they who'd pushed him to her. She knew all about him, of course, a brilliant aeronautical engineer, published in respected scientific journals. He currently worked for Arianespace in France, ah, but he had plans, big plans, and she wanted to be part of them. He was also known as a playboy, but to Nevaeh, he was a contradiction in terms — as much as he loved the center stage, none knew about his private life and he never spoke of it.

Nevaeh clutched her cell. "Yes, Monsieur Broussard, thank you for calling me back."

"I look at your email like a sign from God. Dr. Patel, I need your brain."

Her heart began to pound, slow, heavy strokes. "My brain?"

"Your brain. As I said, I hadn't known what I needed, then — an email from the exactly right person. I'd like to make you an offer. I'm starting my own aerospace firm, and I want to put you back into space."

And they talked and talked. He told her he wanted to revolutionize space travel — "starting with dropping the cost to get a rocket into space. It shouldn't cost billions, and it shouldn't have to go through government approval hoops, not if we bring in the raw materials and build them ourselves. And these rockets are going to be reusable, further driving down costs. We will undercut the prices of our competitors, and send rockets up weekly. I would say, if we're successful, we will be able to start shipping supplies to the ISS within five years, and put a manned pod into orbit to dock with the ISS within the decade. And you would be first in line to man the mission. Of course," he continued cheerfully, "this will probably take us ten years, but that's nothing, given my goals."

Ten years? No, she couldn't wait ten years to return to the Numen.

"Dr. Patel? Are you still there?"

"I am, sir." She drew a deep breath. "I think we can do it in five years."

He burst out in a big belly laugh. "I hope that means you still want to come work for me? I promise the salary will be worth your while, loads of vacation — why, you can even join me on my yacht for off-site work anytime you please. I spend a great deal of time on the seas — in addition to my aerospace work. I'm a treasure hunter."

"Yes, sir, I'm aware of that." The world was suddenly bright, full of promise. "Mr. Broussard, I would love to come work for you."

"Excellent. Let's get you on *The Griffon* as soon as possible and we can start our plans. Oh, and it's Galactus, Dr. Patel. The company's name is Galactus."

She told the Numen, "I must know, I must be certain what she did." And they agreed.

She made one last appointment with Dr. Fontaine.

Fontaine met her at the door, smiling. She wore a cream linen blazer and black slacks. She looked fit and sharp, and Nevaeh, still hopeful, complimented her new hairstyle.

Blah, blah, blah, she only wanted the truth, wanted to hear it from Fontaine's mouth.

When they were settled, Dr. Fontaine gave her that sweet, noncommittal smile and said, "How have you been, Nevaeh?"

"I'm quite well, actually. I'm taking a new job, working for Galactus Space Industries. They are starting a program to perfect reusable rockets, which will help drive down the cost of putting material — and people — into space." She paused a moment, crossed her legs, gave Fontaine a smile full of teeth. "As you can imagine, my day-to-day life will be demanding from morning to night — endless responsibilities, endless decisions, deadlines, in other words, constant stress." She paused, leaned forward, lowered her voice. "Dr. Fontaine, if I were schizophrenic, or suffering from delusions or dissociative episodes, would I dare to take on this challenge? Would I dare to work hard to make this company a powerhouse in space exploration?"

Fontaine didn't appear to notice the clip to her words. "I'm thrilled for you. So the REST therapy worked for you?"

"Evidently something worked."

"I am so glad to hear it. A brilliant mind like your own — well, it's wonderful to see you getting back to your life, Dr. Patel."

Was the woman tone-deaf? Nevaeh slowly rose to her feet, leaned over the desk. "Dr. Fontaine, I have only one question."

"Anything."

"Why did you sell me out to Dr. Holloway at NASA?"

The doctor's face grew wary, her eyes shifted away. "I'm sorry?"

"I know you consulted with her. I also know speaking with her was unethical, immoral, and illegal. I should be filing a lawsuit against you, so you wouldn't be able to betray anyone else coming to you seeking help. I should complain to the medical board, make sure your license to practice is revoked."

She saw fear in Fontaine's eyes, and alarm. It was wonderful to see. "I — I —"

Nevaeh straightened, walked slowly to the door. She turned, said over her shoulder, "You sold me out. You are despicable. Do you know, some dark night, when you least expect it, I could slip a knife into your ribs, or poison your evening glass of wine? It would be so simple for me to end you. It's the justice you deserve."

Fontaine's face was white, she was trembling.

Nevaeh said quietly, "Dr. Fontaine, you should pray we don't meet again."

She closed the door quietly behind her. She heard the Numen humming. "Yes," she told them, "I faced down that unethical, deceiving bitch."

Soon, soon. She was restarting her life. Ah, but her goals were clear.

Chapter Forty-One

In Wolfram's account, the Grail is a stone that fell from the heavens. It is by the power of this stone that the phoenix rises from the ashes. Hence Wagner's reference to the *"meteoric stone"* in the mosque at Mecca.

— www.monsalvat.no

Blue Mountain Gulfstream
Somewhere over Israel

Mike jerked awake when they hit turbulence. She saw Nicholas and Grant were still dead to the world, but Broussard's eyes were open. He stretched his arms over his head, nodded to her. He looked clear and calm; the short rest had done him good.

He said quietly, "I must apologize to you and your partner for my shortness with you. You're doing your jobs, and believe me, I

302

do appreciate your help. I have lost so much, I fear I lost my manners as well." He looked down at his clasped hands. "It is not an excuse, but I lost four of my crew, men I've known for years." He paused, then swallowed, and his voice sounded raw with pain. "Devi. If it turns out she betrayed me, well, there has to be a reason. Grant believes her sister was being held as a hostage."

Mike said, "You also lost the — stone."

"Call it by its name, Mike. The Holy Grail."

She nodded. "It's difficult."

"Yes, I know. But it is real and its loss is more than I can bear." He turned away, said no more.

"Jean-Pierre, how did you know the Holy Grail was in the wreckage of the *Flor de la Mar*? Why would something so magical, mystical, if you will, be aboard a ship that went down in the Strait of Malacca?"

He settled more comfortably in his seat, and she saw his powerful intelligence focus on her question. "I've studied the possible whereabouts of the Grail all my life, but really immersed myself for over three years now. And I found the journals of the captain of the *Flor de la Mar,* Afonso de Albuquerque. He spoke of a black stone he carried home from Siam, encased in a great sphere, not of this Earth. He believed it was the cause of the boat going down. No one had ever found the wreckage, and many have tried, since it's known as one of the most valuable in the world. We found it and it does hold an astonishing amount. We retrieved quite a bit over the course of our two weeks of dives, but now, of course, it's lost again."

He looked out the window into darkness, and when he turned back to her his face was alight with excitement. "When we found the sphere, it was precisely as Albuquerque described — large and black, not of this Earth. I believe it to be a natural asteroid of some kind, hollowed out, and those who had it initially knew it was the perfect home for the Grail. The stone was inside the sphere, in a lead-lined box suspended in the center, as if it had been placed in the asteroid and was merely waiting for someone worthy to retrieve it."

"And you were worthy?"

"Yes, although I told the Grail I was only the messenger."

"The messenger?"

"Never mind. You believe Nevaeh is behind all this, that she murdered Devi, stole the Grail. I will tell you over the past three years, Nevaeh and I have discussed the

Grail extensively. She might know as much about it as I do. Her intensity, her desire to find it, rivaled my own. If she was behind this, well, this treachery, this betrayal, she wouldn't be at all worthy, now would she? Thus I cannot believe the Grail would respond to her in any way at all. It would repudiate her, but what this would be like, I have no idea."

"Wouldn't she know that? Why would she take it if it wouldn't gain her anything?"

"Mike, you know everyone has limitless ability to justify their own actions, believe them noble, believe them necessary. If she believed what she was doing was worthy, then I don't believe it would even occur to her the Grail could reject her. I imagine she believes herself more worthy of the Grail than I."

He sat back, closed his eyes a moment. "Listen, Mike, space can make you lose your mind. Just like the ocean. You have to be prepared for the concept of infinity. If you're not, you can easily go mad. Trust me, many do. It's possible Nevaeh did as well. After they brought her back down to Earth, grounded her, she was forced to have multiple meetings with the staff psychiatrist. They wanted to put her on medication to help her deal with the delusions brought on by her near-death experience."

"Ah. I take it you heard my conversation with my coworker?"

"Some, yes."

"So it's possible her bosses at NASA were right. She changed, went mad, up there."

"Possibly. But I will be honest. I never saw anything that would give me pause. The woman is brilliant, focused, amazingly creative. I've always believed genius must be given the time and place to flourish, which is one of the reasons I stay out of the way at Galactus." He took a drink of water, stared out the window at the blackness beyond the plane.

Mike said, "I know one of your goals is to get as many people to space as possible."

"Yes. Do you disapprove? Why?"

"No, I don't. It's just that right now, I am very straightforward, no philosophical meanderings. I have to figure out how your company is tied to a nuclear EMP, and how I can stop it before it goes off and ends up killing millions of people."

He stared at her a moment, slowly nodded. "I can help a little. I heard you asking your coworker about the woman standing behind Nevaeh. Her name is Kiera Byrne, the chief of security at Galactus. Let me say she has eyes only for Nevaeh, not that anyone cares, just a bit more information for you. You should know Kiera is slavishly devoted to Nevaeh. Perhaps dangerously so. If there's anyone I know capable of murder, who finds murder pleasurable, it's Kiera."

Mike looked toward Nicholas. "The moment Nicholas and Grant wake up, we will put together a plan for how to approach Dr. Patel. Jean-Pierre, logically, I believe it's irrefutable. Dr. Patel is involved. She might be the one in charge of it all. No, listen. If she is involved, she believes you dead. She's stolen the Holy Grail. Why? We don't know, you don't know. She probably intends to set off an EMP. Jean-Pierre, do you actually believe the Grail gives immortality?"

"Yes, of course it does."

As he said it, Mike saw his eyes lit with a desperate hope. What was going on here? She said slowly, "If Dr. Patel believes in the Grail, believes it brings immortality to the one who has it, and she was willing to kill to possess it, then she's more dangerous than any of us can imagine."

Broussard waved this away. "When her own people cast her out, I gave her a home, a mission, ample money to accomplish anything she could dream of. Trust. Responsibility. A life, a respected life. If Kiera is devoted to Nevaeh, I could easily say Nevaeh is devoted to me. To think otherwise — I don't think I could bear it." Broussard looked away from her and closed his eyes again.

Mike sent Adam a quick text — Got a name for the woman in the photo. Check out Kiera Byrne, Nevaeh Patel's head of security. She got a bottle of water and settled back in her seat. She'd done all she could for the time being. She knew objectively why Broussard was holding fast to his belief in Patel's innocence. They would simply keep him off his phone until they could prove to him he'd been betrayed.

And time was running out.

CHAPTER FORTY-TWO

T-MINUS 31 HOURS

May 4, 2018
A small amount of radioactive, weapons-grade plutonium about the size of a U.S. quarter is missing from an Idaho university that was using it for research. The amount is too small to make a nuclear bomb, agency spokesman Victor Dricks said, but could be used to make a dirty bomb to spread radioactive contamination.

— Associated Press

FBI New York Field Office
26 Federal Plaza
Adam was alone in the office. He'd been running names and flights for three hours, looking for anything that could tie Nevaeh Patel to the Idaho Research Facility. He was ready to quit, but since it was new code he'd written expressly for this task, and they were

trying to stop a nuke, he was willing to let it run for a full twenty-four hours before admitting defeat.

He'd finished reading the AP report on the missing plutonium in Idaho. He was on his third Red Bull, fingers sore and wrists aching, his eyes burning. When the program dinged to indicate a match had been found, he at first couldn't believe it. Then he punched a fist in the air. Of course he should have known it would work. There it was, a flight manifest — it made him sit up, heart revving.

The manifest was for a private jet company out of Duluth specializing in deadhead flights — when the plane was empty of passengers but needed to be moved to a new airport for a client pickup — and allowed the empty seats to be sold at the last minute at a fraction of normal cost so the planes wouldn't fly empty and waste more fuel.

This particular flight, in July of 2015, originated in London, England, and ended in Boise, Idaho, where it picked up a full load of passengers and continued to Los Angeles.

There was one listed passenger on the London-to-Boise leg of the flight. The passenger's name was K. R. Byrne.

The moment Adam saw it, he knew he

had her. K. R. Byrne.

Kiera Rachel Byrne.

Bingo.

Nevaeh Patel's bodyguard had gone to Idaho the same week the scientist was killed? Was this when the plutonium had gone missing? What about Dr. Patel? Had she been there as well, taken a separate flight? Using a fake ID and passport?

Adam sent a message to Mike's computer, telling her what he'd found, then he set about tracing the rest of Byrne's whereabouts. Knowing she traveled under the name K. R. Byrne helped. He adjusted his coding and waited.

Sure enough, he was able to find another flight, this one a return, a week after the incoming flight. It went to Cuba, then directly to French Guiana, and two days later, back to London.

Had Kiera Byrne taken the stolen plutonium to South America and stashed it there until they were ready to use it? Three years was a long time to keep something so volatile hidden. But it wasn't like she could take it to France and keep it in her desk at work.

Yes, Guiana made sense — it's where the signature was spotted by the U.S. Strategic Command nuclear division. So how had she kept it hidden for so long? Where had it been? Did she give the plutonium over to a terror organization that in turn made her the bomb? French Guiana was north of Brazil — not exactly a hotbed of insurgency, but close enough to Venezuela, where there were many reports of bourgeoning terror organizations.

He went back to the travel schedule of K. R. Byrne.

She was a busy woman. He had to assume most of the legitimate travel she did was based around guarding her boss, who also traveled a great deal. For the most part, they flew on one of the three Galactus Lear jets, regular jaunts between Lyon and French Guiana for launches of Galactus rockets. Those were easily searchable, registered flights, all assigned to one of three tail numbers. No, they weren't hiding or doing anything shifty on those flights.

But Byrne herself continued to make random trips here and there, some to the U.S., some to other European destinations, a few to more exotic locales, like India and Sri Lanka. There was even one flight into the heart of Nepal.

Either she had an inordinate amount of vacation time to burn, or Patel had sent her to scout, plan, get ready for the launch of the nuke, put together the source material to be taken to Guiana and attached to the plutonium. Were the two involved with a terrorist organization?

He created a chart of the flights with their dates, and was about to send it to Mike and Nicholas when he saw a flight to Corsica, with both Patel and Byrne on board. It was August 18, 2015. Adam stared at two grainy photographs that came up with it. The first showed Patel and Byrne sitting at a table at the Hotel Corsica restaurant at 10 p.m. local time, and a man sitting at the bar, looking at them. In the second, the three were sitting together in an outdoor café.

Who was he? Adam felt a niggling recognition. He called up a series of terrorist photos, most of them barely recognizable, but he was certain. It was Khaleed Al-Asaad sitting at the bar. Well, the database gave it an 85 percent match.

Adam pulled the face from the photo, lined it up side-by-side with Al-Asaad's last known photograph. The database program ran, lining the screen with red, diagramming the two faces, measuring angles and giving comparisons.

It was Al-Asaad all right, though Adam thought he'd probably had some surgery to alter his looks. His chin wasn't as strong, nor his nose, and his cheeks were rounder. But the basic measurements — pupillary distance, the set of his ears — these couldn't be falsified. The program finished running and gave him an official match confirmation. This was Al-Asaad and he was there meeting with Patel and Byrne.

Al-Asaad was on the terror watch list for suspected activity with Al-Qaeda from well back in the early 2010s. And he was on record calling for a nuclear strike against the United States, and known for trying to buy a suitcase bomb. He'd been off-grid for several years, assumed to be killed by the CIA in one of the cave bombings in the Afghan War.

But here he was, in 2015, on the coast of Corsica, drinking a glass of wine at a bar, alive and well. Nicholas and Mike were going to love this. So the renowned and respected, possibly crazy, Dr. Nevaeh Patel was in league with one big scary terrorist for sure — Al-Asaad — and that was why her minion had stolen the plutonium from the Idaho facility.

He reached for the phone, but Gray walked in at the same moment, hair standing on end.

"Did you sleep here?"

Gray nodded. "Didn't feel like fighting

the traffic. Why do you look like you're about to burst?"

"Check this out."

Adam turned the screen and explained what he'd done.

Gray said, "So, Al-Asaad isn't dead. That's a bummer. Where's he been all this time? I'll tell you, Adam, if he has anything to do with this EMP, we're in trouble. I have a call with Strategic Command shortly. They're the ones who've been tracking the satellite to see if they can find it. What we know so far: Dr. Patel lied when she said it didn't make orbit, it did. Only it's not in the place it was supposed to be. Looks like someone with serious hacking skills managed to reroute the satellite. It wasn't damaged."

"Patel claims Galactus has been sabotaged. She made a statement earlier."

Gray said, "Sabotage. Clever. A story like that could buy her some time."

"You think she launched it with code meant to move it from its original elliptical to another spot?"

"Exactly."

"You know, if Strategic Command can locate the satellite, I might be able to break into the programming and shut it down."

"Finding it seems to be an issue. Space is

a pretty big place, and it's a small satellite."

"I was about to call Nicholas and Mike, tell them about Al-Asaad's involvement —"

"Let them sleep. There's nothing they can do from the air anyway. You can tell them when they land. Right now, you need to get some rest, too. No, don't argue with me. Go grab a bunk, sleep for a few hours. Cross my heart, if something happens, I will come get you."

Adam stood, dropping candy wrappers and crumbs on the keyboard. An empty can of Red Bull spun away with a clatter. Gray laughed.

"See? Man cannot live on junk food alone. Drink some water, for heaven's sake, and while you're asleep, I'll see if we can't track Al-Asaad."

CHAPTER FORTY-THREE

Lyon, France
Galactus Headquarters
2013

Nevaeh had to admit her boss and the founder of Galactus, Jean-Pierre Broussard, was proving to be a witty, brilliant man, but unavailable on a day-to-day basis. And this was why he had her, and she intended to prove herself as quickly as possible. She was happy being there, being back at work, using her mind to solve problems instead of obsessing over those who had destroyed her. She had hope, new hope, and she knew she'd figure out how to get herself back with the Numen. She was happy, optimistic.

Her first day on the job, she began the design work for a new space module that could carry people. She sketched and ran numbers and printed up 3-D models. She spent weeks refining every aspect, discussing options and possible flaws with the Numen. It was interesting how they always agreed with her, tossing her back the same questions she'd asked them, which, of course, made her think and rethink.

Finally, after six months, she knew she had something stable and sustainable to bring to Jean-Pierre — their very own manned spacecraft, designed for orbit, docking with the International Space Station, and eventual landings on the moon.

It was going to cost billions, but she could make it work. She would get them into space — and she would be on the first rocket there. The Numen were as excited about it as she was.

Jean-Pierre loved the idea, approved it immediately. The timeline they attached was nine years. Nine years, even less than the time that he'd originally planned. Still, nine years. She wept when she told the Numen and they wept with her. She told them she had to cut it back, it was far too long, and they readily agreed with her, but how? They had no answer.

Jean-Pierre gave her a raise and they had a party on the yacht.

But she also had to run the company. There were board meetings, staff meetings, meetings with the distributors and the buyers, the people she was purchasing the raw materials from. She had to travel, extensively, to Russia and India and China and Malaysia, to other areas of Europe, and to meet up with Jean-Pierre as he floated around the world looking for treasure.

He was funding the company, funding her personal plans, so she could hardly complain. But all the busywork and management took away from her time to work on their manned spacecraft. She had to cut the nine years down. By a lot.

The years had slipped by. They built the rockets in-house, in a factory she'd designed on the Galactus campus, then shipped them by boat to French Guiana to launch. The first blew up. So did the second. The third made orbit, and the celebration was insane.

Kiera Byrne, Nevaeh's new head of security, had short spiked red hair and long legs, and a brain. She was quiet, more taciturn, really, so very young. Nevaeh learned quickly enough she was also ruthless and bloodthirsty. Ah, but Kiera never left her side, and she felt safe, and then she began to feel more.

In 2014, she bought her own house, a beautiful chateau she'd purchased and renovated in her spare time near their Lyon headquarters. She'd bought her own sensory deprivation flotation tank as well, and used it nightly to decompress and unwind and report to the Numen what she was thinking, what she was doing. If she was angry about something, they were angry along with her, if excited, they hummed and congratulated her. It was her favorite time of the day. She spoke of the insanity in space, so many satellites hovering over Earth, and they agreed, they hated the noise, the constant interference. She'd wondered aloud, "How can I quiet space so we can speak all the time rather than in my chamber?" And they said, *You must find another way.* And she knew that, spoke of it all the time to them, but she didn't know how to do it yet.

She said to them in the blank darkness, "We're a small company. It's going to take time. We're going to have to invent some of the mechanics for this, they don't exist yet. We have to build, and test, and test some more. Development of this nature takes time." But she knew the Numen were getting impatient because she was, too. "How do I do this, short of setting off some sort of nuclear blast to take out the grids — eliminate all the wretched noise so you can —" She stopped, whispered, "You were able to get past the stationary geosynchronous satellites. You came to me at the space station. But I see now it's the space between the Earth and the space station that is too crowded to let you through. *I know you are in need. This plan — this blast —* it would be simple, really. A nuclear blast at, say, three hundred kilometers would send an electromagnetic pulse through the surrounding atmosphere. Depending on the yield produced by the bomb, the EMP would allow for a rather large area to be taken off the grid. But I have less chance of getting my hands on plutonium than I do moving up the manned program schedule." What to do, what to do? What? They didn't want to wait, she knew it.

She told Kiera about the Numen in 2014, her trusted Kiera, who loved her, believed in her, trusted her completely. Kiera was the closest thing Nevaeh had to a friend. She knew Kiera was not her intellectual equal, but she was dead serious about keeping Nevaeh safe, her shadow at all times. Wherever she was, Kiera was close by. Every time she glanced up, Kiera would go into motion, making sure she had everything she needed. Had their relationship bloomed into love? Nevaeh didn't know, didn't really care. Kiera made her happy.

After a few years of extraordinary discretion, Nevaeh decided it would be easier if

Kiera moved into the chateau. They had separate rooms, and outwardly, nothing changed. Kiera was still her bodyguard by day. Now, she was there for her at night, too.

They dined together most evenings when Nevaeh was in France, and whenever Nevaeh got up to visit the deprivation pod, Kiera stood guard.

She swore nightly to the Numen she was working as hard and fast as she could, and they listened, always listened. And agreed, yes, she was working hard. But she didn't see any way to make Galactus's manned spacecraft program move any quicker. It was already three years behind schedule, simply because the legitimate work was piling up. She sometimes felt getting back to space wasn't ever going to happen.

It was Kiera who made her revisit the idea about the EMP.

It was a quiet winter's night, with snow billowing across the estate and a fire roaring in the dining room grate. Over dinner and an excellent bottle of Bordeaux, Kiera unexpectedly began to talk about her past. She was from Ireland, which Nevaeh had known the moment they met, her lilt was a dead giveaway. She'd gotten into close protection because she was good with guns, good in a fight, had a double black belt in karate, and had mastered several other martial art disciplines. But that evening, gauzy with wine, she loosened up and talked more than she ever had, about things Nevaeh didn't know — about her mother, who was in jail for bombing a supermarket in Kerry. Her father, who was dead by the hand of his rival. Admitted her greatest shame, and pride — her parents had been part of the IRA.

Fascinated, Nevaeh listened as Kiera talked long into the night of the hardships of being the child of freedom fighters. They'd taught her so much about how to survive. How to fight. The many moves to stay ahead of the police, the secret meetings in the middle of the night, of a child tracked and frightened, of the bombs she'd grown up around.

As it turned out, Kiera knew quite a bit about bombs.

Later, in the velvety darkness, as she was twined around her lover, the Numen came to Nevaeh's dreams. It wasn't a regular occurrence — they preferred to speak to her in the utter silent emptiness of the deprivation chamber — but in moments of duress or joy, they would appear, their voices great harmonies, merging into a single voice, and she told them about Kiera and how she knew all about bombs, and maybe she could help, and they agreed. Kiera knew about bombs, she could help.

Nevaeh woke the next morning with a plan. And she whispered to the Numen, "If I can't come to you, then you can come to me. Let me tell you about it and you can tell me what you think." And the Numen rejoiced and agreed it was the solution.

And that meant she and Kiera had to get their hands on some plutonium.

She could get nuclear material, she could get a bomb on a satellite. And because of Nevaeh's genius, Galactus's reusable rockets could take a satellite with the bomb aboard to space, a satellite she could program to be in exactly the right spot in orbit, where it would be detonated at the perfect time, forcing a massive electromagnetic pulse through the atmosphere and down to Earth, taking offline both the satellites in orbit and the electrical grids across a continent. Everything she needed she could get, including the plutonium.

And all the satellites in space would be knocked offline, and there would be blessed silence both in space and on Earth. And the Numen would be able to come for her. And when she told them, the Numen rejoiced.

But she worried. They were immortal, they'd felt it to her, and she wasn't. And then Broussard began telling her about the Holy Grail. And time passed, and she began to tell the Numen about her growing belief in the Holy Grail, or the Heaven Stone, as she preferred to call it, since the Numen were, after all, in the heavens. She told them about her studies and discussions with Broussard, and how she knew to her soul he would find it, in the Strait of Malacca, on a shipwreck known as the *Flor de la Mar.*

And when she told them the Heaven Stone would make the one who had it immortal, they rejoiced with her. The bomb's EMP would create enough of a channel for them to collect both Nevaeh and the Heaven Stone. This was what they wanted, wasn't it? They hummed, they were so happy. Nevaeh, with Kiera by her side, began to implement their plan.

CHAPTER FORTY-FOUR

New York
July 2015

Dr. Claire Fontaine lived on West 69th. Nevaeh was pleased the large glass building backed to a quiet alley, dark even though it was still daylight, where no cameras pointed. She now waited in the alley, wearing black, blending into the shadows, listening to the squeal of tires and the footsteps. The heat was making sweat prickle on the back of her neck.

You're fine. Breathe. Relax. She will come.

Fontaine kept to a schedule, Kiera assured her.

Monday through Thursday, she came home at 4:30 every day, put on running gear, took a loop around Central Park, then returned home at 6 p.m. and disappeared into her apartment for the rest of the night.

Fridays were different. Fontaine exchanged work clothes for dinner and dancing, went out in heels and a little black dress. Nevaeh had read Kiera's dossier thoroughly — sometimes it was a date, sometimes it was a charity event, the symphony or a ballet, when the season was appropriate.

For someone so smart, she is seriously stupid to keep to such a rigorous — predictable — schedule. When she had told this to the Numen, she would swear she heard laughter. *And will you kill her, Nevaeh, like you've told us you would? Like she deserves, the traitorous bitch. Kill her, Nevaeh, you want to, that's what you've told us over and over, just do it. Do it tonight.*

And here she came, ponytail bobbing. Nevaeh didn't even bother looking at her watch, she knew it was 6 p.m., on the dot.

When Fontaine went inside, Nevaeh followed. Amazing that such a supposedly intelligent, quite well-to-do woman would live alone in New York without a doorman.

She's reckless and stupid and deserves this, the Numen sang in her ear. Hadn't she told them the same thing so many times?

Nevaeh took the stairs, waited until she heard Fontaine's door lock.

She had a key — of course, Kiera had managed it, bless her. When Nevaeh had visited the first time, letting herself in, she'd spent half the afternoon in the apartment, gloves on, touching all of Dr. Fontaine's lovely things. Books, china figurines, art.

A lonely existence.

You were lonely once. We found you.

Yes, you did, and I found you and now you're with me all the time.

Nevaeh could hear the shower running.

She crept on silent feet to the bathroom. She had a knife in her pocket but she didn't want to have to use it. She'd discussed it with the Numen, worried she might get stuck herself, and they agreed. Fontaine was in shape, strong, could easily disarm Nevaeh if she wasn't careful. No, she needed a surprise attack, and again, the Numen agreed.

She flexed her fingers in the gloves, felt blood racing through her veins. She was excited, she was ready, more than ready. At last. She picked up the large, heavy ashtray on the console table by the bedroom door, settled it firmly in her hand, got a good grip on it. She'd seen the ashtray on her visit and had told the Numen she had to be careful to hit her on the side of the head, not her face. And they'd agreed.

One deep breath, then she was through the door. The room was steamy. Fontaine was singing quietly to herself, some lame song Nevaeh remembered from the seventies.

She ripped open the curtain, waited for Fontaine to turn to look at her, her face a rictus of terror. Nevaeh smiled and slammed the ashtray into the side of Dr. Claire Fontaine's head. Water sprayed everywhere, and a stream of red began running down the side of her head, temple to chin, mixing with the water and face soap.

Fontaine fell, her head resting on the edge of the tub. Nevaeh came down on her knees, watched the blood pour from the wound in her head.

She leaned close. "Hello, you treacherous cow."

Fontaine's eyes ran red with her blood, but Nevaeh knew she recognized her. She managed to whisper, "You? Why?"

"You aren't surprised, are you? Really? You knew you'd have to pay for your deceit, for your betrayal. Did you and Holloway have a good laugh together?"

"No — no." Her eyes rolled back in her head and she was gone.

I did it, I did it.

Yes, you did, she deserved it, but now you've won, and she's dead.

Fontaine rested exactly where she would have had she slipped and fallen in the shower and hit her head. An arm dangled and blood began to pool.

Ten minutes after she'd let herself in, Nevaeh was walking down the stairs, her bag heavier, but her heart light. She'd killed one of her betrayers. The Numen had understood and approved.

She ducked out the back entrance, walked four short blocks east into Central Park, and lost herself in the crowds. Fifteen minutes later, on the east side of the park, she hailed a cab. He dropped her at the W hotel in Midtown. After he pulled away, she walked to the Maxwell Hotel instead, went inside, changed clothes, disposed of the old clothes and the ashtray, then grabbed another cab for the ride to Teterboro for her flight to Boise.

What a lovely week it was shaping up to be.

Chapter Forty-Five

T-MINUS 30 HOURS

I named my company Galactus after the Marvel comic book character. That may seem silly to some of you, but Galactus is an ancient being, and is also known as the World Eater. What name could be more fitting for an aerospace company that will be changing the way the people of Earth move through the universe?

— Jean-Pierre Broussard,
founder and CEO,
Galactus Space Industries,
Annual Meeting, 2013

Galactus Headquarters
Lyon, France
The plane landed hard on the Lyon airstrip, jarring everyone awake. Mike stretched and grabbed her phone immediately, grateful to Poppy for the gift, shocked there weren't

any calls. With a raised brow, she dialed into the office, to Adam's number. Gray answered.

"You're safe on the ground, I take it?"

"We are."

"We have things to tell you, but you'll want to be on a secure line. Get to Galactus, set up an encrypted channel. We'll fill you in then. Oh, and we have a trap set on Nevaeh Patel's and Kiera Byrne's phones, but neither one is turned on. The moment they go live, we will be able to track them. Both were last used in Lyon, so chances are they're still there. Be careful, Mike. I don't like this. More's going on than we know."

"Will do, Gray. Thanks for being so cryptic."

"Anytime," and he was gone. Nicholas handed her a cup of coffee. He was scruffy and needed to shave, just how she liked him. He smelled like salt from the ocean despite his attempts to clean up in the plane's shower. She smoothed back his hair, touched his cheek.

He said, "Another fifteen minutes won't matter, but I would like to know what they've found out."

"Gray was very focused, operational. Whatever it is, it's important."

Grant joined them, pouring down coffee

and smiling. "You lot made quite an impression on my boss. Congratulations, that's hard to do. Fentriss is by-the-book, very old-school."

Mike said, "Well, sure he is impressed. I mean, Grant, you did tell him we were ninjas, right?"

"Oh yes, and maybe he thinks so now, too."

An SUV waited for them on the tarmac. Broussard said nothing, only nodded to them. They climbed in, and the SUV wound its way from the small airport to the outskirts of Lyon to the Galactus headquarters and campus. It was dark, the roads deserted, but the moon was high and nearly full, and Mike could see the French countryside.

She said, "I bet it's beautiful in the daylight and not at all industrial."

"Many do expect us to be in a more manufacturing area," Broussard said, "but when I purchased this land I knew it was perfect for my company. I wanted a spot out of the way, off the beaten path, as you like to say. Oh look, media. Even though it's dark. I'm going to duck down now."

He did. They passed several media trucks from the major international news organizations, satellite dishes on top of the vehicles pointed at the sky. The vans were in front of a small café, all of them unmanned.

Grant said, "There's luck. Everyone's on a nap break, it seems."

Their SUV slid past, no one the wiser.

When they pulled up onto the lovely, lush Galactus campus, Broussard asked the driver to take them to the front gates. He proceeded to unlock it using a series of numbers on an electronic keypad, and the gates swung open.

The grounds were deserted, not surprising for the middle of the night. No lights were on in the building.

It wasn't only that. Something felt wrong. Nicholas glanced at Mike, noticed Grant shifted in his seat, got the weapon Poppy had provided at the ready.

Nicholas said, "Jean-Pierre, does the idea of sabotage ring true to you?"

Broussard shrugged. "It's possible, I guess. All right, I have to admit, shutting down the campus doesn't seem like the logical thing for Nevaeh to do."

Hallelujah, maybe he was coming around, at last. Mike said, "It makes perfect sense if she had something to do — like set off a nuclear weapon — she'd want to do it in privacy. Be on guard, people. She could be in there, fortified. Go carefully."

Broussard, to her relief, kept his mouth shut.

They all climbed out of the SUV at the Galactus entrance. Nicholas and Grant cleared the area. At their nod, Broussard walked to the front doors and unlocked them. The interior lights automatically came on. There was no night security, no one anywhere. Broussard went directly to a room just inside the doors. Nicholas knew the media would notice the sudden lights, but it couldn't be helped. If Patel was here, if she had backup with her, they weren't going to have the advantage of surprise much longer.

He pointed. "These screens here? They feature our latest security — a laser-guided, heat-sensor motion tracker — it allows the guards to see any movement on all the floors and points the cameras in the direction needed. When it's set to secure mode, as it is now, if a mouse moves across a hallway or stairwell, the software can home in on it instantly." He waited. The cameras remained stationary, the screens empty. "No, there's nothing. She's not here. No one is."

Nicholas asked, "Could she be somewhere else on the campus?"

"She could, but all her work is here, in

335

the headquarters building. No, the campus is shut down, and that includes our manufacturing buildings."

They left the security center and walked into the grand lobby, with its pristine white walls. Mike looked toward the winding upward ramps. She said, "I thought this was familiar. It's like the Guggenheim museum in New York. Very nice, Jean-Pierre."

He grinned at her. "Yes. Now look up."

Mike stared at the huge model of the solar system hanging from the blackened ceiling, obviously representing the vastness of space. It was amazing.

"All of you, follow me. We must get to my office. With any luck, we'll find out Nevaeh doesn't have anything to do with this." They rode a near-silent elevator to the top floor.

Loyalty, Nicholas thought. When you believed in the loyalty of a person, it was hard to let go, to accept betrayal.

Broussard said, "I haven't been here in a few months. Like I said, I work from the boat — worked, that is. Nevaeh's office is adjacent to this one. Feel free to look in, though don't be surprised by her seeming chaos. To gain access to her computer, we will need an override from mine. The entire campus can be controlled from my system. I've never felt fully comfortable ceding control to an IT department. They run most things on campus, but the mainframe has a separate control from here."

He swung open the office doors and gestured them inside. Lights immediately came on. The room fit with the rest of the building: white, anonymous, except for large color photographs of the various rockets and a number of shots of Earth from different angles in space.

Mike went to the adjoining office — Broussard wasn't kidding, it was chaos. Books and papers stacked sky high, covering the desk, chairs, bookshelves. Broussard soon joined her.

"How does she find anything?"

He shrugged. "She knows where everything is, and gets very, very angry if anyone messes with her things."

"Can you give us access to her computer now? Our people will search it remotely. Oh, yes, I'm going to need to set up a secure call."

"Certainly. You can use my conference room. It's right through there."

He pointed to a door off his own office, across the expanse of clean white room. She felt better immediately being out of Nevaeh's office. She couldn't imagine existing in such a mess.

Mike saw a triptych of paintings showing the Grail legends on the far wall of the conference room. Compared to everything else in the room — no, the entire building — they were old-fashioned. She stopped to study them.

Broussard said, "We're not sure who painted these. Even though they're unsigned, I'm betting it was Arthur Hughes. He did paintings of Galahad. To me it stands to reason he would do some of Parzival, the Grail knight who features in Wolfram's story of the Heaven Stone — the Holy Grail. Beautiful, aren't they? I found them only two years ago. They'd been hidden away in a private collection."

"Yes, they're lovely."

"They represent perfectly what I salvaged from the *Flor de la Mar*," he said simply. They were golds and greens on parchment, the first showing a black sphere, large enough for a man to step inside, the second the sphere cracking open and heaven's light escaping, and the third, a greenish-black stone, the size of a man's hand, rising from the split in the black sphere, just out of the grasp of a man in a suit of armor.

The people in the painting watched in awe, their faces turned to the light. How could it be possible? Mike wondered. But the evidence was staring her in the face.

He said, "I've always thought the Heaven Stone — the Holy Grail — was made of moldavite, a rare substance created by meteor strikes. But oddly enough, when I held the stone in the palm of my hand, it was very light, weighed almost nothing. I'd given Devi a necklace made of moldavite stones the night she —" He broke off, quickly walked away.

One more thing Mike needed to learn about now — moldavite.

She heard Nicholas and Grant come into the conference room and start peppering Broussard with questions about Nevaeh. She tuned them out and put in her earbuds. She didn't want Broussard listening to the other end of the call.

She opened her laptop, scrambled her phone, hooked into its encrypted secure signal. Adam's face popped up on her screen, looking very serious indeed.

"Where are you?"

"At the Galactus headquarters, in Broussard's conference room. What's wrong? Gray said there was an issue."

"We have an idea of what might be going on. Is Nicholas with you?"

"Yes, and Grant and Broussard. What's happening?"

"We found two photos of Nevaeh Patel, Kiera Byrne, and a terrorist named Khaleed Al-Asaad. Both times they were in Corsica. You've heard of him, right?"

"Holy crap, you're kidding me. That bloodthirsty, murdering terrorist Al-Asaad is still alive? He's involved?"

"Yep."

Gray's face came onto the screen. Adam had looped him into the chat.

Gray said, "The photos were taken in Corsica in 2015 and 2016. Listen to this: We know Kiera Byrne flew to Boise in 2015. The Boise field office has contacted the local authorities and they're looking again at the death of Dr. Linton, the scientist from the Idaho Research Facility. The original ruling was murder-suicide. Linton killed his wife then himself.

"We believe Byrne stole or paid off Dr. Linton to give her the plutonium, killed both him and his wife, and then Byrne and Patel handed it off to Al-Asaad to make the nuke. Which means at their cozy get-togethers on Corsica, they made a deal. Get Al-Asaad the plutonium and he'd arrange for scientists on his payroll to make the nuke. We believe Al-Asaad paid Patel millions for the plutonium with the promise she'd use one of Broussard's rockets to hijack a satellite and send the bomb to space, with the intention of setting it off to cause an EMP. Bring down the West, bring down the world, it doesn't seem to matter much to terrorist organizations. And they can afford it, what with all the oil money funneled into their pockets in the Middle East.

"Adam's been using the NGI database hooked into CCTV from all possible locations, searching everywhere for Al-Asaad, and we think we've spotted him."

Mike's heart began to pound, shooting adrenaline into her system. She couldn't believe he was alive. "Where? Where is he?"

"Khaleed Al-Asaad is in Lyon."

CHAPTER FORTY-SIX

Mike was starting to shout out to Nicholas when Gray continued. "So why is he in Lyon? A final meet with Patel? Or maybe Al-Asaad found out Broussard is alive and came to kill him, on Patel's orders. Or on his own? We simply don't know. So be careful, Mike. We don't know how many people Al-Asaad might have with him. My own feeling is he knows Broussard's alive and will do whatever it takes to kill him. Why? Now, that's uncertain, sorry, I can't be more definitive."

"Thank you, Gray. We're safe right now. We're inside Galactus, and it's all been cordoned off since there's plenty of media in the surrounding area. Surely he wouldn't make a run at us here. But if you locate him, holler, and we'll do our best to bring him in. Or take him down."

She hoped she sounded more certain than she felt. Al-Asaad here? His reputation, before his supposed termination by the CIA, was terrifying. Suicide bombers in Jerusalem, bombs blowing up buses in London, bombs ripping trains off the tracks in France. Everyone had been relieved when word came he was dead. But he wasn't. It was all a ruse. He was alive and he'd managed to have his scientists make a nuclear bomb to go off in space above the Earth, with the plutonium Kiera Byrne had stolen from the Idaho Research Facility in 2015. Or was it both Patel and Byrne?

Gray said, "We have a satellite on you, watching. Now, what are you guys doing at Galactus?"

"We're getting into Patel's computer, seeing if there's anything to tell us where she is. You're going to receive an open channel here shortly. We need you to pull everything you can find from her systems. Has her phone come online yet?"

"Not yet. We're —"

She heard a pinging noise, like firecrackers muffled inside a pillowcase — *Small arms fire, semiautomatic weapon.*

She said calmly, "Gray, Adam, I have to go. There's gunfire somewhere close by. I suppose Al-Asaad figured out where Broussard is. Do find out why he personally wants

Broussard dead. Did Patel pay him or what?"

She broke off the call, slammed her laptop shut. She heard Grant shouting to Nicholas. She pulled her Glock off its clip, did a press-check, saw a bullet was in the chamber.

Nicholas already had his Glock in his hand. "Evidently some of Broussard's security are breaking into the building. Grant and Broussard are watching it on the cameras in his office."

Mike yelled, "It's not Broussard's security — Gray and Adam just told me — it's Khaleed Al-Asaad and his thugs. They want Broussard dead. Why? Probably Patel ordered it. I'll tell you all of it later."

Nicholas blinked at that, slowly nodded. "Al-Asaad? Okay, we need to get Jean-Pierre to a safe place while we deal with Al-Asaad. We need more weapons, too."

They found Grant and Broussard standing at the windows in his office. Broussard said, without looking up, "Those men are not my security. I don't know who they are."

Mike said, "It's Al-Asaad and — I don't know how many men are with him."

Grant said, "But I thought he was long dead."

"No, he's far from dead. I'll give you the

details later. Al-Asaad broke through the gates and is coming to kill us. Jean-Pierre, can you give us more weapons?"

Mike heard three shots, closer now. A single look of panic crossed Broussard's face and then it was gone. He cleared his throat, pulled on his leader skin, and became utterly calm.

"At the end of the hall there is a security outpost. I don't know what they have in there, but here's the key." He fumbled a key from his desk drawer, tossed it to Nicholas. Nicholas and Grant were out the door, their pounding footsteps loud in the hallway. Mike said, "We want to keep you safe, Jean-Pierre. What's the most difficult area to penetrate?"

"R&D, but it's in the basement. If they get in, we're trapped, and there's only one egress. There's a chopper on the roof. Wait, Mike — Al-Asaad — he's that terrorist, isn't he? Why would he want to kill me?"

Mike said, "Patel's orders."

She heard him suck in his breath, then Nicholas stepped into the open doorway, loaded down with weapons. He grabbed Broussard's arm. "Let's get to the roof."

Grant handed over several guns to Mike. She strapped them on, threw an ammunition belt around her shoulders, and accepted a comms unit, placing the earwig in her ear. "I don't suppose you found any Kevlar?"

"Sorry."

"Let's go," Nicholas shouted.

There was a massive flash, and a pop, and the room began to fill with smoke. The jitter of automatic weapons fire started, and Mike felt hot bullets speeding past.

"Flash-bangs!" Nicholas shouted, dragging her back against the wall.

"I know, I'm still seeing stars."

Grant said, "They shot one through the window. They can see us. Jean-Pierre, kill the lights!"

Broussard, calm as a judge, reached up and typed a few commands into the computer, and the building's lights went out, darkness was complete. The firing stopped.

Grant said, "Someone want to tell me why we're under attack by Al-Asaad, of all people?"

Mike said, "Jean-Pierre, you called your secretary, Claudette. It seems likely Patel was tracing her phone, in case you managed to escape the explosion on the yacht and got in touch with her."

Another battery of bullets, but nowhere close. Nicholas said, "They're shooting in the dark. We can't wait until they get into the building. Where are the stairs to the roof?"

"We have to go out into the gallery. We'll be exposed."

"If we can stay down, the concrete knee walls might block us if we crawl."

Nicholas went first. The white knee wall around the spiraling ramps was high enough for him to crouch down and belly crawl. Mike went next, then Broussard. Grant took up the rear. He had a set of night-vision goggles on now, was scanning and relaying enemy positions in a steady stream in Mike's ear.

"They're at the doors, they have a shaped charge on them, they have it set —" He ripped off the NVGs. "Crap! It's going to go off in less than ten seconds —"

The doors exploded inward, glass shattering and spraying all over. They used the distraction to scurry on hands and knees across the gallery.

They could hear booted steps, at least four pairs, by the sound of them, working in concert, no shouts or calls from ten stories below them. These terrorists were trained. They knew how to breach a building, and do it quickly.

The four of them crouched against the door that would lead them to the stairs to the roof.

Nicholas whispered, "The minute we open this door we give away our position. Mike, you and Jean-Pierre go first. Grant and I will hold them off. Get to the roof. Jean-Pierre, I assume you can pilot that helicopter?"

Broussard shook his head. "I'm sorry. I'm not a pilot."

Grant said, "I am. I'll go with Jean-Pierre. Mike, you and Nicholas hold them off. When you hear the rotors turning, get up to the roof as fast as you can."

Nicholas was more than grateful they'd found the M4s. He and Mike had them in their hands, their Glocks back in their holsters. There was two feet of glass railing above the knee wall, and Mike risked a quick look.

A bullet smashed into the barrier.

Nicholas yelled, "Go, go!" and angled his weapon down, firing in short bursts as Grant and Broussard pushed through the door and pounded up the stairs.

A barrage of gunfire came directly at their position. Mike had never been so thankful for thick concrete. It didn't matter plaster shards and cement were chipped free and raining down from the wall behind them. They took turns shooting down. Mike got one terrorist as he ran up the winding ramp. Before she could be relieved — down to three now — six more well-armed men flooded into the vast entrance.

"Well, crap. They have replacements."

Nicholas nodded grimly. Suddenly, Grant was behind them. Mike jerked and very nearly shot him.

"Don't shoot. The keys. Jean-Pierre's keys. We need them. The door to the roof is locked and I can't shoot through it, it's steel. I have to get back to his office."

Nicholas was silent a moment, then a half smile crossed his face. He pointed to the installation of planets, dangling just below their position.

"Mike, how sturdy do you think the structure is?"

"The planets? You're joking. No, Nicholas, don't even think about it."

But Nicholas had already wedged the M4 under his arm, swung the strap around so it wouldn't get in the way. He looked at Grant.

"There's no other way back to Broussard's office, the wall is blown out. Just wait, pin them down. I'm going to climb across, and get the roof door key from his office. Back in no time at all."

Mike grabbed his arm. "Nicholas, don't be insane. You don't know it will hold your weight. Your mother would kill me if anything happened to you."

"Don't fret, just look at all those beams and trusses. Those bolts are meant for heavy usage. All those planets, they're far from light. It'll hold."

Grant grinned at him. "By the way, you have a grenade in there," he said, and pointed to the vest Nicholas was wearing. "Drop it on them from above, it will buy you some time to cross. When you're ready to come back, flash us with your phone, and we'll cover you. Ready?"

Nicholas nodded, gave Mike a last smile, said, "Steady on," and jumped onto the installation.

CHAPTER FORTY-SEVEN

The planets were stout and steady, happy to hold his weight. Nicholas crawled through the outer planets first, Pluto, Jupiter. Good to know Broussard wanted Pluto to stay a planet. He shook his head, realized when the power was on in the building, the planets must move. Cool touch. He saw the counterweight bar on the far side — not only did the planets move, they moved in their designated orbits.

As he drew closer to the counterweight, he heard a grinding noise, a soft, mechanical sound, and Nicholas realized no, they weren't dependent on the electricity, but were moving, gently, slowly, but moving. Had he accidentally hit a switch, or were they in perpetual slow motion and he hadn't noticed it before?

Bloody great. Obviously, his weight had altered the movement, and the whole mechanism was in motion around him, faster now, the planets starting to whir as they gently twirled and spun.

He heard a gasp, realized it came from Mike, but ignored it. Al-Asaad's men hadn't realized he was up there yet. All their firepower focused on the gallery. It wasn't going to take them long to realize the mechanism was in motion, and if they looked up — he was a sitting duck.

Nicholas edged closer to the center. Hand, foot, step. Hand, foot, step. The steel-frame trusses were strong, he just had to make sure he placed his feet in the right spots, grabbed hold of the truss above him. If he hadn't been as tall as he was, this would have been more of a tightrope walk. At least he could grip above as he walked along the trusses. As he crossed onto the other side, his weight made the planets around him move a bit faster than he liked. A planet was swinging toward him, he needed to get out of its way.

Three fast steps and he was across. He blew out a breath, vaulted over the railing, and ran down the hallway to duck into Broussard's office. He saw the keys on the desk, pocketed them, and started back.

The gunfire was fast and furious. He saw Mike and Grant taking turns shooting down to the foyer. They had Al-Asaad's men pinned, it seemed — they couldn't move. They couldn't get to the ramps that wound to the upper levels of the building, they'd be shot from above by Mike and Grant. Some good luck for the good guys.

When he stepped onto Pluto, he heard a metallic groan. Not good. The trusses had held his weight across, but now they were protesting? Not fair. He needed to hurry.

Mike heard the change in the metal and her heart froze. Nicholas was two hundred feet in the air, suspended over a shooting gallery. If he fell, he was dead.

She wanted to scream, *Go back, go back.* No, this was Nicholas, and he had to do this, he could do this, if only he could get back across without the mechanism breaking apart.

A bullet zinged an inch from Nicholas's hand, and then there were more, and shouts. He'd been spotted.

He cursed. If he could just get back across — but the gunfire was heavy now, sustained, both from Mike and Grant and from Al-Asaad's men. He was sheltered behind Earth, but it was going to move through the elliptical and expose him within a minute.

Grant yelled something at him, pointing at his chest. Nicholas grinned like a maniac, pulled the pin, and dropped the grenade.

The explosion was deafening. He heard screams. But the blast also shot a wave of power upward, and the concussion knocked Nicholas off the truss.

He was falling, falling.

He landed, hard, on the top of Jupiter, swinging wildly, loose now from the rest. Thank heavens, Jupiter was the largest of the bunch. He was sprawled over it and rode it around in a circle, trying to gauge how to get off the sphere and onto the ramp. The planet would swing close, then swing away.

He saw a loose cable above him, one meant to hold the planet in the proper place, but it had snapped, torn free by either the blast or gunfire, and as he swung below it again, he took a deep breath and jumped toward it, grabbed it, and hung there for a minute.

Mike was shouting at him, but he couldn't make out her words. He clung on for dear life. When Jupiter passed beneath him again, he used it for momentum. He kicked off and swung across the twelve-foot expanse like Tarzan.

Too soon, he realized the cable wasn't long enough. He wasn't going to make it, his hands were already slipping. When he came close to the glass railing, he leaped toward it, catching one hand on the edge.

His other arm dangled, and he dropped his M4.

He couldn't pull himself up, his hand was slipping. Then Mike was there, hauling him over the railing. Glass cut his chest and legs, but he ignored it. She dragged him onto the ramp.

He rolled and came up to see a bearded man running toward them, his gun raised. He dove for Mike as a gun went off.

Another shot and the man fell on his face. Grant had killed one of Al-Asaad's men who'd managed to sneak up the ramp.

Mike's heart kettledrummed in her chest, she couldn't breathe. *Get it together, get it together. Nicholas is safe.* When she realized what had happened, she yelled to Grant, "Thanks. Too close."

Grant laid down fire as Nicholas and Mike ran to the roof door, where Broussard was waiting. Mike took the key from Nicholas's bloody hand, managed to unlock the door.

Nicholas and Mike took turns shooting down the stairwell while Grant got the chopper going and Broussard got himself strapped in. The rotors began to whip, and they slammed the door closed and ran full speed across the roof, leaping into the helicopter as Grant lifted off. They landed in a heap.

She stared at him and started to laugh. "You're a bloody mess."

Nicholas gave her a crazed grin. "Only scratches from the broken glass, Mike."

She couldn't seem to stop laughing. Between hiccups, she got out, "You are an idiot, you know that?" But her eyes were bright, adrenaline riding her high. Broussard was in the front seat, breathing hard, staring at them.

Grant looked over his shoulder. "Good thing Jupiter was there to catch you. If you'd fallen on Uranus, you'd have been in real trouble."

And they all started to laugh.

CHAPTER FORTY-EIGHT

The ground disappeared beneath them. Grant said, "In all seriousness, guys, that was entirely too close. Where to?"

Mike said, "We didn't get into Patel's computer. We need to access it. Jean-Pierre, do your employees work from home, log into your systems remotely?"

Broussard turned in his seat. He had himself well in hand, as if a shoot-out with terrorists was only another walk in the park. "Yes, of course."

"Good. Tell us where Nevaeh Patel lives, and we'll try to access her files from her home computer."

He gave them an address, and Nicholas turned it into coordinates for Grant. Five minutes later, they set down on the lawn of a lovely country manor house. The sun was starting to rise, hitting the rooftop with gentle beams, making the stone glow yellow. Mike realized suddenly she felt bone weary. Two hours of sleep, a chopper crash, and a shoot-out was a lot for one day, even for her adrenaline-junkie-trained body. Nicholas and Grant had to be in the same shape as she was.

As the rotors spun down, Broussard said, "So much for surprising Dr. Patel."

Grant said, "Well, there are no lights on, nor any lights turning on. If someone set a chopper down on my lawn, it might wake me. She's most likely not here. We're breaking in?"

Nicholas nodded. "No choice. We need to get to her computer."

"Then let's hurry," Mike said. "Al-Asaad's men will track us, and I'd prefer not to have another shoot-out with them."

Broussard led them to Patel's garden door. "I haven't been here in over a year, but I know where she used to leave a key. It's difficult — how could she get caught up with a terrorist like Al-Asaad? And he's paying her? So after he builds the bomb, she'll put it into space? To explode and cause an EMP. Why?"

"We don't know the why yet, Jean-Pierre, but —" Nicholas's mobile rang. He looked at the screen, looked again. "It's my mum," he said blankly. "Hello, Mum? Ah, I'm sort of busy right now —"

"Nicholas, I know it's early and I probably woke you, but I had to tell you. I think I understand why Mr. Able was murdered. I discovered his sister was sneaking around with this Satanist cult leader in London. Mr. Able found out —"

"Mum, sounds like you've got it covered. I'm really sorry, but I have to go," and he punched off. He looked at them. "Ah, my mother's up to her ears in a murder mystery back home."

Mike hugged herself, she laughed so hard.

Nicholas's phone rang again. Nicholas said, "Okay, this call's from New York. Hello, Adam."

Adam and Gray were both on the line. Gray said, "Good, you're okay. What happened? We saw a team make entry, and picked up a heat bloom from an explosion."

"Grenade. We got a few of the terrorists. Are the local authorities on it yet?"

"Yes, full response at Galactus. Al-Asaad's team scattered when the chopper took off."

Nicholas said, "I think Al-Asaad will realize it makes sense for us to come to Patel's house, looking for her, which means we don't have much time. We're about to break into the house and access her computer, since we were chased out of Galactus before we were able to hook in. Can you redirect your eyes our way?"

He gave them the address and Gray waved at Lia Scott, their communications expert, who stepped away to have the satellite moved.

"Let us know if anyone comes for us, all right?"

Adam said, "Will do. I assume you'll be hooking me up to this off-site computer? I'm on standby, let me know when you're secure."

Mike put the comms unit back in her ear. "Grant, you keep watch. We'll go inside with Jean-Pierre and find the computer. Shout if anything, or anyone, happens by. We hardly need the Lyon *flics* on our backs right now."

Grant said, "Copy that."

Broussard gave her an arched eyebrow. " *'Flics'?* You've worked France before, haven't you? I thought the FBI was supposed to be an American-soil organization."

Mike adjusted her ponytail. Little bits of debris from the shot-out knee wall rained down onto the flagstones. "We're part of a special unit. We get to travel the world stopping bad guys. Now, Jean-Pierre, let's get inside and access Patel's computer."

Broussard unlocked the garden door, and they slipped inside. Nicholas used the flashlight on his phone instead of turning on the lights. Soon there would be enough light from outdoors to show them the way, but inside, with the curtains drawn, the rooms were dark.

Broussard looked around, confused. "It's like she's gone away for the season. She's closed up the house entirely."

Mike asked, "Where is her office?"

"I am not sure. I've only ever been downstairs. I don't recall seeing it."

Nicholas led them through the kitchen, a great hall, and up the staircase. "Spread out," he said, and they all went in different directions.

Mike found the office on the third floor. The room was beautiful: blond wood, floor-to-ceiling bookshelves, with a ladder allowing the occupant to get to the top levels. Half library, half office, and out the large windows, a view of beautiful gardens.

Patel's computer was a twenty-seven-inch iMac desktop, sitting on a desk devoid of anything but a mouse. Completely the opposite of her workspace at Galactus. Interesting.

Mike booted up the computer and called Adam.

"Okay, I'm here. What do you want me to do?"

"Computer?"

"iMac."

"Do you have the jump drive with the program Nicholas likes to use to break passwords?"

"Oh, yes. Hold on, it's in my bag."

She found the small jump drive, plugged it into the back of the screen. She toggled the mouse and the computer came on.

"Great, give it a few minutes, then we'll be in."

She could see the program running, the password box filling and emptying over and over, and then Adam said, "Got it. Open sesame."

The screen came to life. There was a super-high-resolution photo of Earth, close enough to see the layers of atmosphere and the curve of the planet. It was not the standard photo that came with an iMac's software. Mike wondered if it had been taken by Patel from the space station.

Files began flashing on the screen, and Mike sat back and waited, drumming her fingers on the desk.

Nicholas stuck his head in. "You all set?"

"Adam's running the files now."

"That will take a while. Come here, I want to show you something."

"Adam, I'll be right back."

His voice floated through the speaker of

her phone, distracted. "All good, Mike. Gonna take me a minute here anyway."

She stashed the phone in her back pocket and Nicholas walked her down the stairs to the second floor, where the living quarters were. His shirt was bloody, and Mike reached for him, wiping at the biggest stain. "We have to get you cleaned up. Surely there's a bathroom."

"Yeah, I'll clean up in a minute. Patel and Byrne don't share rooms. They each have their own. Byrne has a computer here, though, and I was able to force my way in. I'm scanning it now, and I think we might find some answers."

She followed him into a large bedroom with a separate sitting area. The room looked more like a high-end hotel suite, perfectly decorated in creams and blues, well balanced between priceless antiques and modern furniture. She had to hand it to them, Kiera Byrne and Nevaeh Patel had good taste.

"It's strange, it feels like they're basically roommates. Whatever, this is a pretty elaborate setup."

"Jean-Pierre said Byrne is incredibly protective, whatever that really means."

"It doesn't matter. From all we know, Byrne is going to fight to the death to protect Patel. What did you find?"

He sat her down in front of the computer, eased in next to her, and started opening files, moving her through his theories. "Schematics for the nuclear EMP. And here's a lengthy correspondence with someone who certainly seems to be — guess who? None other than our buddy Al-Asaad."

Mike said, "That seals it. They were working out their deal in their two recorded meets in Corsica. In 2015 and 2016. Of course, the plutonium was stolen in 2015. I suppose the meet in 2016 was finalizing everything, making the money deal and the delivery. I wonder how much Al-Asaad paid them? Millions?"

Nicholas said, "I wonder how they got hooked up with a terrorist?"

Mike said, "That's easy. Kiera was raised in the shadow of the IRA. Bombings, killings, you name it. She had contacts, don't doubt it."

"They probably communicated on the dark web. These emails are all coded, I'm running my encryption program on them right now. See? They date back to 2015, before the plutonium was stolen from Idaho, before their first meet in Corsica. Looks like Al-Asaad was looking for a way to build and launch a nuclear EMP himself, and Kiera Byrne and Patel had the solutions."

"Nicholas, I don't understand why Patel would do this. I mean, are we about to have a coordinated terrorist attack?"

His face was stark. "I think so, yes."

"We have to let New York know."

"I already have. I cloned the hard drive and sent it to Gray. He's running the analysis now."

"So what's our next step?"

"This."

He flipped to another screen and Mike saw what looked like a huge eggshell broken in half, with a massive telescope sticking out like a snout. It was surrounded by thick vegetation, palm trees, and unfamiliar lush green plants.

"What's this?"

"This, Michaela, is a refracting telescope. I think Patel built her own observatory somewhere. Using lots of Al-Asaad's money to supplement what she doubtless stole from Galactus."

"Why? To what end?"

"To this end. Listen."

Mike heard a woman's voice, hyper with joy. She was speaking jerkily, quickly. *"Everything is in place. I have the Heaven Stone so*

I am now immortal, so I can be one with you and live forever. I've placed the bomb aboard the satellite, the countdown is underway. Two more days, and there will be no more noise in the heavens, no more noise on Earth. And you will come to me."

A long pause.

Then, *"Yes, I will be high on my mountaintop awaiting you. In two days, at the apex of the lunar eclipse, the skies will glow with an explosion of such magnitude that, like I said, all the satellites will go dead, and then the world around us will be dark and silent, as I came to believe you wanted. That will be your moment, that is when you will be able to enter Earth's atmosphere unharmed. Earth will be open to you, and I will welcome you and we will begin our journey to save Earth."*

Another pause. This one even longer.

"Yes, we will bring peace to Earth together. I will rule, you at my side, my confidants, my advisers. No one will ever betray me again, all will revere me — and you."

He hit stop.

Mike said, "What in the world?"

"Out of this world, actually." Nicholas started running through the files. "There are hundreds of these recordings, all different. I sampled several from each year beginning in 2014, and there's a gradual change in Patel's attitude, in her plans. She begins speaking with optimism, nothing can stop her, can stop them, then gradually she becomes bitter, people betray her, her anger runs deep and deeper. She's frustrated."

"She sounded crazy."

"Yes. It seems Byrne's been recording her boss's conversations with — someone. What's strange is it's an open channel, but there's no one on the other end, no one I can hear, at least. Patel is having a conversation, but no one's talking back to her."

"Or maybe we're missing whoever is responding? Can the tapes be enhanced?"

"I'll send it to Gray and see if he can work his magic on it, but I don't know. What we have to do now, though, is figure out where this mountaintop she mentions might be. That's where she is, and she has the means to set off the nuke and cause the EMP."

"Well," Mike said, taking off her glasses and polishing them with the hem of her shirt, "this isn't a biggie. All we have to do is find a monster observatory with an unregistered telescope, and we find Patel. Only one problem. If this was recorded yesterday — I don't think we can have more than a day before she sets it off. When is the apex of the lunar eclipse?"

Nicholas opened a search engine. "Slightly

different times from different regions, but
—" He cursed under his breath. "We don't
have long, Mike. It's going to happen early
tomorrow morning."

Mike heard footsteps running toward
them, jumped to her feet, M4 at the ready.
It was Broussard, shouting, "They're here,
they're here. Al-Asaad's found us."

CHAPTER FORTY-NINE

Nicholas said, "Bloody hell, I'd hoped we'd have more time. Mike, give me your comms."

She handed her comms to Nicholas, who started shouting orders to Grant. Jean-Pierre came into the room. "Jean-Pierre, we'll have backup here shortly. Listen to me now. Did Dr. Patel ever talk to you about building her own observatory? Or purchasing an industrial-grade telescope?"

He looked taken aback. "An observatory? A telescope? Wait, I remember she did mention wanting to do something down the road, for educational purposes — she wanted to teach students about space from her perspective as a former astronaut. But it would take more money than she possibly has, grants, land somewhere. There would be records."

"Did she say where she wanted to build it?"

He shook his head.

The *rat-a-tat-tat* of gunfire started up. Mike gently shoved Broussard toward a chair. "Please stay here."

"No, absolutely not. I'm going with you. I'm not about to sit here and wait for them to come kill me. Give me a weapon, this is my fight, too."

Mike's phone started to ring. She gave him a long look, handed him a pistol. She grabbed her phone. Adam was still on the open line. She said, "Tell me what's happening."

"Satellite shows five bogeys at the back gate and — wait — five more at the front. And the Lyon police have been dispatched, someone tipped them off to your possible address. It's going to take them ten, fifteen minutes to get to you, though, you're well outside of the city limits."

"We're running low on ammo. Our attackers, they don't have air support, do they?"

"Not that I can see. They drove, they're not on foot."

"So if we can get to the helicopter, we can get away."

Mike heard Nicholas yelling, "Mike! Get down here!"

"Gotta go, Adam. Keep an eye out. And start looking for a high-end private observatory, on a mountaintop, probably funded by Dr. Patel herself. Maybe the answers will be in her computer files. Talk soon."

She grabbed Broussard's arm. "Let's go. We're all in this together now."

Nicholas and Grant had set up a barrier at the garden door, and were trying to figure out the best way to get back to the helicopter when Mike and Broussard ran out of the kitchen.

Mike said, "Adam says there are another five at the front. So they've got us on both sides."

Nicholas said, "I'm with you, Mike. We'll take the front. Jean-Pierre, you're with Grant. We only have to hold them off for, say, ten minutes, then I'm praying the police will be here."

Mike and Nicholas ran through the house and took up positions in the drawing room windows that gave out onto the sweeping front lawn.

Mike said, "These French doors are hardly going to hold up to a gunfight. If they breach, we're sunk."

"Well, you're an excellent shot, Agent Caine. I'll give you the right side, I'll take the left. Maybe we can catch them by surprise."

Mike glanced out past the edge of the

curtain. Nicholas went to the other side of the room, a good twenty feet away.

"They're making a straight-on approach, right up the hedgerow along the path. Ready?"

"As I ever will be."

She knocked a hole in the window pane and started shooting. She caught two, who went down and didn't move again, and the remaining three scattered, running away from her fire, directly into Nicholas's path. He picked them off, one, two, then a third man was left alone. He took off running back toward the gate. Mike pinged him in the upper thigh, and he dropped in the grass, writhing in pain. Just as quickly, he grew still.

"Good shooting, Mike."

They heard yelling from the back of the house, shouts and calls.

Nicholas said, "Grant needs help. You go, I'll stay here just in case there are more of them out there."

She ran back through the house to Grant's position, only to see Jean-Pierre on his back, a large red stain spreading across his chest.

She yelled, "Nicholas! We need you," and to Grant, "What happened?" She dropped to her knees and started putting pressure on the wound.

"Ricochet in the window. I took out three, but there's two more, and one of them's a damn good shot."

Broussard groaned. "Some help I am, you should have made me stay upstairs," and he gave her a heartbreaking smile.

Glass shattered around them. Grant called, "Mike, move him, I can't get a proper stance."

"Hold on." She dragged Broussard ten feet into the room. The wound was high up in his left chest, almost collarbone level. The blood leak was slow and steady, not gushing. "Lucky," she murmured to him. "You're going to be okay, I promise."

Nicholas came skidding into the room, cursed, then ripped off his already ruined shirt and tossed it to Mike.

"More pressure!"

She saw the blood starting to leak out his back. "I think you got even luckier, it looks like the bullet went through. Still, it's bleeding heavily. We need to get you to a hospital. My guys said the Lyon police are on their way."

"It hurts, I think I might —" Broussard shuddered and passed out. A blessing because it gave Mike the chance to really get the pressure to the right depth. The bleeding was slowing. She felt for Broussard's pulse — slow, a bit bumpy, but strong enough for the moment.

"Grant, do you have any hemostatic gauze in your bag?"

"QuikClot? Yes, my bag's on the back table there."

Nicholas shot three times out the window, then rushed to the bag, tossed it at Mike, and said, "For heaven's sake, Mike, get this on him and make another call for help. We're down to our last magazines."

They saw another man running wildly toward them, spraying the house with bullets. Suddenly, he was down. They stared at each other. Who had shot him? Not the Lyon police, they weren't here yet.

The gunfire slowed from outside. As they searched to find the shooter who'd killed the terrorist, they saw a man walking slowly toward the house, his hands laced on top of his head.

"Bloody hell, what the devil is this? Is he surrendering?"

Grant yelled at Nicholas, "Careful, careful, don't show yourself. He might be wearing a vest. We don't need him blowing us up. I think we should take him out."

As if the man knew what they were thinking, he ripped open his shirt, showing only dark skin and hair, and immediately clapped his hands back on top of his head.

Grant was shocked. "Bugger me sideways, mate, that's Al-Asaad himself! I recognize his photo. What is he up to?"

"You've got to be wrong, Grant," Nicholas said, crowding him away from the window.

"No, I'm sure. That's Al-Asaad approaching the door, hands up, shirt open, no bomb."

Mike squeezed in beside Nicholas. "Look, now he's getting on his knees. He still has his hands on his head, fingers laced, now he's down, face in the dirt."

"It's a trap, got to be," Grant said. "The minute we open the door, his remaining people will rush us."

"I don't think he has any remaining people," Nicholas said.

A voice shouted out, "Agents Drummond, Caine? May I have a word?"

The man sounded like a bloody American. What on earth was going on here?

Nicholas shouted, "Who are you?"

The man called back, "You probably know me as Khaleed Al-Asaad." And now they could hear the Southern in his voice. "But my real name is Vince Mills. I'm CIA."

CHAPTER FIFTY

Mike circled the man, his face still pressed against the ground, trying to figure out what was going on. CIA? Yeah, right. She wasn't about to take his word for it. She ordered him up, marched him into the dining room, and handcuffed him to a chair. He didn't say a word as she tied his legs to the chair. It wouldn't stop him from breaking free, but it would slow him down long enough so she could shoot him.

They stood back and eyed the man. He was dark as an Arab, with a full black beard, and go figure — he had a frigging Southern accent. Nicholas said, "All right, you're American and you claim you're CIA. Yet you attacked us, twice, and you weren't exactly firing blanks. You were trying to kill us, all of us. Why?"

Mills said, "Sorry about that, it wasn't intentional — well, it was intentional by my betraying captain, but I didn't intend it.

Here's what happened. I was told Broussard had escaped dying and Patel wanted him dead. She told me he was headed to Lyon, to Galactus. I don't know how she discovered that, but I told her I'd go after him. What I didn't tell her was I wanted to capture him, question him, see what he knew about this mess, if he knew where Patel and Byrne were.

"I guess Patel — or Kiera Byrne, more likely — made a sideways deal with my captain to make sure Broussard was killed this time. I couldn't believe it — he and my men betrayed me! *Me* — Al-Asaad! The meanest terrorist bugger imaginable." He sounded so outraged, Mike wanted to laugh. Instead, she kicked his leg. "Get on with this fine tale of yours."

"So I get to Galactus with ideas of capture, and my son-of-a-bitch captain and the men, unbeknownst to me, were there to kill him.

"He wasn't alone, there were you three. I didn't know who you were, maybe cohorts. My men started firing and then, of course, you guys fired back. Then everything went to hell in a handbasket."

He shrugged, had the gall to grin up at Mike.

She nearly punched him.

377

"I was trying to find out who you were, and my men figured they had a free pass to kill the lot of you along with Broussard. Then you managed to escape. I had no alternative but to come after you. You could have all been in on it together with Patel and she was double-crossing you, I just didn't know. I didn't find out who you were until a couple of minutes ago. You'd already taken down nearly all the men, including that treacherous captain of mine, and it was my pleasure to remove the last one. And then I surrendered.

"Hey, really good shooting. Gotta say, those individuals aren't — weren't — very nice, and some were new, but still fairly well trained. Unfortunately, as it turns out, as I already said, they weren't loyal to me but to my captain who talked them over, probably paid them." Another grin. "And here we are."

Nicholas stared down at Mills, his eyes narrowed, his arms crossed. He looked royally pissed. "You're going to have to make me believe you, mate. I'm having a hard time fathoming how this all worked."

"I'll fill in all the blanks, answer all your questions, but first, do you know where Kiera Byrne and Nevaeh Patel are?"

"We don't. We're looking for them right now."

"I assume you know about the nuke?"

"Yes, we do. How do you?"

"I'm supposed to. I'm CIA, as I told you. I've been deep undercover, playing Al-Asaad for two years now. Tough gig." Mills sounded almost chipper, and Nicholas wanted to boot him in the jaw. He was furious. Nobody had bothered alerting them about this undercover CIA nutter?

Vince Mills recognized the rage, didn't want to have his head knocked off, and said fast, "Kiera Byrne has been working with Khaleed Al-Asaad — that is, she's been working with me. No, don't shoot me. Here's what happened: Nearly three years ago, we — a CIA team — managed to kill Al-Asaad. Before we announced to the world we'd killed a major terrorist and received our just kudos, we heard about a theft of plutonium from the Idaho Research Facility. Only we knew about it, and we kept it under wraps.

"Then we heard chatter about a new player looking for someone to make a nuclear bomb. They had the plutonium, but not the nuclear material and expertise. The CIA decided Al-Asaad was the perfect go-between. I wasn't going to say no. The bombings, all the attacks, keeping him in character so the world still believed he was out there. Granted, there were a few bombings that were the doing of various unsavory people in the region, but we claimed responsibility.

"It wasn't hard. We made sure to have me in the vicinity, doctored a few photos, put out a massive online propaganda campaign. You know how easy it is to spread disinformation through the Internet, Drummond. I've been playing a top terrorist for the past two years. Look at me. I've got the thick wild beard, coal-dark eyes, and heavy brows. I blend right in.

"My assignment was to make contact, make a deal with them. I would pay them for the plutonium, build the bomb for them, let them inspect it to their heart's content, then arrest them at the last minute, hijack the nuke before they could blow up New York or whatever their target. They never told me." He took his first breath, shrugged.

"So I resurfaced as Al-Asaad and eventually managed to net both Kiera Byrne and Dr. Nevaeh Patel, as you already appear to know, which doesn't say much for CIA security. We struck a deal and they gave me the plutonium and I built the bomb. It had to be for real because I knew Patel was brilliant and she'd know if I'd screwed something up so it wouldn't work, plus none of us knew if Patel was really the one behind the entire deal — we were thinking North Korea — which is why I simply couldn't arrest both her and Byrne at the get-go. I had to play it out, find out the identity of this unknown person or country. Of course, turns out Patel was the head of the hydra.

"So now you know the whole story, and while all of this is fun, we need to find Patel and Byrne, because I'll bet they have the means to set off this bomb and wreak serious havoc."

Mike said, "Where'd the money come from to build the nuke?"

Mills looked embarrassed. "Well, a lot of it came from Al-Asaad because the CIA wanted the bomb built so they could nab Patel — or North Korea or whoever. For a while, we suspected Broussard. But, of course, he was clueless."

Mike said, "So over the two years, you funneled tons of money to Kiera Byrne and Dr. Nevaeh Patel."

"Listen, not very much at all came out of the taxpayers' wallets. You wouldn't believe how deep the pockets are of those sheikhs who have all the oil. When I told them it was a nuke and I'd blow up something big to cripple the demonic West, I got whatever I asked for."

Mike and Nicholas looked at each other. Mills hurried into speech. "And then I found out Patel was putting the nuke on a satellite."

Mike said, sarcasm riding high, "You had the nuke. You had this great plan. Tell us, how did Patel get her hands on the nuke?"

Mills said fast, "By the time we realized Patel was the brain behind the nuke, it was too late. She paid another terrorist group to steal it and then she acted fast, faster than we'd expected, and before we could bring her down, the nuke was launched aboard a Galactus satellite into space. And the bummer is I have no idea where she plans to detonate the bomb. And that's why I wanted to question Broussard. But hey, we'll find the satellite and bring both it and the nuke back to Earth. All will be well."

Mike could only stare at him. "You — the CIA — allowed a nuke to be made. On purpose. Are you a total idiot?"

"Maybe the decision-making along the line wasn't the best, but that's in the past. Now is what's important. We have to find Patel and stop her before a massive nuclear EMP disrupts all our communications, shuts down the electrical grid, and we're down and in chaos. I don't want to think about what would happen."

Nicholas said, "So you people march the world to the bitter edge, then assume you can make everything all right? I can't believe you — the CIA — pushed it this far. Who cares if there was someone behind Patel, like North Korea? You should have arrested both Patel and Byrne immediately."

Mills shook his head. "Trust me, in retrospect, we should have, but we wanted more than Patel and Byrne. Not only did we believe there was a bigger force behind them, we knew there were a half dozen major terrorist groups involved, and we wanted all of them, and that meant waiting."

Grant spoke for the first time. "The CIA set up this terrorist cover to get their hands on the stolen plutonium?"

"And who are you, boyo?"

Nicholas said, "You will tell him what he wants to know or I will personally ship you back to Syria or wherever your play-cave is."

Mills paused a moment, and Mike knew the instant he believed Nicholas. "Oh, all right. Yes, since 2015, as soon as we realized the scope of the theft of the plutonium, and we found out Kiera Byrne was involved, the op went into action. I met Patel a short time later, in Corsica. She's the brains of the two of them, but don't get me wrong, Kiera's tough and street smart, dangerous as a snake, but kinda cute, I thought, and well, hot."

Mike said, "You're saying you slept with her?"

"Well, yeah, but come to find out she really doesn't swing that way. Look, I never meant to hurt you guys, or Broussard. Hey, guys — ah, girl — you do know this is highly classified, need-to-know only."

Nicholas said in a voice as dry as sand, "Trust me, we have clearance."

"Yeah, I know who you guys are. But this one? He's a civilian."

Mike got in his face. "Agent Drummond is a nice man. Me, not so much. You will tell Mr. Thornton everything he wants to know. You will tell the Easter Bunny everything if I tell you to, or I'll pull out your tongue." And she leaned even closer, and whispered, "Fear me."

Mills believed her. "All right, whatever you say. Listen, I'm really Vince Mills, CIA. My dad's name is Bob Mills, he's a straight-up Virginian, a bank manager, but my mother is Pakistani and I inherited both her looks and her language skills. Got recruited by the Company in college and have been in the field undercover pretty much my whole career, working in the Middle East theater. Really, guys, how many times do I have to repeat myself?"

"As many times as we want," Mike said. "Now, shut up."

Nicholas studied Vince Mills, nice American name. His story rang true, it did sound like a typical CIA maneuver. He said, "We have to confirm this."

"We're running out of time here. Oh, all right, call Langley, talk to my boss, Mr. Grace. Actually, you know him, don't you?"

A strange European *wa-a wa-a* siren's wail began to grow louder. Mike glanced out the window. The Lyon police and first responders were coming up the road toward the drive. Big surprise — it was littered with bodies.

Mills said, "Now, if you don't mind, I need you to keep the police off my back while I have a chat with Mr. Broussard. He's got to know where Patel and Byrne have gone."

Nicholas said, "We already told you, he doesn't know. And you're not even going to say hello to him until we confirm your identity. He was shot, needs to go to hospital."

Mills went to stand, realized he couldn't. "Then hurry up and call Langley, talk to Mr. Grace. Time's a-wastin'."

Nicholas said, "Grant, cover him, please. Mike, with me."

Grant pulled Nicholas to one side, said, "We need to get Broussard to hospital. He's still unconscious, his pulse is too sketchy."

"I hear you. Give us a moment."

In the kitchen, Nicholas pulled his hands through his hair. Little bits of dirt and glass rained down on Patel's floors. "I hate this — that character is CIA, and what's worse, I believe him. Imagine, playing the notorious terrorist Al-Asaad, working with Byrne and Patel. And we didn't know a blessed thing about it."

Mike said, "Nicholas, why would anyone bother telling us? Imagine, his handler is Carlton Grace. A multiyear undercover op in a terror organization sounds just like him. We need to confirm Mills's story. Get Adam on the phone."

Adam's voice came through. "Good timing, was about to call you. I think I have a lead on the telescope."

CHAPTER FIFTY-ONE

T-MINUS 20 HOURS

Nicholas said, "Tell me."

"It was delivered to Colombo, Sri Lanka, in 2016. I traced it to a mountain, dead center in the middle of the country. And there's a very good chance Patel is there, too. She has a set of architectural drawings on her computer, very detailed, and there are several references to 'Aquarius.' I think that might be the name of her observatory. I've sent them to you. Nicholas, you're going to want to check this out. I found them in an old cache. They'd been deleted, were several years old. The files were degraded. I don't have an exact location.

"But I did match a tail number of a deadheading jet that landed in Colombo, Sri Lanka, a couple of days ago. Her name wasn't listed, and I'm trying to get their CCTV to look for a facial match. But my gut says it's her."

"Sloppy of her. Sounds like she's not trying to cover her tracks anymore. Good job, Adam, thank you. Listen, I have an emergency. We need to verify a set of bona fides with Carlton Grace from CIA. Get him for us, I don't care where he is. Crash their mainframe, break down the doors, whatever you need to do. We must speak with him immediately. If you get any resistance, call the White House, get Vice President Sloan on the phone, and tell her it's life or death."

"Jeez, okay. What are we confirming?"

"Just get me Grace. I'll handle the rest."

"Copy that. I'll ring you back when I have him."

And he was gone.

Nicholas smiled at Mike. "I'm so glad Adam came into the light." He had his tablet out, found the map. "Well, Sri Lanka is one of the places that will experience the full lunar eclipse." He looked up, stared at Mike. "My God, she's timed this down to the minute and place. What are the odds, Mike? Surely this is where we'll find the controls to the nuke. But you know, my biggest question is, why is she doing this?"

"I might be making a leap here, Nicholas. But say Patel wasn't happy about being sacked from NASA. Could she be trying to get revenge on them somehow? Or maybe she blames her co-astronauts on the ISS."

Nicholas said, "I don't think you're far afield. From the snippets of her conversations with — we still don't have a clue who — she got progressively more angry, more bitter. There was hate there, and then, later, the thirst for power. Are we talking revenge, too? Could she be going after the International Space Station? Can you imagine a nuclear bomb going off in space, taking out the space station? It would halt a huge swath of the space program in its tracks. Not to mention the astronauts aboard who would die, and decades of research destroyed. The space station is hardened against solar flares and other types of natural EMPs, but a bomb of this magnitude — I'm not sure they could survive it, even with precautions. And assuming it doesn't take a direct hit, if it couldn't be powered because of an EMP, it would degrade into orbit and fall to Earth."

Mike nodded. "We'd better look at its orbit, see where it's going to be at the apex of the lunar eclipse.

He typed it in. "You nailed it. The ISS will be passing over the Sri Lanka area moments after the eclipse begins its hour and a half of totality."

"Here's my question. If she's in Sri Lanka, and the ISS will be overhead and the moon will be in eclipse — and assuming the nuke is in a low Earth orbit — won't she be directly in the line of the blast? That would make it a suicide mission."

"I don't know, Mike. We're going to have to hunt her down, see what all this is really about."

"Yep, find out everything before the bomb goes off. Hey, not all that much for us to do. And we have that bearded idiot in there to contend with."

The sirens wailed to an ear-splitting crescendo, then squawked as they shut off suddenly. There were shouts from the front lawn.

Nicholas said, "They saw the bodies, I assume."

"This is insane." Mike cursed. Nicholas was so shocked, he stared at her. "Sorry, but like you, I know Mills is telling the truth. And I'd really like to belt him. And Carlton Grace. Hey, the whole lot of them for dealing this down to the wire."

"Agreed, but first things first. Let's focus on getting Broussard patched up and safe. Then we can deal with Mills — and Patel."

They heard Mills arguing with Grant even before they got back to the dining room.

"Don't you understand? You have to let me loose, if they see me there's a good chance they're going to take one look and see Khaleed Al-Asaad. They'll take me into custody and sort through the reality later. It'll blow this entire operation. Look, there's a nuke, and we've got to stop it."

Nicholas said from the doorway, "Grant, let's play it this way. Go let in the police. Mike and I will take care of him."

Grant gestured at his dirty, bloody clothes. "We'll be lucky if they don't cuff me on sight."

Nicholas smiled. "You're married to Kitsune. I'm betting you can talk your way out of anything."

Nicholas took off the restraints, pulled Mills to his feet, and marched him from the room, Mike covering him. She was down to the last few bullets in her magazine, but that was enough to take out this bozo if he tried anything.

Grant was yelling out the door now, "I don't speak French, I'm a British citizen, I work for Blue Mountain. We have a wounded man here, we need a medic and an ambulance, stat."

Mike said, "I hear one of the police speaking English. Good. No one's going to shoot Grant, not right away, at least."

Nicholas pushed Mills into a small parlor off the dining room, shoved him into a chair. "Don't move a muscle."

"No need to get rough, Agent Drummond. I'm on your side."

"Trust me, it's to your benefit to shut up, mate. It's been a bloody long twenty-four hours and I don't see it getting any better."

"Time is running out. If the nuke goes off —"

"I told you to shut up."

Nicholas's phone rang, a 202 area code. D.C. "Yes?"

"Agent Drummond? Carlton Grace. Didn't expect our paths to cross again so soon."

"Nor did I. We're secure, I assume?"

"Yes. Speak your mind, and make it fast, I'm busy here."

"I have Vince Mills here, he told us a wild-hair tale only you bozos at the CIA could come up with. Do you claim him?"

Grace started to chuckle. "However did you manage to hook up with Vinny? And what's he doing telling you his name?"

"He's told us everything. Like you, evidently, we're also on the trail of this nuke EMP. Are we on the same page now?"

A sharp breath, then Grace sighed. "Why am I not surprised you're involved, Drummond? We're getting down to the wire. Anything you can do to help secure the nuke, our resources and assets are yours. Mills has been on the hunt for two years now. He's legit. He almost had eyes on it, too, until last week when everything went south. How'd you get involved?"

"Through Jean-Pierre Broussard. A friend is on his security detail. They were on the yacht that went down. We went for the friend, got wrapped up in stopping this nuke."

"Wait. Broussard is alive?"

"Yes."

"Excellent. Does he know where Patel is going to detonate it?"

"He doesn't. But we're nearly certain it's in Sri Lanka. There's a lunar eclipse at one a.m. there, and we think the EMP may be timed to go off at the eclipse's apex. Small problem: We don't have a specific location outside of central Sri Lanka yet, and we're in Lyon, France, right now. By my calculations, seeing as it's eight a.m. now and it's at least a ten-hour flight, plus a three-hour time differential in their favor, I don't know how we're going to make it in time to stop it. And this is assuming she is indeed in Sri Lanka."

"We can rally some assets. Help you track

them, and if they're found, get you there. We have people on the ground in Sri Lanka. We can send them along with you."

"That's a lot to coordinate."

Grace said simply, "I'm a good coordinator. It's what I do best. How do you propose tracking them?"

"I could make a cell phone call sharing the good news Jean-Pierre Broussard is alive. That would do it. Especially if the call came from Patel and Byrne's business partner, Al-Asaad."

Grace said, "We've tried it. She'll scramble the call. They've always been exceedingly careful with their communications. We've never been able to pinpoint Byrne, it's part of our problems with this. They're very smart."

"I'm not worried about what she says. I want to verify she's in Sri Lanka. A call from a trusted source, with the infrastructure in place to capture its location, or at least triangulate —"

"I know what you're thinking. She uses a satellite phone that has tracking, yes, but she always, always has it turned off. And you know a satellite's tracking is much broader than a cell phone tower. When she has the tracker off, we have one chance, only one, that the phone might register a single ping before it scrambles. Thing is, the ping is rerouted multiple times. So far, we've never been able to capture it. We've tried this before, following Byrne. She's never had the GPS on. She's been very careful."

"We have nothing to lose trying again, and this time, we'll use a deencryption tool of my own design. See if it works."

There was a slight pause, then, "You're telling me you have better toys than the CIA?"

"Not better, necessarily. Different."

"By all means, then, let's try. What sort of gear would you need?"

Nicholas said, "I need the brand and age of the sat phone, and a computer line."

"You know, if this works, you may have to share the protocol with us. Ah, in the spirit of national security. Be at the Mont Verdun Air Base in an hour. I'll have everything you need waiting. Now, may I speak to Vince?"

Nicholas turned on the speaker. "Talk away."

Grace said, "Privately, Drummond."

"Sorry, Mr. Grace."

"Fine. Have it your way." Grace changed to Arabic, had a short, terse conversation with Mills. Nicholas caught a few words — he was by no means fluent, but he'd spent enough time in the Middle East to understand a bit — *help, trust,* and a highly idiomatic version of *don't cock it up.*

Then there was a click. Grace was gone.

"Might we dispense with the handcuffs now, Drummond? We need to get to the airbase pronto."

"You have a plan for waltzing past the Lyon police, do you?"

"Waltzing, no." He gestured toward the window, thought a moment, then grinned. "But I assume there might be a few gurneys and body bags out there, don't you?"

CHAPTER FIFTY-TWO

Boise, Idaho
July 2015

Nevaeh stood near Paulie's diner, rain striking her like pellets. She was wearing a low-brimmed hat and sunglasses, but no raincoat. No matter, she was here to do a job and there was nothing that could stop her.

She glanced at her watch. Three minutes late.

Is he going to bail on us? After all the work, the planning? No, no way. Kiera has his wife tied up and gagged, her life depends on him showing up.

There. A light blue Ford pickup pulled into the lot. Nevaeh took a last glance around the diner, stepped from the shadows, and got into the passenger seat, slammed the door.

She never looked at him, only said, "All right. Let's go."

"No way, not until I know my wife is all right."

Nevaeh turned, leveled a look at him. "She'll be dead within the minute if you don't start driving. Now."

He put the truck in gear.

"Drive faster. The sooner we finish this exchange the sooner you get to see your wife. You shouldn't have tried to back out, it was a serious mistake on your part."

He was quiet, driving carefully, maddeningly slow. "How much do you know about plutonium?"

"Enough to know I've paid you handsomely to bring it to me. And that's all you need to know."

"I'm going to lose my job if they ever find out I've stolen the plutonium. Maybe even go to jail."

"Really? You're worried about losing your job now? Going to jail? It didn't seem to bother you when I paid you one hundred thousand dollars."

"How are you planning to get this on a plane? Unless you have a private jet — oh, of course you do." He sighed deeply, kept driving. Slow, too slow. She wanted to slam her fist into his skinny jaw, get his attention.

His hands were white on the wheel. The wipers slapped against the windshield, merely spreading the intense rain over the glass instead of clearing it away.

"You're going to build a nuke, aren't you?"

She heard the fear in his voice, the awful knowledge that he would be responsible. "Yes, but rest assured, it's not going to hurt anyone. It's a deterrent, nothing more. We can't have these yahoo countries threatening the United States and Europe with their own versions. And our governments can't be openly building deterrents, or else it would seem like an open threat. They've hired us to go this back route. You've done your country a great service, Eddie. Anyone tries to strike us, you'll be a hero."

"But my wife —"

"Your wife will be fine if you give me the plutonium and keep your mouth shut."

"But if someone gets ahold of the plutonium, builds a nuke, then — you're talking about a lot of lives. This much plutonium — the yield of the bomb could take out the population of Brooklyn if it's mishandled."

Nevaeh smiled sweetly. "You're a gambler, Eddie. It's how we found you in the first place. You made yourself a target. Your debts have grown so large there is no recovering from it, and you knew this, so you agreed to sell us the plutonium to get yourself out of debt. And so far, you've been doing everything right, and if you keep it up, you're going to get the money to wipe your slate clean, and see your wife.

"This is all you need to know. Keep driving."

Finally, Dr. Edward Linton turned off the divided highway into what looked like an endless field of corn. After bumping a mile up the road, Nevaeh saw a small barn. He pulled to the front.

He said, "Wait here," but she ignored him, got out of the car, ducked her head to keep the rain out of her eyes. He slid open the barn door. The space was long empty but still smelled of old hay and manure. Inside, a four-foot-by-three-foot lead-lined box rested on top of a roughhewn table. It was surprisingly small, considering. Small, but heavy.

"This is it? The plutonium?"

"It is."

Nevaeh said, "Thank you, Eddie. You've been most useful." The suppressed gun kicked in her hand, there so quickly he didn't even have a chance to register that she'd drawn it from the holster inside her belt.

Eddie fell, sprawled onto the leftover wisps of hay, blood leaking from his head.

It only took her a few minutes to clean

the scene, collect Eddie's blood in a Tupperware container, stash his body in his truck. The lead box was heavy, but Nevaeh was strong, and she quickly had it wrestled into the back of Eddie's truck, alongside his cooling body.

She plopped his baseball cap on her head and set out for his house.

Poor Eddie. He didn't even know his wife had been dead for hours. Like she'd let them live. For a smart man, a frigging scientist, he'd made very poor decisions.

Nevaeh stopped his truck by her car and stashed the box in the trunk. Imagine, what was inside that box would punch a hole in the atmosphere.

All hail technology.

When she reached Dr. Linton's house, she pulled into the garage. Kiera was inside. She had turned the air conditioner to its lowest setting; the house was freezing, helping the crime-scene narrative she was about to create.

"Glad you're here, I'm nearly frozen. Is he dead?"

"As a doornail. Help me get him into place."

They carried Eddie's body into the living room, sat him across from his wife. Nevaeh turned the air back to its normal setting, watched Kiera doctor the scene to her liking. She placed the gun in his hand and took one shot to make sure there was gunpowder residue spread on him. She microwaved the blood, then spread it until the blood pool was just so. The note, crumpled and bloody on his chest, was the finishing touch.

Everyone knew the Lintons were having money troubles. Would he do such a thing — a murder-suicide? Not out of the bounds of reason. Such a terrible event. Good plan.

Finally, they wiped down everything, even though they were both wearing gloves, and went over Eddie's truck. Kiera put the keys in the sun visor and locked the doors. They jogged through the cornfields, wet with the heavy rain, back to their car.

Kiera said, "It's a long drive. Why don't I take the wheel first, so you can get some sleep?"

Nevaeh nodded and tossed her the keys. She watched the skyline of Boise disappear in the rearview as they started south. Then she closed her eyes. *It's done. Finally, things are beginning to fall into place.*

She heard a soft sibilant voice whisper against her ear, *Yes, everything is falling into place. It is all you told us it would be.*

CHAPTER FIFTY-THREE

Houston
July 2015

The road trip from Boise to Houston was long, twenty-eight hours, through Utah and the southwest tip of Colorado before smoothing into the long flatlands along the Texas highway. They'd stopped overnight at a motel in Four Corners, the area where the borders of Utah, Colorado, New Mexico, and Arizona touched, but Nevaeh couldn't sleep more than a couple of hours. She was vibrating with excitement and anticipation, and the Numen were as well. She'd gone over in detail her need to destroy the people who'd destroyed her, and they'd agreed.

Soon, she'd bring them to Earth. And the beginning was in a box in the trunk of the car.

Finally, in the early evening of the second day, they saw the lights of Houston.

Nevaeh knew Rebecca Holloway's address from a long-ago party during astronaut training. She lived in an ostentatious Spanish-style five-bedroom near the Bay Oaks Country Club in Clear Lake, full of travertine floors and a giant lagoon pool in the backyard. Holloway was childless — probably a good thing, she had little compassion and no discernible maternal instincts, rare for a psychiatrist — and her ex-husband worked in the oil business, traveled out of town when he wasn't drunk at the clubhouse.

Poor, lonely Dr. Holloway, all alone in that massive house.

Nevaeh couldn't help but smile.

The drive was gated, but the gate wasn't too tall. Thank goodness there was no one at the little gatehouse at the entrance to the neighborhood — it was only for show. The neighbors here weren't on top of each other, either. Not as easy to slip in unnoticed as it had been in New York, but easy enough.

Kiera pulled to the curb several blocks away, turned and asked, "Are you absolutely sure you don't want me?"

"We've been over this. Now, I will see you at our arranged meeting site in one hour. If I have a problem, I'll call."

Nevaeh climbed out of the car. She was

dressed in jogging clothes, black leggings and a black top, and a baseball cap, her hair tucked inside. She imagined there would be security cameras, so she was very careful approaching the house.

It was nearly ten o'clock, fully dark now. Perfect. She inserted her earbuds and jogged to Holloway's gate. She waited, heard nothing, saw no one. She slipped over the black metal gate and made her way to the back door.

She had a gun with her, but she didn't want to use it. Actually striking down Fontaine had been so satisfying, much more so than simply shooting Eddie.

Another accident, that would do it.

Nevaeh was inside the house two minutes later. Kiera had done reconnaissance on Holloway, too. If she was sticking to her routine, Holloway should be getting ready for bed now, in good time to get up tomorrow and maybe ruin another astronaut's life. Nevaeh went upstairs slowly, her sneakers silent on the carpeted treads. She didn't hear anything. She looked through the rooms on the second floor, but no one was there.

She knew Holloway was here, she'd seen two cars in the garage. Where was the bitch?

She made her way back downstairs, looking into every room — so many, musty with disuse, and no one here but her.

Nevaeh went through the kitchen, silently opened the back door, and stared out onto the patio. She heard music, the strains of a Chopin étude.

She stood in the shadows and watched Rebecca Holloway methodically swim laps. Her strokes were smooth and steady. She normally swam in the morning before work. Why the change in her schedule?

Nevaeh went to the deep end, lay down on her stomach, and waited. When Holloway started to tuck and turn, Nevaeh reached out a hand and grabbed a hank of Holloway's streaming dark hair.

Surprised, Holloway gasped and jerked, brought up flailing arms, but Nevaeh had a brutal grip on her long hair and pulled hard, brought her head out of the water. She stared into Holloway's shocked eyes. She saw the recognition, then only a brief instant of relief, gone quickly enough.

"Hello, Dr. Holloway. I'll bet you never expected to see me, did you? Did you know I killed Dr. Fontaine? Both of you conferred and decided I was crazy. You always hated me, didn't you? Made up stories about me because you were jealous. You tried your best to destroy me, but you didn't. And now

I'm going to kill you."

Holloway began fighting her in earnest, and she was strong. No choice. Nevaeh quickly brought up her gun and struck her hard on the side of the head. It didn't knock her out, but it stunned her. Nevaeh leaned close, twisted Holloway's long hair around her fist. "I waited to kill you last, my dessert, you could say. I thought about killing Franklin, but decided his only crime was his weakness. He was afraid of you. But I'm not."

Holloway stared up at her with blind eyes. "You think I betrayed you? That I lied? I didn't, I didn't. I only did my job. You were crazy then, you're crazier now. You can't kill me, you —"

"Goodbye, you worthless bitch." Nevaeh shoved her head underwater and held her down, difficult because even stunned, the woman was amazingly strong. Finally Holloway slowly weakened, finally she stopped thrashing. Another minute, Nevaeh counted it off in her head, then one more for good measure. She was smiling, singing under her breath, *"Ding, dong, the witch is dead."*

She let her go and shoved. She slowly rose, pulled the wet strands of black hair from between her fingers. She was soaked from Holloway's struggling, even her hair was wet. Who cared? She watched Holloway float away, barely disturbing the surface, then, ever so slowly, she watched her sink to the bottom of the pool.

Nevaeh breathed in the hot, humid night air. She felt exhilarated.

Such a terrible accident. Poor Dr. Holloway had drowned in her beautiful Olympic-size swimming pool.

Poor old Rebecca.

She sang to the Numen as she climbed back over the gate, *"She's dead, she's dead, she's dead."* And the Numen sang back to her, *Yes, she's dead, she's dead, she's dead.*

CHAPTER FIFTY-FOUR

T-MINUS 18 HOURS

CIA Headquarters
Langley, Virginia

Carlton Grace paced his office as he waited for the telecon to start. He had a briefing at the White House in forty minutes and he needed as much background as he could get to fill in the blanks on Nevaeh Patel.

If only Strategic Command could find the satellite. If they knew for sure whether Patel had the means to blow it up remotely, or if it was on some sort of timer. Then again, they weren't used to dealing with actual EMP threats. Who knew what Patel and Byrne had managed to come up with?

He gulped down some water and forced himself to stop glancing at his watch. Then he closed his eyes. *Too long, you waited too long. It's your fault, your fault, if the bomb goes off.*

Finally, the screen flickered to life and a man with gray hair and a matching mustache, wearing a yellow short-sleeved button-down, came into view. He had on thin silver wire-rimmed glasses and looked like everyone's favorite grandfather. It was the famed NASA flight director himself, Dr. Franklin Norgate.

"Mr. Grace? I understand you're CIA. What's the matter? They said this was an emergency. What's happening?"

"I apologize for disturbing you at home but we need to talk about your former astronaut Nevaeh Patel. I know you were asked to make available the tapes showing her spacewalk. You've signed the nondisclosure?"

"I have, though it's hardly necessary. I have clearance."

"Not for this, you don't. We are tracking the movements of a nuclear EMP and we think Dr. Patel is behind it. You look shocked, and I don't blame you. But believe me when I say she's been playing a long game and we're out of time. I need to know her state of mind, see if I can get any clues to what she's up to, and you're the one who knew her best. You're also the reason she's no longer an astronaut, which could mean you're in danger."

Norgate was shaking his head in disbelief. "No, this can't be true, there's no way. Yes, nearly a decade ago, Nevaeh was disturbed, angry she'd been grounded, but for her to set off a nuclear EMP? It's a long way from hearing voices in space to destroying a large segment of society."

"It is, Mr. Norgate, no question, but here are the facts: She managed to stow the bomb on a satellite that was launched on July 14, and her company, Galactus, claims the satellite wasn't inserted into orbit. We believe this was a lie. We believe she programmed it to be on a different, unexpected elliptical. We also believe it is designed to go off during the apex of the lunar eclipse tonight, which is going to coincide with the passage of the International Space Station over Nepal. We are making an educated guess as to where it's going to go off, but the information we've pulled together is sound. Now, I need the tapes from her spacewalk. She claimed she met up with space aliens and they saved her life. And I need the tapes immediately."

"Yes, yes, I have the tapes ready." He moved out of the camera's view and a screen flickered to life.

Norgate fast-forwarded through the six hours of footage to the moment Patel

411

drifted away. "I know it's hard to see everything, the cameras missed a portion of the event when they repositioned. It's a full fifteen seconds of her spinning, then she resists the spin, turns, and comes back to the hand rungs."

"Okay. So how'd she do it?"

"Remember, this was early on, things are tighter now, so we will never have this happen again. You can see she and Verlander get their lines crossed somehow, and she tries to get them untangled. The cables snap, and with the sudden pressure, the trailing line breaks. Somehow, she released the main safety line when she was doing that. Or maybe it yanked free, we don't know. Her third failsafe was a jet pack — what's known as Simplified Aid for EVA Rescue, or SAFER. It's basically a life preserver for astronauts. According to her colleagues, she activated it and propelled herself in the right direction. It was a smart move, gutsy. If she'd activated when she was facing the wrong direction she could have shot herself farther away from the ISS and Verlander wouldn't have been there to catch her. We couldn't move the robotic arm to save her in time, either. It was a fluke, and we were lucky she made it back in one piece. We changed a few things on the suits and our procedures afterward to make sure it never happens again."

He chewed a lip, then said, "Watch where I point, okay?" Norgate rewound the video, hit play. "See here? The video should show the vapor from the SAFER. It's nitrogen gas propulsion. There is none. But by the time anyone thought to check, the pack had been reset. We have no way to prove or disprove she actually used it. She claimed it didn't work, that the — Numen, she calls them — pushed her back to the hand rungs. We've never told anyone that fact, Mr. Grace. I trust you will only use it if absolutely necessary."

Grace said, "Back up. So it's possible she's been telling the truth all this time?"

"I'm supposed to say no, absolutely not."

"I see. Let's hear what her fellow astronauts are saying."

Norgate hit play. Patel's voice was clear on the tape.

"How do you know my name?"

Grace said, "She's talking to someone, who's she talking to?"

"We don't know. It wasn't an appropriate response to anything anyone was saying to her. She's wearing what we call a Snoopy cap, which allows for regular communication with the ISS and command. She wasn't talking to us, responding to us, or otherwise in conversation with us."

Patel again: *"I will tell them. Thank you for saving my life."*

Norgate said, "Then she's back on the hand grip. Verlander grabbed her, maneuvered her into the airlock. We hastened the depressurization, blew out Verlander's eardrums doing it, but we got her back inside the station. Doc checked her over, we talked to her extensively. Or tried. She wasn't making sense, but we assumed that was part of the — event." He paused, face strained in recall. "It was a bad day."

"There's an understatement. What was she saying?"

"She was talking about 'new men.' We didn't know until later she meant the Numen. Dictionary says Numen are a divine spirit. Knowing the stress this event caused, we chalked it up to her panicking, losing her breath, having a few moments of hypoxia which caused a hallucination, though she said she didn't see anything, only felt their presence and heard the words."

"Did anyone talk to her fellow astronauts on the space station? What did they say about the incident?"

"Sure, everyone was thoroughly debriefed. We take accidents seriously, Mr. Grace.

When she came back in, she was talking crazy, so we made the decision to sedate her. When she woke up, she kept insisting there were beings outside the space station. An alien race who wanted to bring us peace. We did a full workup, of course, but it didn't show anything. She couldn't shake it. The decision was made to end her mission early, rotate her off the space station when the next round of astronauts came up. She had another few months on her tour, but by then — her actions were colored by this event. We had no choice but to bring her home."

"Who made that decision?"

"Our flight psychiatrist, Dr. Rebecca Holloway. She worked closely with Nevaeh and all the team from the beginning of their mission two years earlier. You can't talk to her, though. She's deceased, drowned in her pool. She'd recently been through a divorce, so they looked at her husband, but found nothing. He was out of town. They ruled it an accidental drowning.

"Anyway, once Nevaeh was back on Earth, Dr. Holloway spent a lot of time with her, then decided to ground her. Nevaeh didn't take it well. She quit, and I didn't hear from her for a year. She came back out of the blue asking to be assigned a new mission.

to space she was devastated."

Grace said, "Just so you know, we think it's very likely Dr. Holloway was murdered. We have a record of Dr. Patel and her bodyguard in Houston the week Holloway died. They were also in Idaho the same week. She left behind two bodies, one of which was the research scientist who worked at the Idaho Research Facility. Made it look like a murder-suicide."

"The Idaho Research Facility, they're the ones who've been in the news this week for misplacing some plutonium?"

"The very same."

Franklin said, "You think Nevaeh had something to do with all these deaths? That's preposterous."

"Were you aware Dr. Claire Fontaine is also dead? She's the psychiatrist Patel consulted a year after she was grounded, before she came and talked to you. Patel and her bodyguard were in New York the same time of Fontaine's death. She, too, was ruled an accidental death, a slip in the shower. But we believe Patel murdered her."

Norgate was silent a moment. "I don't know, really, but I do know Dr. Holloway was jealous of Patel, perhaps treated her unfairly, and that's why Nevaeh went to

New York to this other psychiatrist. She and Holloway spoke."

"Patel saw this as a betrayal and so she murdered her. Revenge. Makes sense."

Franklin rubbed a hand across his face. "I can't accept it, I can't —"

"Considering the attack on Jean-Pierre Broussard and his ship a few days ago, I would have to say the pattern is evident. Did she ever feel you betrayed her, Dr. Norgate?"

"No, not really."

Grace said, "If Patel is capable of stealing plutonium to have a nuke made, she is fully capable of murdering millions. She's capable of murdering you as well."

Norgate looked devastated. "I haven't talked to her in almost six years. But I'll tell you this. If she's been planning to set off a nuke, she'll have thought through every permutation. She's brilliant, scary brilliant. If she doesn't have every tool at her disposal, then she's fully capable of obtaining whatever she needs to make this happen."

CHAPTER FIFTY-FIVE

T-MINUS 18 HOURS

Nevaeh Patel's Chateau
Lyon, France

Mike was relieved to see Broussard not only conscious again but also getting back some color. She asked the pink-cheeked French EMT whose name tag read D. LOUÇON, "How's he doing?"

In heavily accented English, Louçon said, "Well, I think. The bullet passed through below his collarbone, just here. It is most likely cracked, and I believe his lung to be impacted as well, though it has not fully collapsed. He will need surgery."

Mike nodded, said to Broussard, "You heard that? You're going to be okay, only a bit of surgery. Are you up to talking to me, Jean-Pierre?"

"Of course. What can I do, Mike?"

"Tell me how you knew where to find the

Flor de la Mar."

"Three years of intense study, and some natural supposition, I suppose. And luck."

"So no maps, nothing physical? Gut instinct?"

He managed a weak smile. "I certainly consulted many old maps. And journals. The *Flor de la Mar* is one of the richest lost ships in history, as you already know. Many people have searched for it. I spent three years studying its possible whereabouts. Why do you want to know this now?"

"Jean-Pierre, did it emit some sort of electrical charge that enabled you to locate it?"

"No, but the Holy Grail did."

"You know from the moment you touched the stone? How?"

"I just knew. And it did have a charge to it, I suppose one could call it electrical. But it was really something else entirely. I felt like the clock had turned back. I was young again, invincible, strong, ready to take on anything, and I felt a sense of rightness, of peace." He thought back, remembered how his knee no longer ached. "It was as if all my blood rose to the surface in greeting, and the stone vibrated in response. I suppose the very best description is it was like holding a purring cat, so it definitely must have been giving off some sort of audible vibration. You'd have to have an extremely sensitive microphone to pick it up, though. I don't know if anything exists so powerful that it could pick up the Grail's heartbeat from afar."

"You speak of it as if it were alive, in some way."

"Oh, it is, not in the way you believe, not a human sort of alive, but when I held it, I felt like it was becoming part of me. You know only those who are selfless, those who are worthy, can claim the Grail. I know I am not worthy." He looked at her closely, drew a breath. "Mike, I told the Grail I wasn't worthy, I was only the messenger, but still it favored me. But the person to whom the Grail must truly belong is more than worthy, she's pure, incandescent, a bright light." His breath hitched.

"Who is this person, Jean-Pierre?"

"It's my daughter, Emilie. She is dying. She has la sclérose latérale amyotrophique."

"I'm sorry, I don't understand. What is that in English?"

He said, "It is amyotrophic lateral sclerosis. It's called ALS, Mike, a death sentence. Nothing can help. It can kill quickly, in months, or it can go years, like Stephen Hawking. When Emilie's leg muscles became weak — we learned it is the most common symptom to begin ALS — she was diagnosed. I didn't know what to do. I railed against fate. It was so unfair, why my daughter? Why Emilie, she is so honorable, kind, humble. She was studying medicine at the Sorbonne. She is only twenty-one.

"All my wealth, all my resources, yet I could do nothing in the face of this unrelenting, merciless disease. I realized the Holy Grail was her only hope. I knew the Grail would call to her, welcome her, cure her. Make her immortal? I don't know. From the day of her diagnosis, every waking hour, I studied and searched. And I found it." He choked. "And now it's gone again. Stolen. Mike, Emilie must have it, and soon. She is now bedridden, can barely raise her arms. Soon she won't be able to feed herself, then she will not be able to breathe, and then she will die of suffocation.

"Please, Mike, promise me you will find Patel — yes, I believe you now — there could be no other, it had to be her. She is behind the theft of the Grail and my attempted murder. And the deaths of some of my crew? Yes, she is responsible." He swallowed. "And poor Devi. Please, you must get me back the Grail. For my daughter.

For Emilie."

Mike closed her hand over his, squeezed. "I will do my best, Jean-Pierre. Both Nicholas and I will. Now think a moment: Do you believe it's possible the Grail will give off some sort of vibrations to help us locate it?"

Grant stepped into the room. "I felt something when you brought the stone out of the sphere, Jean-Pierre. I don't know if it was a vibration, exactly, or a hum, it was incredibly subtle, could even have been mistaken for the running of the motors on the boat under sail, but I did feel something. When you put it back in its lead box, the vibrations stopped."

Mike said, "So if Patel takes it out of its box, it could be traced."

Broussard said, "Perhaps. Do you have any idea where she is?"

Mike said, "We think she's in Sri Lanka. Adam traced the sale of a massive telescope to a company called Aquarius, which we believe she owns. There is an undocumented observatory there. He's nailing down the exact spot. Jean-Pierre, this took some years to build, and millions of dollars."

"So she's stolen from me. And the rest?"

"Possibly from terrorists. Now, we want to draw her out, verify exactly where she is.

I'm thinking if we can let her know you're alive, we can trace her. Your secretary —"

"Yes, that is a good plan. No, better to use Alys, Nevaeh's secretary. All we need to do is tell her I'm alive and Al-Asaad tried to blow up Galactus, and she'll call Nevaeh immediately to tell her."

"And while they talk," Grant said, "we will trace Dr. Patel's location."

The EMT approached them. "I must take Mr. Broussard to the hospital now."

Mike touched Broussard lightly on the arm. "By the time you wake up from surgery, we will have stopped her. I swear I will try to find the Grail, sir. For Emilie."

"Thank you, Mike. I was a fool, didn't oversee Nevaeh like I should have. And she betrayed me. Remember, she is very thorough, very smart. As for Kiera Byrne, I've heard rumors she's as dangerous as Nevaeh is smart. She was trained in the IRA camps when she was young, so she knows explosives as well as small arms. My secretary, Claudette, can get you a profile so you can at least see what you're dealing with."

"Thank you for the warning, and the offer. We'll call her, have her send it to Nicholas's phone. We will succeed, Jean-Pierre. We must."

When the EMTs wheeled Broussard away,

Mike said to Grant, "We have to get Mills out of here. He suggested a body bag. It's not a bad idea. The CIA has arranged for us to go to an airbase near here now. Are you with us?"

Grant cursed, dashed his fingers through his hair. "I want to, Mike, but the fact is Fentriss would have my butt in a sling if I left Broussard's side. Does he still need protection? I don't know. That CIA idiot, Mills, said he was betrayed by his captain. Maybe this terrorist has others willing to try to kill him. So I must stick close to him.

"Please stay in touch, and if you need anything, you let me know and I'll do my best to help." He gave her a quick hug. "Now, go find Patel and the Holy Grail. For Emilie." He walked away after Broussard, said over his shoulder, "Hey, you might want to punch out Mills. The yahoo."

Nicholas and Mike gave their statements to the Lyon police, gave them Pierre Menard's name and number at Interpol, and promised to talk more as soon as they could return. The fact that they appeared to have saved Jean-Pierre Broussard from terrorists helped. The police guaranteed to guard Mr. Broussard from further possible attacks while he was in the hospital.

It was easy enough to lift a body bag from the coroner's truck, since the responders were distracted by the nine bodies Mike, Nicholas, and Grant had left scattered across Patel's estate, these in addition to the dead team at Galactus. And easier still to carry Mills out into the backyard and put him in the back of the waiting SUV, summoned by the CIA — Carlton Grace. The driver, wearing wraparound black sunglasses, black jacket, white shirt, and tie, was behind the wheel, tapping his fingers impatiently. Mike gave him a look, then quickly called Claudette, who agreed to manage the calls between Alys and Patel. Adam set a trap on both their phones so he could monitor where they connected, hoping if Nicholas's attempt with the satellite phone failed, they could at least try to have a generalized location for Patel.

Mike and Nicholas shared a glance before getting into the SUV. Grant had given Nicholas his go-bag holding all his tactical equipment. Nicholas sat in the back, going through the bag, seeing what they had to work with.

A voice came from behind the back seats. "Hey, someone want to get me out of here?"

Mike looked over her shoulder at Nicholas, winked, called out, "Sorry, Vinny, several more police cars are right ahead of us, you'll have to wait."

Muffled curses, and Nicholas smiled at the clear road ahead. Then he turned his attention back to the go-bag.

Mike asked, "Anything interesting in there? Striped undies, a photo of Kitsune?"

Nicholas spread all the goodies out on the back seat: extra magazines, of which there were only three, two guns, a variety of medical goods, a Taser, and a high-intensity flashlight that could blind anyone approaching from up to twenty feet away.

He laughed. "I've looked through it, no underwear at all and no photo of Kitsune. A few handy items, yes, but not nearly enough. We'll have to load up. There's no way we're heading into the abyss after these two madwomen without more."

"I doubt Grant was thinking about how to stop a nuke and two crazy women when he packed for his cruise on *The Griffon*. Um, about the crazy women. Assuming Patel and Byrne are in Sri Lanka, how, exactly, can we make it there in time?"

"I'm not worrying about it. Grace has to figure it out. I'm more worried about how we stop a nuke. I have to assume it's on some sort of timer, if she's trying to make it coincide with the lunar eclipse and the passing of the International Space Station. If I can narrow down their location, I could conceivably jam the signal, but I'll have to be on-site to pull it off. Once I'm in the system, I'll be able to see what sort of fail-safes she has in the software." He looked at his grandfather's Breitling. "The eclipse is in sixteen hours."

"I spoke with Broussard about the Grail. It emits a signature I believe must be electrical in nature, so I'm thinking we need some sort of air-based sonar. If we can focus on its signature, we might find them quicker. Wherever the stone is, Nevaeh Patel won't be far away."

"A good idea, though again, we'd have to be close, on-site, for it to work. What does the Grail have to do with setting off the EMP? Why else would she have gone to such lengths to steal the stone from Broussard's yacht?"

"I don't know, Nicholas. But we'll find out."

Mills said from the body bag, "Children, I know all. Let me out and I'll even tell you."

"Hey, it looks clear ahead, no more police cars," Mike said. "Open him up, Nicholas, see what Mr. Brain has to say."

CHAPTER FIFTY-SIX

T-MINUS 16 HOURS

Lyon–Mont Verdun Air Base (*Base Aérienne 942*) is located to the northwest of Lyon. It is a center for air defense operations transferred to the site from the now-deactivated headquarters of the French Air Force at Taverny Air Base — BA921 near Paris, with an underground alternate strategic command center hardened against chemical and nuclear attack.

— Wikipedia

Mont Verdun Air Base
Lyon, France
The rolling hills of Lyon were Irish green from so much rain. And the vineyards, they stretched on either side of the road, as far as the eye could see.

"How far?" Mike asked their driver.

"Twenty minutes. You three look like

leftovers. Take a nap, I'll wake you up when we get to Mont Verdun."

Within moments, all three were asleep.

It seemed like only a second had passed when their driver called out, "Nearly there."

Mills stirred and yawned. "What's the countdown?"

Mike turned, said, "We're about sixteen hours out from the eclipse."

"I'm thinking we should probably scramble some jets for world leaders, just in case."

Mike's eyebrows went up. "You want them in the air?"

"Hey, Air Force One is hardened against an EMP."

Mike said, "Seriously, guys, if we start putting world leaders in secure bunkers or in their jets, everyone will know something bad is up and the panic will ripple across the world, causing as much damage as the EMP, if not more. Our only choice is to stop this before it goes off."

Mills said, "You know, depending on how high above the Earth it is when it detonates, a nuclear EMP wouldn't necessarily burn the Earth or cause great mushroom clouds of fallout."

Mike said, "I thought you were going to tell us something we didn't know. Well, not that I expected it. No, but as we've discussed, it could shut down all the communication signals from the satellites near the explosion, which would cascade through the cellular and radio signals. Anything using electricity to generate power would be disabled. If it's high enough, it's going to affect global communications satellites; low enough, and there will be an impact to Earth itself."

Mills nodded. "True. People could die from the initial blast depending on its strength and position in orbit — as you've said, the closer to Earth, the worse the situation would be. Without communications, fresh water, food distribution, any way to get news —"

"Anarchy, within three days."

"Yes," Mills said, "and complete chaos. But here's the bigger issue. *Where* it goes off. You realize the lunar eclipse is at its apex tonight over Nepal, right?"

Both Nicholas and Mike stared at him.

"I was holding back, now I'll give you the good stuff. Say Patel has her blast go off above Nepal. Say, thirty kilometers up. A HEMP — high-altitude EMP — in that area of space would knock out the electrical grids in China, India, southwest Russia, all of the countries that end in '-stan,' and most of the Middle East. Now, a few of these countries are probably hardened against such an attack. I am not one for looking on the dark side of things, but if Russia or China think the U.S. has set off an EMP designed to knock them back to the Middle Ages, they might not take it so well. Because not only would it take out the electronics in that fourteen-hundred-square-kilometer area on Earth, it would also annihilate any satellites in its path.

"Now, were I a feisty country, forever in the shadow of the U.S., and I'm hit by an EMP, I would be mighty pissed off. I might even decide to shoot off an EMP of my own in retaliation, this one above Montana, and the next thing you know, we're all up the creek. This is bigger than a single explosion. This is the beginnings of World War Three — a nuclear nightmare scenario. The thing is, no one's been testing the effects of HEMPs on Earth. This is just what we know because of the science. And it's the best-case scenario."

Mike was shaking her head. "I get that Patel is pissed at NASA for kicking her out of the astronaut program, but why does she want to cause catastrophic damage? Why does she hate the world?"

Mills shook his head. "I hope we get to her in time to ask."

They heard the deafening *whoosh* of the planes before they saw them — four French air force jets were flying low and close, skimming the trees.

Shortly, they pulled up in front of a guardhouse similar to those she'd seen at the entrance to every military installation she'd ever been on. The soldiers were dressed in camouflage fatigues, small black berets cocked on their heads. They carried automatic weapons with an ease born of long handling.

The SUV was directed to the tarmac, and parked next to a small hangar. The driver got out and disappeared. Mills opened the door and stepped out, rubbed his jaw. "I can't wait to get rid of this thing. I don't want anyone to mistake me for Khaleed Al-Asaad ever again. I sure hope there's a razor and some water on the plane. Everyone ready for some fun? There's our transport. This is the CIA, folks. Isn't Mr. Grace amazing?"

Mike looked to the four jets parked on the tarmac, and her face split into a wide smile. "Oh, you're kidding. We get to fly in those?"

The four jets were big, no, massive gray ghosts with tons of armament. She couldn't believe it. Always, since her earliest childhood, Mike had wanted to ride in one of these babies, pull big G's.

They were escorted inside the hangar. Their driver was standing next to a card table set up with a laptop and a T1 line. Nicholas was relieved. Relying on Wi-Fi was too dangerous, and being hardwired into the base's communications system would make life much easier.

He secured a line to Adam, whose face popped up on the computer. He had dark circles under his eyes.

"I'm ready and waiting to trace Patel's phone. I don't know if this is going to work, Nicholas. If Patel doesn't have the GPS turned on, it's going to be hard to locate the signal."

"We only have one chance at this. You found the facility in Sri Lanka for us. Do you believe she's there?"

"Well, yes. It's off-grid, it's private, and it's cost her a lot of money over the years. I'd put our chances at 50 percent. Maybe 75 percent."

"We're looking for a squawk, a link, anything that might show this phone on the grid for even the barest hint of a moment. If we can confirm she's anywhere near there, I'm comfortable heading to Sri Lanka immediately."

They could hear Adam talking on the other line, then he came back. "Here's the number to track. Alys is going to make the call in five minutes. She'll keep it simple. She doesn't know there's a problem outside of the headquarters being attacked. She won't be able to warn Patel about anything."

Nicholas glanced at his watch. They were running out of time. He said, "Here goes nothing," and typed in Nevaeh's sat phone number. He launched his tracking protocol and waited.

CHAPTER FIFTY-SEVEN

Nicholas listened to the one-sided call with one ear, typing frantically, searching, searching. The program he'd written could examine five square miles at a time for a satellite phone signature, regardless of the GPS signal. But five square miles at a time to cover a twenty-five-thousand-square-mile country was going to take a while.

He decided to narrow down the search to the main routes leading from Colombo to the coordinates Adam had for Aquarius. With a smaller grid, the program began to run faster.

A small pinprick of light came online, then faded just as quickly.

"There!"

The map overlay came back on-screen.

Mike said, "Adam, did you see it? Was that her sat phone?"

"I am seeing it, and I'm running it now. Yes, that was her phone. It registered when the call dropped. Damn, Nicholas, that's a pretty cool program."

"Where are they exactly?"

"They're outside of Colombo, in the mountains. It's right where Aquarius is supposed to be."

Nicholas said, "Confirmation enough for me. Let's go."

"More than enough," Mills said, and pumped his fist. "This Adam obviously belongs in the CIA."

Nicholas said, "Yeah, right. Hold on. Adam, you taped the conversation she had, yes? I want to be one hundred percent sure she isn't using some sort of fake GPS system to send people off the trail. Run the protocol again, and this time, back-trace it to France and lay in voice recognition, see if we can tap in from the other end. Let's make sure it was Patel, and she's really in Sri Lanka."

Typing, whistling, then Adam said, "It's for real. The voice profiles match up, and I was able to get a specific locale for the sat phone, down to a hundred yards."

"Good job. We'll be in touch."

Nicholas tossed the headphones down, uploaded a program into the computer, then ejected the thumb drive. The program launched and erased the computer's hard drive. Not necessarily polite, but there was no sense leaving tracks behind. They wouldn't know it, but the next time someone tried to power up this machine, they'd find absolutely nothing. He wasn't willing to give the CIA his brainchildren.

Mike was nearly dancing with excitement. "Can we go now? Right now? Hey, where's Mills?"

Mills came out of the hangar, yelling at the top of his lungs at Nicholas, "Did you erase that computer?"

"What? No idea what you're talking about, mate."

"Bugger off, you British bastard."

Nicholas laughed. "Okay, Vinny, are we on, or what?"

Mills said, "Oh yeah, we're on. But you pull a trick like that again and you'll be left behind."

Nicholas only grinned at him.

Outside the hangar, the pilots were milling about their jets, relaxed, wearing jumpsuits that made them look like bugs, strange arms and legs sticking out. One came over to them. "*Madame, messieurs,* I am Captain Rousseau. We have received orders to bring you to Sri Lanka. I understand you are in something of a *ruée* — ah, yes, you are in a rush. These are F2 Rafales. These are the fastest planes we have. Eighty-five hundred kilometers from here to Sri Lanka, we are going to have you there in a little less than four hours. We will have to refuel on the way, of course."

Mike said, "Four hours is good. But landing will cost us time."

"Oh, we will not have to make a landing. You see the arm right there?" He pointed at a long, thin pole that stuck out of the right side of each plane near the clear glass hood. "We will refuel in the air. It will require very little time. We will do it two times. There is one issue. The winds are going to be pretty rough, flying into a typhoon is not gentle." A sly grin moved across the captain's face. "I hope you did not eat any breakfast, did you?"

Mike grinned back. "As a matter of fact, nope. I'm starving, too."

"Good. Let us get you ready to fly. The things you need are inside the hangar."

"Let's do it."

They did all the necessary prep, got dressed in their flight suits, briefed on their flight plan and mission. Nicholas was shaking his head at her. "Imagine, you wanting to fly heavy G's."

"Oh, yeah. This part I'm going to love."

He tweaked her ponytail. "Keep your wits

about you, Dame Michaela. Don't have too much fun."

They each climbed the ladder and wedged themselves into the tiny, hard second seat of their jets.

Mike was riding with Captain Rousseau. Nicholas would be in the second jet. She gave him a crazed grin and a thumbs-up.

Mills was in the lead jet. A fourth jet was geared up, and would be flying with them. As what, a guard? Or to try to save them if one of them got shot down?

Rousseau did a series of checks in French with his pilots, then spoke to Mike, his voice strong and clear across the comms in her ear attached to her helmet.

"Are you ready, *Madame Agent* ma'am?"

"You better believe it. I've wanted to ride in an F-14 for years, but they're retired now. This baby? She's beautiful."

He laughed, gave her an interested look, very French, and she smiled back at him. "We will see how you feel when we are pulling five G's. Do not forget the bags tucked by your right knee. The weather near the landing site is deteriorating, and we will be feeling every bump. There is no shame to feel sick. Most people do the first time."

Mike was rubbing her hands together. She didn't care if she barfed in Technicolor into her own shoe. This was going to be a blast. "Let's go!"

As they started to roll toward the runway, Nicholas came across her comms.

"Mike, you okay?"

"Never better."

"Bloody hell, you're still altogether too excited." She heard the smile in his voice, knew he was excited, too. The best part was they'd be in Sri Lanka with hours to spare to look for Patel and Aquarius. And the Holy Grail. For Emilie.

She said into her comms, "Adam sent me some files. I'm going to put on my earbuds and listen to more recent private tapes Byrne transcribed of her boss in her deprivation chamber. Hopefully I'll find out who was in the chamber with her, who she was talking to. I'll also go through her personnel folder, see if I can find any clues to why she's doing this."

There was the roar of the engines, then a downright whoop of joy as the jet roared into the sky.

Nicholas said, "I daresay my pilot is a nutter."

CHAPTER FIFTY-EIGHT

T-MINUS 16 HOURS

Aquarius Observatory
Sri Lanka

The incessant ringing of her sat phone woke her. Nevaeh rolled over to pick it up, annoyed since she'd made it clear all were to remain silent. A surprise, it was Alys.

She turned on the sat phone and ran the scrambling program. When she was certain she was secure, she said, "Yes, Alys? What is it?"

"I have the most wonderful news. Monsieur Broussard has been found alive. It is on the television."

"What?" Nevaeh's heart hammered in her throat. How was this possible? Jean-Pierre Broussard was dead, dead and gone, she'd even paid that terrorist to go against Al-Asaad to kill Broussard at Galactus.

Kiera said, "What is it?" and Nevaeh

shook her head and held up a finger. She said to Alys, "They found *The Griffon*? I thought it had sunk."

"It did, it went down completely, but Monsieur Broussard and most of his crew were able to get to lifeboats, and were rescued. Is this not the most wonderful news? I knew you would want to know right away."

No, it was not wonderful frigging news. What had happened? How had he escaped?

But she said aloud, "Yes, of course it is. Where is he?"

"He is here, in Lyon, at the hospital."

"Jean-Pierre is in Lyon? But how is this possible? I thought *The Griffon* was somewhere near Malaysia. What was he doing in Lyon? At headquarters?"

Kiera stiffened next to her, then frantically began tapping on her phone.

"I do not know the whole story, Dr. Patel. I only know he was saved, and escorted back by his close protection team. There was a break-in at Galactus, terrorists, shooting. An explosion. They are saying the terrorist known as Khaleed Al-Asaad is responsible. Many people are dead, though not our people. They were all safe, at home, as you wished. You were right to close headquarters. But why would terrorists attack Galactus?"

"It is an excellent question, Alys. We shall have to work with the authorities on an answer."

"Dr. Patel, as soon as I heard, I knew I needed to call you. Monsieur Broussard is in surgery and Claudette won't disclose anything else to me. What should I do? The media wants a comment from the company."

"I will speak to Claudette myself. Put me through."

Kiera put a warning hand on Nevaeh's thigh, said quietly, "We don't know what's happening. They might be tracing this call."

Nevaeh waved her hand at the high canopy of trees out the bedroom window. "We are safe. No one can find us here. And I scrambled the call, as always."

Broussard's secretary came on the line. "Dr. Patel? Where are you?"

"I'm at the spaceport, of course, handling the next launch. Is it true what Alys said? Jean-Pierre lives?"

Claudette's voice was cool. "Really? You're at the spaceport?"

"Yes, I took the Quints jet here as planned."

"We need you back at headquarters, Dr.

Patel, immediately."

"You didn't answer me, Claudette. Is Mr. Broussard alive or not? Alys said the media is reporting he's in Lyon, in the hospital."

Another small pause. "Yes, he is alive."

Nevaeh tried to sound as delighted as possible. "It is wonderful news. I've been worried sick."

"When can you return, Dr. Patel?"

"As soon as possible. Our pilots are not here. Please send the plane for me, Claudette. With luck, I will be home by nightfall. And Claudette, thank you for calling Alys and having her contact me. Now, a statement must be coordinated. The release should say —"

"Mr. Broussard has already drafted the statement for me, Dr. Patel."

Why hadn't he called her himself? Well, he was in surgery, but why did he pick Claudette?

"Very good. Again, I will try to be back to Lyon by this evening. You can coordinate anything else through Alys until my return."

"Yes, ma'am."

She clicked off. Alys came back on the line.

Alys said, "Do you have any instructions for me? Headquarters is a disaster, someone will have to coordinate a cleanup and renovation."

"Feel free to start discussing a solution with Claudette. In the meantime, I am going to call the hospital and see if I can speak to Jean-Pierre. I will be in touch."

She clicked off and sat back, stared at Kiera. She shook her head back and forth, she struck her fist against her open palm. "I can't believe it. He's alive. The son of a bitch somehow managed to survive Devi's drug and our missile. He even managed to escape the attack at Galactus."

Kiera said, "I gave Devi the correct dosages. Devi mustn't have given them enough. She was weak."

Nevaeh took a breath, forcing back the rage. Her first instinct was to lash out at Kiera, but she needed her. Nevaeh knew a time would come when a decision would have to be made about Kiera Byrne, but for the next several hours, she could put it off.

"Do not make excuses, Kiera. Threatening the life of Devi's sister should have ensured her complete cooperation. Perhaps you didn't give her enough ketamine to do the job. Evidently many of them awoke from the drug before *The Griffon* went down and managed to get off safely.

"Now there is a chance they can trace us,

do you understand? Not only is Broussard alive, Al-Asaad went after him believing he knew where his bomb was hidden. And we barely managed to hijack it. What do you propose we do about him?"

Kiera snorted. "It won't matter what Al-Asaad does now. He's going to get what he wants, what all his terrorist buddies want, only he won't be targeting it. The bomb will go off, the electrical grids will be disabled. Planes will fall from the sky, and he'll take credit, you can be sure of that. And he will never be able to track us here."

"He isn't as stupid as you think, Kiera. I've often wondered if there was something more to him. He was too smart, slippery." She shrugged. "I still can't believe Broussard survived the missile, survived Galactus. The captain I bribed should have killed him, he had enough men."

Kiera looked impatient. "Look, Nevaeh, I don't know what happened and neither do you. And it's too late to care. We're committed."

But Nevaeh's mind was still squirreling about. "That bastard, Broussard, is not stupid, nor are his people. They will realize quickly enough we aren't at the spaceport, and they will come looking for us."

Kiera laid a hand on her arm. "Calm

yourself. By then it will be too late. They think you're in French Guiana. We are on the other side of the world. Even if they figure out where we are, no one can reach us in time. The detonation will happen well before anyone could possibly arrive. Besides, we're about to be enveloped by a typhoon. We will be well protected here in the mountains. Even if they were able to find us, no one could penetrate the facility, especially through a storm of this magnitude."

Nevaeh stared out the window at the relentless rain, trying to gain control. Kiera said again, "Nevaeh, believe me. It doesn't matter. There's no way to stop us now."

Nevaeh slowly nodded. Kiera was right. It didn't matter now.

CHAPTER FIFTY-NINE

T-MINUS 12 HOURS

Air Force Base Katunayake
Colombo, Sri Lanka
July 27

Once on the ground in Sri Lanka, Mike peeled herself from the seat of the jet and accepted Captain Rousseau's hand to help her down the ladder to the tarmac.

He hadn't been kidding, they'd made good time, just under four hours. Refueling had been an insane experience — they were hovering so close to the huge fuel jet, a Boeing KC-135 Stratotanker, according to Captain Rousseau, watching the tube snake down and attach itself — a probe-and-drogue system it was called, again supplied by Rousseau. Then, in only a minute, they were topped up and ready to fly. Doing all of this at Mach 1 was something she'd never forget as long as she lived.

And she hadn't barfed once, even when he took her for a few barrel rolls for the fun of it, curse him. She had gotten extremely light-headed a couple of times when they pulled extreme G's, but had managed to hold herself together, breathing deeply and shutting her eyes. She'd never felt anything so incredible as flying at 1,500 miles per hour. And the world below had not, shockingly, been a blur. No, it was stunningly beautiful, the view afforded by the Perspex bubble far-ranging, much better than riding in the window seat of a commercial airliner.

But now, it was time to refocus. They had twelve hours until the lunar eclipse. And in that time they had to find Patel and Byrne, and the facility named Aquarius. And shut off a freaking bomb before part of the world turned into chaos.

Then, to her surprise, Captain Rousseau had taken her hand and asked her to dinner. When was she coming back to Lyon? Nicholas overheard this, and said in an expressionless voice, "This has been amazing, Captain Rousseau. I would be pleased to join you." And he beamed at the captain and shook his hand.

Rousseau understood instantly. He was French, after all.

"Of all things," Mike said, appalled, as

they walked away. "Doesn't he realize what we have to do? Talk about crappy timing. I mean look at this mess." Rain was pouring from the gray skies. At least they'd managed to land before the worst bands arrived, but the wind was picking up, making the palms sway and bend. Even so, the crows of Sri Lanka were everywhere. Big and glossy, with blue-black feathers and cacophonous caws, so loud and pervasive Mike felt the hair on the back of her neck stand on end. Even on the tarmac, even in the rain, they crowded around and lined up on the hangar roofs like silent gargoyles.

As they walked to the hangar, Nicholas had to bat away two who were dive-bombing his head.

Mike laughed. "They think your hair is one of their enemies from another clan. It's almost as black as their feathers."

"I guess there aren't any blond crows, a pity." He tugged on his shirt. "It's hot and wet."

"Really? This is exactly like New York in a heat wave, facing down an early nor'easter. High humidity, big threat of rain."

"A threat of rain?" Sheets of water were pouring off the eaves of the hangar. "You hardly have Category Four typhoons heading into the city. And I've never known New

York to smell like this. Do your heat waves often carry spices and curry on the breeze?"

She nodded. "In some spots. Hey, Nicholas, we're on an adventure, remember? And here we are, of all places, in Sri Lanka. Everything's different, everything's new." She shook out her ponytail, sending droplets of water to splash on him. "Just you wait to hear what I found out from Kiera Byrne's transcriptions of Patel's discussions in the deprivation chamber — you're not going to believe it."

The wind was so strong now they could scarcely hear each other. They ran the last hundred feet to the hangar, the hot, spicy air billowing around them. Even though it was raining, perspiration beaded on Mike's forehead. "Then again, maybe right now I'd prefer the London fog and rain. At least you don't sweat."

"My mum always told me ladies never sweat, they glow."

"Tell me the next time we're facing off at the gym. I'll show you how I can glow."

Vince Mills was already conversing with a group of tough-looking men and women who'd just entered the hangar next to their plane. At their curious glances, she said, "Looks like our arrival hasn't gone unnoticed. Hopefully they're on our side.

451

We're going to need all the help we can get. Listen, Nicholas, before they join us, let me tell you what I found out about Patel. Here's the bottom line: When Jean-Pierre told her about his search for the Holy Grail three years ago, she quickly became obsessed. She desperately wanted to get her hands on the Grail because it fits in with her plan to set off the nuke in space, causing the EMP."

"But how? To what end? Why does she need the Grail?"

"Let's get more distance from the CIA folk. Believe me, this is private." She leaned close. "She believes, as does Jean-Pierre, the Holy Grail will give her immortality. She must be immortal because she believes her 'friends' are. She's counting on the explosion to knock a hole in the atmosphere so her 'friends' can come get her. Her 'friends' are the same beings she claims saved her life when she was detached from her tether on the space station all those years ago. The Numen. It all started out kumbaya, with the Numen assuring Patel they'd bring peace to the world, no more war, no more famine, no more hate. But her conversations changed as she changed, became bitter, more angry. The last several years, she's wanted to rule the Earth with the Numen's help. She wants power, she wants ultimate control. There's lots more, but that's the short version."

He stared at her. "This is all about little green aliens?"

"It would be cool if they were green, but Dr. Patel never mentioned what they looked like or their color. I don't think she ever knew."

"Well, this answers a lot of questions."

"Indeed it does. Now, Carl Grace sent over their dossier on Kiera Byrne. Nicholas, she's seriously bad news. However did she pass the background check to become the security chief at Galactus?"

CHAPTER SIXTY

That was an excellent question. Nicholas said, "I'm thinking Patel decided she wanted Byrne, got her approved."

"Bypassed all their protocols? She managed to keep from them that Byrne had done time? I know, a few arrests for petty things. But there was a big one in 2010. She was twenty. They found her in an alley right after a supermarket blew up in Derry, caught her with a weapon and bomb-making materials. She did two years, then was released."

"So she's twenty-eight, twenty-nine now. What else?"

"She's a chip off the old block. Her mother died in jail for a bombing in 1990. Also a supermarket. Her mother was an actress, then an activist, then an outspoken member of Sinn Fein. She booby-trapped a car in Belfast, rigged it to explode when three members of Parliament were driving by. She was scheduled for release under the Good Friday Agreement in 1998 but died a couple of months before she would have been freed. Byrne learned at the knee of a master, for sure. Explosives and extensive weapons training, and it looks like she went off-grid in South America for a time before she joined Patel's security detail in 2014."

"What was she doing in South America?"

"Unknown at this time, but one source thinks she met local terrorists and these are the people who eventually hooked her up with the big bad terrorist Khaleed Al-Asaad — sorry, the idiot Vince Mills — in one of the ISIS training camps in Venezuela. They were in the same area at the same time. Hey, my phone's not working. Do you have a signal?"

He looked at his. "Yes."

"That's a relief. Let's check in with Adam and Gray, fill them in about Byrne, and see if they have anything new for us. Or any warnings about what's to come before we head to Aquarius."

Nicholas flicked up the antenna for the sat phone and dialed in.

Gray answered, "You two survived your ride, I take it?"

Mike said, "We did. It was amazing. What's happening there?"

455

"Oh, you know. Nothing major. We're just at Defcon Three. Everyone is mobilizing in case a nuke goes off."

Nicholas said, "Okay, that's good. Listen, Gray, I have an idea. I haven't had much time to analyze it since we didn't exactly have Wi-Fi on the flight, but if the military is already raising the threat levels, then I'd like to give them a suggestion, should it be possible."

"I'm all ears."

"A nuclear bomb needs a trigger in order to explode and create fission, correct? And the fission part is what we'd like to avoid at all cost. If fission happens, the nuke goes off and the EMP follows."

"Yes, as far as I know."

"So if the bomb were destroyed before the trigger went off, we could avoid the nuclear explosion entirely. We could blow up the bomb and not set off the nuke."

"Theoretically, I suppose you're right. As far as I know, at least."

"So if we were able to identify the satellite the nuke is on, we could conceivably destroy it before the bomb went off."

"Conceivably." He didn't sound convinced.

"Since the military is now alerted, why don't you have a quick chat with one of your friends, see about moving a defense satellite into place above the area where we believe our rogue satellite is going to be, and if Mike and I can't stop this in time from the ground, the military can shoot it with a laser. There are satellites with that sort of capability, yes?"

"Whoa, dude. You are so far above our pay grades on this one — I don't think I can make that happen. I mean, I could — again, theoretically — take control of a satellite, but I kind of like my job. We'd need to go to the White House for orders for something of that magnitude."

"Gray, I don't mean for you to do it. We'd need to get the military to handle this. I think it's something worth pursuing. In case we can't get it stopped from the ground, or worse, don't make it to Patel's installation in time, as long as we can identify where the satellite is, we can come at it from a different direction, as you Yanks like to say."

Gray thought it out. "Okay. It's a solid plan. I always prefer having a backup when it comes to stopping a nuclear bomb. But I think you should talk to the White House directly. I can scramble a call between you and them."

"Good idea. And you better inform Grace from CIA about this as well. We're here with

457

his people, and it's their coordination that allowed us to even be here in time. Oh, and you might want to loop in NASA."

"NASA? Why?"

"We think there's an additional target. The space station will be passing through the area where we think the nuke is set to go off, at the moment of the lunar eclipse. It's possible the space station is a target, considering Patel's previous situation with them. Perhaps they could undertake a change of course, if given enough warning. We'd hate to see the ISS be collateral damage."

Gray said a very bad word. "Can you imagine what Zachery will say when he finds out what he's missed?"

"No, nor do I want to imagine it."

"Okay, hang tight. Let me wrangle up some folks for you to talk to."

Nicholas put the phone in his pocket and shrugged at Mike. "All we can do is try."

Mike said, "It's a brilliant idea, though. We have to hope they have enough time to move every piece of the puzzle into place, and our assumptions are right. But if they are, then we have two shots to stop this nuke. I like two much better than only one."

"I do as well." He waved at the windswept, rainy scene outside the hangar. "We simply might not make it in time."

Chapter Sixty-One

Mills walked across the hangar to join them. He gestured toward the group of heavily armed people.

"These are some of the best we have in-country. They know about Aquarius. The locals call it *Taru Pratimāva,* which our guide explained means 'Statue to the Stars' in the Sinhala language."

Mike said, "Hey, being two-toned is better than looking like a terrorist. Did you plug any drains getting rid of all that beard hair?"

"Har, har," Mills said as he rubbed his hand over his face. "Three minutes and a mirror, that was all I needed."

Nicholas said, "I'm going to want to talk to our guide."

"There'll be plenty of time. It's going to be at least three hours in the trucks. We can't fly, everything is grounded and there's no place to land."

Nicholas looked at his Breitling. "Cutting it rather fine, aren't we? I'm sure we could find something close —"

"I've seen the radar — the storm is too intense. We need to get moving right away if we have any hope of making it out before the roads become impassable. Things are going to get dicey. We'll take three vehicles. You'll ride with me, get filled in. I hope you FBI wusses are up for this."

Nicholas laughed, remembering how Mills had calmly walked toward Patel's house, his hands on his head. They could have shot him dead. Even though he was an idiot, he had guts. So, instead of slugging his very white lower face, Nicholas merely said, "We'll see. We have to talk to both our bosses, we might as well do it together. Let's get on the road. Put the guide in our truck, too."

Mike looked around the hangar at all the grounded aircraft. "I wish Grant was here. He'd fly into the storm."

Nicholas thought he probably would, in a heartbeat.

Their guide walked up to them and introduced himself, hand outstretched. His round face was deeply seamed, his thick hair an odd color between red and brown, maybe a bit of yellow in there as well. "I am

Bernard Arndt. Normally I would take you to the Union so you could rest and have refreshments, but I understand you are in a hurry. I will get us safely to *Taru Pratimāva*. I have lived on the island my whole life."

Mike said, "I wasn't expecting a name like Arndt. Are you Dutch?"

"Yes, madam. My people are Dutch Burghers, many of whom fled during the civil war. It is only me and my wife and children, and my brother and his children, now. Ceylon has changed. We've suffered so many losses, the war, the tsunami. Forty-seven thousand souls, gone in a single event. Many of my people left but I stayed. Ceylon is my home. Let us go."

"You can call me Mike. This is Nicholas. And as for him" — she nodded toward Vince Mills — "exactly what he is, I'm not sure yet."

"Then call me Bernard."

They all piled into the vehicle and said hello to their driver, Samuel, an older man with shaggy black hair and aviator glasses, who was chewing on a toothpick and only gave them a nod. The caravan set off, winding out of Colombo toward the mountainous nature preserves in the middle of the country. It was slow going. Their wipers were on high, the water splashing across the glass so hard it was difficult to see out the windshield.

Bernard gave them a quick lesson in Sri Lankan colonialism and the recent civil war, which explained why the military was on the streets and there were tons of roadblocks — choke points, really, cutting the trucks off from the remainder of the street, which meant they could be easily overpowered if they didn't meet with the approval of the soldiers manning the gates. IDs were shown again and again and again to soldiers bedraggled by the rain, and even though the winds were picking up and the streets were becoming waterlogged, trishaws and cars made for near gridlock.

Finally, after an hour of stops and starts and a final warning of the roads' deterioration by a small group of soldiers who looked to Mike to be about seventeen, they were out of the city and winding into the mountains.

Bernard said, "Now, Aquarius. The facility was under construction for several years. They even had roads built into the area. It sits on the edge of the nature preserve, with tall fencing, electrified, not unlike a military installation. It runs on generators, so cutting the electricity isn't an option, everything will power up within moments. There are guards — many ex-military — armed with automatic weapons, who patrol the grounds. With a typhoon of this magnitude nearly upon us, it is possible they will take shelter, assuming no one would dare try to breach the facility in such bad weather."

Mike said, "What's our best entry point?"

Bernard opened his tablet and brought up several photos. "As you can see, there is only one road in, and there is a guard tower in this location, as well as an electrified gate."

She groaned. "Those fences are ten feet tall, with razor wire. Not exactly what I want to be scaling in a typhoon."

"Yes, I agree it would be most difficult. The best way in is to be let in. We can't force our way through the gate unless we are able to both turn off the electrical grid and destabilize the generators, and this could be too challenging."

Nicholas said, "I could do it —" but Bernard raised a hand.

"It won't be necessary."

Mike grinned. "Bribery, then. That'll work."

Bernard laughed. "When we were made aware *guests* were coming" — he looked pointedly at Mills, who gave him a feral grin — "we rotated an asset onto guard duty. One of the gate guards was suddenly taken ill, and our asset was next on the roster for duty. He will meet us at the gate and make sure it is opened."

Mike arched an eyebrow at Arndt. "Now that's handy. However did you manage to have an asset in place already?"

"It is my brother's son. He doesn't work for your government, he works for mine. He has been assigned to this facility since its inception. Though there has not seemed to be anything illegal happening, the fact the owners set up such extreme protections for the facility so closely set off warning bells. My government took the steps they thought necessary to protect our people in the event the facility did end up being an illegal operation of some kind. There are several buildings on the property, and the main building, in the center, has a retractable roof. This is where the telescope lives."

"Is the telescope why they call it 'Statue to the Stars'?"

"Yes, exactly. It is massive. It took three days to maneuver it into place with a crane brought in especially for the job. It's been finished for a little over a year now. Oh yes, the woman who owns Aquarius is rarely in residence."

Nicholas said, "She is there now, though, right?"

"Oh, yes."

"You brains should've asked that first," Mills said. He didn't wait for Mike or Nicholas to try for a comeback. "Bernard, there are plans, blueprints, documents we can use to ascertain where our targets are, yes?"

Bernard shook his head. "Unfortunately, the office holding those documents burned down. For some reason, the plans for the facility have never been entered digitally, so all we have to go on is what we know from my nephew, and the lore surrounding the construction."

"Lore?"

"Yes. You must understand, the locals shun this place. They fear it is evil."

Mike asked, "Why?"

"There were several accidents when it was being built. Three local men disappeared. One or two bodies were found in the rivers, as if they'd slipped in and drowned, but the bodies had been — interfered with. And it is claimed the bodies of animals have been found on the site as well. Something that kills lives on the land. *Napaurau ātamaya,* or *avatārayak.* An evil spirit, or a ghost."

Mike said, "What do you think it is?"

Bernard grinned. "I am an educated man. I don't believe in ghost stories or phantom evils. There are leopards, boars, bears, and venomous snakes roaming free in this area. They are all natural, explainable deaths, at least to me."

"How would large predators get inside the fence?"

"We are talking one hundred square kilometers of land. Nature finds a way."

Bernard leaned forward and said a few brief words in Sinhala to their driver, Samuel, who sped up a bit.

Mike said, "I wonder what the dates would show if the deaths were matched up to Byrne's and Patel's stays here?"

Nicholas said, "You think Kiera or Patel is the evil ghost?"

"Well, we're talking a lot of dead people — a murdered psychiatrist in New York, a murdered psychiatrist at NASA, a murdered scientist in Idaho. I have a feeling Patel murdered those people. As for Kiera Byrne, her profile shows her to be dangerous, volatile. I'm also betting on a sadist. Take your pick." She turned to Vinny. "Hey, Al-Asaad, you met with Kiera many times over the past two years, right? What would you say about her?"

Mills said, "I would say I wouldn't want to marry her, that's for sure."

Nicholas looked at his watch. "We're slowing again. How long is it now, Bernard?"

"We're still a full hour away. As the crow flies, the facility is there" — he pointed to the east, through a thick canopy of trees — "approximately ten kilometers. But we must follow the roads, which wind up the mountain in switchbacks, which is why it takes longer. The heavy rain is making it worse. In monsoon season the roads often disappear under mud. We've only just finished monsoon. A typhoon on top of it will cause major destruction throughout the southwest of the country. We must be careful. This is why we go so slowly." He added, "It is not only the snakes and leopards that kill here. Ceylon can be a very dangerous place."

They rode in silence for a few minutes, then Mike said, "If the apex of the lunar eclipse has the moon over Nepal, we're still close enough that if the nuke goes off, Sri Lanka will be affected."

"Absolutely."

"That means, then, that Patel is looking for her friends, the Numen, to protect her, to possibly come for her, but she's convinced she'll be safe. But here's the question. If the nuke goes off in a low Earth orbit, then Aquarius would be offline, unless she's managed to protect it with some sort of massive Faraday cage, which I suppose could have been built into the roofs of the buildings. What do you think?"

Nicholas said, "It's very possible she doesn't care. She'll be with her saviors. Bugger me, I wish we had those blueprints. Since we have only another hour — hopefully —" he said to Vinny and Bernard, "let me tell you about the weird stuff you don't know —"

Mike felt the SUV shift, then heave and jerk, heard Samuel cry out — and, suddenly, they were falling.

CHAPTER SIXTY-TWO

Mike had the breath knocked out of her when she was slammed against the safety belt. Something crashed into her leg, then her shoulder. She was disoriented, couldn't see, only heard curses and yells, the sounds of metal being crushed. The scent of loam and mud filled her nostrils. A hand grabbed hers and she realized it was Nicholas and he was shouting at her. "I've got you." He said it over and over. Oddly, she relaxed, stopped fighting against the seat belt and the frantic pitching and twisting of the car. She realized the SUV had slid off the road and they were rocketing down a steep hill. But then, suddenly, they hit something and the SUV flipped and they were sliding down the hill upside down on a vast sea of mud. A window shattered and water and mud flowed in. It was only her and Nicholas in the back seat. Where were Bernard and Vinny?

The SUV slammed against a large tree and shuddered to a stop. She opened her eyes to see Samuel slumped over the wheel, his aviator glasses askew over sightless eyes, a tree branch through his chest. She must have screamed because Nicholas squeezed her hand. She heard his voice, garbled to her ears. "Are you hurt, are you okay?"

Finally, she was together enough to whisper, "I'm okay, I'm still in my seat belt. Nicholas, Samuel, the tree branch. He's hurt badly. We have to help him."

"I'm sorry, Mike, he's dead."

Of course he was, she simply didn't want to accept it.

"We got caught in a mudslide?"

"Yes. I think Mills and Bernard were thrown out." Nicholas leaned downward and pressed two fingers into the driver's neck. He'd known he was dead, but he'd had to try. He undid his safety belt, landing hard on what was now the floor of the SUV. "We've got to get out of here."

They heard Mills and Bernard yelling.

Nicholas shouted, "We're alive! We'll need help up the hill, though." And to Mike, he said, "We're filling up fast with mud."

She took one last look at Samuel, said a prayer for him, then held on as Nicholas cut her free from the belt. She fell against him. He hugged her tight to his chest.

After a moment, she said, "I never thought of meeting upside down in a mudslide."

"I don't want you to get bored, Agent Caine. Now, let's get out of here."

They maneuvered out of the truck onto the muddy wet ground. The rain was slamming down, the winds howled, and ankle-deep mud sucked at their boots. It was dark and somehow they had to make it up the steep slope. Nicholas said, "We slid at least fifty feet straight down the hill. If the SUV hadn't hit the tree, we might have landed at the bottom of the mountain, then good luck getting us back up."

Mike raised her face, let the rain clean off the mud.

Nicholas called, "Hurry up there, mate," and Vinny's face appeared over the edge of the cliff, his beardless jawline white as a specter's in the darkness.

He shouted, "Bad news. The road's washed out ahead. We can't get the SUVs any farther. We're going to have to go in overland, carrying our gear, so salvage what you can from our vehicle. We're coming to get you."

Nicholas looked down at his watch, wiped off the mud, and said, "Bloody hell," followed by a few more choice phrases under his breath. "Five miles through the bloody jungle, in a bloody typhoon, in the bloody dark? With gear? We're never going to make it in time."

Mike shook his arm. "Stop that. We're going to make it. We're trained professionals, to us five miles is nothing."

He pulled a huge machete from the back of the SUV and handed it over, handle first. "Fine. You want to be an optimist? You can lead."

She took the heavy blade, swung it in front of her a few times in dramatic Zorro fashion, grimaced only slightly at the bruises across her chest from the safety belt. "Not a problem. All right, boyo, follow me."

It took them twenty minutes to get up the hill, hand over hand on a rope let down by Vinny and Bernard, then another ten minutes to get everyone geared up and ready for the trek. Nicholas was able to reach Adam with the sat phone, and he triangulated their position to Aquarius and mapped the easiest route. It was slightly longer than five miles, but Adam didn't think it would be as dangerous as the more direct route.

They were about to sign off and get underway when Adam said, "Hey, hold on. I see another option. Looking farther east, there's an older road leading to the facility, one I assume they stopped using when they built the main thoroughfare. If you can reach it, you'll have a straighter shot in. It's basically a path now, you couldn't get a vehicle through it, but on foot, it will be manageable. It's two klicks to your west, then another three and some change to the gate."

Bernard said, "We must be very careful if we choose that path. Tamil Tiger rebels once controlled the area. There could be IEDs along the route, left over from their camps. They were defeated and the area cleared, but I can't be certain we'll be safe."

Mike swiped her hand over her face. "We can do it, Bernard. It is the shortest, quickest route, and believe me, time is of the essence. We'll be careful."

Vinny said, "It's come to this? I'm actually agreeing with an FBI agent? Maybe I lost my macho when I shaved off my beard. Yeah, we have to chance it."

Bernard said, "All right. It's been ten years — If you feel the risk is worth it, then this is the way we'll go."

Adam pushed the route to Nicholas's phone. He said to the others, "I have the new route, we're heading in. Adam, keep an eye out. And when do we talk to the White

House?"

Gray answered, his voice hyper even though he had to be dragging. "Hey, team. Afraid that's being handled by the CIA — Carlton Grace. They liked your idea, Nicholas, and they're moving forward. You won't believe this, but it's too classified for even the FBI to know about. We've been looped out. I'm going to keep my ear to the ground, see what I can find out."

"That figures. Copy that, Gray. We'll be in touch."

Adam said, "I'll keep watching you, Nicholas, we have a stationary satellite and the feed is relatively clear. We'll be following the heat signatures. The rain is making it hard to see you, so if a bear comes out of the woods I won't be able to warn you. Do me a favor and squawk your phone every five minutes, just in case we lose sight of you in the trees."

"Will do, Adam. Thanks."

Nicholas turned to Mills. "We're out of the loop? Only the CIA? I'm tempted, if a bear comes along, to throw you in its path."

Vinny had the gall to laugh. "Long live the CIA, the true power in the world."

It was close, but Mike didn't belt him.

CHAPTER SIXTY-THREE

T-MINUS 2 HOURS

The White House
Washington, D.C.

Carl Grace presented his ID at the gatehouse to the White House grounds. The agent looked it over carefully, even shined a black light on it, verifying its unseen markers. Since the attempts on President Jefferson Bradley's and Vice President Callan Sloan's lives last month, White House security had been tight as a drum. No Secret Service detail wanted to lose a president.

As the CIA's counterterrorism director, Grace was well known to the gatehouse, and to the agent inside. He was half-annoyed at how long it was taking, and half-pleased. If only they were as careful with the people who weren't supposed to be on the grounds.

Finally, the agent handed him back his ID

and waved him through. He parked in the side lot and went in the portico doors.

He was surprised to see Callan Sloan waiting for him.

"Madam Vice President."

"Carl. We're in the Situation Room."

She turned and he followed, stepped through the door at the end of the room, then down the concrete stairs to the Situation Room.

Inside, President Bradley and a dozen advisers were studying a screen showing a satellite view of Sri Lanka, and another showing a scattering of photos. Dr. Nevaeh Patel's and Kiera Byrne's faces stared at him — one older woman with dark hair in a ponytail and black glasses, the other younger, red-headed. Grace had always believed Byrne could tear a man's head off and go eat a sandwich. As for Patel, she looked like a terrifyingly smart dominatrix who could wield a whip with the best of them. He saw no mercy in those dark eyes of hers.

Bradley stood, shook Grace's hand. "Thanks for coming, Carl. You know everyone?"

Grace glanced around the room. In addition to the president and vice president, the assortment of men and women included the president's chief of staff, the head of NASA, and a couple of spit-shined men in uniform from the DOD.

Bradley said, "The joint chief is on one open line, and we have General Clarke from Strategic Command on another. They're tracking the satellite where they think the nuke might be. Have a seat, they're about to brief us on what they know. Go ahead, Command."

A third screen flashed up and Grace saw the interior of another situation room, knew this one was in Florida, well away from D.C. He also knew Callan Sloan shouldn't be here. Protocol dictated the vice president and the president be separated in times of a national security crisis. But he also knew Sloan wouldn't leave Bradley's side, even with a gun to her head, succession plan be damned. He liked that about her. She was tough, loyal, and smart.

The general said, "We think we found the right satellite, the one launched on the fourteenth. It's in the right orbit to be the P-Tel Communications satellite. The specs match. From what we can tell, despite the official word from Galactus, the satellite *was* successfully launched in orbit, only it was inserted in a completely different elliptical, which is why we didn't pick up on it sooner.

Like you, we understood the satellite missed its orbital window and had fallen back to Earth. We also would have been looking for it in the wrong orbit entirely, much higher than this. It was certainly never activated by P-Tel Communications, though I did receive a report they did in fact attempt to communicate with it.

"We've come to believe Dr. Patel managed to recode the satellite's computer system and hijack the motherboard from the ground. Instead of the satellite inserting in a geosynchronous orbit at twenty-two thousand miles above Earth, she sent it into a low Earth orbit at two hundred and fifty miles, where it has been moving, silently, into position — right here." The screen changed to a map, showing the ley lines of the satellite's orbit, looping sine waves that ended up converging in a single spot. "Its current position puts it two hundred and sixty-seven miles above Earth, in the general vicinity of Nepal."

Vice President Sloan said, "Nepal is nowhere near Sri Lanka and Patel's facility. Why there?"

"No idea, ma'am. But it's in the general region where the eclipse can best be viewed. We're assuming the eclipse has something to do with all of this."

Sloan turned to Grace. "We have assets on the ground in Sri Lanka now, correct?"

Grace said, "Correct, ma'am. There is also a Category Four typhoon making landfall in the area where our assets are located. Currently, they are here."

The screen showed a canopy of trees with a small bloom of heat signatures. Grace could see nine blobs of red.

"The facility is close by. As of last check-in, they're making excellent time, though they had a problem with a mudslide and are doing ingress on foot. My assets are working with Agents Drummond and Caine from the New York FBI Field Office. Their Covert Eyes team tracked the facility based on the purchase and subsequent shipment of an industrial-grade telescope, incredibly detailed. We are relying on this team to deactivate the nuclear sequence from the ground."

Bradley couldn't believe it. "Drummond and Caine? They're there?" He shook his head. "Leave it to them to be involved in this. And thank all that's holy they are — there are few people on this earth I believe more capable of stopping this than those two. Now, is there a reason we haven't simply dropped a bomb on Dr. Patel's facility? Wouldn't that stop the countdown?"

Grace said, "Unfortunately, sir, we have no idea what sort of backups she has in place. A bomb could set it off. Patel has been plotting this for years, certainly before she stole the plutonium in 2015. You can bet they've taken every precaution, covered all the bases."

He drew in a deep breath, then spit it out, "I believe our best course of action is to let our people on the ground attempt to stop the explosion."

DOD spoke up. "But just in case, Mr. Grace, Drummond's idea about eliminating the satellite carrying the nuke is sound. Should we determine the satellite does in fact carry a nuclear explosive, we can attempt to move the X-37B — the Orbital Test Vehicle — into place to intercept. Assuming, of course, it's in the proper orbit, and can get there in time."

The president rubbed his chin. "I'm no nuclear scientist, so explain to me how blowing up the satellite carrying the nuclear bomb won't set it off?"

General Thomas Monroe, the chief of staff, said, "There's an interior trigger that must be set off so that the two chambers of plutonium can collide and react with one another, resulting in a nuclear explosion. Fission. Avoid the fission, avoid the explosion. Understand, sir, it's not as simple as lighting a stick of dynamite and tossing it at the bomb. This must be a precision strike."

"Then let's get an ICBM loaded and up there. The Orbital Test Vehicle can be a backup, assuming it's capable of such a feat."

"We're at the outer limit of the ICBM's range, sir. And all of this is assuming we can find the satellite among all the space junk floating around up there. We think we know where it is, but until we positively identify the satellite carrying the nuke, sir, we can't take any offensive measures."

"Well, Thomas, figure it out. We're running out of time."

"These are precise calculations, sir. The math is being run as we speak." He coughed. "We aren't one hundred percent sure we can get the numbers to work in time."

Vice President Sloan sighed deeply. "And the space station? It would be compromised should an EMP go off in its orbit, yes?"

Henry Castelli, the head of NASA, said, "Yes. Though the ISS is hardened against a natural EMP event, solar flares and the like, we can't chance it. Anything else in the area not already hardened will be compromised. As a result, ISS has been given instructions to deviate from course and they have laid in new navigation. They'll be out of the way, farther north, as safe as we can make them, very soon. The thing is, this course correction is already being quietly reported in the community. Enthusiasts who watch would certainly have noticed the new course, and people love to talk. We don't have more than an hour before it gets into the public domain. Once it starts trending on Twitter, all bets are off. We'd like to avoid a panic, if at all possible."

Bradley looked to a countdown clock running in the top left corner. "Come up with an excuse — space junk in their way or something. That'll give the armchair astronomers something to buy."

"Sir, it's not that. I'm concerned that if Dr. Patel realizes the space station has moved off course, it will give away our knowledge the bomb exists and is in play. And that could mean she might blow it early."

Bradley slowly nodded. "Ah. Good point. We have a little more than one hour until the apex of the lunar eclipse in the area over Nepal. Is there a chance we're wrong about this timing?"

"Anything's possible, sir," Castelli said. "It's the unfortunate part of this, we don't know for sure."

"And your people, Carl? Their operation depends on them reaching this jungle-bound facility. Do they have the proper tools to stop this?"

"They do, sir. I don't need to remind you, Drummond and Caine are formidable weapons, exactly what we need for shutting down the computers. Drummond's hacking skills are top-notch. We don't have anyone better. And Caine is capable of handling the physical side of things, should a fight ensue. Combine the two of them with my people, and we're sending in a missile strike team, just warm-blooded instead of mechanical. And as you can see, they are very close."

The red heat blooms were in fact close to the main gate.

The president said, "I can't believe we don't have any other options in place to handle this threat."

Grace said, "We can only be so proactive, sir, when dealing with a nuke two hundred and fifty miles above the Earth on a rogue satellite we aren't yet sure we've accurately traced."

Bradley slammed his fist on the table. "We're going to change this, trust me. We are never going to have this situation on my watch again, do you understand?"

"Happy to hear it, sir," the chief of staff said. "Get Congress on board and we have a deal."

Bradley said, "Good, all right. I know Drummond and Caine well, I would trust them with my life. But there's no reason why we can't have a backup, just in case. Callan?"

Sloan nodded.

Bradley said, "Then it's settled." He said to the chief of staff, "Move our missile defense batteries into place in case things go south and Russia or China decide to lob a nuke our way in retaliation. Get the ICBMs ready for a launch. Even if this is out of their range, I want to be prepared. We must be ready in case our other attempts to stop this fail. But I do not want things getting that far down the road, am I understood? You verify you've indeed found this rogue satellite, get the air force on the horn, talk to their Rapid Capabilities Office, and tell them to get the Orbital Test Vehicle on the move to intercept and destroy. And tell your people to tune up their calculators, find that satellite. That's an order."

General Clarke spoke from Strategic Command. "Yes, sir. It's more like running a billion calculations per second through a supercomputer than punching in some numbers, but — we're on it."

Sloan watched the red dots moving on the screen. "Even if the team makes it inside the gates, they're facing an armed force, and they're in the northwest wall of a typhoon."

Castelli, NASA, said, "A slight bit of good news." He popped the storm satellite view on a small quarter of the screen. "Here's the most recent view from space. The eye of the storm will be on them soon, and they'll have about an hour of relative calm to get this thing stopped. I fear all we can do is wish them Godspeed."

And at that moment, the screen showing the team's progress toward the Aquarius Observatory bloomed bright white.

Bradley cried, "What's that white? What just happened?"

Grace looked from the screen to his president, feeling the first bursts of panic in his chest. "An explosion of some kind, sir."

CHAPTER SIXTY-FOUR

T-MINUS 1 HOUR 10 MINUTES

Nearing the Aquarius Observatory
Sri Lanka

It was fully dark now, the storm eerie and keening above, making the treetops whip around. Debris rained down on them with every step, and the ground was slippery muck. It was wet and miserable.

Nicholas's satellite phone showed they were nearing the road, which meant a clear shot to the gates, a blessed relief for their screaming legs.

Nicholas said, "I think we need to split into two groups, come at the gate from two sides."

Mills agreed and he, his five CIA agents, and Bernard split off.

Mike pulled up, leaned against a trunk, and shut off the flashlight to save the battery. They had to shout to be heard, even with their comms.

"The winds are getting stronger. I want to get inside the facility before the worst hits."

"Agreed. Catch your breath, then off we go. By my estimation, we're nearly to the road. Though the forest is giving us cover from the worst of the winds. I wish we'd thought to pack goggles. We'll be maybe thirty yards away from Bernard and Vinny when we get to the gates."

She pushed off the tree, turned the Maglite back on. This time Nicholas went first, hacking with the machete. They took three steps, and the forest in front of them exploded.

Nicholas was thrown backward into Mike, and they both hit the ground hard.

Mike was on her hands and knees a moment later, head up, gun in her hand. Nicholas wasn't quite as quick. She cleared the zone ahead, stepped back to his side, searching for fresh blood or broken bones. His eyes were open, no pain she could see.

Nicholas sucked in a big breath. "I'm okay, give me a second." He put a finger in his ear and cracked open his mouth. "I can't hear you."

"I'm not saying anything."

"Your mouth is moving."

"I'm cursing Nevaeh Patel to hell and

back. What happened?"

"I don't know. Let's go — carefully."

She hauled him to his knees, then to his feet. He swayed for a moment, then got his footing and nodded.

Twenty yards farther and the trees thinned. They saw a smoking crater. It looked like a war zone, bodies scattered around, the stench of death thick in the air. There were three people on their knees or staggering to their feet and four on the ground.

They saw Mills on his side, unmoving. One of his CIA agents was beside him, covered in blood, now quickly being washed away. Bernard was on his knees, giving CPR to another agent. Mike knelt with him while Nicholas checked the other three, one of whom was unconscious.

Bernard's face was grim, blood-streaked from a cut on his head. He'd lost his helmet, was sheltering the agent with his body. He shouted, "Hit an IED. Mills was on point. It exploded right in front of him, he took the brunt of the blast. They are supposed to be on the roads, not in the forest."

Mike pressed her palm against the man's chest. After a moment, she felt his heart stutter against her hand. "He's alive." She closed her eyes a moment.

Bernard helped the man sit up. "I don't know how stable he is, and we can't get help for anyone. Is Mills — ?"

Nicholas was standing next to her now. "Mills is alive, but he's in bad shape. The lucky bugger's unconscious, and that's a very good thing. He has a piece of shrapnel in his thigh. I'm afraid it could be wedged against the artery. If we try to remove it without the proper medical tools, he could bleed to death. We've got a tourniquet in place and stabilized the wound so we can get him to shelter. Bernard, we have to move, and move now. Are you okay?"

Bernard nodded, but stayed kneeling in the mud. "We have two dead and two more wounded. There is no way we can carry this many people. We will build a quick shelter and stay here while you two continue into the facility."

"You're going to be stuck out in the storm."

"We have the proper gear. The forest is cutting the wind."

A massive gust blew through, and Mike stumbled. Not two feet away, a tree creaked and uprooted, and fell heavily, scattering mud and leaves everywhere.

Mike said, "Absolutely not. The storm is getting worse. You have to come with us. We can't leave you here. Just to the gates, to shelter."

One of Mills's men, Honeycut, stumbled toward them. "She's right, we have to go, the worst of the storm is about on us. We can carry the wounded."

Honeycut pulled Bernard to his feet and set him toward the road. "We estimate we're less than half a klick from the gates. Can you manage Tomkins here? We'll take Mills."

Nicholas handed Mike his gear, holding back his weapon, ducked down and lifted Tomkins in a fireman's carry. Once Nicholas had his feet and was braced against the wind, he nodded.

Honeycut looked at Mike. "You have to lead us. Watch for anything white — on the road, in the bushes. That's what this one looked like, a piece of dirty white cloth, like a flag, planted. We think it was marked for removal and someone missed it."

"Copy that."

The going was slow. Mike was careful where she stepped. Mud squelched underfoot, her clothes were sodden, rain dripping in her eyes. She was royally pissed and worried, no, scared to death was more like it. Ten minutes later, the path, miraculously, was clear.

She shouted over the wind, "We're at the

road," and soon they were all with her. Mills wasn't looking good, his head slumped on his teammate's shoulder. They'd covered his leg with a tarp and she couldn't see any additional bleeding but couldn't imagine the jostling of being carried through the woods was doing the leg any good.

Tomkins, the man Nicholas carried, had come to and was insisting on trying to walk.

"Sorry, mate, you'll slow us down. Only a few more minutes and we'll be at the gatehouse."

Mike counted, they were down to three capable souls. Counting herself and Nicholas, that made five in all — against Patel's army. Granted, the teams were armed to the hilt, chest rigs full of gear and ammo, but this wasn't good.

With luck, Bernard's nephew would join them, making an even six. Two teams. The element of surprise was their best hope, but the IED exploding had to have drawn attention. Maybe they'd mistaken it for a blown transformer?

They set off again, moving quickly now, trotting up the road, gear as silent as they could make it. Mike's mantra — *We have to succeed, we have to succeed.* She felt her heart leap when they turned the last curve and saw the gatehouse. It looked deserted.

She called out, "Bernard?"

When he came up beside her, she said, "Do you have a signal to give your nephew?"

"I'm supposed to call him, but the phones are no longer working, the cellular signals cut off by the wind. I will have to approach myself. No, do not worry, I will do so under the pretext of checking on him."

"I'll cover you. Be careful. Oh, yes, tell me what he looks like."

Bernard pointed at his strangely colored hair. "He looks like me, Agent Caine. You won't have any trouble recognizing him." And he set off toward the gatehouse at a trot.

Nicholas gently set Tomkins on the ground and joined her, weapon out. They edged closer, took tactical stances, and waited.

Mike said, "If there's a gunshot —"

"Stop worrying. Bernard seems confident."

A moment later, Bernard crept back to their position. "He is there, and ready to let us in. But he will need his two compatriots paid, he's promised them money to help."

Nicholas said, "Fine, whatever they want. I have money in my belt."

"A thousand American dollars each."

Nicholas rolled his eyes but took off his belt, where he'd stashed several one-hundred-dollar bills. "I only have fifteen hundred dollars American. It will have to do."

Bernard nodded, took the cash, and trotted back to the gatehouse. Within moments, they heard a grinding noise and stepped out of the bushes to see the great gates to the facility breaking apart like a wax seal cracking in two.

Mike saw that in the center of each gate was half the astrological symbol for Aquarius. When the gates were closed, the insignia would complete the sign — two highly stylized lines that looked like mountains, or waves of water, carved into a round gold seal ten feet across. When she looked closer, she could see all twelve astrological signs carved into the edges of the central disk.

Nicholas said, "Well, we know we're in the right place at least."

Mike said, "The cameras just started to swivel. Look there."

Nicholas looked up. CCTV cameras were pointing in their direction.

"Let's hope it's from the gatehouse and not the main facility. We don't want Patel and Byrne to know we're here. If we don't have surprise on our side, we're sunk."

Bernard was waving to them, and they moved forward. He said quietly, "The cameras to the main facility have been temporarily blocked out. If you can get in quickly, they will close the gates, then perhaps no one will know we're here."

They slipped through the crack in the gates.

Nicholas said, "Looks like they have it set to seem like the gates may have blown open with the winds, but it can't work for long. No way they aren't going to notice a group of people coming in."

Mills moaned with each step his guys took, a good sign, Mike thought. They'd leave him behind in the shelter of the gate-house. She wasn't sure what she thought of Mills — Vinny — but he was as ready to leap into pits of hell as they were, and she had to admire that. In the gatehouse stood two men, both looked scared. She watched Bernard hand over the cash. That lightened their mood. A younger version of Bernard came forward to hug his uncle.

They heard the gates clang back shut, and the hum of electricity sounded like bees in her ears.

Nicholas said, "We're in."

CHAPTER SIXTY-FIVE

T-MINUS 60 MINUTES

Aquarius Observatory
Sri Lanka

It was nearly time to prepare herself.

Nevaeh left the command center and walked the long concrete halls to her private quarters. She brushed her hair and changed into a long, flowing white gown that looked like a Roman toga, fitting, she thought, to meet the gods. She looked at herself in the mirror. She looked older, not as she had when she'd first met the Numen years before. And they hadn't aged, of course. They were immortal. Wasn't she now immortal also? Would she begin to look younger with the Heaven Stone in her possession? It was hers, only hers. And surely this magic stone would realize she was worthy, that she'd done only what had to be done. Surely it would applaud her goal and the Numen's goals and judge them magnificent.

But why then was the Heaven Stone so heavy, so very cold when she touched it, even when she squeezed it in her hand? It never warmed. It remained completely inert, like a simple rock. A very heavy rock, and that wasn't natural. What did it mean? No, she had to believe once she was with the Numen, the Heaven Stone would recognize them as blessed, recognize the worthiness of their goal, and would grant her immortality and that which she wanted most, if it hadn't already, simply with her possession of it.

Nevaeh stared at herself in the mirror. She wound her long hair into an elegant topknot, looked again in the mirror, and nodded. Yes, she looked older, much older.

She crossed her bedroom, with its floor-to-ceiling windows that gave out onto the dense jungle, and watched the dark skies and pelting rain. It was worrisome for such a tempest to rise up now, of all times. No, it wouldn't be a problem, not for the Numen. They were gods, they could do anything once she'd rid space of all the junk man had jettisoned into it. She looked down at her watch. She now had fifty minutes until the explosion. Time to recheck every variable.

The halls were oddly silent, as was the command center. There was only the sound of her heels clicking on the floors and the moaning of the winds. Suddenly, the winds quieted and she realized the eye must be upon them. Amazing how much noise the rain and wind had been making. Even inside her concrete palace, the noise had been deafening. The silence was disconcerting. For a moment, only a moment, it unnerved her.

She sat down at her computer, looked at the weather radar, pleased to see they were on the edge of the eye-wall. A few quick calculations; it would be calm for an hour, and then — everything would change.

She looked at the moon's position. The eclipse had already started, though the cloud cover hid it from her view. No matter, she was pleased to see totality was going to occur within the window of time the storm was going to be passing through. Now that the eye was here, she would have a clear view of the eclipse. This particular celestial event was a long one, almost one hundred minutes, extended in length because of the distance from Earth to the moon. A blood moon, in the farthest position in its elliptical away from Earth, and a lunar eclipse, all at the same moment — and this was why Nevaeh had chosen tonight for her bomb. Even Mars was shining bright, brighter than it ever had before. A miracle. An omen. The god of war favored her, of course he did. Did the Numen recognize Mars? She shook her head at herself.

As she'd planned, the space station would pass through just as the bomb went off. Well, they'd taken the space station from her, she would return the favor, with the Numen's blessing.

It was exceptional timing. The only thing she hadn't foreseen was the typhoon, but even it was behaving, as if the Numen had created the storm to help hide her from her enemies.

Of course, she'd hardened Aquarius against the EMP, with every precaution taken to make sure they weren't blown off-line when the blast occurred and the waves of radiation burst through the atmosphere. The facility was at a state of readiness, everyone on alert. Despite the storm, she'd ordered her security forces stationed around the perimeter of the main grounds. Kiera was in charge of them. She knew Kiera was capable of handling anything that might happen so Nevaeh could have this moment for herself. Even now, she knew Kiera was walking around the facility, making sure everything was safe and secure.

But she wasn't taking any chances. On the off chance Aquarius went offline at the wrong moment, the satellite's onboard computer could operate autonomously. As much as she was looking forward to the pleasure of pressing the button and setting off the trigger, if she or her systems were somehow disabled, her failsafe would kick in and the bomb would go off anyway.

She'd thought of everything. Everything. She was a genius, and she'd had years to plan. There was nothing stopping this countdown. Nothing.

The programs were running flawlessly. She walked to her prized telescope in the next room. Since the eye of the storm was upon them, she felt safe opening the roof for a moment to admire the eclipse. It took five minutes for the domed roof to retract — five minutes she spent getting into position.

Her telescope was magnificent. Modeled after the VLT — Very Large Telescope — in Chile, with its state-of-the-art adaptive-optics module, it gave her the clearest imaginable view of the planets and satellites, nearly as impressive as images from the Hubble Space Telescope. Of course, it was unheard of for a private citizen to have this level of technology. But as Nevaeh had learned, money could fix anything, and she'd been able to have the telescope built and installed without a problem, without a trace. She'd stolen, skimmed money from Galactus, and used shell companies, fake names, and a series of numbered bank accounts run through multiple countries. And she almost forgot — *Thank you, Khaleed Al-Asaad, for your small but important financial contribution.*

No one knew she was here. No one knew Dr. Nevaeh Patel was behind the secret Aquarius Observatory. Even the men who'd worked to build the facility didn't know who she was, only the assumed name she gave them, Dr. Colombo, like their nearest city.

She climbed into the seat, settling her white toga around her as it whirred to life, moving into place until she was lying back at a perfect 32.7-degree angle, not lying down but comfortably reclined on her back. The ocular lens moved into position and the control panel rose and locked in front of her. She could program the telescope to look wherever in the universe she wanted.

She'd often looked for signs of the Numen, never finding a trace, but she knew they would be corporeal when they came to her. Wouldn't they? Or would they make her like them? And what would that be?

She smiled at her questions, not really caring. She wanted to see her eclipse.

She pressed a button on the control panel. The lights dimmed until the huge circular room was black. She closed her eyes, allowing them to adjust to the sudden darkness, opened them, then looked through the ocular lens.

The darkening moon was visible, as she'd hoped. It was incredible to see the red-tinged shadow caused by the Earth's atmosphere settle like a dusky pink sunset on the face of the moon. Even more incredible to know the Earth was passing between the sun and the moon, causing this shadow to move across the entire mass. The shape of the moon was unique in this moment, a view rarely seen, and it brought tears to her eyes.

How many people were staring in awe at the skies? She'd done so as a child, as a young woman, as an adult — stared up into the sky at celestial events with wonder, with hope, knowing one day, if she did everything right, she would be among the stars. Their ancestors must have been terrified at such a sight — the moon growing dark, then becoming drenched in red. Unexplainable, so for many it became an evil portent of what was to come.

As an astronaut, she'd been in orbit during an eclipse, had seen the moon's shadow move across the Earth from the window of the space station.

She said softly, "You are coming to me."

The Numen spoke as one, their voice clear as the tolling of bells. *Yes, we are coming to you.*

A small chime sounded, a warning that a door had been opened into her sanctuary.

She called, "Go away. I'm working."

Kiera raced into the room, calling for the lights to come on. They blazed to life, and she saw Nevaeh lying back, dressed in white, looking ready for a Roman orgy.

Had she been talking to the Numen again? No time, no time. She ran to Patel and tried to pull her off the chair. "Someone has breached the gates. You've got to get up."

Nevaeh stared at her. "What did you say? Someone is here? That's impossible. Through a typhoon? Through the jungle? Through our gates?"

Kiera shook her. "Yes, yes, they're inside the gates! I need to get you secure."

No time, no time. Kiera slapped at the button to close the roof of the observatory as she ran with Nevaeh through the door.

She didn't realize she'd missed the button.

The roof stayed open.

CHAPTER SIXTY-SIX

T-MINUS 40 MINUTES

Nicholas and Mike called in to Adam, who answered before the first ring ended. "What blew up? Are you okay?"

"It was an IED," Nicholas said. "We have two casualties and two injuries on the team. We're going to need a medevac. Vince Mills, the CIA agent, is hurt badly. Mike and I are all right, we were behind the main group. I don't know how you get someone to authorize a chopper to come up here, Mills said everything was grounded, which is why we drove in the first place, but someone has to do it, or he'll die."

"I'm on it. Grace is on the other line freaking out. Let me tell him, hang on."

Mike shouted, "Grace is on the other line? What's that about? Adam, what's going on there?"

Nicholas gestured at the other CIA agents.

"I would assume Grace is watching his team."

Adam came back. "Yes, many more than Grace are watching. The White House Situation Room has all of this being broadcast live, so make sure you wave at the satellite next time you're outside. They're working their end to help you knock out this nuke, trying to identify the satellite. There's a ton of classified stuff happening. You'll be happy to know the International Space Station has changed course and if the EMP goes off, they'll be okay — one win."

Mike said, "Good. The winds have calmed, Adam. Are we in the eye?"

"Yes. If the countdown coincides with the peak totality of the eclipse, you have exactly forty minutes. The eye will finish passing over you in forty-five minutes, so you have no time to waste. I've been watching the satellite feed, and the roof of the observatory opened about fifteen minutes ago and the telescope moved. As far as I can see, the roof is still open."

Nicholas shot Mike a look, rubbed his hands together. "We've always had good luck with roof entries. Well, maybe some good luck."

Mike said, "If the team can draw the guards' attention to the main entrance, we can get past them undetected and go in through the roof. Adam, we're signing off, but we have comms. Shout if we're about to run into trouble."

"Will do. The president and vice president say good luck — and get this stopped, or else."

"Or else what?"

"Well, that was implied. They'd probably have you pay triple taxes or something. Lia's going to take over now. See you on comms."

A moment later, their earwigs in place, Lia Scott's voice crackled to life.

"Hey, you two. I'm going to walk you in, Adam's going to keep working the computer. When you're ready, let me know."

"Copy that. Good to hear your voice, Lia."

Nicholas grabbed Bernard and Honeycut. Mills was too out of it, so Nicholas was going to have to take over his CIA team.

He said, "Here's the plan. Honeycut, you take your crew and head straight at them. Draw the guard's attention away from the observatory. Mike and I will circle the periphery and head in. The roof is open but we have no idea for how long. We have to move now. We've called in a medevac for Mills and anyone else who ends up needing help off the mountain."

Bernard said, "I will stay and coordinate

the rescue."

Mike shook his hand. "Thank you, Bernard. You've been a lifesaver."

He smiled, gave her a short bow. "You as well, I hope."

Mike pulled on gloves and cleaned her glasses as Nicholas and Honeycut worked out a few final details. She went through her weapons, realized she was missing something vital.

"Rope?" she asked Bernard's nephew. He yanked open a locker and tossed her a perfectly bundled tactical rappelling rope. "Excellent, exactly what I needed. Thanks."

She tied the rope around her waist and yanked her hands on her belt to make sure it was on good and tight, then turned her M4 around and strapped it in place. She had double holsters on her legs, checked her Glocks and her M4. She dug into Mills's bag, found a Ka-Bar knife, strapped it inside her leg, stuffed one Glock into her belt. Satisfied, she crossed her hands on top of her M4, grinned at Nicholas. "Shall we?"

"One moment," Honeycut said, and handed Nicholas a night-vision monocular. Nicholas pulled the strap onto his head then topped it with a backward baseball cap to hold it in place. Honeycut nodded, then turned his attention to Mike.

"Your hair's going to shine in the lights. Take this," and he tossed her a black watch cap. She stuffed her hair under it, reset her comms, nodded her thanks. Her heart was beating hard in her chest. As for Nicholas, he was as loaded down with weapons as she was. He looked ready to wrestle a bear, and maybe he'd take him down.

She said, "Everyone ready?" Nods all around. "Good, let's roll," and one by one, the CIA operatives slipped into the night. After a count of five, she and Nicholas followed, heading in the opposite direction.

The air was still, incredibly humid, wet and thick. She felt like she was walking with a wet washcloth draped over her mouth and nose. Nicholas was in front of her. All she could hear was his breath, coming a little harder than normal. *Adrenaline,* she thought. *He's as ramped up as I am.*

"Hey, Lia. We're on the move."

"I see you. Head to your west forty feet, then stop. There's a guard behind the tree but he's looking in the other direction. Move quiet."

They made their way from tree to tree on cats' feet, thankful the heavy rains had made the ground soft, but still they had to take care, the mud sucked at their boots. Finally, they hit the cement paths that curved around the facility.

There was a burst of gunfire from Honeycut and the other CIA agents. Mike started to move, but Lia said, "Wait, wait, guards are responding to the gunfire, they'll be passing in front of you in three, two, one —" And a squad of six men ran past them, all dressed in black. Lia said, "Go. Now!" and they took off, sprinting in the opposite direction, toward the observatory.

It was almost half a mile from the gates to the building. They ran quickly, crouched low, trying to blend into the night around them.

They were almost there when Lia shouted, "Stop! Guard."

A man stepped into their path, weapon in his hand, his mouth open in surprise. He was starting to raise his weapon when Nicholas leaped on him, took him down. The man hadn't had time to make a sound. He fell hard on the cement, headfirst. He didn't move.

Lia said, "You're clear. Keep moving."

Nicholas took the man's guns, stuffed them into his belt, and they jogged the rest of the way to the observatory. It was only two stories high, a relief. Mike attached a hook to the rope and tossed it to the roof in a beautiful parabola. It hooked on the edge of the roof, and she yanked hard on it, setting it in place.

Nicholas said, "Nice one. Look up."

She did, and the sight took her breath away. The moon was disappearing in a red haze, the Earth's shadow pushing across the face like the moon was being eaten by darkness, one sliver at a time.

He squeezed her shoulder. "You go first."

Mike slung the M4 to her back and started to climb.

CHAPTER SIXTY-SEVEN

T-MINUS 20 MINUTES

Mike planted her feet against the building and hauled herself up the rope, one hand over the other, blessing all those days in the gym. Nicholas was right behind her. She tried to regulate her breathing, but by the time they hit the roof, she was panting. It was hot, the gear was heavy, she'd just scaled two stories. And there was more to come. She was grateful the rain had let up for a while, though without the winds to wash the air clean, the forest smelled of must and rot.

The roofline led to a gravel top that worked as a moat surrounding the observatory dome itself, which rose one hundred feet above them. Nicholas scrambled over the edge, blew out a deep breath.

Mike pointed at the dome. "It's still open at the top, about a fifty-foot gap across. You ready to climb some more?"

Nicholas had his night-vision monocular on, swept his head around the roofline. "Look over there."

She followed his finger. On the far edge of the dome, she could make out a black metal staircase. It blended with the roof of the observatory so perfectly she could barely see it in the dark.

"Oh joy, now it's time for the StairMaster. Bring the rope, we can rappel in from the top."

He smothered a laugh and they crept across the gravel-topped roof to the stairs.

The metal staircase clanked and rang out as they started up, but the gunfight happening on the other side of the campus covered any noise they made. Nicholas looked up once, saw the moon was taking on an almost orangish hue as the eclipse moved closer and closer to totality.

He said quietly, "It's beautiful. Wish we were sitting on a beach watching this, champagne in hand."

Mike said, "You and me both, maybe you feeding me some grapes. Weren't we supposed to be having our last day in Rome right now?" She gave a manic grin, and shrugged. "Oh well. Come on, one more flight and we're there."

When they were in position, Mike tied the rappelling hook to the staircase, and they shimmied up the remainder of the dome's exterior. It was like climbing a cracked-open eggshell, if the eggshell had a square wainscoting pattern on it, the edges of which were excellent foot- and handholds. It took a few minutes to scale the dome, but they finally reached the open top and looked down.

There was a massive telescope above a reclined chair. The room was brightly lit, but empty, as far as they could see.

Mike said, "No guards. We can go in."

Nicholas nodded and wrapped the rope around his arm, positioning himself to give Mike the first ride down. She grabbed the rope and set her feet. She was about to go when he yanked back on the rope and she sailed out of position and slammed facefirst on the roof.

Nicholas whispered, "Sorry. Door opened."

They scrambled back to the edge of the opening. As they watched, a tall red-headed woman stepped into the room. It was Kiera Byrne. She scanned the grounds and looked up, but Mike had swung back out of sight. She was looking for intruders. Not good.

They heard a loud click, then gears started

grinding and the roof began to close.

"Crap. Nicholas, we have to go in now."

"Lia, advise."

"Guys, she's still in there. She's walking the periphery, she's out of my sight now."

"The roof is closing, we don't have a choice. I don't see any other way in."

Lia said, "Wait, I can see her again. She's returned to the door."

Mike snuck a glance over the edge. The side of the roof they were on was sliding inward, shortening their rope. "We gotta go, Nicholas. Now. Or we'll end up jumping."

He nodded once, and she slung her M4 back into place, put one hand on the trigger in case she had to come in shooting, secured her other on the rope.

"I'm right behind you," he said, and she started in.

Byrne was just getting through the door when Mike started down. She held her breath and prayed, sliding closer and closer, and she knew the rope was going to run out with ten feet to go, fifteen now — as the roof's two halves slid closer together. No help for it, she had to jump.

She tried to land quietly, and nearly managed it even with all the gear and a fifteen-foot drop onto the white tile floor, but the mud on her boots gave her away. She slipped as she landed, clanking hard to the tiles. Byrne, already aware someone had gotten inside the gates, heard her and whirled around.

Nicholas landed next to Mike and got off three shots. Byrne was already shouting for the guards as she disappeared out the door, slamming it behind her. A wailing, high-pitched alarm sounded.

The roof closed, and the Klaxon shriek grew louder. They were inside, yes, but they'd lost the element of surprise.

"Nicholas, is there another way out of here?"

"I don't know. Blueprints, Lia? Anything?"

Adam came across their comms. "I see only one door, but what I found is old, Nicholas, looks like a prototype."

Nicholas said a few choice words. Mike said, "We gotta go, she's going to come back with an army."

"Keep to the walls."

They ran across the room to the nearest wall, then made their way to the door. Nicholas counted down from three, put his hand on the knob.

"Here goes nothing." He flung open the door.

The hallway exploded in gunfire.

CHAPTER SIXTY-EIGHT

T-MINUS 10 MINUTES

Kiera ran into the control center, yelling. "We have to go, Nevaeh, we have to get you out of here. They're inside. They want to stop you, stop the countdown. I don't know who they are, I saw only an armed man and woman in the observatory. They're here to kill you, I know it. We must leave."

Nevaeh smiled at her. "Calm yourself, Kiera. Only ten minutes now and everything will be over. They can't do anything. Wait, you'll see. And I have this." Nevaeh reached into a hidden pocket of her toga and managed to pull out the Heaven Stone with both hands. "Don't worry, with the stone, I am untouchable. I am immortal. Let them come. It won't matter."

Kiera looked at the ugly dark stone now weighing down Nevaeh's hands, clasped beneath it to hold it. Why hadn't its weight ripped open the toga? This was supposed to be the Holy Grail? It was nothing, a stupid rock, but how could it weigh so very much? Nothing made sense. She finally faced that her mentor, her lover, the single person she'd willingly give her life for, was insane. Kiera thought of all the conversations she'd transcribed when Nevaeh was in her sensory deprivation chamber — all one-sided — but with pauses, like Nevaeh was listening to someone talk back to her. The Numen? These aliens Nevaeh believed in utterly? Believed they were coming for her once she set off the nuke? But if they were real, why couldn't Kiera hear them? And now, Nevaeh truly believed this ridiculous hunk of rock meant something important, like immortality?

Still, Kiera loved her, wanted to save her. She shook her shoulders. "Listen to me, there are people outside, and the man and woman who've managed to infiltrate through the roof. It's my fault, my fault. I worried, and so I went back to double-check the roof was closed and they were already in. The only thing that matters now is your safety. Not the nuke, not this bloody stone. Whatever you believe it is, whatever Broussard believes it is, it can't help you, can't help us. The stone — it's too heavy to take.

Leave it. It doesn't matter. Come now, you must."

Nevaeh looked sad as she took Kiera's hand. "And where will we go, Kiera? The eye of the storm will pass soon and then the typhoon will be upon us again. We can't drive down the mountain or fly out. No. There is no choice. You have to fight, you have to stop them, just long enough for the bomb to explode and the Numen to come. Trust me one last time. They will come. They promised." She rubbed the Grail. "The Heaven Stone. I know it will come to life for me, it must. I know it will come to recognize my worthiness, recognize I'm the only one destined to guide the world with the Numen at my side."

Kiera paced away, then back again, trying to figure out what to say, how to convince her. "You must listen to me. Look, I appreciate that you have this — belief, this fantasy — I'm sorry, Nevaeh, but that's all it is, a fantasy, maybe a delusion. Whatever it is, it's not real. I'm real and you're real, but the rest of it?" She shook her head. "We can't waste any more time, I must get you to safety."

Nevaeh slapped her hard, panting, her rage was so great. "How dare you? You believe I'm insane? You, the only person I've trusted over the years with my love, with my life, with my secrets? You're like that lying, jealous bitch Holloway at NASA, that miserable traitorous cow in New York. And now you're betraying me, Kiera? You?"

Kiera's cheek burned, but it didn't matter. "Nevaeh, you wanted to kill the people who hurt you, I get that. You want to clear out all the junk in space — silence the heavens for these aliens — the Numen, you said. I do get all of it. I understand. But now you have to stop this absurd belief that this stupid rock you're holding is something special when it's only like a rock you could pick up in your garden. It doesn't mean anything, it doesn't have any more reality or power than these aliens, the Numen. No one from outer space is coming, believe me. But someone else is and this someone is coming to destroy us. Do you understand? We must leave, now, while we still can."

All Nevaeh could hear was Kiera's contempt. How long had she only humored her? Should she kill her now and be done with it? Or let the Numen end her? Yes, she would let the Numen deal with her. She said, her voice infinitely calm, "You will lead the team to stop whoever has come. Leave me now. I will be fine."

"No, no, you can't stay here, they'll kill you."

Nevaeh shrugged. "Let them try. Now, if you're nearly as capable as you claim to be, you'll be able to stop them. Are you responsible for their being here? Did you somehow give away our location? No, don't argue. Quit your sniveling. Get out there and deal with your mistakes." She shoved Kiera toward the doors. "Go!"

Kiera stared at her, unwilling to believe what she'd said. She saw no forgiveness on Nevaeh's face, only implacable — what? Resolve? No, belief, fanatic belief, that she was going to meet up with this alien species.

"Go!"

She hesitated only a moment before running from the control center. She looked back once to see Nevaeh staring after her, no expression on her face. Nevaeh didn't care. Not about her, in any case. It hit Kiera hard, and she ran.

When Kiera was gone, Nevaeh calmly pressed a series of commands into her keyboard, and a huge steel door slid shut behind her. She checked her command module once more, pleased to see the countdown proceeding as planned. As her very own flight director, she said aloud,

"Flight, all is nominal," then laughed and rubbed the Heaven Stone. Why didn't it warm at her touch? Why didn't it seem to recognize her? Welcome her?

It would. It would. She glanced once more at her countdown clock. Ten minutes. Ten minutes until her life changed forever, until the world changed forever. And the Numen agreed and sang to her in their sibilant single voice, *The world will change forever, the world will change forever.*

CHAPTER SIXTY-NINE

T-MINUS 8 MINUTES

The white-tile hallways branched out in a labyrinth of corridors in every direction. Mike saw a head pull back around a corner twenty feet ahead and moved steadily forward, shooting rhythmically, smoothly, driving back the gunfire until Nicholas was at her side.

When the firing stopped, she whispered, "Reloading."

"Let them. I saw a sign back in another corridor. Let's go this way, I think it might take us to Patel's command center."

They walked down the hallway, clearing it of three more of Patel's guards, moving deeper into the facility.

The gunfire abruptly stopped. They looked at each other. Too easy.

She whispered, "We can't be sure if the rest of the team made it inside. We could be alone in here, Nicholas."

"Yes, and we're running out of time. We're going to have to split up. I'm not sure now about that bloody sign, and these hallways are a maze. Who knows where they're leading us. We need to find the control center and shut this computer system down."

"Yes, but we have to find our way there. Adam, can you help us? Which direction? Which way?"

Silence.

Mike said, "Hey, where's Lia? Are all our comms down?"

Nicholas tapped his, checked his satellite phone. "Everything is down. Something in here is interfering with the signal. This place is supposed to be ready to withstand a massive EMP, so there's a good chance it's the facility itself."

"I'd rather not split up. We have to keep moving. We'll find the command center."

They jogged down the hallway. Mike said, "I've counted seven dead guards. There must be more guards than this."

"Agreed. Many more. They've taken cover someplace."

They came to another split. There were two directions they could take at this point. Two completely identical, unknown paths.

Nicholas looked around for some sort of

markings or directions, found nothing. He looked up at the ceiling. It was smooth white, with no breaks. But there was a slight seam in the panel above him.

"Hold on. What's this? Can you give me a boost?"

Mike dropped to all fours and Nicholas stepped on her back, pushed on the ceiling with both hands. It gave a bit at the edge and he shoved harder, knocking a full section aside. It clattered to the floor, but still, even with the noise, there was still no gunfire from the guards.

He pulled Mike to her feet and made a stirrup from his hands. "I'm going to lift you up. Look at the rafters, tell me what you see."

"What am I looking for?"

"Cables. Phone lines, telecom lines, anything cable oriented. Tell me which direction they go."

She said, "Don't get me shot," and stepped into his hands. He lifted her easily and she stuck her head into the darkness. "Maglite." He passed it to her, and she shined it all around her.

She saw steel rafters running the length of the building and tried to orient herself. They'd come from the observatory, which was definitely behind them. She played the light until she saw familiar cables. They were running away from her at a thirty-degree angle. She called down, "I got it, let me down."

"Cables?"

"Tons of them. We need to head that way." She pointed down the left-hand hall. "It's leading straight from the observatory toward something, and the mess of cables are thick."

"Good job. Let's go."

They started down the hallway, weapons up. Still, there was no return fire. Mike whispered, "It's as if the guards have laid down their weapons and aren't trying to defend this place anymore. Something's wrong. Where did they go?"

"Maybe we tagged them all."

"No way. Look." She pointed out a few scattered blood droplets on the floor. "See the pattern? Elliptical drops — whoever we hit was on the run. But on the run to where?"

"I bet the guards have retreated to a certain section, probably the command center, and they'll be setting up a final defense to keep us occupied until time runs out. Let's keep moving."

Three more steps, and a door flew open in front of them. It slammed into Mike's shoulder, and she stumbled.

Kiera Byrne stepped into the hallway.

Nicholas started for her but she dodged expertly, jumped up into the air, and grabbed hold of the top of the door and swung at him, kicking him as she went. The blow caught him in the chest and he spun to the ground, momentarily stunned.

Mike was back on her feet, her M4 at the ready, but Kiera kicked out from the door and landed right on top of her. Mike stumbled but stayed on her feet. Kiera tumbled gracefully to the floor. Mike's M4 clattered to the floor behind Kiera. How had she managed to knock the gun from her shoulder and send it spinning away? She was fast, flexible, had the moves of a gymnast. Kiera whipped around and faced her. "Hey, little girl, who are you? You think you can hurt me? Think you can stop this? Come on, let's play." And she waggled her fingers at Mike.

Nicholas was back up but he couldn't shoot, he couldn't take the chance of hitting Mike.

Mike shouted, "Nicholas, go! Shut it down, I've got this crazy bitch!"

He was torn for a moment, but she screamed, "Go!" at him again and he took off running. Mike could handle herself. He had to stop this bomb.

CHAPTER SEVENTY

Mike and Kiera faced off. Kiera was taller, weighed more, and was probably as good at martial arts as Mike was at shooting. She was formidable. Still, no choice, Mike had to stop her. "You're a hard woman to find, Kiera Byrne. Yeah, I wanna play. I'm the woman who's going to kick your butt from here to eternity."

Kiera laughed in her face. "Whoever you are, you've got a mouth. I like that. Now I'm going to slam your teeth down your throat. Okay, come on, let's dance."

Kiera launched herself at Mike with a cry, her hands a blur.

Mike absorbed the impact of the first hit with her forearm, the second with her shoulder, leaning into the punches instead of backing away. This surprised Kiera, who was used to people running away from her berserker charge. Her momentum carried her two feet past Mike. Mike whirled and kicked her in the hip on the way by. Kiera smacked into the wall, felt a sharp hit of pain.

Mike heard the crunch of bone, excellent. But which bone had she broken? She didn't wait, threw another roundhouse kick, catching Kiera behind the knees.

But now Kiera was ready. She flipped over backward instead of falling, another acrobatic move, and landed lightly on the balls of her feet. She came again, arms a blur, punching, kicking, trying to catch Mike's forearm and twist it, which would surely break it in two. Mike was faster, Kiera was bigger, but they were well matched. They brawled down the hallway, both landing hard punches and kicks but neither delivering the killing blow.

Mike knew time was running out. She had to end this. She pulled together everything she had, stepped into a punch, took it on the jaw, and managed to yank up with her elbow. She caught Kiera square in the nose and shoved upward. She spun and delivered a left jab with a satisfying crunch followed by spurting blood. Kiera stumbled backward. Mike grabbed her Ka-Bar from its sheath.

Kiera swiped the blood away with her sleeve. "So you want to play with a knife now? My favorite weapon." And Kiera grinned. The adrenaline was pumping so hard the break in her arm didn't even hurt, at least not now, when it mattered. Kiera knew how to fight someone with a knife — either take it away or jam it inside of them. She attacked.

Mike was ready, held the knife's thick hilt tight inside her fist, blade out, ready to punch and slice, a dangerous combination. The Ka-Bar dug into Kiera's shoulder, but it didn't seem to faze her. She slammed her fist into Mike's head, twirled and hit her in the breastbone. Mike landed heavily on her back, and Kiera was above her, ready to jump down on her, teeth bared. Mike kicked up into Kiera's face with both legs. She missed her face but hit her in the chest. A sharp zing went up her leg from her ankle — not again — and she knew she was in trouble. She could fight fine with two legs, but now she was going to have trouble standing.

She made herself stand, she was ready, she had to be. She had to go for it. Mike slammed her head back into Kiera's face, grabbed her hair, whipped her hand around her shoulder, and jerked her arm back toward herself as hard as she could. One single frozen moment — Mike plunged the knife deep into Kiera's shoulder, shoved away from her.

Kiera collapsed backward, blood spurting from her shoulder, hot and thick. Wait, she moved. How?

Kiera suddenly flipped over, her weight taking Mike down. Mike landed on her back, and Kiera wrapped her hands around Mike's throat. Squeezed, squeezed, squeezed, until Mike was seeing stars. No choice, she released her grip on the knife in Kiera's shoulder and slammed her arms into Kiera's once, twice, and finally, felt her grip begin to loosen. She kneed Kiera in the stomach, shoved her over her head, and managed to get out from under her and roll to her feet.

Kiera landed face-first and stopped moving. Blood was everywhere, on the white tile, on the walls, on Mike. She saw the tip of her Ka-Bar visible through the other woman's ribs, sticking out of her back.

It was over.

Mike tried to swallow, finally managed to roll over on hands and knees. She gagged a few times before she could breathe again. Blood was dripping from her mouth. Finally, she got to her feet, staggered a little, wiped her mouth on her sleeve. She ran her fingers over her teeth, all still in place.

Good. But her ankle, did she break it this time? She tested it, put her weight on it, and wanted to scream as pain shot through her. She gritted her teeth. She'd deal with it later.

She stepped over Kiera and followed Nicholas's path.

She could hear the wind start to pick up again outside.

No time, no time left.

Mike ran down the hall, dragging her foot, calling Nicholas's name.

CHAPTER SEVENTY-ONE

T-MINUS 6 MINUTES

Nicholas forced himself to stop before he turned into the last hallway. He used the reflection on the face of his phone to see around the corner. There were four guards grouped in front of a steel door with a biometric panel on its right side.

They were expecting a frontal assault. In front of them lay four men, two of them obviously dead, the other two moaning. He realized they'd expected to be inside the command center, but instead, there was now a steel door keeping them out. And they were stuck in the open with no cover.

Nicholas called, "Your mistress has left you to die. We have no desire to kill all of you, but we will if you fight back. We can handle this like gentlemen. Drop your weapons, put your hands on your heads, take your wounded men, and walk away.

You have thirty seconds to comply before we start shooting down the hall. Trust me when I say I am an excellent shot, and I have more men behind me."

There was a murmur, then one of the men called back, "You are friends with Bernard?"

"Yes."

"Okay. Don't shoot."

He looked around the corner to see the four men, their hands on their heads.

Nicholas said, "Take your men. Leave. Now."

The men grabbed the wounded soldiers and carried them out fireman style. They left their guns on the floor. He sent a thank-you prayer heavenward and ran to the biometric panel. Where was Mike? He couldn't wait, no time. He had to get inside. He had a preprogrammed biometric reader in the pocket of his vest that would override the palm prints approved to open this door and put his in place. He inserted the micro thumb drive into the reader. Moments later, the image of a palm appeared on the glass, and as he watched, it morphed into the outline of his own hand. He slapped his hand into place and the steel door unlocked, opened smoothly.

He rolled onto the floor in a ball, expecting a barrage of gunfire, but there was nothing, only the quiet whirring of computers and gears. He slammed against a console.

Where was Nevaeh Patel? He'd expected her to be here, but the room was empty.

He stared at the computers. They were as high-end as any he'd seen. Liquid plasma screens crowded together on the walls, giving several different views. The command center was offset so the programmer could move from table to table. One side was organized, clean and sharp, the other was reminiscent of the interiors of the International Space Station he'd seen in photographs and interviews, cords and panels set up haphazardly, papers everywhere, all the screens showing different programs running.

Which one was responsible for the satellite's motherboard?

He wished his comms worked, but it didn't matter. Neither he nor Adam were astrophysicists.

No help for it. He started moving left to right, systematically, reading the running programs. One was telemetry, one was an orbital path, and he stopped to study that screen. It was just as important for them to figure out where the satellite was as it was for him to get the bomb countdown stopped. He looked at his watch — he had less than six minutes to stop it.

At that moment, his comms came back on with a deafening squawk, and he heard Adam shouting in his ear. "Nicholas, Nicholas, can you hear us? We can finally hear you, you're muttering those great British curse words. If you can hear us, give us a sit rep."

He shouted back, "Yes, I can hear you again. Thank God, Adam. I'm looking at a screen right now and I've got the orbital path. Is this where the satellite is right now?"

He read off a series of coordinates, and Adam said, "I've got it, we're mapping it now. Can you turn off the bomb?"

Nicholas looked at his watch — five and a half minutes to go. "Well, I'm in the command center. Can't find Patel, and Mike is somewhere out in the halls going head-to-head with Kiera Byrne."

"We've heard a lot of fighting, but I think she's okay, I heard her cussing up a blue streak about her ankle. The bomb, Nicholas. You have to turn off the bomb. We can't stop it from here, can't get the Orbital Test Vehicle into place in time. It's all up to you."

"Problem is I can't tell which bloody setup is to the satellite's motherboard."

"Well, keep looking, and hurry up. The White House is panicking, they're about to get on the phone to Moscow and Beijing to warn them, and they'd rather not have to do that."

"I'm looking. Wait, I think this is it."

He sat on the stool and dug into the code. "It is, I've got it. Bloody hell, Adam, it's in remote mode. I don't think I can —"

A voice behind him said, "What do you think you're doing? Get away from there."

He whirled around, saw the gun before he registered the woman holding it. He dove to the side, sent the stool spinning away, but it was too late. He had only a heartbeat to register he'd found Nevaeh Patel before the bullet struck him and the pain began, so sharp and intense it took his breath away. He went down.

CHAPTER SEVENTY-TWO

Nevaeh stared dispassionately down at the man. He wasn't dead, he was breathing, but he'd be dead soon. She heard shouting, realized he was wearing an earwig. She knelt down, took it out of his ear, and listened.

"Nicholas, Nicholas, report! We heard a gunshot, are you hit? Are you hit?"

She said, "Whoever you are, oh yes, he's hit. He's down for the count."

She dropped the earwig to the tile floor, smashed it with her shoe. The remote shouting stopped.

She saw the man, Nicholas, was bleeding, the bullet had caught him in the upper arm. She pressed her foot against the wound until he groaned in pain.

"Your name is Nicholas? And just who are you, you gorgeous creature?"

Nicholas tried to lunge at her, but she was fast and he was light-headed from the pain. He could feel the bullet, knew it had gone through his arm and into his chest, right in the notch where his body armor met his underarm. He couldn't tell how deep it was, but he knew it had to be bad, he was having trouble breathing. It had hit a lung.

He knew he had to get up, he had to stop the countdown. He tried to push himself to his knees and Patel started to laugh at him.

"Hurts, does it? I've not been shot, but Kiera told me the pain is incredible, like hot pokers shoving into you over and over."

He managed to grab hold of the counter that held the multiple command and control modules.

He got some air in his lungs, not much, maybe he'd gotten lucky — again — and the bullet wasn't in his lung. He looked over at the older woman, fit, tall, glossy black hair, wearing, strangely, a Roman-style toga. "Why are you doing this? Trying to set off a nuclear EMP, hurting thousands, and eventually millions of innocent people the world over?"

"Unlike you, I am doing this to change our screwed-up world, to stop all the fighting, the incessant wars. I will bring peace, no matter what is necessary to do so. The Numen will be beside me. I have the Heaven Stone, thanks to Jean-Pierre, and it will come to obey me, to do what I require of it.

I have the satellite in place, the bomb will go off shortly, and the Numen will come to me. They will reward me.

"I met them in space, did you know? Is that why you're here? Did those bastards at NASA send you? Well, let me tell you, the moment the bomb goes off, the space station will be the first casualty. They're going to be in exactly the right spot —"

"No, they won't. They've been alerted to the danger and altered course two hours ago."

Nicholas watched this woman go from dreamy to psycho in a heartbeat. Even her voice changed, no longer eerily calm, it was vicious, cruel.

"How is that possible? Who are you?"

"I'm Special Agent Nicholas Drummond, FBI. And it's time to end this insanity, Dr. Patel. Listen to me, please. Your actions could start another world war. Help me end this. Help me turn it off."

Nevaeh sneered, but her voice calmed, and she sounded like a professor he'd once had. "You poor stupid boy. I'm bringing peace to this corrupt world. As for the EMP, the Numen require silence. Our presence in space, all our technology and satellites — they cannot communicate with us. Only with me. You know as well as I do the world now worships itself, the age of Me, everyone staring at their cell phone screens, no one really present. It must end, or civilization as we know it will cease to exist. The Numen — through me — will bring back peace, prosperity, and the communications structure will revert back. We don't need all this science, all this technology. Look what it's done, look at the harm it's caused. The world is on fire. The Numen and I — we have a chance to stop it.

"And with that end will come peace. Do you know I was the first one to fulfill NASA's grand mission? The one thing they claim to want more than anything is to make contact with an exoplanetary species, and that's what I did. And I am the one who is going to bring them back to Earth. I alone will be responsible for first contact."

The pain thudded in his chest, but he couldn't let it grind him under.

She smiled. "There's nothing you can do. It's all over. The launch computer takes over in five seconds, and we are no longer in control. So sit back and enjoy the silence. It will last forever."

He had to get up, he had to stop this, but before he could get to his feet, she was out of sight. He collapsed back onto the floor, trying to catch his breath.

Clinically, he knew what was happening. His lung was filling with blood. He needed a chest tube.

He needed Mike.

But he had no idea where she was.

He dragged himself to the command module, pulled himself to his knees. He was bleeding on the keyboard, not good. He fumbled his hands into place and started to type. He had to stop the bomb.

CHAPTER SEVENTY-THREE

T-MINUS 3 MINUTES

Nevaeh shot him again, in the chest, even though she knew there was nothing he could do. She walked quickly out of the command center and back to her bedroom, shutting doors behind her as she went, the Heaven Stone in her hands, dragging her down. Why did it seem so much heavier than it had even ten minutes ago?

On the wall in her bathroom, she pressed her hand into a slight groove and a biometric panel rose from the gap, rotated into place. The surface was coded to her handprint alone, so even if they made it through all of her doors in the next minute — impossible, but Nevaeh was an astronaut, redundancies were her calling — no one could follow her.

The door opened with a click. The small lit passageway would lead her back to the observatory. She shut the door behind her, used her handprint to close and lock the biometric mechanism so it would slide away and no one else could find it, and followed the small hallway, repeating the same steps to open the door to the observatory.

When she was safe inside the circular room again, she activated the shield she'd designed to drop steel cages across both doors. They clanged into place. She was alone. No one could get in, and, most importantly, no one could stop her now.

She glanced at her watch, moved to the wall, and set the timer to open the roof in eight seconds. She took her seat again, setting the Heaven Stone in her lap. It hurt it was so heavy. No, it had to be her imagination. She had to be patient. Soon now. The telescope's command module swung into place in front of her.

The countdown continued to move ever forward, winding down to the moment she'd be back with her friends. Would they appear at her side immediately after the bomb went off? Or would it take them a few minutes to let the reverberations of the EMP make their way through the orbit before they came?

Interesting that she hadn't thought of this before, or thought to ask.

She waited patiently, lightly rubbing the Heaven Stone, so heavy on her legs. She ignored the shouts and calls and gunshots she heard outside the room. Soon, none of this would matter.

When the roof opened, she smiled up at the shadowed bloodred moon in the sky above her. The eclipse was at almost 100 percent. Soon now, very soon, the bomb would go off, only two more minutes to complete totality.

With a beatific smile, she turned her face to the heavens. "It is time. I am ready."

Chapter Seventy-Four

T-MINUS 2 MINUTES

Mike had to get the door open to the command center, but how? She'd put her hand on the biometric panel, but nothing had happened. Now, nearly frantic, she slapped it, pressed every button she saw, but still nothing. She called out Nicholas's name again, but no answer. Was the room soundproofed?

There had to be a different way in. Her comms crackled to life.

"Mike? It's Adam. Can you hear me?"

"I hear you. What's going on? I can't get inside the command center but I know Nicholas did. I called out, but I don't think he can hear me."

She heard Adam start shouting, then Gray came on the comms, calm and cool.

"Mike, we've lost comms with Nicholas. We believe Patel shot him. She spoke to us,

545

then she must have smashed his comms. We need to get you in there. You're going to have to stop this, and her.

She heard her voice as if from a long way away. "Gray, do you know if he's alive?"

"We don't know. Mike, we have to get you inside, now."

"What do I do?"

"Look for a panel."

"There's a panel, I've put my hand on it a hundred times now, and it's not opening. I'm trying to break in and I can't do it."

"Okay, take a breath. It's programmable. I'm going to need you —"

"There's no way, Gray. I'm not the computer whiz you guys are."

It hit her then. She looked up. The ceiling.

"Hold on, I'm going to try something else."

She didn't hesitate. She piled up the two dead bodies the soldiers had left and used them as a stepping stool to climb up to the ceiling. She shoved the panel above her head and it gave way.

Her arms screamed as she pulled herself up into the rafters. The steel door to the command center reached all the way to the ceiling above her, but there was a tiny gap on either side, fifteen feet to the left and to the right of her current position. Rafters spread out like metal ribs in five-foot increments.

"Okay, Gray, can you hear me? I'm in the ceiling, I'm going to try and get around this door from above."

"Mike, we're under a minute — hurry!"

She didn't think, she just did it. She jumped the five feet from the first rafter to the second, almost falling off. The pain in her ankle shooting up her leg took her breath away, plus the mud on her boots made each step slippery. No time to take off her boots, and her ankle needed the support. She jumped more carefully the second time, landing better, and jumped again, to where she could see the sliver of light.

"This better work."

The gap between the steel and the girder that made the wall was small, but she had a runner's build. She eyed the gap, realized there was no way to make it through with all her gear. She shucked off the tactical vest, put a gun in her waistband at the small of her back, and squeezed herself into the gap, past the steel door.

She barely made it.

Once on the other side of the steel wall, she danced her way back two rafters, then dropped to her knees and used the butt of the gun to bang a hole in the ceiling large enough to drop through. The ceiling material fell to the floor and she braced herself for a retaliatory shot, but nothing came.

She stuck her head down through the hole and saw an empty room. But it was definitely the command center.

She dropped in, landing on her good foot.

"Nicholas!" Then she saw him lying on his side. She ran across the room, her heart pounding in her ears. He was still breathing.

"Come on, Nicholas, you've gotta get up and turn off the nuke."

"I'm — trying —" he gasped out, and she saw the keyboard on the floor next to him. "I shut down the failsafe on the satellite. But the countdown didn't stop —"

"Which one is running the bomb?"

He pointed. She pulled her Glock from the small of her back and emptied the entire magazine into the computer.

Thirteen shots.

An explosion rattled the building, and she dropped to her knees. Threw herself over Nicholas. It hadn't worked, she'd failed.

She heard cries and shouts, smelled smoke, and realized the explosion was on the ground, not in the sky. Mills's men must have blown off a door to get in.

She looked at the countdown clock. It wasn't moving anymore, read 00:00:01:03.

She reared back. Nicholas was white, his breathing labored, and there was blood covering his chest. But he gave her a half smile. "Shooting the sucker — never would have — thought of that. You're — such a show-off."

She drew in a deep breath. "Where are you hit?"

"Lung," and his voice sounded hollow, breathless. "Then she shot me in the chest, hit my Kevlar." Mike spoke calmly into her comms. "The countdown has stopped. Gray, Adam, Lia, anyone there? Nicholas needs a medic, immediately. It — it's not good. I think he's lung-shot."

"Copy that."

She brushed Nicholas's hair back from his forehead. "I don't know if we stopped the nuke, but it stopped the countdown. You turned it off from the ground?"

"Yes. It should have stopped the countdown, too."

"So we'll never know if it was you who stopped it, or me. I'll go with me. My shooting has always been better than your computer skills."

He tried to laugh, but only his jerky hollow breathing sounded in the silence.

"Mills's guys are now inside, that was the explosion we heard." Nicholas was getting paler by the minute. She got back on her comms. "Were you able to get anyone up here? If so, divert them into the building, now. Hurry."

But it was Carl Grace's voice that came back to her.

"Medic is on his way in. Keep Drummond comfortable. No reports of any bomb going off in the atmosphere as of yet. Whatever you two did, well done, agents."

"You get someone in here to help my partner, and we'll call it even."

"They're on their way. You have to get Dr. Patel into custody."

"I'm out of bullets and left my gear in the ceiling. And my partner is down. Let someone else get her." As she spoke, she was easing Nicholas out of the heavy gear he was wearing. When she got it off him, he could breathe more easily. Nicholas sucked in air. "Don't worry about me. Mike, go. She might have a separate override. Go get Patel. Be careful, she's quite mad, utterly over the edge."

She leaned down and kissed him. "I will. You're going to be okay. Do you hear me?" She took his gun, shoved it into her pants.

"How do I get out of here?"

He pointed. "To the right of where you came in. She went through a door there, down the hallway. I'm low on bullets, too, but there's a tranquilizer gun in the pocket of my vest. In case."

Mike pulled out the tranq gun and shoved it in her pocket. With a last pat on his shoulder, she went to the steel door, punched the button. The doors slid open, and she stepped out into the hall.

CHAPTER SEVENTY-FIVE

T-MINUS 00:00:01:03

Nevaeh waited.

Nothing happened.

She opened her eyes, saw the clock no longer counting down, it was now running forward. The bomb had to have exploded, but where were the Numen? There were no lights in the sky to announce their arrival, only the keening of the wind, eerie and mournful, and the first drops of rain coming through the open roof with the passing of the eye. The blood moon was obscured by dark, angry clouds for a moment, then they raced past. The moon shined brightly down. And still, nothing.

She didn't know what to think. Was there some sort of problem? Hadn't the EMP blown all the satellites dead? Surely that had happened, but what was wrong? Where were they?

She slid out of her chair, staggered as she set the heavy Heaven Stone down on the floor. She ran to the roof's control, shut it so her telescope wouldn't be ruined.

But the rest of her was screaming inside.

This wasn't happening. She had programmed the computers herself. Once the flight computer took over the countdown there was no stopping it. Was there? And she'd shot that agent dead. But it hadn't gone off, she was sure of it now.

She ran toward the control center. She would set off the bomb herself.

The doors to the command center slid open. Yes, there was the FBI agent on the floor where she'd left him, but the steel door that led out of the command center was open, and a woman — not Kiera — was running out of it.

Nicholas saw Patel and yelled, "Mike!"

He wasn't dead? How could that be? Patel watched the woman jerk around. She was wearing a black watch cap, ripped pants and shirt.

"Bitch! You're dead, like your friend here will be dead very soon now."

And Nevaeh charged her, raising her gun as she ran.

How odd, Mike was thinking as Patel came toward her. The woman was wearing, of all things, what looked like a white Roman toga. Her eyes were quite mad, Nicholas was right about that.

Mike pulled out the tranq gun and pulled the trigger.

Nevaeh felt a single sharp pain, but only for a moment, nothing more than a bee sting really, and then she began to feel — happy. Happier than she'd felt in so many years, since she'd first met the Numen. She smiled. They'd come. They'd brought incredible light. It flooded over her, encased her. She whispered, "You came for me. At last."

She hadn't failed. She knew blessed victory, she'd done it. The world would be hers now. Ah, what she would do, the Numen at her side. And they sang to her, *Yes, Nevaeh, what we will do together. Together.*

A white light shined bright on her face. Nevaeh looked up into the blurred face of a woman kneeling over her. She seemed to be floating above her. "You're not Kiera."

"No, I'm not. She's dead."

Nevaeh smiled. "Oh no, that can't be right. No one could kill Kiera." Then she was drawn inward again, and the light sharpened, hurt her eyes.

The woman was shaking her now, peeling back her eyelids, feeling her pulse. She was talking, Nevaeh could hear words, but they made no sense. The room filled with figures and she felt joy overcome the pain. They were here. The Numen had come for her.

They gathered her up in their arms, and she was being carried. She felt safe, loved. She felt blessed warmth, tenderness. Was that a heartbeat she heard against her face? Did the Numen have hearts just there? She whispered, "Thank you. I am ready."

They didn't answer.

She closed her eyes, settled into the strong arms that held her, and let the waves of warmth carry her away.

CHAPTER SEVENTY-SIX

Mike didn't watch Mills's team carry Nevaeh out of the control room. She was leaning over Nicholas, checking the wound. "Okay, you hang in here with me, you hear? Oh, yes, Patel — you're right, she is certifiable."

His teeth were gritted.

"I know, it hurts like bloody hell. Help's on the way —"

Suddenly, his cell phone sang out, "Rule, Britannia!" And she nearly jumped a foot. She fumbled, found his cell, answered.

"Nicholas? It's your mother. I've solved it, it was Mr. Able's wife who killed him. She was the lover —"

What to do, what to say? "Mrs. Drummond, I'm sorry, but Nicholas isn't available right now. Congratulations on solving the crime. He always says you're a whiz. I'm sorry, but I have to go. He'll get back to you." And she punched off, fast.

Surprisingly, Nicholas looked like he wanted to laugh, but couldn't. "I heard. She did it. Not surprised. Thank you, Mike."

Mike looked up to see Poppy Bennet stride, not walk, into the control center, a phalanx of men on her heels. She was dressed in camo assault gear that looked like it had been made for the runway in Milan.

Mike laughed. "Nice duds, Poppy. I need to visit your designer."

"I'll give you her name. None of the regular gear fits me right, so I have it made. Word is you stopped the bomb from going off, you shot the sucker to death. Good job."

"You were the ones who blew the door? I'll tell you, I was sure it was the nuke going off. Medics? Tell me you brought medics."

"Oh yes, we can't have anything happen to Agent Drummond."

Mike watched a medic, or a doctor, Mike didn't know which, work on Nicholas. Another, thankfully, gave him morphine. A third fitted an oxygen mask over his face. Poppy said, "Grant was in touch with your New York headquarters. He told us everything that was happening. Fentriss wanted to have a backup for you, so we diverted back and sent up a relief team. When the eye hit, we flew in with a couple of medics

557

and another team. Though it seems like all you needed was the medics. Are you hurt? You're limping."

"Ah, I broke my ankle a few weeks back, only a hairline fracture, and I think I've re-cracked it. It's Nicholas who was hurt." She swallowed down tears. She felt Poppy squeeze her arm and say, "Nicholas will be okay. These guys are great. Let's get you looked at, too."

Nicholas, morphine now swimming happily in his veins, smiled up at her. "Hey, Poppy? Thanks. Glad you're here."

"Me, too. Now, Agent Drummond, you keep quiet for the moment until John here says it's okay for you to talk." She said to Mike, "I saw Dr. Patel being carried out. She was, of all things, singing, well, more like humming, happy as a lark. What did you do to her?"

"I got her with the tranq gun. She came flying at me, screaming like a banshee, and I shot her."

"Good enough. She's out of this world, will be for a while. Those tranqs can last up to four hours."

"She was already out of this world," Nicholas said, then shut his mouth at the stab of pain.

Mike took his hand, held it hard.

The medic said, "Don't worry, he's going to live. I'm going to reinflate his lung now. Hang on tight, boss," he said to Nicholas, "I can't guarantee the morphine will mask all the pain." In went the chest tube. It didn't seem to bother Nicholas, he smiled up at her.

"Good, all done. Great stuff, morphine. Hang on, tough guy, we're going to get you out of here. I predict a healthy future for you." He said to Mike and Poppy, "Okay, he's as stable as I can make him. We're going to have to wait out the rest of this storm before we head back to Colombo. Keep him calm, it will be over in a couple of hours."

"Copy that," Poppy said. "You want to take a look at her ankle?"

The medic pushed and prodded, which made Mike want to kick him in the face, declared the ankle was only sprained, and wrapped it up. He offered her a pain pill, but seeing the dreamy look on Nicholas's face, she figured one of them needed to be solid in the here and now, and reluctantly declined.

Nicholas's eyes were closed. She pulled his head into her lap, smoothing his hair, leaned down, and kissed his forehead. "We did it, partner."

"I'll never forget you shooting the motherboard to death. Got me hot."

She kissed him again. "Everything gets you hot," and he smiled, and she went on whispering silly things in his ear until he fell asleep.

Epilogue I

Jean-Pierre Broussard ran up the stairs and down the long hallway toward his daughter's room. He paused a moment at the door, breathing light shallow breaths until the pain in his shoulder subsided. Then he gave a light knock and walked in.

Her nurse was seated beside her bed, reading a book.

Emilie lay quiet on her back. She wasn't asleep, her beautiful eyes were open. She heard him and slowly, with difficulty, turned her head to face him. Her eyes filled with pleasure. "Papa."

He was at her side in a moment. He sat down, leaned over, and kissed her. He looked into her beloved young face, lightly ran his fingers through her beautiful hair.

The nurse started to say something, but

Broussard waved her off. "Please leave us. I wish to be alone with my daughter."

"I am so glad you are here, Papa. No one tells me anything, but I knew, I knew in my heart something was wrong, something bad happened to you —"

"Shush, *ma petite,* it's nothing. I'm here and I have a grand present for you. Emilie, you will be completely well in but an instant of time."

He gently cupped her white hands around the Holy Grail.

EPILOGUE II

The big black FBI SUV pulled to the curb, and Nicholas sighed with satisfaction. "Home at last. I'm counting on you, Mike, to protect me from Nigel's wrath."

Mike slapped his leg. "Not a chance I'd leave you to him, not in your current pathetic invalid state."

"Who are you calling a pathetic invalid? You look as bad as I do."

That was the truth.

They both stepped gingerly from the SUV and thanked their driver, Agent Franks, a dour older agent who looked like he'd rather take them to the Lenox Hill Hospital emergency room. Franks started to hand over their bags, but Nigel burst out the front door and beat him to it.

He grabbed the bags, then dropped them to the sidewalk. He took Nicholas's hand to

563

hold him still, and examined him closely. He finally said, "Well, you're alive and walking, that's something."

"Nigel, I'm more than alive. Stop fussing. I really am fine now."

"Well, neither of you look fine. Let's get you inside, I've made tea, or perhaps something with a bit more bite would be more appropriate for the situation."

Mike gave him a hug. "Really, I look worse than I am, and Nicholas looks better than he should. What would be more appropriate?"

Nicholas said, "I hope you're talking about Talisker, beginning with a double."

Nigel looked them up and down — Mike back in the boot to help her ankle heal faster, bruises on her jaw and a black eye, and Nicholas with his arm in a sling, beard stubble, looking battered. He shook his head at the two of them. "Come inside and let's get you set up. The library, I think, the light's good right now. Then, once you're settled, I suppose you'll tell me what you've been up to these past few days? I've spoken to Gray and Adam, of course, but I want to hear it from your mouths."

"I can tell you faster than Nicholas. We stopped a bomb exploding in Sri Lanka, we received über thanks from the president, we were debriefed and discharged from the hospital in Colombo, Blue Mountain flew us back to Lyon where we handed over the Holy Grail — yes, that's what I said — to Jean-Pierre Broussard. Broussard left the hospital and flew immediately to Paris and to give the Grail to his dying daughter. He called earlier, deliriously happy, said she was well again. So yes, the Holy Grail is very real. Broussard thanked us until I finally had to tell him to go replace his magnificent treasure-hunting yacht, if he could talk the insurance company into footing the bill.

"Then we met with Grant, who was going to go home to Kitsune and tell her the whole story, well, maybe, parts might stand even her hair on end, and finally Nicholas and I boarded a plane home, courtesy of the CIA. I bet Mr. Zachery is going to love that. The end."

Nicholas's laugh was pathetic, but he tried. The doctors had told him the bullet wound would ache every once in a while. He wondered how long he'd be tied to a desk.

He said, "Talk about succinct. Just a bit more. In between calls with the White House, the CIA, the FBI, and a host of other people, all who wanted to either congratulate us or dress us down, we did manage to catch some sleep. All in all, we're alive and plan to stay that way."

Nigel said as he shepherded them inside and into the elevator, "Of all things, a CIA agent was here yesterday. He dropped off some papers he said you'd need to sign when you got home. His name was Mills, and he looked like he'd been through a war like you two. He limped. He looked around the house, said he might have known you were rich since you were such a prick. He said though that since you'd saved the world a lot of grief and suffering, he wouldn't hold your prickness against you."

Nicholas laughed. "So I'm a prick? He's an idiot. You said Vinny looked pathetic? He was limping? Serves him right, even though I'm glad he's up and about. What's this paperwork?"

After Nigel settled them in Nicholas's library, Nicholas on one of the leather sofas, Mike beside him, he handed them the papers Mills had brought to the house.

He was back quickly, carrying a tray with a steaming pot of tea on it, a full bottle of Talisker, and two shot glasses that didn't go very well with the Royal Doulton china cups.

Nicholas opened the package from Mills as Mike poured them each a double shot of

Scotch whisky. The tea wasn't touched, but Mike did say, "Pretty cups, the Gorgeous Rebecca would like them."

They toasted each other, slugged down the whisky nonstop. Mike gasped for breath, felt fire all the way to her belly. Nicholas, curse him, was grinning at her. "Another one, please."

She poured them both another shot while Nicholas read the papers. He burst out, "Bloody hell, you're not going to believe this, Mike. The bloody CIA, namely Carlton Grace, wants to pay me for my program that, I must say, very elegantly erases a computer's hard drive in a nanosecond. Remember the one I erased in Lyon before we jetted off to Sri Lanka? And that idiot Vinny was foaming at the mouth? That's what he's talking about. I guess Vinny went whining to Grace. Ah, here's a note from Grace at the bottom. 'Dear Agent Drummond, you sell the CIA this program and we will consider our two agencies even.' "

Mike drank down the rest of her whisky, wheezed a bit, then yelled, "Even? Did that CIA yahoo really have the gall to say we'd be even? As soon as my ankle's well again, I'm going down to Langley and give him a piece of my mind. Well, no, I need all my brain, but I could go down and punch him out."

Nicholas tried not to laugh, it hurt too much. He managed to get out, "Alas, you did get to fly in a jet and get refueled in midair, all thanks to Mr. Grace, CIA."

She poured them another shot. "Yeah, so pulling five G's was a really big deal, but still, we kept that idiot Al-Asaad — Vinny — alive, doesn't that count for something?"

Nigel stuck his head in the library. "I have a roast in the oven, I'm going to check it now. Dinner is at seven o'clock. You two get some rest, and then I'll feed you and you can fill in all the very fine details I'm sure you neglected to tell me." He eyed them, said, "Or, the two of you can continue drinking that amazing Talisker and I'll simply put both of you to bed when you pass out."

Nicholas tossed down the rest of his whisky, handed Mike his glass, watched her pour two more. She said, "I don't want to stop drinking and I want to keep yelling at the CIA."

They heard Nigel laugh outside the library.

Nicholas said, "I bet he's off to call his father at home. Then Horne and my parents will discuss everything, down to the five G's we pulled and your emptying your magazine into the motherboard to a nuke. Wait, they don't know that yet."

Mike held up her glass, gave him a silly grin. "I'll drink to that."

By the time Mike called her parents, she was very content with her world, and so mellow she could have danced the tango on her sprained ankle and not felt a thing. She gave them a finely edited rendition of what had happened, in a soft, blurry voice. Her father didn't believe her for a minute, probably knew she was drunk, and the Gorgeous Rebecca wanted to hear more about Jean-Pierre Broussard.

When she punched off, she sat back, took a sip of the incredible Talisker. "It's like we're an old married couple, having drinks at the end of the day. I'm all sort of relaxed, how about you?"

She was met with a light snore.

She moved over to him, lightly touched her fingers to the dent in his chin. "Do you think we'll ever have a normal life?"

He took her hand in his, but before he could say anything, his cell rang. He fumbled it out of his pocket, looked down at the name, and groaned. "I need to take this," he said, and drank down the rest of the whisky in his glass. "Mike, I don't want to be alone for this. I'm turning on the speaker. Hello, sir, how was the retreat?"

Sky News
"In breaking news today, we've learned the president and CEO of Galactus Space Technologies, Dr. Nevaeh Patel, one of the first female astronauts to stay in space for almost six months, has been arrested on charges of treason and terrorism in the failed attempt to set off a nuclear bomb in space. NASA reported such an explosion would have affected large portions of the Asian peninsula, southern Russia, and the Middle East, possibly devastating the electrical grids and taking out the International Space Station. Authorities report the terrorist attack was stopped by the combined efforts of American FBI and CIA agents in cooperation with the governments of France, Malaysia, Thailand, Sri Lanka, and Singapore. We will have more on this story as facts are released.

"More news from the space world: Scientists in Canada today reported the very first contact from their new twelve-billion-pound telescope, a low-frequency wave radio signal from deep in outer space. The signal, known as a fast radio burst, lasted only milliseconds, but was caught by the Canadian

Hydrogen Intensity Mapping Experiment telescope, which is designed to search the depths of outer space for contact from alien civilizations. Scientists say a fast radio burst has only occurred a handful of times before. They believe this signal is exceptionally powerful, and will be monitoring the telescope for more.

"Stay tuned for more from Sky News on this busy news day."

ABOUT THE AUTHORS

Catherine Coulter is the #1 *New York Times* bestselling author of eighty-four novels, including the FBI Thriller series and the Brit in the FBI international thriller series, cowritten with J.T. Ellison. Coulter lives in Sausalito, California, with her Übermensch husband and their two noble cats, Peyton and Eli. You can reach her at ReadMoi@gmail.com or visit Facebook .com/CatherineCoulterBooks.

New York Times bestselling author **J.T. Ellison** writes dark psychological thrillers and pens the Brit in the FBI series with #1 *New York Times* bestselling author Catherine Coulter. With millions of books in print, her work has won critical acclaim, prestigious awards, and has been published in 27 countries. She is also the Emmy-award-winning cohost of the premier literary television show *A Word on Words*. Ellison lives in Nashville with her husband and twin kittens. Visit JTEllison.com for more information, and follow her on Twitter and Instagram @ThrillerChick or Facebook.com/ JTEllison14.

CPSIA information can be obtained
at www.ICGtesting.com
Printed in the USA
BVHW042038050220
571582BV00009B/83

9 781432 861810